HOOKED ON A CALIFORNIA KINGPIN

A BBW ARRANGED MARRIAGE

MASTERPIECE

 Created with Vellum

SUBSCRIBE

.

Interested in keeping up with more releases from S.Yvonne Presents? To be notified first on upcoming releases, exclusive sneak peaks, and contest to win prizes. Please subscribe to her mailing list by texting Syvonnepresents to 22828

CONTACT THE AUTHOR!

Hey Pieces! It means so much to me to get your honest
feedback. Please feel free to join my private readers group on
Facebook! **Masterpiece Readers**
Join my mailing list by texting **Masterpiecebooks** altogether
to the number 22828!
Contact me on any of my social media handles as well!

FACEBOOK- AUTHORESS
MASTERPIECE & MASTERPIECE
READS

FACEBOOK PRIVATE GROUP FOR UPDATES-
MASTERPIECE READERS

Instagram- authoress_masterpiece & masterpiece_lgee

Email – masterpiece3541@outlook.com

SYNOPSIS

Meet Sovereign aka Queen, coldly calculated, and troubled. She is beautiful mixed with the street smarts to elevate her gang to the next level. Sovereign sacrificed so much for her and her little sister Empress aka Clapback at the age of thirteen. Her parents were murdered leaving Sovereign no choice but to step up to the plate and become a young adult. She roamed the streets and created a gang until the love of her life betrayed her leaving her in a bind with multiple disloyal men on her team. Blinded by love can truly be your downfall when thinking a person has your best interest when they truly don't. They call Sovereign treacherous when really the people surrounding her are the ones that's plotting. Her heart is on reserve, until she meets Malice aka Inferno. That butterfly feeling comes and then they clash hard. Inferno runs a syndicate in the states and reigns as a Kingpin in California. Sovereigns' grandmother and Inferno's father is trying to create a new alliance called the "Golden Triangle" in Mexico. The only way to build this strong foundation is marriage. How can two impulsive and powerful individuals come together under such a union? Toxic and selfish ways come out to play as drama unfolds at a fast pace. Before Sovereign realizes it, she's hooked on a California Kingpin and stuck in an arranged marriage.

PROLOGUE

*M*elvin writhe in pain as he laid in a puddle of blood. Through swollen eyes, he laid eyes on the only woman he tried his hardest to protect. He simpered lowly and sniffed back dried-up blood as he tried to focus in on his wife whom he succeeded at hiding for the past six years from a woman more powerful than any man or woman in the states.

"You fucked up Mel, just like that nigga Manny fucked up by fucking Gina." Clapback always liked to compare serious situations to her all-time favorite movie Scarface.

"When my sister gets here, I don't know how she will go about this shit... you should beg for mercy and hope that she kills you instantly. See, I know Sovereign though... she gone do some cold shit like you did to her. Queen is the coldest bitch known to mankind. Bitch ain't got a heart and she thrives off a weak niggas blood." Clapback taunted as Melvin released a bowel movement that was too pungent to inhale. Clapback's face balled up and she almost stumbled backward to get away from Melvin's naked body and waste that stained the warehouse's ground.

"Got dayum you stank!" Clapback took a few steps back and stood next to Murk'um with a disgusted look on her face. Melvin ignored Clapback's pestering and desperately squirmed and moved his body slowly while lying on his belly. His eyes were swollen shut from being pistol-whipped by Murkum's Ak-47. He struggled with his eyesight and tried his best to see a clear view of his wife's battered lifeless body.

"Neeta, please wake up baby." He could no longer fight back the tears that kept his dry face lubricated. A vein popped out of his neck as he chewed on his bottom lip. Grabbing at Neeta's left ankle, he pulled himself as close as he could and rested his head alongside her. He could feel movement from her swollen stomach and sadness engulfed him all over again. His baby was still alive and kicking. He grabbed Neeta's wrist and a little hope plummeted throughout him. She had a faint pulse, his stomach dropped at the sound of heels hitting the concrete and heavy footsteps. He smelled her before he could lay eyes on the devious woman, he'd dealt with for the past six years.

"Melvin, Melvin." Sovereign rocked a permanent glare on her round chubby face. Her velvety cinnamon skin tone had a permanent glow and was baby-soft to the touch. Sovereign's catlike eye shape tightened at the sight before her, and she turned and nodded at the men that flanked her curvaceous sides. A tall lanky OB-GYN, a friend of the family, gave her a light nervous smile as he rubbed his hands throughout his salt and pepper hair. He sat his big briefcase down and gave orders to his nurses. Sovereign's men got to work as they silently set up a big white folding table in the center of the empty warehouse. They dragged Neeta's body away from Melvin's hands and picked her up laying her on her back for Sovereign's doctor to start his work.

Sovereign aka Queen had been going hard the past six

years, trying to avoid the very thing she never wanted. She knew sooner or later to be the true Queen of at least five states, she would have to face the woman who took over and raised her and Empress aka Clapback. Empress was Sovereign's hard-headed sister. Since the age of thirteen Sovereign and her sister roamed the streets of L.A trying to survive and duck child services. Sovereign was mature and smart. At age thirteen she turned heads and had a lot of dope dealers taking advantage, which she knew. She sacrificed her innocence in order to survive being in the streets which turned her cold. By the time her grandmother came to the states to look for her and Empress, Sovereign was already turned out and addicted to money; she had a million ways to make and obtain it.

Her Abuela, was a legend, a Queen pin of Mexico. She ran her cartels and did big business in the state of California. Miguella was the mother of Miguel, Sovereign's father. Of course, she was seeking out revenge in a way that would have multiple cities covered in blood. She hated the fact that her only son came to California and fell in love with a black chick that was straight from the hood. To her, Sovereign's mother was classless and weak. She wasn't good enough for her son that held top ranking in her country. She only started to accept Sovereignty when she became pregnant with Sovereign. As time went on, Miguella expanded and supplied lots of drugs to the states for Miguel so that he could live in luxury and provide for her grandkids the proper way.

What Sovereign didn't know was that her Abuela, Miguella was waiting for the perfect time to collect on what was promised to her; an arranged marriage that would connect two powerful families together. Abuela was getting older and was ready to step down. The only thing was Sovereign was out of control, leaving home and running into

3

trouble. At the age of fifteen she was running the streets and paving her own way. Once she turned eighteen, she had her own crime and drug organization that took over multiple cities. She fell in love once or so she thought, turned out the man she thought she had fallen hard for was an enemy.

This whole situation would for sure turn her heart colder than Alaska and make her treat the next and every other man with a cold vendetta. She looked down at Melvin and remembered all the lies he laid up and told her. She remembered how he was the only one that knew her secret of not being able to conceive.

She desperately wanted to carry a baby for him and start a family. Late nights to early mornings hustling with Melvin had them growing close. When she was sixteen, he was the one that saved her from being gang raped by a bunch of older men. He was the only man that got to see the raw her. So, his betrayal had anger and hurt that felt like pain running through her veins. Like the strong woman she remained to be, she stood over him with a blank face. Her heart thumped in her chest, she wanted to break down, but she would never show her team, including her baby sister an ounce of weakness.

"I got to give you a round of applause Melvin. You had me fooled for the longest. I mean, besides the good head and good dick you coughed up on a regular. I should've listened to Clapback's obnoxious ass and never put you on the team. I always wondered how Dboi knew about every fuckin' hit we placed on his operations." She paused and shook her head as her right-hand man Peep passed her a lit blunt.

He placed it between her succulent thick lips, and she took a couple of puffs. Murk'um walked up with black gloves and a big raincoat and assisted her with putting the gloves on while Peep stood close allowing her to hit the blunt to calm

4

her nerves a little. Bundy stood back observing, that was something he always did. He was the extra set of eyes that Sovereign needed to catch things that she didn't see coming. Bundy's love for Sovereign was deep, he couldn't help himself when it came to Queen. He loved her strength and the way she was determined to elevate the people around her that pledged loyalty. If Queen would give him the okay to kill Melvin, a man he never trusted or liked, he would do so without even blinking.

Clapback watched it all unfold and knew her sister needed some sort of deliverance for the dark evil things she did to people for punishment. She knew her sister better than she knew herself. Ever since their parents were murdered her sister was the only provider and mother figure, she knew of beside her grandmother whom Queen ended up walking away from.

Once Sovereign's large raincoat concealed her all-white Prada dress she stepped away from the men as Bundy finally stepped out of the shadows, handing her a water hose.

"You fucked up bad Melvin, revenge for me will be sweet." She looked over at doctor O' Ryan's handiwork and chuckled. Neeta's stomach was being cut wide open, she had to be dead by now.

"Roll this bitch nigga over. I want him to look me in my eyes." She didn't direct what she said to anyone in particular. She never had to; people knew when she gave a demand their life depended on making it happen at the snap of her fingers.

"You came after me with a vengeance Melvin. You almost succeeded, all those marriage proposals and gifts from my money." She spat out angrily, they held him up and she gave him a wide smile. Her hazel brown eyes penetrated Melvin's soul. He heard a baby cry out and his heart leaped and then sped up. Sovereign fought to remain *focused, but other thoughts came surging to the forefront of her brain.*

The things that Melvin knew about her didn't sit to well with her. The love she had for this man, now had her disgusted to her core. A lot of money was now missing from her, enough money to set her back. She prided herself with the power she obtained and how much money she made because of her own mastermind.

"I... loved you, Queen." She looked around and laughed sharply. He said "Loved" as if she did something to him to make him fall out of love with her. As if she didn't give this man her heart and soul only for him to fumble the shit like she meant nothing. To lie and pretend like she was the right woman for him had her standing above him feeling sick.

She laughed hard and grabbed her stomach and bent over dramatically. Stomping her stiletto heels into the concrete she laughed for what felt like a long time to Melvin. Sovereign always appeared deranged; what people didn't know was that she used laughing as a coping mechanism. Instead of crying, she laughed hard enough to wipe the tears from her chubby round face. For years she learned how to mask a lot of things that crushed her on the insides and ate away at what she had left of being kind of normal.

Melvin's stomach clenched out of fear. In seconds she stood up straight and her face dropped instantly. She was back with the same hard glare she gave on a day-to-day basis. Her face was blank and void of any emotions. That's the shit that made people nervous about her. Nobody around her could determine Queen's mood.

She squeezed the heavy-duty metal nozzle on the water hose and squeezed as the water shot out fast on Melvin's face. He choked and panicked; he couldn't catch his breath as the water hit his face at a rapid pace. It felt like he was drown-

ing, he didn't think that Queen had it in her to torture him like she was doing now.

"You love that gorilla looking bitch, huh? Drop that nigga." She spat and released the nozzle, the water stopped immediately. Stepping around his bowels, she stood over him. He offered a haunted facial expression. Dr. O' Ryan walked up with a small bundle of joy wrapped inside of a pink blanket. He cautiously handed the baby to Queen, and she cradled the baby while smiling down at her.

"Thank you, Melvin." She beamed at the baby. I can't conceive, so I see this as a gift in disguise. That is the only mercy that I will show... The woman you love is dead, her stomach is cut open but at least you leave behind a beautiful baby girl. You thought you had me but Melvin, I had you... you weren't shit but a kept nigga, the truth always reveals itself."

"You treacherous fat bitch!" Melvin struggled with his words, but they were clear enough for her to know exactly what he had said.

"Yes, that is exactly what I am Melvin. I'm so fucking treacherous, and I won't stop at you, Melvin. See, I know now that your father was behind the hit of my mother and father. I will keep you alive until you sing like a bird. You will talk Melvin; I know your loyalty is strong for that bitch ass daddy of yours. Don't you dare say shit about him being dead, it's been confirmed the bastard is alive. You will lead him to me. You will spend, I don't know a month maybe a year or a decade in this shitty-ass warehouse. You will be fed through an IV just to keep your ass alive. Every day you will wake up in pain and go to sleep in pain. I'm going to make you wish like hell you never tried to play a treacherous game with me." She sighed like she was exhausted from talking. Queen never

did much talking; when she did, it was always in short sentences.

"I've talked enough now... I need to get my daughter to the hospital." She rocked the baby in her arms and smiled down at her.

"Murk'um please assist our new guest. Make him feel at home." She smiled and walked out with her team behind her. Clapback stood behind for a while, if Queen was able to see the look on her sister's face, she would've killed her too. Clapback had a look that showed sad emotions and indecisiveness. She turned on her heels slowly and went to catch up with Queen, fixing her face and checking her feelings.

SOVEREIGN AKA QUEEN, MARTINEZ

*T*wo **years later**

"Queen? You thought about what we talked about baby?" I looked at Deontae's handsome face and raised my brows.

"You want a male BBL? Nigga do I look like a sugar momma or a trick?" I clicked my teeth then looked up at the ceiling to see the time. Today was collection day, I was sure that Empress was already suited and booted with Murk'um making their rounds around the city. I desperately needed to elevate because the money I spent on a daily kept me under a million. I wanted a few M's in my safe for security. The people that I had running traps and clocking in with me ate well. I wasn't selfish but it was time to step my shit up.

"Nah baby, they do some sort of ab surgery. Oh, that shit called abdominal etching. Shit ain't nothing but ten racks. That ain't nothing to you baby." He smiled and I slid out of the bed, still naked and high as a giraffe's pussy. See that was the problem, yea, I had dough. I just needed more. Never in my life have I tricked on a nigga. This was the exact reason why I linked with niggas away from where I lived.

"Dee, I think you take my kindness and smooth words for weakness. You think, because I'm a fat chick, that I would trick on you. I knew you were a broke nigga when I met you, driving ya bitch car. I only got at you because I saw those thick ass lips and wanted to see how they felt between my legs." I took a deep breath and sighed. It felt like I was talking too much to a man that I wouldn't remember within a month's worth of time. I walked away and went to start the shower to clean myself up.

Deontae was fine as fuck and a freak nigga. He was tall and lanky, with thick ass lips that wrapped around my clit like a suction cup. His dick was average, it was enough to hit my spot and put in enough work. I made a mental note to stop fucking with random ass niggas. I didn't want any attachments to the opposite sex, but I had needs and cravings that only the opposite sex could handle for me.

Today was a different kind of day for me. I was still mourning the loss of my daughter. I had to put my feelings to the side in case I needed to kill a nigga for not having my money. F.Y.F was my organization full of roughneck niggas and bitches that wanted nothing but the money and the street cred. *Fuck Yo Feelings* was well known and respected from the suburbs to the hoods.

"Can you at least think about it?" Deontae stood right at the bathroom door, looking pitiful.

"Nigga no." I stepped in the shower and eyed the gun that I had tucked inside before Deontae arrived. I didn't trust anyone, not a soul. That's how I survived when it was just me and Clapback. The people that claimed to be there and have my back were now dead by the hands of me. I didn't have an ounce of pity in the world for a soul. The world didn't have one for me.

"By the time I clean my ass, you need to disappear." I

closed the shower curtains and sighed. I was now disgusted with this nigga. I couldn't believe he had the nerve to beg me like a bitch begged a nigga to be flewed out. "That's how you gone play me?" I opened the shower curtains up and we had a long stare off as the water beat down my body. I broke the serious glare and smiled brightly at him.

"Deontae... if you were smart, which you are not. You would have played your cards right and just maybe you could've gotten that BBL that you were just begging me for. I like my men naturally fine, not enhanced by a plastic surgeon." I closed the curtain back up and hoped that he left like he was told. I hadn't run across a stubborn needy nigga in a long time. Deontae was too damn anxious to squeeze me out of money. There was only one man that I allowed that close to me. That man was missing from a failed plan and disloyal individuals surrounding me. I used to want the type of love that my father showed my mom.

That was until I realized that it was a new time in day. The new generation seemed to follow along with what everybody else was doing. Whatever social media instructed them to do, they followed that shit to the tee.

"That shit ain't attractive Ma, you all aggressive and shit. You might as well get a strap on and start fucking on bitches. I mean, a nigga fine as fuck. What nigga like me gon' fuck with a bitch like you? You need to start paying what the fuck you weigh and lose that uppity ass attitude." I chuckled lowly and winked at my teal beretta. Opening the shower curtain for the third and last time, I reached for my beretta and made sure to keep it concealed.

"Deontae, it sounds like you're begging me to fuck you with a strap on." I paused and smiled, running my stiletto nails through my scalp. "Hmm, what color dick you want me to use on you baby. You will get brownie points if you pick teal. It's my favorite color." I winked at him to taunt him since he was trying so hard to taunt me. Soon as he picked up his right foot to move further in the bathroom, I shook my head no.

"Deontae, don't cause me extra money baby." I really wanted him to think about this shit. If he took another step, I was ready to blow his fucking brains out. It was Sunday, I didn't want to kill on the Lord's day. Deontae was making shit hard. The fee that I would have to pay my clean-up crew and the hotels worker to get rid of footage would be the same fee that equaled up to Deontae's BBL.

"Bitch, the hood might fear you, but I don't! You just a regular, smegular ass fat bitch! Think you too high and mighty!" He picked up his left foot and put it right in front of the other and that's when I pushed back the shower curtains and aimed for the center of his head making him piss himself and push his long skinny arms above his head.

"Nah nigga. I am high and mighty. They call me Queen which you already knew. The rumors are true. The only time a muthafucka gets to know my government name is when I'm sending them to heaven or hell. Whichever place you are about to go to, because only God can judge you. Tell them other muthafuckas that got laid out by me.... Sovereign said heeeeyyyy." I couldn't hold back my laugh as I carefully stepped out the shower. My body was dripping wet, and I wished somebody could get a picture of me in this very moment because I knew for a fact that I was looking sexy as fuck.

"Queen, wait! I'm..."

Pop!

One shot to the dome. I wished like hell that I could empty the clip in him. I didn't want to bring too much attention to have the cops notified. Then again, they wouldn't call the cops because in the hood people had fireworks all year long. With just one gunshot they wouldn't be able to tell if it was a gunshot or a damn firework.

"You is a sorry muthafucka! Got me killing on the Lord's day. Now I gotta spend some unnecessary money to clean this shit up." I spit on him then sat my gun on the bathroom counter to finish my damn shower.

That was niggas for you, they couldn't take rejection for shit. Yet they loved rejecting multiple women and playing games.

After I showered, I dried off and got dressed. My hair was still wet and sticking to my damn back. I made a mental note to have it trimmed by a couple of inches. My hair was now flowing a little past my curvy backside. I loved my hair stopping a couple of inches above my ass. I rocked an all-black Prada dress with the matching black boots. After making sure all my jewelry was back on. I went in my Prada bag and sprayed my favorite Dolce and Gabbana Light Blue perfume and applied a thin coat of nude gloss. Today my curly mane would look wild once it dried up, but I didn't give a damn.

Excitement flowed through me; I was ready to hit the blocks. I enjoyed watching and making money. I came a long way and although I didn't consider myself at the top yet because my money needed to be stepped up, tremendously. Muthafuckas still knew not to test or step to F.Y.F gang.

Before leaving out the room, I placed a call to Xavier. When he answered, I said nothing. I hung up which was code and shot him a text with my address and room number. Picking up my personal phone, I wired him eighty-five hundred. He knew exactly what to do to make it all go away.

Valet pulled my teal blue Porsche truck around to the front. I hopped in and pulled out fast. It was already ten am and I knew the block was jumping. Summertime would be approaching soon, to me that was the best time. I made the most money because everybody in they momma name was out and about.

I pulled my Porsche right in front of the trap house that sat a couple of houses down from Rowley Park. Rowley Park was a neighborhood park that we met up at on Sundays to talk and connect with one another after a busy ass week. Nobody sold drugs on Sundays. I gave my squad the opportunity to chill and be with their family. Hitting the alarm on my truck, I walked up the raggedy ass steps and took in my surroundings. Kids casually played basketball in the middle of the street.

I could see the park directly across from the house I was about to walk into, I was ready to see the amount of money I had.

You could literally smell the aroma of different foods being cooked. I think the main reason, I gained a lot of respect was because I didn't have the heart of my gang doing average gang-banging shit. They assisted in any way possible when it came to elders and women. I had them cooking up and bagging shit in the hood. If we had local crackheads that wanted to cop, I had men for that. More importantly, my drugs went to suburban rich areas. It was the main reason why I didn't too much care for the other thugs that called themselves getting money. Pouring drugs into their community to make us go up against one another.

Anybody that stepped on my toes, had to answer to me. So far, I kept a low profile, and I wasn't as flashy. To be honest a lot of people didn't even believe that I was the head bitch in charge. In their eyes, I was a stupid bitch running my man operation. I let them think whatever it was they needed to think to keep the pigs off my ass.

To further make what they thought to be true in their dumb brains, I purchased a store and named it Sovereignty's after my mom. It was for dermatologists and estheticians; I actually loved popping pimples but didn't have the time to go get me a degree. I would spend a lot of time there whenever I had free time to do so.

To most, I looked like a pretty ass chubby chick, I took more after my mother looks. My skin tone was a toffee color. What really gave my mixed race away was my hair type. It came straight from my father's side. My sister, Empress, looked and could pass for full Mexican. She was the spitting image of my father, and she ended up being tall and thin. I was short standing at five feet, I had thick thighs, a stomach, and double-D titties. My weight was well portioned, I wasn't sloppy fat.

Pulling out my second set of keys, I let myself in, giving Murk'um and my sister a simple head nod as they sat on the couch pushing money through the money counting machine that sat on the coffee table. I turned back around to the door and locked all five locks that was attached and closed the security gate that they had opened which pissed me the fuck off, instantly.

"Why the fuck is this open?" I looked at both of them. I didn't feel like dealing with my sister smart ass mouth, so my eyes fixated on Murk'um. He was chocolate and handsome as hell, the ladies were crazy over him. He was as loyal as they came but always seemed to get caught up in my sister's bullshit. I knew he had a crush on her, but he respected my "No mixing business, with pleasure" rule. That didn't stop the two of them being tight, something like best friends. So, I let it ride, they seemed to balance each other out.

"Sovereign- my bad, I mean Queen... We left the gate opened because we knew you were on the way." Clapback answered for Murk'um. My baby sister was indeed my soft spot, I didn't expose that, but she was the one person that I would risk it all for. I might have never expressed it much, but I loved her whole heartily. I made the sacrifices that I did at a young age so that she never had to see what it felt like to be mistreated and handled wrong like I was. I snapped my eyes to her then back at Murk'um.

"Y'all know that I don't give a fuck about that. What if the police busted this bitch down before I arrived?" I asked and was answered by silence, so I continued. "This security gate is in place for situations like that. If they were to come, that security gate would give you slow muthafuckas an extra five minutes to get my money to safety. Don't make this stupid ass mistake again. Am I clear?"

"Yes Queen." They answered at the same time. To them, I was too uptight, to strict, and maybe paranoid. In my mind, I was only trying to stay on top and ahead of people that could possibly be plotting.

"How's the dough looking?" I asked them both, this was the moment of truth. If my money wasn't right today, then tomorrow someone would have to start making funeral arrangements for their loved ones.

"Well, seem like that nigga Flow been skimming. He claims that the college kids haven't been wanting the pills like that. Said he had a slow week, so he was short of two thousand. Besides that, this week we brought in forty-eight thousand." My jaw ticked and I instantly started to laugh lowly until it turned into a full-blown laugh.

"Forty-eight thousand? So, you telling me after all that shit that we dished out…Forty-eight thousand close to fifty if Flow wasn't short of two racks was all we would have made in a week? My estimation was eighty this week when I gave ya'll all that shit to distribute." I was getting madder by the second.

"Queen, you showing too much love on the product. You need to double up the percentage. Its niggas out here charging triple of what you charging, a double wouldn't hurt." Clapback cut in, I side eyed her. She kept pressing for us to up the price, I was taking it into consideration, but I needed more time to think on it. I was well known for good pure product for a cheap good price and that's what was starting to make my clientele expand. The problem was, I needed more product and at a cheaper price.

"You know, if you stopped running from our Abuela, she would help." Empress rolled her eyes.

"Bitch, I don't run from shit. Watch your mouth Em... you're pushing it." I warned as I started to pace back and forth. I was so close to pushing my money to a little over a million. It seemed like every time I was close to reaching that goal then bullshit would come my way. I still had to pay the people on my payroll, including the pigs that turned a blind eye to my operations. Everything caused a pretty penny when people thought you had it like that.

"My apologies, Abuela has been in town for the past two days. I told you; she is requesting a sit down with you. You know how that shit goes when she feels disrespected. Just hear her out please Queen." She gave me those puppy dog eyes so I nodded my head at her. It wasn't an answer, but it would shut her up from begging. I loved my Abuela, but I didn't want to sit down with her. I knew what she wanted, and I didn't want to bend on that.

"Murk'um tell Peep, to let that nigga Flow enjoy his Sunday afternoon and evening. Soon as the clock strikes one, I want him on the nasty ground of my warehouse with a couple of opened wombs. Keep him breathing, you know the get down." He nodded his head as I finally went down the hallway to check on the workers that we had bagging shit up in different rooms. This was my main head quarter, we prepared shit for the new week to come. The workers that I did have on Sundays got paid extra to work for two to three hours.

This was a three-bedroom fixer upper house, so I bought it for cheap. My credit was good, so the mortgage was low on this particular property. My mind went back to Flow, he was a fast talker and sneaky as fuck. He knew the rules when he copped pills from me. The rules remained in place for a reason. A couple hundred didn't really bother me much. Anything over a thousand was worth more to me than his life. No way in hell was I about to let him slide. It was either he coughed up my two thousand or he would be a dead man walking. No other way around it.

I went back into the front, I recounted all of the money by myself right in front of Clapback and Murk'um. When I said I didn't trust a soul I meant that. I let them count and touch money first. I would always be the final person to get the last count. Once we were done doing everything that needed to be done, we walked out the house with gym bags. Murk'um loaded them into my trunk while I stood and watched. This was the routine that I had become used to. Murk'um would follow me to my house, and I would store the money in my safe. Before we would even reach my house, we would detour a couple times to make sure no one was following us. Once my trunk was closed, I noticed a Lincoln town car pull onto the block with two other town cars close behind.

"Shit." I gritted not ready to deal with Abuela.

"I told you; you know how she gets." Clapback smiled. She loved and cherished our Abuela. Abuela spoiled her rotten. I tossed her messy ass the keys to my Porsche, I also gave her a knowing look. I would get off into Em's ass later. It was only her that ran her mouth telling our Abuela my whereabouts. Soon as the car came to a stop, I wasted no time walking towards the first town car. I didn't need Abuela making a scene with her men.

Before the driver could get out and open the door for me, I opened it myself, still feeling tight about the fact that my seventy-four-year-old grandmother, pulled up to one of my trap houses. Soon as my eyes connected with hers, she smiled and lifted her glass of wine to her thin lips. She would never be the one to speak first so out of respect, I pushed my attitude away and forced a fake smile.

"Abuela, what a pleasant surprise." My smile dropped fast. She still said nothing as she tapped the headrest.

"Hector, take me on a tour while I talk to mi Nieta." He said nothing as he pressed a button to make the petition rise up slowly.

"Still very classless, Nieta." Which meant granddaughter in Spanish. I gave her all of my attention and remained quiet. There was no use of speaking when she clearly already had her speech figured out. Hector finally started to drive as I kept my eyes on Abeula. She still looked good to be in her seventies. Her hair was pulled up into a neat bun with loose curls framing her face. She had a couple of wrinkles that told on her age, but she was very beautiful. We shared the same hazel brown eyes and nose. Her gaze was out the window, with her champagne flute locked in her hand.

"Mi hijo (*My son*) was very stubborn like ju. He cost me millions of dolares, by marrying ju mama,'" she smiled then placed her light brown orbs on me. Her gaze could make one of the toughest men known to mankind fold.

"Ju see, I had a powerful woman that he was supposed to marry to link dos familia's together." Her thick accent was strong. Everything she said was very slow and deliberate so you could understand exactly what it was she was saying. Abuela never repeated herself.

"I have billions... and I have to pass it on soon. Your Abuela is getting old, I want to travel di world. Ju see?" Her french tip short nails drummed against the glass flute; her eyes darkened. I cleared my throat and fixed my posture out of respect.

"What does that have to do with me, Abuela?"

"Toda! (*Everything!*)" squinting her eyes and raising her voice meant that this whole conversation was going to go left. I was getting it out of the mud. I had my own supplier and soon I would be able to do distribution once she stopped being stubborn and let me cop all my shit from her.

"Ju think, the way you move is smart?" She tapped her forehead with her index finger. "Killing a man, with no men? Trusting an ex-enemy like Xavier to clean ju mess?" My stomach tightened and started to twist. I have never known Xavier to be an enemy. In my eyes he was solid.

"Si mijo, nothing concerning my blood gets past me. I've been watching you very closely. I must say, I'm not impressed." She tooted that thick nose of hers heavenward and shook her head.

"Where is Xavier?" I tried to keep my voice calm. At all times I tried my hardest to remain respectful. This was my Abuela, but if she killed Xavier then that would be fucked up on my end. Xavier was the only clean-up person I knew who had a crew that could make things happen at the snap of my fingers. Not only that, I paid him well.

"In di river with the pigs that you had on your low budget payroll. Xavier was using all evidence and giving it over to di sergeant. The money ju sent, is back in your account."

"So now, I guess... I owe you?" I sighed ready for her to hit me with the bullshit.

"Mijo... you have owed me since the day, ju was born. You have the rest of this week to get your affairs in order. Empress will run things until ju return." She finally broke the intense stare down and smiled wide at me. The smile pained me because it mirrored my father's wide smile.

"Return from where?" I raised my arched brow.

"Mexico, there you will be groomed by me and a couple of others. Your organization here is falling apart. You are borderline broke. Ju are a Martinez. A petty savings like yours is shameful." She cleared her throat then looked out the window. I could see that we were pulling into my private condo compound. "Look at me, Sovereign... Si, you will live up to ju name. Make me proud and your Papa. I have so much dolares that I'm ready to walk away and turn all my contacts and connections over to ju. All di power, all di muscle will be in your possession. Di policia, will never look ju way." She smiled again.

"What is the catch, Abuela?" This was the part I knew I wouldn't like.

"Casamiento (Marriage)."

INFERNO

*M*alice Ashonti Ruiz
Heavy chatter could be heard loud and clear as I walked down the long hallway. To my right side was my henchman, to the left was my right hand. My jaw flexed as anger soared through me like an eagle in the sky searching for his prey. The closer I got to my father's meeting room, the more anxious I got to break a nigga fuckin' neck. Niggas got real comfortable around here since my old man wasn't up and moving around like he normally would. I came down to Mexico because my father sent for me. My father and I were business partners, but above all, he was still my father.

"Try to go in there with an open mind Inferno. You can't walk up in there killing niggas like you do back home." Killa stopped me in my tracks, little did he know, nothing he said could possibly stop me from what I was about to go in this meeting room and do. "Speaking of back home, we still got a little situation. We will speak on that when we back on the jet." I shook my head no. Taking a deep pull from my blunt, I

22

inhaled deeply and held my breath for a couple of seconds to long before releasing the rest.

"We talk about it here. I don't know when we leaving. A lot of shit needs to be put in order. You know my bitch ass siblings ain't gone see to things running smooth for my old man." That was the truth, the only reason why I even fucked with one of my brothers and kept him alive was for the sake of my father and his third wife. My father had a total of six wives, my mother included. My mom was still married but separated from my father when I was fifteen, she took me to Cali and tried to give me a better life. Her struggling and running from my father didn't help with that. I still ended up in the streets. With a father like mine, he saw to it that I had all the tools I needed. He kept his distance to a certain extent for my mom's sake.

In his mind she would come back home one day but I knew that wouldn't happen ever again. My mom was a strong black woman and stood firm on whatever or however she felt. She was fierce and believed on standing on her own two feet not letting anybody control or manipulate her. She claimed she once played a fool out of love but that ended when my father kept breaking her heart.

"That situation should have been handled before we got here, Killa. I told you to end whoever stepped in my way. Being that you didn't we will speak upon that later when we get off of this fuckin' compound." I picked my feet up and Killa along with Big B followed closely behind me.

I could just smell the lighter fluid and matches. The tips of my numb discolored fingertips were ready to strike a match and watch a muthafucka writhe in pain until they took their last breath. It was a big fuckin' thing to slack off, then fuck off in my father's multi-million-dollar operation. Now, it was a kick to a man's nut sack and a nasty spit to the face, to turn around and act like the Ruiz cartel was ran by a pussy.

My father was the toughest of the tough, a fair but lethal man. I came here to get things in line whether he wanted me to or not. I was a Ruiz, and that shit was a reflection of me.

"Hola Papi." I took a couple of steps back to allow six inches of space. Tilting my head slightly to the side, I shook my head no. That was a fair enough warning. To a regular broke nigga, the sight of Callista would've had a nigga crazy. To me, she was nothing but a reminder on why I could only use these hoes for nothing more than catching my nutritionist nut.

Instead of taking heed to my warning, she stepped even closer. Maybe it was my ugly ass bluish, greenish eyes that had this bitch acting stupid. She attempted to touch me, and I grabbed her up by her throat. My sharp pinky nail penetrated her neck drawing blood. Whimpering only made the shit worse, she squirmed as I eyed her like the venereal disease, she gave me when I was twenty. The only thing that kept her breathing after that day was my father's close-knit relationship with her father.

"Chill, Inferno." Killa's face could be seen through my peripheral. Keeping a firm grip on her neck, I eyed him for a couple of seconds before I decided to speak.

"You taking the wrong chances today, Kill. That's a strike, don't make it to fuckin' three. You know I get amnesia quick and forget who a muthafucka is." That was the truth. I loved Killa to death, did time with the nigga in jail, and he held me down until my father had his cartel men break me out of that bitch with no traces of me ever even being there. I took Killa with me because he saved me from an attack that could have ended my life. In my eyes, everybody needed to learn and abide by whatever position I gave them in my life.

"Malice, pleaseeee." Her watery eyes didn't move me at all.

"Callista? What is the number one rule when you and I cross paths?" Her pale face was now red, I shook her a little until her silk-curly hair fell onto her face.

"Act like you're a ghost." I nodded.

"Would you like to say rule number two? Because we both know that rule would mean paving your grave." I pushed her away from me like the trash she was. There was no need to look her way, I could hear her gasping and coughing. The sound of her expensive heels could be heard running away. Good, fucking hoe.

Adjusting my tie and readjusting my dick inside of these tight-ass trousers, I picked my feet up and made my way to the double doors. I hated wearing suits and dress clothes. My father wouldn't have it any other way. I respected his way whenever I was in his space.

Big B, stepped up to the huge double doors. Looking my way for the okay to proceed, I could tell his big burly ass felt congested in the suit he had to wear today. Pushing the door open, I stepped in, and silence immediately swept over the room. I could smell the fear, it was the wrong move to make. Fear seemed to feed me rage. My eyes swept the room from left to right. I met eyes with a lot of unsure, pussy mutha-fuckas. They told on themselves with pitiful looks covered all over their faces.

I forced a fake genuine smile and opened my arms like I was here to accept and reward these fuck niggas.

"Gentlemen, please don't stop all the chattering and laughing on my account." I snapped my fingers, with my hand out. Big B smiled and handed me my flamethrower cannon. It weighed about twenty pounds; it wasn't as big as the ones that I used back home. This one would get the job done. Placing it on my shoulder, I started to pace the forty-five hundred square foot meeting room.

I estimated twenty-five men, maybe ten would live to see another fucking day. Clicking my tongue, I started picking brains.

"Inferno?" A short chubby greasy, muthafucka had the nerve to speak my name like he was infatuated. Looking at Killa and nodding my head, he pulled his gun from his dress pants and blew his head off. His brains splattered onto the man that sat next to him. The gentleman that occupied his seat started to sob and shake.

"Mi, hermano(*brother*)!" I clicked my tongue and Killa shot him too.

"Anybody else ready to speak out of turn?" Silence. I picked up my feet and kept walking.

"See the silence, I can accept because that tells me... that you, tamale-eating muthafuckas is thinking about the hit that was placed on the Don. If you muthafuckas were smart, you would do your very best to protect the head of this organization. You all failed. Now, who knows? A sick evil half-breed nigga like me might take over. Ju know, no me detendre' *(I won't stop).*" I stopped right behind Jose, my father's henchman that looked like he was shaking in anger.

"Jose? Do you have something to say?" I placed my free hand on his shoulder, I could feel the steam coming off of him. I wanted to laugh but I was trying to respect my so-called elder. Getting close to his ear, I spoke lowly. "You and I will have a talk outside of this room. You may leave." I stood up straight and watched him stand and walk out.

Right now, I wasn't thinking too clearly, pain resonated in my chest. The sight of my father crushed me. I have never been crushed; this was a first for me. I was used to seeing my father standing strong and unfazed. Jose sitting perfectly without a scratch nowhere in sight had me ready to torch his fucking face to my satisfaction. My father wouldn't like that, so I gave him a pass for now. I eyed the all-gold throne-like seat, it resonated at the head of the one-hundred-inch table. Something was going on, I needed to get my temper under control to be able to see clearer. I could smell a rat and all I needed was some rich strong cheese to spot them out.

"My father was shot three times. You all sit in his home, laughing and talking when his wounds haven't even stopped leaking blood. Killa and Big B walked towards the throne and stood on each side as Big B pulled the heavy golden chair out for me to take a seat. They knew that the only way for me to level out and think level-headed was for me to take a seat. What they didn't understand is if I sat in that chair, it would mean to these men, that I was stepping into my father's shoes.

"Somebody better start talking… make sure when you speak, that it's of something very important." I gripped the handle of my flamethrower and started to eye every man that sat around the table.

"We only answer to di Don." I pointed my flamethrower in the no-name man's direction and pressed my finger underneath the clutch.

"No answer to me?" I raised my thick brows and smirked. His Adam's apple moved up and down. "You're scared but not that scared to test me. Hmmm… that's interesting. Big B, do me the honors." Everyone watched with wide eyes. Big B pulled a clear bottle that looked like water, out of his suit jacket. He marched around the table until he was standing directly behind no name. Taking the top of the lighter fluid and grabbing a handful of the man's curly hair, he tilted his head back, then started pouring the fluid all over his face. The

27

remainder of fluid was dosed over his hair. Visibly trembling and squeezing his eyes shut from them burning. The panic all over his face was noted.

"Seems like to me, you all need structure. I'm never the one to knock what my old man has established within his cartel. However, you all need an example of what the results are for not taking great care of your Don."

I squeezed the trigger; the gas, I smelled first. Soon as the fire ignited, my eyes lit up. The flame immediately picked up on the fluid and started melting his face like a candle. The pungent smell had everyone but me, using their shirts as a mask. This shit never got old to me; I loved playing with fire since a youngin'. It's how I got my name Inferno. The older I got the more obsessed I became with flames.

By now everybody was up on their feet moving far from the table. The smell of burnt hair annoyed me but the sight of him lying limp on the table with fire blazing off his body had me anxious to pick another pussy nigga, for the same treatment.

"One of you niggas, fetch a fire extinguisher. Clean this shit up." I handed Big B my flamethrower and took a seat on the chaise that was close to the floor-to-ceiling window. Pulling the blunt from behind my ear, I used my lighter torch to spark it. The crackling and popping, sounded like music to my ears.

"It's getting hot in hurr." I nodded my head, singing.

"So hot!" Big B's raspy voice sounded off as the adlibs, he kept a nonchalant look on his face.

"So, take off all ya clothes," I mumbled and inhaled my blunt.

"Y'all niggas is sick." Killa shook his head and pulled his own blunt out.

"Fuck y'all looking at?" I frowned and chuckled when all

eyes snapped away from mine. Someone was going answer to my father's failed assassin.

"Excuse me, Mr. Ruiz, your father is awoke, and would like to speak with you now." Saved by the bell, I nodded my head and watched a man walk in with a fire extinguisher. I stood to my feet and nodded to my two men to follow behind me.

"We smell like smoke." Killa's pretty boy ass complained as I handed my blunt off to Big B. Ignoring Killa, I picked up my feet and made my way down the hallway to get to my father. When I first arrived here, nurses were tending to him. I couldn't stand the sight of him like that, it almost broke me down to my knees. I couldn't even find my voice to ask where he had been shot, I just knew it was three times.

I took the steps three at a time, one thing about Mexico is, it had beautiful mansions overlooking the ocean. My father's estate sat up high giving you the best view of Mexico. Coming back brought back memories of my childhood. My father showered all of his kids with love, he always knew that out of all his kids that I would follow right behind him. I knew at a young age how powerful my father was. I saw it every day and every time we left the house. Grown men would bow their heads whenever he appeared. Most was too scared to look him in the eyes. I attended all of my father's weddings and thought it was normal. None of his wives except my mother got the courtesy of living here in this house.

I was his firstborn, and after the fifth kid, I stopped counting how many he produced. That fifth kid was the reason my mother left and went back to California. I remember spending my summers in Mexico and going right back to California. I was close with two of my sisters, the others looked at me like I was the special kid. They were jealous that our father put my mother first before their mothers. I didn't give a damn; I also didn't care to get to know any of them.

By my siblings and their mothers, they treated me differently and looked at me oddly. I was the only kid from my father mixed with half Mexican and black. I took after my black roots more. My skin tone was the color of Frappuccino, my eyes came from my father. Everything else was on my beautiful mom.

"Mi hijo (*my son*)," my father gave me a weak smile. I remained quiet for a while. It's what I did when I needed to think and take something in. Right now, I was observing my father closely. I walked further into the dimly lit room. They had lots of pillows piled up behind him. My father was fifty-three years old and didn't look a day over thirty. His curly black hair didn't have not even one piece of gray added to it.

"How many men, ju kill?" He laughed lowly. I finally cracked a smile and bowed my head until both of our foreheads were touching. Standing up, I pulled a chair close to his bedside. Killa and Big B showed respect and shook his free hand. I noticed his left hand had heavy bandaging.

"Just one pops, I really want to kill all." I gritted. Leaving out the fact that one of my men killed two brothers, I was still telling the truth because the fact was that I only killed one. I wished like hell he wasn't close to Callista's father. I wanted to kill her ass too. She didn't take no for an answer, and she always tried her hardest to get back in my good graces no matter how much she knew that I despised her.

"Controla tu ira (*Control your anger*)." He gave me a serious look.

"I will, once I know what is going on." His eyes lowered, he looked away from me. This was big, I could see the uncertainty on my father's face.

"Kill and B, let me and my father speak." They moved out the room and shut the door behind them. My father cleared his throat.

"I'm trying to rebuild the golden triangle. El Munchio, is not happy with me. I lost his alliance over the gun trades to the Dominican Republic and Cuba. I agreed to Herion because moving it is easier. I will not supply the Republic or Cuba. They don't respect us." He paused, the room was filled with a comfortable silence. I thought to myself, why my father didn't warn me about this. He was just as big as El Munchio, my father took pride in running one of the biggest cartels in Mexico. He constantly took care of his people and made sure the poor had food as well as money. He provided legal jobs for men and women that needed to provide for their families. He stood on standards his reputation proceeded him.

El Munchio, was the opposite. On his side of Mexico, he ran things eviler. He took from the poor and flooded his cities with the same drugs that he distributed to other countries. Women were treated like sex slaves; he sold and did whatever he saw fit without having any morals. My father had a strong alliance with El Munchio's cartel and Nueva's cartel. Together, all three of them called themselves the golden triangle. Other cartels respected them and made sure to steer clear as well.

"I don't know if it was Nueva." My father coughed lightly. "I lost his alliance too, ju know he follows closely behind El Munchio. Too scared to make his own decisions as a man. His virgin daughter married El Munchio's son, so they are tied as a family."

I shook my head at that, arranged marriages were something that went on here a lot. To merge powerful families together and make them stronger. I was glad that my father never sprung that type of shit on me. Things were too complicated here in Mexico. If some shit like this happened in California, then I would wipe the whole operation out, within a couple of days to be exact.

"How did the attackers look? Where was Jose?" I pressed on. I needed way more information than what my old man was giving.

"Jose covered a meeting. I didn't need him at my daughter's christening. They attacked there. I don't know how they looked Malice." I could see the anger behind his eyes. Him not knowing infuriated him more.

"You still having kids. How many now Papa?" I raised my brows.

"Sixteen, three died. Leaving me with thirteen. Ju know, ju should get to know them all. I finally got all of my wives under the same roof in the City of Angels. Well not all, except your mother she would never go for that, and I wouldn't expect her to." I shook my head quickly, agreeing to what he said. My father was selfish when it came to my mom. He only wanted my mom to himself.

"Why they can't stay here?" I pestered.

"I don't want to have a heart attack. I visit on weekends. Plus, ju will stay here." Ignoring what he said because no way in hell was I about to stay here when I had my own list of problems back home. I was in the middle of a drug war. Taking over wasn't as easy as I thought. There was one particular gang that was bowing out gracefully no matter how many people I took out they seemed to multiply.

"Where all were you shot at Pa?" His stomach had a bandage, so I assumed there.

"My stomach, hand, and leg. No main arteries. I might have to walk with a cane. Nothing major." He shrugged like it was nothing but every time he moved, I could tell it pained him. "Mi hijo, I need ju." I wanted to drop my head in defeat.

Him needing me, could be too much. It could mean doing some shit that I wasn't willing to do.

"I need to create a new triangle. I have one already aligned; I need a third. Without strong alliances, ju know what would happen. The next hit, could be... I dunno... successful." That stirred something in me. I wouldn't know what to do if I lost my old man.

"You have to help with the third alliance. I need ju here to train and learn more about the cartel. Ju still can go back and forth between here and California. You would be a filthy rich man." I liked the sound of that. "I don't plan on retiring until another five years. You can run things, but I will remain head of it all until I hand it over to ju. Your temper and thinking has to get better."

I nodded my head in agreement. A man was blind if he didn't acknowledge what he had to fix or make better for himself.

"What else comes with this?"

"Ju will need to get married... within a couple of weeks. My third alliance is with the Martinez cartel. She will be retiring, and her granddaughter will step into her shoes very soon which will give us a tight tie with that very powerful cartel."

My heart dropped into my ass, suddenly the room felt stuffy and everything else my father said didn't sound so clear. Me getting married to a bitch that I didn't know, was some crazy shit. I wouldn't be faithful to her; I was faithful to the streets and moving big drugs. I never thought about marriage, nor did I want the shit. A nigga like me needed to be free and not tied down. Women could be worse than men, hard to trust and sneaky as fuck.

Callista was the prime example of that. She served as a reminder to never fall for a bitch with a fat ass and pretty face. Niggas always seemed to become blinded when it came to women. My father was proof of that, he was in his fifties still having fucking kids. Had he been more focused on his fucking cartel then we probably wouldn't even be discussing my freedom as a single man.

KENYA MONROE

J watched Inferno stand on the balcony overlooking the city. He always stood in a way that made him appear humble yet powerful. Shirtless, with only Versace briefs on, he stood tall as hell in all his fine glory. I kept asking how did I score a man like him but then if I stepped back and looked at myself in the mirror I knew why. I had curves that put the average chick to shame. My light sun-kissed complexion always made the toughest men bow down to their knees and give me whatever it was I asked for.

"Yeah." He spoke into the phone as I tried to quiet my lustful thoughts, to ear hustle what his conversation was about. He walked away from the balcony and took a seat on the chaise that sat in the corner of our massive bedroom. Stretching his long caramel legs before him and laying his hand on his washboard abs had me licking my lips and thanking the man above.

"I thought you were coming to meet my parents." A desperate bitch whined into the phone. All Inferno offered was a soft chuckle giving his answer.

"Listen, Inferno... I love you baby. I want us to work

something out. This baby I'm carrying will bring us closer than you think." She sobbed softly.

"The baby will bring me to become a good father. I don't want to be your man Mi'elle. I'm the nigga that gives you good dick." He looked over at me and winked his eyes and grabbed his juicy dick through his boxers causing me to squeeze my own thighs tight.

"Plus, I'll be a married man soon." My stomach dropped as he eyed me very carefully while tucking his juicy bottom lip into his mouth. "That baby ain't mine, Mi'elle. I wrap up every time and even after I never leave the opportunity for a bitch to sneak and stuff my shit up their pussy. Once the DNA is cleared, I'll be a distant memory for you."

"Bye Malice." She hung up. I didn't know what to say so I busied myself with my phone. Inferno let out a deep chuckle and tossed his phone to the side as he laid his head back and sighed.

"Yeah." Again, he answered his phone with agitation laced in his tone of voice. This was anytime we spent time together. His phone rang nonstop, somebody always needed something from him. His nonchalant attitude always made him appear like he didn't give a fuck.

"Why you answering like that nigga."

"Killa get to it nigga. I'm tryna relax for a couple of seconds before I start making moves in the city." I slightly rolled my eyes at the sound of Killa's voice.

"Her name is Queen; she owns a clinic off Rodeo called Sovereignty. In a couple of days, she supposes to celebrate her sister's birthday at a club."

"Bet, set me up an appointment at her clinic before it closes. The night of the celebration we snatch her ass up."

"You not coming to the annual toy drive in south central today?" Killa asked sounding shocked.

"Do I ever?" Those thick sexy eyebrows of his raised and Killa chuckled into the phone. That was very likely of Inferno, he always gave back to the community and never boasted, or liked the attention that came with it. You would never catch this man on social media bragging and recording himself feeding the homeless. He loved staying anonymous for his own special reasons. I don't even think he realized how big of a blessing he was to so many people.

"Bet nigga." Killa caught on to Inferno's silence and hung the phone up. Now those big two-toned eyes were focusing on me as he licked his full set of lips.

"You got something you need to be doing." I already knew what that meant. My heart felt like it was starting to thump instead of beat normally. Why couldn't he see that the only thing I wanted to do was him.

I was in love with him, from his natural curly lashes down to his big prominent beautiful eyes. The burnt mark along his chiseled jawline added roughness to his perfect-looking face.

Inferno stood and slid his boxers down then walked across the room dick limp and all swinging with precision hitting his muscular thighs. He paused in front of the mirror to take in his appearance then looked at me. His eyes swept over me fast, I wished I could read his thoughts to somehow know what it was he was thinking.

"You about to leave." I held my breath.

"No, I want to fuck you, feed you, then go over the numbers." His smile always looked like a sneer, but it still fit him. Our friendship meant everything to me, but I still wanted more. I wanted to be his woman.

"Come shower with me." He disappeared into the bathroom. Shortly after, I heard the shower water start up. Being a part of Inferno's syndicate came with lots of benefits. I was his accountant and close friend. I watched him mature even more over the years. With each year that went by my feelings blossomed even more for him. My loyalty was a hundred percent and I dedicated myself to him and only him. Inferno was hot and cold with affection, most times he appeared as a friend but days like this felt like he was something more. All of his close comrades respected me except one, most assumed that I was the main lady in his life which felt good.

"Kenya, out of your thoughts. A lot has to be done today." That never changed, things had to be done every day. I played my role well in this business that I had going with Inferno. I played his assistant, accountant, friend, and fuck buddy, I also created plenty of ways to clean up lots of his money. The list was long when it came to the things I had to do for this syndicate. My bank account was laced, and I had no complaints. I liked to believe that I was the main leading lady in his life but deep down I knew at any given moment that could change with the snap of his burnt rough fingertips.

I strip down where I stood and walked slowly into the bathroom, I counted each second, careful not to make him wait a moment too long. Was this what my life consisted of? Should I be shameful to willingly give myself to a man that didn't want me in the same ways that I wanted him. Sometimes it was so painful that I had to force my own tears down. I made my bed and had to lay in it. Showing too much emotion would make him push back from me. I already had to keep my chin lifted up when I knew of the nights that he chose to lay with someone else.

Inferno was a lot of things and people from the outside looking in felt like he lived up to his government name a hundred percent. Malice was cold and very calculated with everything he did. I never saw the killer side of him, but I saw it in his eyes when someone had him vexed. I'd heard horrific stories on the news, and they just could never place a face with the crime scene. Somehow, I always knew that it was him. Anything connected with arson and a person being burnt alive always had something to do with Inferno.

I stepped behind him in the shower and softly placed my hands flat on his well-defined back which had several tattoos covering up his rugged toffee skin tone. He turned around to face me, with a hard soapy dick. I slowly dropped down to my knees and allowed the water to wash away the soap before I took the head into my mouth. Closing my eyes and taking him all the way to the back of my throat. I relaxed a little and breathed through my nose.

Inferno's sex drive was impeccable for a thirty-two-year-old man, his sperm tasted good without any disgusting after-taste. Whenever I sucked his beautiful long dick, I did it with pride like I was trying to win the best-sucking dick award. I wanted him to always remember me and never forget who brought him down to the best orgasm. Looking down at his pedicured toes, I smiled on the inside as they curled. Hearing the animalistic grunts encouraged me to go harder. I gathered more salvia and left it idle in my throat as I swallowed and gargled his dick.

"Fuck Monroe, ease the fuck up." He gritted but I wouldn't in fact, I could feel the veins in his shaft swell up on top of my tongue and got super excited. Before I could trace my tongue down to his tight balls, he grabbed me by the neck and pulled me up to my feet.

Placing a soft kiss to my forehead we stared at one another for a couple of seconds. I wanted to get emotional, but I was too afraid to show the worry in my eyes. I couldn't ignore the fact that he mentioned marriage. How could he decide to get married when he was currently staring at me like I was the only woman in his life that he wanted to commit to?

Still saying nothing, he lifted my one hundred and fifty pounds with ease. My legs spread wide open for him as he entered me raw. Dick feeling me to the brim, the pleasure outweighed the pain from his long length inside of me.

"Uhhhh, baby." I fought to catch my breath and close my mouth, but I just couldn't.

"Mmmhmm." His sex face was so fucking sexy it made my pussy contract even more around his girth. The only thing that could be heard was our skin slapping and my pussy spitting out for him and only him.

"Look at me Monroe, with yo sexy ass." My eyes landed on his juicy cinnamon lips. I wanted to kiss him so bad, but I knew that was big violation for him. The most I ever got was quick pecks. "You ain't got to say it, just show a nigga you love me, sexy." The ruggedness of his fingers gripped my ass, he spread each cheek apart to push in deeper. My eyes were flickering, and I didn't know how long I could maintain eye contact with him.

"Cum with me baby." His voice held need and it made my insides stir for him. The kind of dick this man delivered wasn't normal and he wondered why he had women that was only one night stands tatt his name a million times. This was trophy type of dick, the kind you wanted to put inside of a lock box and keep hidden away from the world.

My mouth fell open, but nothing came out. My stomach cramped up along with my feet, I released right along with Inferno as he held me tight for what felt like an eternity. Once my breathing returned to normal, he placed me down slowly and gave me his back to look at.

"What do you want to eat?" It was a simple question that had me nibbling on my bottom lip. When he turned to stare at me, my breath got caught in my throat and I somehow started to choke feeling more stupid in front of him. After all these years of dealing with Inferno, I couldn't seem to adjust to how fine this man was. I was smitten all the time and found myself lusting and feeling silly in love.

Malice Ashonti Ruiz was one of a fucking kind. There wasn't a man alive, walking this earth that had any resemblance close to him. He had his own signature walk, he talked differently and the way he made his moves out in the streets made him a different type of gangsta. I kept praying that one-day God would bless me. I wanted God to open this man's eyes up to see that I was the woman for him. My parents and all my peers would be very disappointed if they knew the truth and what I was really out here doing. I didn't give a damn because this was the life I chose. At the end of it all, I chose my soon-to-be man Inferno.

"Kenya? You keep doing that spacing-out shit. I don't got time for it. What's up with you?" he raised one brow as I snapped out of my thoughts.

"You, umm… getting married?" I was surprised myself. I never really questioned him. I sure as hell didn't want to make it seem like I was ear-hustling. He said the shit right in front of me. I wanted to know who the bitch was so I could carefully plot a way to kill her ass.

I wasn't a killer but being around someone like Inferno made me wonder what it would feel like to kill. I wasn't killing anyone I hope I wasn't that far gone off this man that I was ready and willing to catch my first body. I picked up my towel and grabbed the dove soap and started to bathe myself. That gave me something to do other than feeling nervous from his hard stare. Inferno had a way of making a person feel really small. I saw the look of irritation cross his eyes and dropped my head, looking at my white toes.

"Nothing to worry about Kenya. It's business that has nothing to do with you." I wanted to press him further, that thick deep accent was laced in every word he spoke which indicated to me that I irked him by speaking up on the conversation I heard.

"I got love for you Monroe, as a friend you know that. Don't ever confuse it and step out of place. Think about what you want to eat. Don't worry about who I'm marrying because it won't change shit with you and I." I swallowed down hard and blinked away the tears.

"This is all we will ever be?" My bottom lip quivered at the reality. I became pissed with myself. I sounded like the woman that was crying on the phone to him earlier. I always tried to appear strong and unbothered by the things Inferno did because I didn't want him to leave me. I don't think I could possibly live without him.

"Yes, Kenya. This is all we will ever be. If this is too much for you don't open the door the next time I knock. I promise you will keep your job and this nice penthouse that I pay for every month. You can even get married and start a family. We will always remain friends. If it's my heart that you seek, then stop trying to find it. I'm dead inside when it comes to those things." He left me in the shower without even turning to see the hurt he had cost me.

SOVEREIGN AKA QUEEN

*T*oday was F.Y.F.'s meeting day, I had a lot weighing me down and the main thing was thoughts of Abuela. I wanted no part in getting married, after dealing with Melvin and hiding the heartbreak that I suffered from. I didn't want to dedicate or submit to no nigga. I was my own woman, I stood ten toes down when shit got bad for me, and I never asked for a helping fucking hand. Deep down, I knew I didn't have a choice. My Abuela was deadly and powerful. When she asked you to do something, it was more like she was telling you. I wasn't letting what I took years and time to build go down the fucking drain.

I thought of a thousand ways to get out of this so-called arranged marriage shit and came up empty-handed. I needed the money, although I had a good amount now. Compared to what I could've had was petty compared to the money my Abuela possessed along with her power. Melvin put me and my crew in the hole. Not only did he lie and play me hard he stole so much fucking money right underneath my nose. The love for him turned into hate easily. He infiltrated my crew and had multiple disloyal people working alongside of him while pledging their allegiance to me.

I hated him so bad I wanted him dead but didn't want to give him an easy death so the torture I had in place for him ended up failing. I lost money and the daughter that I snatched away from his wife. I ended up loving the little girl with all of my heart. It all backfired and everything started to collapse around me. I still was trying to put the puzzle to the many pieces that was missing when it came to Melvin and my daughter. That night will forever hunt me, it was the reason I didn't get the proper rest I needed at night.

One main thing that I learned from the situation was to never react so fast off anger. The night I discovered Melvin missing, I went on a rampage of killing, I didn't ask the questions that needed to be asked that night. Till this day I wondered how he was able to escape along with the baby. I killed anyone that looked guilty and whomever I thought had a hand in it. I often wondered was any of the men still lurking around and where the fuck was Melvin. He was out somewhere just living life right after he betrayed me. I knew my Abuela had the resources that would lead me right to him, I just needed to play my cards right.

I no longer felt like I was playing chess, shit started to feel like a petty tournament of checkers. I had to majorly step my shit up and gain the power I needed to be the rightful queen.

I tried my very best to ease my nerves and thoughts as my soldiers started to walk in. Some had nervous looks while others looked confident. I eyed my sister and shook my head because her eyes were glued to Murk'um. I kept a blank facial expression but was starting to burn up at the thought of her falling for this nigga. Love almost disgusted me, it was for the weak and blinded you from seeing what was supposed to be seen. I made a mental note to have a side conversation with Murk'um.

I didn't give a fuck about who Empress gave her pussy to, she was a grown-ass woman and so was Murk'um. When it came to my business and running a smooth operation, business mixed with pleasure was a big fuckin' no. It was either, they stopped whatever the fuck they had going on, or go get down with another crew.

My eyes scanned the room, silence immediately took over. I planned on getting something more sufficient for us to meet up at to go over things for the gang. For now, the back of my clinic had to be where we got down to business at. I had a huge empty room located in the back of my clinic where all equipment and product were held for the estheticians that worked here. It was after hours now, and I had everyone park in the back. I made the crew travel from L.A to Rodeo drive to meet up at Sovereignty's. I loved my clinic and took pride in it. It gave me something different other than being in the streets.

I had folding chairs all around, it was about fifteen of us here. The only people I let come here were the ones in charge of handing me my money at the end of each week. They were responsible for their own private crews, meaning one fuck up and they took the fall or the bullet.

"Clapback, run the week down to me." I looked down at my iced-out Rolex watch and clicked my tongue three times to let her know not to ramble and get to the point.

"Money is good like the survival of every nigga in this room." She smiled and took a small tote from her blunt then passed it to Murk'um.

"Murk'um finish running shit down, I don't have time for Clapback's antics." I took my eyes off her and focused on Murk'um.

"What the fuck is that supposed to mean?" I cracked my neck, Empress had me ready to snap her neck for speaking to me recklessly, especially in front of all my men. Behind closed doors I let her get away with a lot because I was to blame for her being so damn spoiled.

"It means nothing." I winked at her and gave Murk'um my full attention.

"Like Clapback said Queen, things as far as the money is good, very good. I think we need to up the ante to see more of it. Then we have that constant problem from that so called syndicate shit. A nigga named Killa been pulling up asking the niggas for a meeting with the head of F.Y.F. He keeps saying his boss wants us to step in line with his syndicate or else we will all get laid down. So far you have two funerals to pay for." He licked his dry black lips, and I took my eyes off him. Placing my elbows on the rickety folding table, I thought for a couple of seconds. I didn't want to show my emotions, but I was pissed the fuck off.

I didn't know who this so-called syndicate belonged to or why its boss was starting to fuck with me. I didn't have enough soldiers for a fucking war. War would mean more guns and more bodies dropping. Whenever a loyal soldier got killed it was my duty to bury them. I constantly talked to these niggas about getting life insurance so it would be less out of my pocket. Black people were really stubborn when it came to getting themselves some coverage in case they died. Most felt like it was jinxing themselves. I was about to make that important and a necessity in our next meeting. One of my main niggas sold life insurance so I was about to sit all these niggas down and force them to sign up for the shit.

"Okay, I'll let you know after this meeting what moves we gone make. However, F.Y.F ain't getting down with no niggas, nor do we fall in line." I watched everybody nod their heads in agreement, I couldn't afford a war, but I was no punk bitch. Niggas knew that my nuts were just as big as theirs. I was almost positive that it was a young and dumb nigga trying to move reckless and make a name for himself by thinking he was gone punk my fucking crew.

"I don't know Queen, whomever this nigga is seems like a big deal." Clapback smiled, and I finally gave her the attention she was asking for. I held my hand out and looked at my perfect French tip nails.

"How would you know Clap? Instagram?" I raised my arched right eyebrow at her and smirked when her mouth clamped shut. She spent too much time on social media, that shit kept her brains in the clouds. A couple of my men murmured and chuckled. I gave them a stern look and it seized immediately.

"Do tell, do tell… I'm pretty sure we all would like to know where you got this valid information from." I urged her, I loved the hell out of my sister but when it came to being smart, she lacked that. Her beauty was undeniable, but her brain was the size of a fucking piece of grain.

"I didn't say it was valid, I said he seems-"

"Like a big deal, right? What would make you think that?" I spat sarcastically, she needed to learn how to just shut the fuck up and follow my lead at these meetings. She stayed trying to prove something to all the niggas and bitches that truly didn't give a fuck. Clapback loved having bragging rights. I was her bragging right, she thought that when we had these meetings that she had a place right next to me and which she somewhat did. I trusted her more than anyone in this room. When it came to my money and my crew, I had the final say so. Her job was to be the overseeing person when my hands were too tied. She would relay messages and do the big pick-ups since she knew exactly where all my safes and stashes were.

Clapback's problem was she sometimes liked to live in some sort of fantasy world. Always giving people the benefit of the doubt. It's why I didn't have a solid right-hand man. Murk'um and Bundy were the niggas that did all my dirty work and forced niggas to bow the fuck down. It was one of the main reasons why I didn't want Empress sinking her teeth in one of the hardest niggas I had on my team. I needed Murk'um alert with no distractions. Empress was that big distraction which was why I planned on nipping whatever her and Murk'um had going on.

"My apologies, boss lady." She curled her lips tight and sat back in her chair. I decided to let her make it. She embarrassed her own self by talking out of term.

"In two weeks, I will be appointing one of you as my lieutenant. I'll be out of town on business. So, the way you move and the things you all do will be taken into consideration. Pick-ups and drop offs will remain the same." My eyes landed on Teddy; he was seventeen with no family. Hungry little nigga, he provided for himself and his two younger siblings since his mom was too strung out. We made eye contact, and he shifted his gaze. I could tell something was bothering him. I hurried up and closed out this meeting so I could pull him to the side and talk to him.

"I leave in two days, tomorrow we celebrate Clapback's birthday so dress to impress." I paused and took in everyone's excitement. That announcement made Empress smile, she probably thought that I had forgotten her special day.

"When I get back in town, be ready to put in that fuckin work. Less sleeping more grinding, I guarantee it's gone pay off majorly. I'm making moves to better the squad. Trust when I say soon as my feet touch back down on Cali soil, each and every one of y'all pockets will be healthy."

I stood to my feet after we talked more business.

"Fuck yo feelings!" I stuck the middle finger up and everyone followed.

"Fuck yo feelings!" They roared as I took a seat.

"Teddy, go into my operating room and get on the examining table." I winked at him. Teddy had bad acne pimples all across his chubby cheeks and nose. I figured I'd get to the bottom of what was going on with him by easing my own anxiety and working on his face a little today after hours.

"Murk'um and Clapback, I need to have a conversation with you two. The rest of you are dismissed." I watched all the men file out of the room. Bundy walked right up to me smiling. Bundy was a big, tall, buff nigga, always making sure I was straight. We all had hard lives and our parents were no longer in the picture. Bundy always made sure I had everything I needed, like now, I needed a blunt and Bundy sat an already rolled blunt right in front of me.

"See you later Queen." I watched his broad shoulders walk out of the room. Once everyone was out. No one else remained but Empress, me, and Murk'um.

"You two stop whatever it is that you have going on. I don't want to hear excuses and whatever else might come out of your mouths. You either stop fucking or walk away from F.Y.F. this is my final warning. Dismissed." Murk'um nodded in agreement, but Empress just had to be the brat of a little sister.

"That's bullshit, Queen!" I stood up and marched her way. I didn't have to say shit because she knew what was about to happen. I halted my hand back and slapped the fuck out of her twice. Grabbing her up by the neck, I aligned my mouth close to her ear so she could hear me clearly. Her outburst confirmed my suspicions. It pissed me off more at the fact of her blatantly going against what I stated from the very beginning. No business mixed with pleasure. Clearly her and Murk'um had been fucking. I looked over at Murk'um with disappointment. I expected more from him.

"Little sis... it seems like you're forgetting who you fucking with. You out of all people know what the fuck I had to go through to get to where I am now. I will end you before I risk losing what the fuck I have built. I love you Empress, but you are no weak spot for me. Understand that the next time you speak out of term and test my authority, I'll put you down like the mutt bitch you are." I stepped back watching her eyes mist over.

I didn't give a damn about hurting her feelings right now. Empress knew what I went through. Instead of her disobeying me, she should have learned from me and the lessons I had to learn when it came to mixing business with pleasure and feelings when it came to Melvin. I could have got down with Bundy after Melvin, but I chose not to. Bundy was sweet and would go to war for me. I knew he would lay his life down on the line without a question as well. I just wasn't willing to risk that and besides his good looks, I felt nothing deep for Bundy.

I walked out of the room because I hated having to go so hard on Empress. I spoiled her and made sure she never went without. Just like a parent having to constantly teach their child a lesson. I constantly had to do that with Empress even though she was grown. She was my baby sister and I cared deeply about her but lately, she had been testing dangerous waters with me. If being a part of F.Y.F was becoming too much to handle for her then she had better let me know. I never wanted her apart of my shit to begin with. I started this shit to make sure we survived.

I made it to the room where Teddy was at. Standing at the room door, pride swelled in me. My clinic was really nice, I had state-of-the-art equipment and really enjoyed working on people's skin care. Most people got disgusted when it came time to pop pimples but since I was young, I enjoyed doing just that. For some odd reason, it relaxed me and relieved my anxiety. When I found myself not being able to sleep at night, I'd pull up a YouTube video and watch a pimple-popping tutorial until my eyes got too heavy and I'd give in to my sleep.

I looked at Teddy and he somehow reminded me of myself when I was younger. He was really a genuine person and had the ambition to get far in life. I wanted that for him as well. I sometimes wish I had that extra push when I was his age. Teddy was seventeen but looked like he was twenty-five. You could look deep in his eyes and tell that he had been through more than what a boy his age should have gone through. As weird as it might've sounded, I loved Teddy like he was a son of mine. I just couldn't take on full responsibility because I had too many other things on my plate.

What I liked most about Teddy is that he had a lot of pride despite his situation. He didn't brag and tell people what all was done for him in order to look cool. He was very humble and respectful, and no matter what he went through he kept his head held high.

I started the steamer to put on his face and started pulling utensils out.

"Talk to me, Teddy." He sighed as I put on my black latex gloves. I cleansed his face and started prepping to pop some of the blackheads that decorated his pecan-colored cheeks.

"I been having to use the money that I've been saving to put with re-up money. I never want to come up short, but

51

moms been stealing again from my stash." I willed myself to remain calm.

"Have you been eating?" I looked down at his dirty Air Force Ones and knew the answer to that. Teddy didn't like too many handouts. He was very stubborn when it came to me trying to help him more when it came to him and his siblings.

"I'm good Queen, you already doing enough paying for my tuition at the private school. I just feel bad as fuck for having the product in the house. My momma comes in and acts like she wants to be a mom for a couple of days. She always wants to act like she getting clean then turn around and steal and remain gone for weeks at a time. Shit doesn't bother me much, but my sisters… that shit crushes them. Their behavior starts getting worse at daycare and school. I know they just acting the fuck out. It's just added stress but I'm good." He winced a little when I applied pressure to the big black head that was right underneath his eye. White puss popped out and I pressed harder to get to the actual black head. That was Teddy's favorite word, *I'm good though.* He would tell you his problems but try his hardest to reassure you that he was just fine.

"You gotta put the work somewhere else Teddy. You can keep it at my house, you just gone have to travel to pick the shit up. How's football going." I tried to brighten up the conversation.

"I dropped that shit for now, daycare fees kicking my ass." My stomach tightened. I knew just how much he loved football. If he wasn't running down on the young niggas, he had in place to move the work that I supplied him with, he was with his siblings or football practice. Things had to be spiraling for him to drop out and I didn't like that.

"You know if all of this is becoming too much Teddy, I

can hire you here. It might not be the same amount of what you make in the streets, but it will be something. You still got to follow your dreams."

I was in his position before and didn't have that much of a choice just like him. I also didn't have someone like me in my life at his age offering something more than just having sex with stranger men to save up to purchase my first brick of cocaine. I wanted to give Teddy options and was hoping that he could make smart choices with what I presented to him. He only told me what he wanted me to know, and I couldn't do anything but respect that shit. It was his life and his decisions and although he was young as hell, I still respected him like a grown man because he was mature and moved like one.

"I can't do that Queen, I got bills and kids to feed. If I can, I'll get back to football soon. I really want to drop out of school, but I know you ain't having that so a nigga doing the best that I can." He opened his eyes a little and stared up at me. I said nothing as I continued to work on his face. We made small talk and when I finished up working on him, I went in my purse and handed him a knot full of money. At first, he didn't want to accept it, but I refused to put it back into my Gucci bag. Once he left, I used that time to clean my private room. I went to the meeting room and saw that Murk'um cleaned up and put the folding chairs away.

After a long day, I was ready to head straight to the hotel I had reserved. I wanted my niggas to rub my ass and feet and feast on me until I passed the hell out. Yes! You heard me very correctly; I had two niggas, and it was truly worth it. I wouldn't call them my boyfriends, but they were my friends, and we did freaky shit together. Aiden and Caiden were fine as fuck and paid. They took over the modeling industry all throughout Hollywood. I made a lot of money off of them as well. I supplied the drugs that they needed, and they brought back the cash.

Half of Hollywood was hooked on drugs, especially the models. They wanted drugs to curve their appetites. I met Aiden and Caiden during my teenage years when I was wild and sleeping around to come up out of poverty. We went to school together and reconnected at a wild college party. I end up getting drunk, but I never got to faded to not know what the fuck I was doing. That same night we ended up getting freaky after I told them a wild fantasy of mine. That fantasy was to have a threesome with twins. I saw the opportunity afterward when we would just hang out for fun. They spoke about modeling and the things that went on in that industry and they easily became runners for me.

I stopped dealing with them sexually when I got with Melvin's bitch ass but never ended my business deal with them. I really looked at the twins like close friends, we always partied hard and enjoyed each other's company. When I didn't want to be alone and wanted to call them to hang, they always came running. They didn't expect much out of me because they still had their own personal lives to live. People on the outside probably viewed us as weird as fuck. Probably thought of me as being a hoe. One thing about having good pussy is that you rarely gave a fuck what people thought.

I didn't suck dick and the twins weren't that big when it came to the sizes of their dicks. They were just freaky as hell, and we had a crazy sexual chemistry that I rocked hard with. I enjoyed my body being explored by four sets of hands. Call it what the fuck you want!

In my eyes I had to pay the cost for a long time to get and do just what the fuck I wanted to. I often wondered what my mom and dad would think of me, especially after all the trials and tribulations I went through just to get to where I am now. I hope they understood that I had no other choice. My Abuela was not our saving grace and when she finally decided to find us and help. She had her own personal reasons that I didn't fuck with. Here it was years later, and I was left with no choice but to comply with her. I needed her back up and her help even though it was hard as hell for me to admit to that.

I had demons that kept me up late at night, I fought hard with them and did everything in my power to stay strong. I wasn't proud of a lot of things; I didn't have magic to erase shit that came with the decisions I made along the way in life. I conditioned my brain and heart a certain way to never feel pain unless it was a bullet to one of my body parts. Empress was grown now; I did the best I could to raise her in a way to not act as blind as she did now. She's the main person along the way that saw how hard we both had it. She saw me at a young age lay down and take dick after dick until it ruined my fucking uterus all for us to have food on the table. Sometimes I sat back and wondered if it was all for nothing.

I did a double-check on the clinic to make sure everything was secure and finally walked towards my car enjoying the night air that caressed my face. My eyes scanned the empty parking lot, I kept my hand inside of my black Nike hoodie and kept checking my surroundings. Usually, Murk'um and Bundy would stay back and make sure I made it to my car safe. Since I dismissed them early, they were long gone. No one was near as far as my eyes could see, but my intuition was telling me that somebody was watching me.

INFERNO

I stood close to the fire, inhaling it, I almost forgot how many times I coughed and shuddered. My throat burned as my eyes flickered in amazement, I felt like I was in a trance like I couldn't snap out of this shit. The sight of fire and the way it flickered and burnt slow had all the blood rushing to the tip of my dick. It was time to put this fucking fire out, but it was just starting to bloom the way I wanted it to. Feeling dizzy and consumed with reluctance, I picked up the fire extinguisher and aimed it at the heart of the fire that I had started in my private chambers that was located underground. I called the west wing of my home "Hades". I loved this area the most, everything was red and black. The smell soon as you got close near Hades smelled like burning wood, smoke, and ash.

Some would say I had a problem, my mom called it Pyromania. My father always backed me up by telling my mom that I was just being a boy and that I would grow out of it. That was a lie because I grew into the shit with no problem. I grew to love and be incited by it. Fire ignited something in me that no one else could. It felt like I had a bond with it, my persona matched it well. Stepping out of what was my chamber, I took the steps as fast as I could to get fresh air from my room.

The steps to get to my chamber was connected to my room walk in closet. I could feel the shift in the air soon as my feet landed onto my carpet and top step. I moved the huge family picture of just me and my parents in front of the door then pushed my heavy ass safe in place. Moving my suits on the rack back in place, I stripped out of the dingy Levi pants and shirt that I had on and tossed them in the hamper. When I entered my room, I instantly could feel the coldness and wind hitting my face. All of my windows were opened, and I was grateful for the fresh air.

After talking with my father and hearing him practically plead with me to fly back to Mexico within the next two days had me feeling on edge. I was always busy, the fact that I had to step up and do more in Mexico would mean more sleepless nights. I was trying to expand my syndicate past the United States and do more. I didn't have a problem with running things in Mexico my big problem was marriage. Sure, it was nothing but a piece of paper, but I just didn't want to be tied to a woman in that way. The only thing I wanted ties with was my money.

After showering, I dressed in all black, the only piece of color that I had on me was a thick Cuban gold chain and a simple twenty-four carat gold watch. I went to my dresser and eyed the different weapons and since Big B would accompany me, I decided on my mini-Flamethrower and desert eagle pistol. As I descended the steps and made my way to the front of my house, I stopped in my tracks to answer my phone.

"Yeah." I waited for Kenya to say what she needed, it was already seven in the evening, and I still had a list of things to do.

"Am I going to the club with you tonight?" Her soft sexy voice was always good to hear.

"No, I'll be handling business tonight." I hung up not waiting for a response. I didn't have the extra time to hear her breathe and think on what to say to me. Kenya was weird but beautiful as fuck, she knew how to suck and fuck me the way that I liked. She wasn't clingy and handled business the way I expected her too. I had love for her but that's exactly where it stopped. The main reason why I treated her with enough respect was because she went above and beyond for me. Sometimes when I looked at her, the thought of her wanting more from me ran rampant in my mind. I hoped like hell she wasn't thinking about pushing for more, that would truly be the day that I ended our personal close relationship.

The line of business I was in, I only had time to release my nut sack and get right back to business. Big B arrived on time; I shook my head at the tight ass clothes he had on. All the money this nigga had he always dressed tacky as hell. He swore he had swag, but the shit always ended up looking stupid as fuck. He was a big buff ass nigga wearing shit that looked two sizes to small and very uncomfortable. Killa complained all the time about his clothes, but I told him that it didn't bother me because I didn't give a fuck what the next nigga did. As long as it didn't affect my money, I wouldn't speak on shit concerning the next man's wardrobe. Big B shook M&M's in his hand like they were dice and threw them back and started crunching down hard like they were his favorite meal.

"Finish that shit before you get inside my car." That was

the greeting I offered him. Everybody knew how much I fucking loved my cars, the car that I picked tonight was my favorite and the market price was worth over twelve million dollars. It was a Rolls Royce Sweptail they only created five of these bitches. My father gifted me this one for my thirtieth birthday and had it delivered. The fiery candy paint red color made me fall in love harder each time I laid eyes on it.

The breeze picked up and I frowned at that, it should've been warming up since it was towards the end of May, summer was right around the corner. With the wind being so ignorant it would fuck with my introduction that I had planned for tonight after leaving the club.

"Killa will be at the club as soon as it opens." I nodded my head and fired up my engine loving the way it roared to life. The night was still young, and my first destination was the infamous café called "Eugene's Palace." Things were moving faster than I expected, and I needed a new attorney. A bad ass attorney to make sure that I didn't encounter any problems with the feds. I liked to stay out of the spotlight and lowkey as possible. I just never knew when a fed was thirsty enough to try and build a case on me. My father had Mexico's police and the entire system inside his back pockets. I didn't pay them shit because they had no clue how far my business went. They probably tried to have a good idea, but they would never have concrete evidence with the way I moved.

Pulling right in front of the café, I eyed valet hard then tossed him my keys. Before stepping into the establishment, I walked around my car and eyed the paint job carefully.

"You like fires?" I asked the young freckle face valet guy that held my keys securely in his pale hands.

"No sir." I watched his Adam's apple move down his throat as he looked everywhere else except for me. I hated that, especially for a man. If a man couldn't look another man in the eyes to me, it was a sign of disrespect and weakness.

"If my car comes back with one scratch, I'm going to properly introduce myself to you. Na'mean?" I winked and walked away with Big B right behind me. We walked through a sea of people until we reached the secluded area in the back. It was deserted with just me and Big B. I checked the time and noted that I was thirty minutes early just to see what kind of attorney this was. Sure, if I set a specific time, I expected whoever I was doing business with to arrive about fifteen minutes before the actual time I set.

I ordered a glass of cognac and ordered appetizers for the table's decoration. I didn't plan on eating anything. I finally stood to my feet when I saw a tall baldhead woman walk towards my table with long oily legs. She favored Serena Williams just skinny as hell with the perfect infectious smile. Pulling out her chair after she greeted me properly, I scooted her up and took a seat across from her.

"It's a pleasure to meet you, Mr. Ruiz." Her big brown eyes sparkled as I offered her a tight smile. I was counting the seconds already, ready to wrap this shit up. It was Kenya's idea that I personally meet up with the person that I would be paying a hefty retainer for.

"Same here, how are you?" I really didn't give a fuck how Ms. Mason was doing. I was ready to cut to the chase but didn't want to appear rude as fuck.

"I'm good, really no complaints. I have to fly out to Chicago tomorrow morning on business. It's kind of hard adjusting to time change when I have to up and leave Cali." She smiled brightly as I thought, *who gives a fuck?*

"So, tell me a little about yourself Malice." She blinked her false lashes and gave me that preppy girl look.

"I prefer Inferno, Ms. Mason." I looked at her blankly.

"If I may ask, how did you find me?" She smiled and picked up the wine that I had ordered five minutes ago for her. I didn't owe her that answer, so I ignored her and picked up my own glass of cognac. Kenya found her and did her own proper research on Ms. Mason. Once it all checked out, I had Kenya situate a meet and greet so here we were. It was very apparent that Ms. Mason wanted to talk a little more about bullshit instead of letting me get right to the point. Women loved to talk and ramble on about a bunch of nothing. Maybe this was her trying to be professional, it was a nice gesture, but she would learn when working with me how simple and easy I liked things. I wasn't into wasting precious time.

Ms. Mason was still waiting on my answer, I chuckled at her and sat my glass down. Big B walked away, and I already knew that he was on his way to get the waitress so she could pour me up another glass of cognac.

"I'm a very busy man Ms. Mason. Do you have the retainer paperwork so I can scan it and sign." Shock was written all over her face, it didn't faze me much. If she kept acting all surprised and stupid, then I wouldn't be signing shit.

"Yes, Inferno. I have the paperwork right here. I just like to get to know my clients. I tried researching you and came up empty handed. What exactly am I dealing with when it comes to you?" Now her face was blank, and my sneer of a smile became evident.

"Again, I'm a very busy man that has my hands into a lot of things Ms. Mason." I looked at my watch then drummed my fingers.

"Okay… so do you need help with copywriting or filing some things?" She was pressing and fishing for more answers than what I was giving. I watched Big B out the corner of my eye stand right back in his position as the waitress walked up with another glass. I took my time and took a sip then placed it down. Placing my elbows on the table I folded my hands.

"I need you to do everything, and when I call you… you better be available for the price that I will be paying you." I eyed her seriously.

"Absolutely Mr. Ruiz." I ignored her slipping up by referring to me again as Mr. Ruiz.

"I'm in my early thirties and in another year, I'm well on my way to becoming a fuckin' billionaire. It's your job to keep the pigs off my dick. Since you're such a fancy ass attorney na'mean?" I sat back a little as I took all of her in, I watched her blank face break and go through a series of emotions.

"I don't work with your kind Mr. Ruiz." Her lips tightened.

"What's my kind Ms. Mason?" Her eyes fell on Big B and widened a little. She was now nervous and trying to choose her words wisely. She leaned close to the table and talked in a hushed tone.

"Drug dealers and murderers, I don't have time for threats and lots of stress." She sat back and eyed her wine glass.

"I take what I do, very serious Ms. Mason and as my attorney you will soon see that." I ate, slept, and breathed this shit. The syndicate would be legendary, it went beyond the petty drugs and all the other bullshit that dumb niggas went after. Sure, the drugs was what made the money, but my hands were twisted into so many other things. All my time was dedicated to bettering my organization and making things better. I wanted to give more opportunities to the less fortunate. California was expensive and there were so many homeless mothers and men that wasn't born with the same golden spoon that I had.

Everyone on my team equally brought something to the

table, of course I was the mastermind. I was ready to expand and bring the syndicate to Mexico and expand even bigger. If I had my way in a couple of years, I would be the backbone of all illegal and legal activities.

"Ms. Mason, I think we are getting off on the wrong foot sweetheart." I made my tone sound more welcoming.

"I'm into creating new opportunities for everyone, you see my business is expanding in ways that you wouldn't be able to comprehend." I already made up my mind that she was the one for this job and I wasn't about to take more time by trying to meet with another attorney.

"How about we not make assumptions about each other and start this meeting over." I didn't want to restart the meeting but again, I was ready to sign the retainer papers and get the fuck out of this place. I had already spent enough time here to begin with. I had other things to do.

I sat with her for another hour and finally went to meet with a crew that had got in line with my syndicate. By the time I arrived at the club, I had a lit blunt dangling between my lips. My section was already reserved and the only person that would be next to me as I sipped slow and peeped out the whole club was Big B. Killa, and the rest of my men were ordered to spread out and act as if I was nonexistent. I already knew how my prey looked. I saw her plenty of times from pictures and me popping up to her clinic and seeing her in passing.

I had to admit, besides the thick dimes and big booty chicks that I went after she just was not my type. Me seeing her as she walked out of her clinic without a care in the world had me watching her a little too long. Her beauty was raw no matter her full figured size. She looked tasty as fuck and had an innocent aura about her. That's what made me intrigued because she didn't look like the type to fight or even get her hands dirty.

What she was doing was beyond brilliant, no one would ever think she was a drug dealing, gun toting, scheming treacherous bitch. She was dangerous in every sense and somewhat smart. Sex appeal leaked from her pores and her scent was tantalizing as fuck. She looked mixed but mainly black.

"That's her sister Clapback." Big B spoke above the loud music as I just nodded my head and looked in the direction. My men knew everything there was to know about F.Y.F down to the bottom members. They weren't as big, but they definitely were rising slowly to the top. Their leader was the mastermind behind it all. Clapback was beautiful, she looked like she was fully Mexican and by the way that she was dressed screamed the need to be fucked.

Looking at her told me everything I needed to know, so it didn't shock me when Killa was able to fuck her and get more information of what I needed to know. The main person that I needed to lay eyes on hadn't appeared. Clapback was the center of attention as everyone cheered her on. She had her hands on her knees and was bent forward shaking her ass. The girl was dangerous, and she knew the effect she had on every man around her. Even Killa looked over at her from his section with hunger in his eyes.

The DJ got on the microphone and screamed happy birthday to Clapback, she held a bottle of Ace of Spades and soaked up the attention that was being given to her. I yawned and looked at my watch. *Where the fuck is this girl?* It was nearing one in the morning, and she still hadn't showed her face.

Suddenly the energy in the club changed and all the attention was dragged towards the entrance of the club. I couldn't see past the big niggas that stood at the entrance but soon as they moved to the side, I found myself readjusting my dick.

"Aw shit the mothafuckin' Queen up in this bitch! Blessing us peasants with her presence turn the fuck up and show some love!" The club held up their middle fingers and cheered. I looked back at Clapback section, and she was sitting with a pleased grin on her face. A look of relief was hidden behind that like she was happy her sister really showed up for her.

Queen face was blank as her eyes surveyed everyone in the club. When she got to the center of the club. "Boss Ass Bitch" remix by Nicki Minaj started playing. Queen eyes landed on me, and that blank facial expression turned into a slight frown as she took her eyes off me. She felt something but didn't know what. She didn't know who the fuck I was because I was not known, and I liked it to stay that way. I stayed out of the spotlight for plenty of reasons. I took her in and admired her curvy frame and how she executed confidence so well. She rocked an all-black two-piece skirt combo. The top curved right underneath her big breast showing off the top of her stomach, the skirt hugged every curve and fell below her knees with a high split on the right. Her hair was bone straight with a part down the middle falling past her curvy ass. She had me wondering what the fuck it would be like to fuck a big chick. I chuckled lowly at my train of thinking and got back focused.

She went and hugged her sister then left her section. I watched her for a little while longer through my dark Cartier glasses. She didn't dance or talk, she sat in her own section with her cup glued to her hands and watched everyone else party and partake in the turn up festivities. When she lit her blunt, I felt her eyes from across the club. She couldn't see me behind my frames, but we were now locked into a stare off. I smiled at her, and she winked at me and looked elsewhere.

Yea, I was gone have fun with Queen, I planned on breaking her the fuck down and making her submit and get her team on board of the syndicate.

QUEEN

"Tell that Peacock-looking bitch to never announce my presence again." I seethed tight lipped to Bundy. That stupid DJ just put a red dot on my forehead, and I was now ready to leave. I planned on making an exit soon as I finished my drink. I watched Bundy stand and pull his jeans up onto his waist as he made his way towards the DJ booth. I was only here to support my sister, show face and leave. Sure, people knew who I was thanks to Empress big mouth boasting ass. Niggas also had F.Y.F tatted on their bodies and made it known what they represented hard which was cool with me.

I scanned the club and my eyes got fixated on the strange nigga that had a dark aura about him. I couldn't see his eyes behind the glasses but sensed that he was definitely watching me. I wondered why. I heard commotion and that's when my eyes landed on my sister Empress arguing with a bitch, what made me angry was it looked like she was arguing about a nigga.

"You know she fucking that nigga Killa." I eyed Murk'um and shook my fucking head. That was the reason she claimed in the meeting that the nigga was a big deal. She was laying with this nigga and didn't even know what he had up his sleeves. I said nothing as I stared hard at Empress. Dragging my eyes back to Murk'um I didn't feel sorry for him at all. In fact, I wanted to slap the shit out of him for not telling me the night of the meeting that Empress was entertaining this Killa nigga.

"Hoes ain't loyal, I warned you. Never mix business with pleasure. It's bad for business, it's still your duty to protect her with your life. Now you in your feelings, get out of them and bring that bitch to me now."

He simply nodded and stood to his feet, when I looked back at the section that occupied Mr. Strange, he was gone. It was something very familiar about him, but I couldn't place it. My intuition was even telling me that it was more to him that would soon reveal itself. I found myself sitting still with thoughts of my parents. Grief always hit me at the wrong times. I could never adjust, I learned to live with it the best way I knew how. I was forced at a young age to survive the best way I could. Some would call it a chip on my shoulder, but it was me realizing that I was left no choice at a young age to survive.

I needed my mother and fathers love and guidance. That was ripped away from me too soon. Their voices still danced in my head along with their scents and smiles. Snapping out of my thoughts, my eyes landed on Empress. She was drunk and beautiful, her angelic face and chinky eyes locked in with mine. Soon as she took the first step, she stumbled and landed right in my lap.

"I love you so much, Queen." She sniffled and backhanded her tears. This was the norm for Empress, especially when she was drunk.

"I love you too, Clapback." I put my arms around her and

cradled her in my arms like a baby. There was no point in me getting on her case tonight about who she had been opening her legs to. Right now, she wanted to be babied.

"You don't act like it." She simpered and I nodded my head in agreement.

"I know." I fixed her hair and eyed Bundy. My eyes went to the exit, and I mouthed to him to get my car. I was taking her ass home. To my house to keep an eye on her. The hard part would be getting her ass out of this club.

"Clapback we about to leave." My thigh started to go numb from her weight. She sat up and then stood on wobbly legs.

"I'm not leaving Queen, the party just getting started." She slurred and hiccupped at the same time, giving me that defiant look that I knew all too well.

"Either you leave with me willingly, or I will have you carried out of here." I never blinked while looking directly at her.

"Fine, one day though Queen you will be forced to change your evil ways. You can't control my life forever." She walked off with Murk'um following close behind. That's what it was like having a little sister. They were spoiled and entitled as hell. Empress was twenty-six years old still throwing tantrums and using certain words to get under my skin. It stopped working a very long time ago. There was a time that I allowed myself to feel things. I would let emotions control who I was until I buried all of that. Living life the way I lived it now helped me to cope and bury my heart into the pits of hell. I handed that broken heart to the devil a long time ago. When he gave it back, it stopped working properly. The only bit of feeling I had left in it was when my mind went back to my parents and the big responsibility I had when it came to raising Empress.

Standing up and allowing my men to walk in front of me, I left out the club through the back where my car was awaiting me. The only thing that seemed to stay on my mind was new ways to make money. I wanted my savings as heavy as I was, sure, I was set but could've had way more. So being at a club partying just didn't do it for me at all.

"Queen! Queen!" I looked to my left and became stuck in place. The night that I turned my first trick came rushing back to me hard. I damn near stumbled on my Red Bottoms and my mouth went dry. Anger flared inside of me and before I could control my anger my gun was out pointing right in the direction of Salem.

He was still very handsome and alluring, the corners of his full pink lips turned up as he stared at me with heavy lust. Throwing his hands up mocking surrender, infuriated me more. My mind went back to the thirteen-year-old desperate me. The night my virginity was snatched away by Salem. At the time he was twenty-three years old. I promised myself when I got older that I would end every trick that fucked me off the worse. Salem was one of them. I used to be best friends with his little sister Saleema. She knew my situation and would try to help me and Empress the best she could.

She thought she was helping me and Empress by telling her older brother that she had lived with at the time about our homeless situation. He offered for us to live there with them and me being desperate and getting tired of finding weird places to sleep at, I jumped at the offer. Empress was eight years of age and always complained about not being comfortable and she seemed to be always hungry.

The first week everything was perfect, Salem took us shopping had us feeling like we were being cared for properly. By the time we got around to week three things took a major turn.

Empress and I finished our dinner with Saleema and took our baths for the night. Saleema had her own room while me and Empress shared a room. Salem and Saleema mom was a crack head so she was never home. I thought it was pretty dope of Salem to always look and dress fly. He stayed with a lot of money and had nice cars. Model like females always came around and some fought over him right in front of the house that we stayed in.

Once Empress was sleep, I did my nightly routine and that was pray to God hard and ask for guidance. My young mind couldn't process what was happening to me and Empress. My heart would ache every single day trying to figure out how I needed to be in order to protect me and my sister. I didn't want to live because I yearned to see my ma and pa faces and feel their embraces. It was on constant repeat in my head rent free that they were never coming back. Blinking back my tears and wiping my face, I stood on weak legs and got into my small ass twin bed. I couldn't complain because at least we had a bed to lay in.

It was hard for me to sleep at night because I kept thinking of ways to make money. I knew by me being thirteen that a job wouldn't hire me and if I returned back to school, I would be turned over to children services. A million what ifs and bizarre thoughts would cross my mind, so sleep became a distant thing.

"What you in here doing?" Salem stood at the entrance to me and Empress small room with only boxers on. I saw a huge bulge that scared me to death in his tight ass briefs. I was already mature and started masturbating at the age of twelve but stopped when my mom caught me and told me that masturbating was like having sex with demons. That scared my young fast ass and I stopped. Every time I laid eyes on Salem yellow ass, I felt attracted to him. He was a pretty boy

and fine as hell. What I didn't know was his intentions to turn my young ass out that night. He had sick plans of pimping me and my sister out to his boss and other high paid drug dealers.

This particular night he made me come to his room and bag up his drugs. He taught me how to weigh and how to eyeball how much the product cost. He paid me five hundred dollars; I knew all about money and what it could get me thanks to my ma and pa. When we were done, he offered me his blunt and his whole dialect changed. His eyes were low and had the same look that other grown men around the way would give me. I was thirteen but could easily pass for sixteen. My boobs were already defined and so was my curves.

Me being heavy set gave me the body of a grown woman. I shook off the uncomfortable feeling thinking that he couldn't have been attracted to my fat ass. I saw the women he laid up with, so I shifted my mind to think that it was the weed that had him high. The weed had me high and giggly too.

"You sexy as fuck Sovereign." He licked those pink lips and my stomach started to churn. It felt like I had to shit, my nerves got super bad. Sure, I had hormones and liked boys, I even explored my own body. I knew that I was still too young for sex so him calling me sexy had me standing up and fake yawning. I tried to tell him that I was ready for bed, and he shook his head no and went to lock his room door.

Salem turned into an ugly monster that night, making me feel conscious of my weight. He scared the living shit out of me. Once he revealed how I would pay him back for all the clothes and me and Empress living here rent-free, my heart sunk into my stomach. Salem's dick was so huge that it ripped me below and after that, I was fair game in his eyes.

I sucked it all up and forced myself to start liking it even though I hated it. This was the only way at that moment to survive. After being pimped out and abused for two years, I saved enough money to run again and never look back. I never could forget his face, and always vowed to get my payback whenever I did see him again.

"Damn, Queen. You sexy as fuck still." He gave me a lopsided grin. Once Murk'um got Empress situated in the car, he walked right up to my side.

"We out in the open Queen. Let him live for now." He gave me pitiful eyes; he knew all about Salem sick ass. I was told that he skipped town when he became wanted by the police for pimping and pandering young girls.

"Yea you right Murk'um." I licked my glossy lips and smiled at Salem as I lowered my gun. I eyed the back of the parking lot, and no one was around. I was ready to take my chances.

"It's good to see you Salem." I turned to walk away, I wanted to get a couple inches away from him because I didn't need his brains splattering all over my expensive outfit. Once I counted to ten, I turned around and aimed my gun at his head.

"Murk'um wants me to let you live... I think he a lil too tipsy from tonight's events. My balls hang lower than you and his. See you in hell, sick nigga."

Pop!

One single shot to the dome had him laid out permanently. I chuckled slowly then my laughing picked up as I doubled over and laughed even harder. I laughed so hard tears escaped each corner of my eyes. I laughed and cried because the night he took my virginity, I got pregnant, and he forced me to get a hood abortion that made me infertile. He deserved to die, and I was ready to pay out more money tonight to make his ass disappear.

Wiping my face and pulling out my burner phone, I scoffed when I realized that Abeula took out my cleaning crew. Seconds later, a Lincoln town car pulled up and three men hopped out dressed in black. My personal phone rung, and I immediately got pissed. Abuela was watching me, and it explained why I had been feeling eerie lately like someone was constantly watching me closely. I answered the unknown number and watched two men carry Salem to the trunk of their car. The third man had his hands tucked deep into his pockets as he entered the back of the club.

"Mi Nieta, still very classless. Ju have a lot to learn. Have you packed your bags to prepare to come to Mexico?" I could hear the smile in her voice as I watched the men cleanse the area of Salem's blood. Gripping the phone tight, I could feel my jaws clenching.

"Why do you have men watching me Abuela?" I could've had Murk'um and Bundy handle this situation. Her having her men help me was putting me at her mercy.

"That's not answering my question, Nieta. So, I will make it very clear. I will see you in two days. The address will be sent to you tomorrow. Please Nieta, don't make me come for you." She hung up and I stood in place for a couple of seconds.

I instructed Bundy to follow me home, I would need him to carry Empress's drunk ass in the house. The whole ride home was quiet, a strong headache was coming to the forefront of my head. I felt like a small burden had been lifted, I laid an enemy to rest and didn't have to pay out money to make it disappear since my Abuela took care of it. Something just wasn't sitting right with her for me, but I had to play along until I found another way to get her off my fucking back.

Pulling up to my house, I instantly frowned. I sat on my

driver's side behind tinted windows and watched Bundy hop out the car from behind me and approach the same gentlemen that was at the club. He was standing in front of his double R vehicle with his hands folded in front of him. Frames hid his eyes but by his posture he was calm. The men that flanked each side of his pulled their guns as Bundy approached midway with his gun pulled. The stranger man crossed his right leg over his left leg and smiled causing me to frown. His smile looked like a sneer, or maybe it just wasn't a smile. After watching them exchange words, I watched Bundy scratch the top of his head and look my way. The stranger kept his face in my direction and in a crazy way it seemed like even when him and Bundy were talking, he looked at me the whole damn time.

Seconds later Bundy approached my side of the car and waited for me to roll down my window. My stomach felt tight, and I wondered who the fuck this nigga was and why did he feel so fucking bold to pop up at my house. He wasn't the only one besides Abuela watching me. Finally getting it over with, I rolled my window down and just stared at Bundy.

"No mixing business with pleasureee, you remember that Queen?" Empress woke up at the wrong time. She sat up from the back seat as I looked at her from my rear-view mirror.

"Shut up, Clapback." I gritted my teeth together.

"Ohhhhh, now I can't talk. You know Bundy has been in loooovvvveee with you forever. You two have something going on." I ignored her and looked Bundy in the eyes. I couldn't lie, whenever I gave Bundy my eyes, he always had a hint of adoration in them for me. Bundy and I was complicated, I never crossed the line with him. I got close to doing so but ended whatever it was we sparked due to business.

Bundy was handsome and very caring when it came to me. As far as the butterfly feeling and liking him more then what I was trying to build never happened for me like it did with Melvin. Hell, I never had the butterflies with Melvin but I sure as hell blindly got feelings for him. Bundy was handsome, caramel complexion, six feet tall with a Greek built body.

"What the fuck does he want, Bundy?" I got to the point, not really liking the fact that a strange man had me feeling very uneasy. The fact that he was where I laid my head at, infuriated me even more.

"He wants you, Queen. Said he just wants to speak with you briefly."

"Okay, get Clapback in the house." He nodded and walked around to Empress side of the car and opened it. I eyed myself in the rear-view mirror and then reached for the glove compartment and pulled my nine-millimeter out and tucked it behind my skirt. The cold metal rested between the top of my ass cheeks.

Opening my door, the cold air hit me first. I deliberately took slow steps and stopped ten inches away from him as he pulled his Cartier frames from his face and handed them to the big, tall scary looking dude next to him. He fixated his eyes on me, and it felt like my heart stopped beating.

"Sovereign, pretty ass name, don't you think?" I said nothing as he let out a small chuckle. His voice lacked emotion and his eyes looked magical as fuck. This man was beautiful with his non-smiling ass. His eyes looked crystal blue with a dash of emerald-green in the middle, those two sets of eyes lacked emotion as well. I eyed the burnt mark along his jawline and wondered how he got that. It gave his handsome perfect looking face a rough-edged sex appeal. I swallowed down my spit and took in the fact that I was outnumbered. I wasn't going to bitch up, if it was my time to go, I was leaving with my chin up.

"You stood in the right exact place that I would prefer you to stand." That sneer took over his handsome face.

"Oh, really?" I maintained a neutral facial expression. He said nothing as he dug into his black Levi looking jeans and pulled out a match book.

"Yes, Sovereign. Really." The guy next to him passed over a Cuban cigar that was already cut at the tip. He began to talk with his cigar tucked comfortably between his thick full pecan and pink two-toned lips. "I think it's time, that I formally introduce myself as your soon to be excellency. Because when it's all said and done, you will fold, bend, and maybe break like the rest of them do. They all refer to me as that even at the ending of their run if they don't comply properly."

I pulled my gun from behind me and fought back the urge to laugh. Who the fuck did this nigga think he was? Talking to me with that thick deep sexy accent and making blind threats. I bit into my bottom lip and looked at his stone covered face and smiled. I wanted to double over in laughter because it was what I did to contain and control my anger. He raised a brow at me and struck his match, this time his eyes lit up like he was eyeing the most beautiful Christmas tree. He looked very intrigued by the fire in an odd way. When his cigar was perfectly lit, he dropped the match and fire erupted and formed into a pathway that led right to me and beautifully formed into a huge circle around me. He picked up his feet and started my way slowly as I secured my gun in my hand and took the safety off. He might've been crazy as fuck, but I had him beat. He walked down the fiery pathway with his eyes glued to me as he hit his cigar.

"My name is Malice Ashonti Ruiz. You will refer to me

as Inferno aka your Excellency." He stepped into the circle and his woodsy aroma hit me first making my thoughts feel like a bunch of jumble. Who was this man? He really had me fucked up in the head. Holding his hand out he caressed the top of the fire with his fingertips. I cringed and fought the urge to pull his hand away. He was off, the man in front of me had the most powerful presence that I have never encountered before not even from my own father. He stood tall like he was at least six foot seven.

"I see, you're speechless, remain that way until I'm done talking. I'm a very busy businessman and every single second is important to me. I will only say this shit once." He placed his right hand that was hot as hell on top of my cold hands and easily removed the gun from out of my grasp and broke it down into three pieces. Tossing it into the fire. He truly had me standing here feeling stuck on fucking stupid.

"I've been sending Killa to reach out to the head organization of F.Y.F, for my syndicate that's building and multiple states. I didn't start building it out here in California first because of too many gangs and killings of black people. My syndicate isn't that messy, it really runs smooth, and everyone falls in line because it's lots of money to be made. I started my business in Vegas first and then worked my way around a couple of other states. The syndicate ranges from politics, real estate, drugs, guns and the list is deeper than that. Since you fall under the category of drugs, I plan to keep things simpler with you. I could have offered more and put you on to more but the way you all move, especially that sister of yours and the enemies you have made for yourself. I have to raise the percentage and tax you a little more. You still will benefit and have better protection. Maybe with the upgraded protection men like me won't be able to get to you like I've done tonight. Then again Sovereign, there isn't another nigga like me on this earth." I licked my lips and shifted my weight. I was angry and turned on at the same time.

"That was a nice introduction. I like the props and all." I looked at the fire that started to blow with the wind. "That shit mad cute, you know?" I stepped closer to him. I didn't stop walking until my double D breast was pressed up against his hard body. I had to tilt my head back to look into his icy eyes. "F.Y.F will never bow down to you are any other nigga that thinks his balls are bigger than mine." He said nothing but his hands did the talking by pulling my skirt up and reaching underneath until he cupped my fat mound. Sneering he gave it a tight squeeze and I could feel my own juices gushing out.

"That's a fat ass pussy, Sovereign. It's hot as fuck, just how I like it to be. I don't feel any balls baby, but your delivery was cute." He mocked me, while sliding my silk panties to the side. His rugged burnt fingertips went up and down, between my thick pussy lips and I shuddered. When I heard a soft chuckle, I stumbled back until he caught me with his free hand. Snatching his hand away from my box, he held his soaked index and middle finger up to his nose and took a long sniff. Flicking his long pink tongue out he lapped then sucked his two fingers clean. I blinked rapidly and stepped back away from his touch. He sniggered and I started to laugh. I was very angry that this man threw me completely off balanced.

"Pussy taste good as fuck, tell me Sovereign… will that thick ass wet pussy go to waste? Get in line, you have one hour to give me an answer." He dug in his pants pocket and stuffed a business card right into my cleavage. Giving me his back, I snatched the card out and balled it up. Aiming for his head, it landed right on his neck and then fell into the fire.

He watched as I listened to the fire crackle and burn the card. I had a look of victory plastered on my face.

"That was the wrong fucking move, Sovereign." He sneered and this time a real smile came through on his face. He looked at his men and gave an order that had me ready to run through the fire and escape. Where the fuck was Bundy?

"Bag and gag that bitch. Place her in the trunk since she's so fucking disrespectful." He looked at me as I flicked him off and smiled right back at him.

"We are going to have some fucking fun, Mi' Amor."

He turned and let his men take over, I gave them the fight of my life until something was placed over my mouth and all consciousness left me.

SOULFUL HURTZ

a **ka Teddy**

Eyeing my sisters warily, I got out of bed stomping my feet at the roaches that scattered upon realizing that there was movement. I woke up every morning at five am like my mind had a built-in alarm clock. Every day that I woke up, I felt more tired than before but had to keep pushing. Money had to be made and I had two mouths to feed. I stretched out the aches that I felt from sleeping in a small ass twin bed and yawned. I weighed about three hundred in some solid change. The bed I slept in was old from when I was five years old. I looked over at the bunk bed that my sisters were on and smiled a little bit. They were constant reminders of why I went so hard.

After showering and handling the rest of my hygiene, I sluggishly made my way to our small roach-infested kitchen. I stopped in the living room and looked down at my mom on the couch with disgust. She had to get her ass up and fuckin' bounce before my sisters saw her and started crying and shouting. I hated her so much for what she put us all through but still loved her at the same time. Instead of starting the pancakes and bacon for my sisters, I decided to wake my mom and kick her out first. I knew with me cooking breakfast, the smell alone would wake my sisters up. I didn't want them starting their day off emotional and still having to go to school.

I had to hustle hard and make moves, school and daycare for the girls was a life saver. It let me move around how I needed to during the day before turning it in early to take care of my siblings.

"Antionette." I shook her frail arm as I eyed her with disgust. "Antionette, get up man!" I raised my voice trying to sound strong and cold but what nigga wanted to see his mom strung out on crack? This shit a different type of pain and I wished my momma was strong and not weak when it came to getting on this shit. My father died when I was two, she met my sister's dad and shit started to spiral out of control. At the time I was eight and knew a change had come over my mom. She used to spoil me hard and tell me daily affirmations. When my sister's dad came into the picture, she became head over heels and lost focus of being a mother. My sister Luv turned two, my mom was strung out and hoeing. She stopped caring that she even had kids and would leave us at home all day and night with no food or lights. By the time Luv turned three, she came home pregnant with Passion. She was so high off crack that when she delivered my second baby sister she laughed and told the nurses that she had a "Passion for crack." Cps got involved and gave custody to Passion's dad. That nigga was a stupid ass drug dealer that was constantly getting high on his own supply. I called him a functioning crack head. He didn't look like he smoked that shit but behind closed doors he shamelessly hit his pipe.

He beat my momma ass constantly then threatened her to

get clean so she could be a good mother and she complied and gained custody back over Luv and Passion and actually started doing what she was supposed to be doing. I was actually happy until a couple months later the nigga that Gerald owed re up money to, sent his goons to break down the door and capped his ass. At the time it was some traumatizing shit to see at a young age. Seeing blood and Gerald's eyes still opened horrified the fuck out of me.

I was happy that his ass was dead too though, and figured my mom would go back to being how she used to be before Gerald came into the picture, but I was wrong as fuck. Right after Gerald's funeral, my mom got high right in front of us when we returned back home. She received a big amount of money from the Victim of a Crime Organization and blew it all on drugs. When I turned fourteen, she stopped paying the rent on the house. That's when I realized that my mom never owned the house that we lived in and Watts. We got evicted and went straight to a women's and kids shelter until they gave her section 8. We only lived in the shelter for three months and they gave her a voucher fast and that's when we moved into the projects.

From that point on everything was on me and I struggled up until I met Queen. At first, I hated her because I had to work off a debt. I stole from one of the niggas that lived next door to me. I was so hungry and weak, tired of hearing my sisters crying because they were hungry too. I didn't have no other options but to climb through Peep's window and take that nigga whole re up money. I knew he sold drugs and had it going on, I figured he wouldn't miss the money. When days went by without Peep saying anything to me. I thought I got away with it and shit was smooth.

A week later, my front door was kicked in. Queen stood at my door with fire dancing in her hazel brown eyes and a gun clutched tight in her hand. When her eyes landed on me and my sisters sitting on our worn-down sofa, eating popcorn while watching The Simpsons. She handed Murk'um her gun and asked for his Gucci belt. She had the girls go to their rooms and whooped my ass with that Gucci belt all around the house until she was breathing heavy and out of breath. From that day forward, I worked off the debt and got to know her more.

Instead of looking at her like an annoying ass boss, I started looking at her in a different light. I had to shake my thoughts of wishing she was my mom. She was full of wisdom and although everybody saw her for a cold, twisted and evil female. I saw her as more. She cared and she never looked at me with disgust or judgmental eyes. Niggas and females constantly made fun of me so much that I started believing the shit they said. It was all talk because I would never let a muthafucka physically hurt me.

I should have beat niggas up and had a comeback for bitches that called me names. I gotten used of verbal abuse at a younger age because of my mother. Whenever she didn't have drugs and whatever else she wanted, I suddenly became fat black and ugly niggas. That shit was the norm and at some point, I stopped giving an actual fuck. The only thing I truly cared about was making sure Luv and Passion had food on the table and warm decent clothes to wear.

I didn't get to experience shit that teens my age got to experience. I looked and felt like a grown ass man. I didn't want handouts and for people to look at a nigga and feel bad. I knew that one day because of my ambitions to get to the money, that the tables would turn.

I looked down at my mom and the same pain that I had been battling and trying my hardest to force out of my system when it came to her kept resurfacing. She had on a t-shirt that looked three sizes too big as drool seeped out the corner of her lips. Her ashen chocolate face looked like she was sleeping good as hell. My mom was beautiful even with sunken cheeks and yellow teeth.

"Wake up man!" I shook her harder as she slowly stirred and simpered. Finally batting her eyes and staring up at me in confusion she sat up on the couch looking around the small living space. She smelled like dried up piss and from the heavy bags under her eyes, she hadn't slept in days while binging hard.

"Shit, Soulful Hurtz! Why you bothering me this early?" I stood back from the pungent smell that hit the air and realized she had pee stains on her gray sweats.

"You got to go, Ma. I don't need the girls waking up for school seeing you."

Mainly Luv, Luv was old enough to understand this shit clearer. She had anger problems and would act out for attention. Seeing my mom would make her not want to go to school just from fear of coming back home and not seeing her again. Passion was nonchalant and never really voiced how she felt but I could tell it bothered her.

"Why? I miss my babies and I want to cook for y'all tonight." I shook my head and fought the urge to grab a cigarette from the kitchen cabinet. I hid them well so the girls wouldn't get curious and try to play with them. My mom stressed me so bad weed just wasn't enough. A roach ran across her foot, and she didn't even flinch to find out what was trekking across her foot. Looking at my mom in such a pitiful state pained me bad. My throat started to burn, and I hated the feeling of fighting back my own tears.

"Fuck, Ma! You gotta stop doing this shit to us. We fuckin' love you and you don't give a fuck." I gritted as my bottom lip trembled. I didn't give a damn how weak I looked,

I just wanted my mom back, I wanted her to be normal and if she couldn't be a mother to me, at least Luv and Passion deserved it. It was already too late in my case. What hurt me the most was seeing my sisters disappointed. Luv was nine years of age and Passion was, seven.

"I care Soulful, that's why I keep coming back. I just need help and I've decided to kick this shit." I heard it before but looking into her glassy eyes made me feel like she was actually shameful. "I can't explain the feeling that shit gives momma, but I'm tired of how it's making things with my kids."

I sighed and ignored the horrid smell coming from her and sat down next to her. My heart beat hard against my chest.

"How can I help you Ma?" I would never give up on her even though I wanted to.

"You can't help me Teddy, I gotta do it myself." I nodded as I continued to stare at her. If she didn't smell so strong, I would pull her in for a tight hug and never let her go.

"Alright Ma, but you got to go. Luv gives me a very hard time. When you pop up and leave without saying shit, Luv's anger is a lot to deal with." My mom smiled and rolled her eyes.

"All she need is her ass whooped, Teddy. You, always soft on them heifers."

"She needs her mom, then a lot of the anger would go away." I reasoned.

"Y'all gone have me, I think I'ma check into that rehab your aunt keeps telling me about. I'm really serious Teddy, I'm going to make up for everything-"

"Mommy?" Luv rubbed her puffy eyes, ridding herself of eye boogers, and blinked a couple of times. Once she really focused and noticed that it was mom, she ran and jumped right into her arms.

"Damn, mommy you stink." She threw her arms around our mom's neck and kissed her all over the face.

"Luv, watch your mouth." I scolded but she ignored me like I wasn't in the same room. She did the normal inspection and checked my mom out from head to toe. She talked to her about school and skipped subjects fast. Luv was breathing hard because she tried to talk fast to get it all out. I knew she did this because she didn't know when she would see our mom again.

Luv led our mom to the bathroom to help her shower and pick clothes out for her. I took time out to go check on Passion. I knew if Luv was up, that Passion had to be up and alert. When I walked in the room Passion was sitting up on the bed with tears in her eyes.

"What's wrong P?" I hate seeing my sisters cry, it fucked with me in the worse way.

"I don't want her to see me." She sniffled.

"Why not?" I sat next to her on the edge of the bed and picked her chin up with my index finger. Passion was beautiful with a nice kinky Afro. Most days I didn't know what to do to her hair, so I wet it and added leave-in conditioner. To top her fro off I would put different color ribbons and bows in it.

"She hates me, and she always leaves because of me." More crocodile tears came down her pretty round chocolate face. I pulled her close and rocked her in my arms.

"That shit ain't true, P. Momma sick, she leaves to make sure she gets better."

"Does she love me?" Her doe-shaped eyes were innocent the hurt behind them is what broke a nigga.

"Of course, she love you, she just don't know how to

show it. She loves all of us and soon she's gone get better." I kissed her forehead and tried my best to reassure her. Although my mom should feel and see the affect, she had on all of us. I sat holding Passion, feeling like it was all my fault. After getting her calm and picking her clothes out for the day I went back to the living room and saw Luv and my mom sitting on the couch. I stood listening to their conversation.

"You got to get off those drugs mommy. Teddy doesn't cook like you and we be missing you." I wanted to laugh because I really couldn't cook for shit, but the girls ate whatever I provided because they didn't like being hungry. Luv was old enough to know what moms was on. Passion still went along with me telling her our mom was sick and I thought Luv still thought that too until now. She boldly expressed herself and I could tell from my mom's posture that she felt bad as hell.

"You look good now mommy. Those drugs make you look old, now you look like a hot girl." She snapped her fingers and smiled. She put too much gel in our mom hair and had it in a loose ponytail. My mom had on black leggings, and one of my big ass pro club shirts. I could smell the dove and baby magic lotion in the room.

"I look like a hot girl, Luv?" My mom smiled.

"Hell yea." Luv cooed with her badass. For once it felt like we were that one happy family that I envied from my peers at school. Shaking off the thought, I made a quick breakfast and got a little happier when Passion emerged from our bedroom to sit next to our mom and talk. Her voice was always low and very timid but to see my mom interacting with the girls. She wasn't high but I was sure within the next hour she would have that strong urge to get high. I just prayed this time around she fought it and brought her ass back home.

I made it to school five minutes late and couldn't concentrate through any of my classes. I kept thinking about how good it felt to get the girls to school, watching them skip and just be in their happy element. Now I was happy and worried as I thought back to Queen and I last conversation. Since my mom got me for my last stash and I had to struggle with coming up with the money for re up. I moved my stash somewhere else in the house but that meant nothing to a crack head. My mom would turn the house upside down to get high if she didn't have the money for it. I told her if she left while we were gone to lock up and if she was to return not to come back high as hell. I didn't like the girls seeing her like that.

"You should ask that nigga, David to the formal dance." I walked by my crush and her ratchet ass homegirls. When we made eye contact, I quickly focused back down on my busted ass Air Force One's. They were used from Goodwill and semi fresh when I got them months back. Now they looked like I personally threw them in a pile of mud.

"Ugh, nigga face look like a crunch bar." One of the hoes stated making the rest of the crew giggle. When I looked up, Jocelyn face was unreadable. This time I didn't shift my gaze, I continued to stare making her shift and look off. She pulled her glasses up the bridge of her nose and gripped her folder and books.

Jocelyn was fine as fuck; she was tall and slim-thick. Freckles adorned her caramel face; she lived in the same projects as me. I wondered how a nerd chick like her could become super popular, but her brother Havoc was well known and I was well acquainted with the nigga because he worked as Queen's ruthless enforcers. Niggas and bitches didn't want no smoke with Jocelyn because they knew her brother was a well-known sniper.

"Nigga boo." I smirked and kept walking towards my

locker to grab my shit and leave. Happy the day was over with, I jogged down the school steps and saw Murk'um double parked with his music blasting and hazards blinking. I usually would wait for Jocelyn to finish chatting with her trout-mouth-ass homegirls. She told me she didn't care if people knew that I would sometime walk her home. I cared though; Jocelyn was just too fuckin' pretty to be seen with a dusty ugly nigga like me. Plus, today I had to put in major work and see what was up with Queen.

Soon as I hopped in Murk'um clean whip, he smiled and handed me the blunt he was smoking. I got right to the point soon as he turned his music down.

"You heard from Queen?" It had only been two days but that was too long. It felt like niggas was giving me the run around when I asked questions. I looked towards the front of the school and locked eyes with Jocelyn, she now stood by herself. Her long thick legs in the jean checkered skirt looked good as fuck on her. The Vans platform shoes had her looking even taller.

"When you gon' tell that broad you feeling her kid?" Murk'um chuckled and pulled away from the school. I high key wanted to tell this nigga that I wanted to get up with him later so I could walk with Jocelyn. I wanted to make sure she made it back to the Jets safe.

"She ain't my speed." I left it at that, then got back on point. "Queen? What's up with her?"

"Shit, why you so worried? You got a crush on her too?" He pestered; I was never the joke around with other niggas type of nigga. I damn sure wasn't buddy buddy with Murk'um either. He supplied me with dope, and I made sure it moved how it was 'posed to. I wasn't really tryna befriend none of these niggas that I dealt business with. I remained quiet until he broke the silence.

"She straight, just got to get some shit straight. She should be back in town in a couple days. The nigga that took her that night just wanted to talk. You know how the bitch gets when she mad. She called us the same night telling us she was safe and that everything needs to run the same as if she was still here. She gotta go outta town on some business shit with her Abuela so ain't no telling when she will be back. The meeting for next week won't be held but Clapback will collect all the dough." I just nodded at that; I didn't really appreciate him calling Queen a bitch, but I let him make it. Yea, Murk'um was a deadly nigga, only when he had a gun on his hip and more than one nigga with him.

In my eyes he wasn't shit but a bitch ass pussy nigga. He would never look Queen in the eyes in disrespect her but when she wasn't around the nigga got real loose lipped. If it came down to it and I ever felt like he would become a problem for the gang, I'd take him out. Especially with Queen, my loyalty to her was concrete. I didn't do too much talking because I liked for niggas to underestimate me because of my age and appearance.

We made it to the storage spot, and I packed my backpack with enough drugs to last me for a full week. Once I was done, I linked with my crew in the projects and dispersed the shit. I didn't care where these niggas moved most of the work as long as it wasn't locally. I didn't need the pigs beating down my door because a nigga snitched. I already put niggas up on game that the suburban areas had the most cash flow. It was a smart move like Queen had said. Less competition when it came to moving work in the hood. Too many niggas in the project were drug dealers trying to come up on top.

If a nigga thought, you were stepping on his toes, or seen that you were on they had no problem offing your ass. I kept a low profile and made my ends. Looking down at my

G shock watch it was nearing six o' clock and the sun started to go down. Luv and Passion should be home by now, so I walked through the projects with my backpack secured with one hand inside my hoodie touching my Glock.

I noticed Jocelyn sitting on her steps while her lame ass nigga got his mack on with her. We locked eyes and I kept pushing past until she called out to me.

"Teddy!" I stopped but didn't turn around to face her. I could smell her strawberry scent approaching and finally turned to face her.

"Yea?" I eyed her down, I slightly pulled my hoodie back a little and looked over her shoulder looking directly at her nigga that mugged me hard. He mouthed dusty ass nigga and I winked at him. If he got stupid, I had no problem blowing his head off, to protect the dope and money I had in my backpack.

"I thought you were walking me home so we could go over all the missing assignments. You know, Soul… if you don't make up these assignments then you can't finish out the year playing football."

"Fuck football, I got plays and moves to make. I'll walk you home tomorrow and we can do the assignments though." I hiked my backpack up. I didn't want to really disappoint her but the only thing I gave a fuck about right now was making ends meet. Only reason why I stayed in school was because Queen insisted that I go. She paid a grip too. I didn't like the uppity ass private school nor the kids there. It felt like I was too grown to even be there even though I was turning eighteen really soon.

"Right, don't let this street shit suck you in, Soulful. I want to help you." She softly said as her eyes batted at me. Her smell was intoxicating as fuck, and I had to remind myself that a girl like Jocelyn would never fuck with a dirty nigga like me.

"I appreciate you; I'll see what I can do. Get back to your nigga, the way he looking at me got me uncomfortable." I was on go and I already heard all about that nigga. He was a stick-up kid, all the jewelry that was on him had been stolen. I didn't want to chance having to pop her nigga.

"Okay but wait for me tomorrow, after school Soulful." She gave me that innocent smile and pulled her glasses up. Touching my forearm softly, she turned and walked away, right into that nigga's arms. I got pissed when he grabbed a handful of ass and winked at me. I couldn't help the angry chuckle that left my mouth. I turned and finished the ten-minute walk to my house.

Arriving home, I stopped at the door when I heard music and good smelling food. It felt too good to be true if it was my mom up in here throwing down like she used to back when I was younger. I let myself in and couldn't hide my smile. My sisters greeted me and got back to doing their thing which was sitting on the couch watching TV. They looked content with their pajamas on and for once they weren't asking me what was for dinner.

I walked out the living room and into the kitchen. My mom had music playing as she took some fried chicken out the frying pan and put it on a paper plate that was laced with paper towels to catch the grease. When she looked at me, she was sober, and I could see the sparkle in her eyes. I was tired as hell and felt relieved that I didn't have to put together another nasty meal. The kitchen and living room were clean and it smelled damn good. I embraced my mom tight to show her my appreciation and went to the back to hide my dope until tomorrow. I just silently prayed that she kept this shit up. Me and the girls needed her more than she knew. I would hustle from sunup to sun down to provide for my mom and sisters just to have my momma home and drug free. The logical and negative side of me knew that it wouldn't be long before she left and went back to the streets. My mom was the first and only woman that kept repeatedly breaking and ripping a niggas heart out.

INFERNO

"Kenya, there are no meetings in the syndicate. Everyone moves how the fuck they're supposed to. You're the major face that plays a big role besides the assistant title and accounting. You work with the public and you do Philanthropy work. Why are you sticking your nose in shit that does not concern you?"

I took a seat at my dining table and gave Kenya my undivided attention. Too many things had to be done before the night was up and here, I am solving a problem that shouldn't need fixing. My syndicate was way different from my father's cartel business. I had brutal men and well-qualified women like Kenya Monroe to work in special fields that accommodated my organization. The syndicate stretched to different groups of individuals with organizations that brought in a certain amount of money. We all had a common interest and that was to stay under the radar. I was the controller of it all and managed to keep shit under wraps like an underground mob. I constantly gave opportunities to different leaders to make more and have more to the point of them not having to get raped by the police that would eventually lead to the feds stopping their money flow and jail time. To have that protection, you needed to be a member of the syndicate and pay a good percentage.

"I don't like that bitch and she's always looking at you like she wants to fuck you."

I stared at Kenya with a little bit of shock. Lately, she had been stepping out of her role and it had to be because of the dick that she had been receiving on the regular. I didn't have time to switch my women out because I was hard at trusting anyone.

"Monroe, Mrs. Glover uses her government job to ship product and make sure it goes untraced for myself and others that are a part of the syndicate. Soon when I take over the cartel in Mexico, she will be responsible for making sure shit ships around the United States." I stroked my beard that I planned on cutting down tomorrow. Standing to my feet, I walked around the cherry oak dining room table and sat at the edge of it.

"Do you think that I'd let you disrespect Mrs. Glover a woman that holds a higher status than you? A woman that is married with kids? Fuck her being married because if I wanted to fuck her or if I was fucking her... what does that have to do with you?"

"Nothing." She cast her eyes down and I lifted her chin up. I had love for Kenya, she was sexy as fuck and to add to all of it she was smart. I didn't regret the kind of relationship that we had. My focus was only on one thing, no sexual relations would shift that focus.

"I don't do meetings unless it is important. I would hate for you to have to recite rules that I set in place for this organization, Kenya. Your pussy is top notch and I love how you take care of business. Never step out of your role are question who I have in place when it comes to my syndicate. Now let yourself out of my home."

I walked away from her, there was more that I wanted to say but would let it rest for now. I went into my office and called my father. I was set to take the private jet to Mexico tomorrow to sit in a meeting with the new Golden Triangle. I didn't want to, but I would do whatever it took to make sure shit was running smooth on my father's end. His protection and alliances meant no more stupid hits on his life.

I dared a muthafucka to test me once it was known that I was part of the cartel. If they knew who stood behind my father, they would tread with light feet.

"Heyyy." A feminine manly tone cooed into the line.

"Put my father on the line." My jaws clenched.

"Oh, hermano mayor." (*Big brother*) he teased. "Is that di way to treat me?" I sneered and chuckled. My brother loved to push buttons that were nonexistent with me.

"Let father know, I will arrive tomorrow." I hung up, vexed that I had to deal with my brother who was always over the top. I didn't have a problem that he was feminine, and my father didn't care either. My problem with him was that he liked to project his gay life onto others. Counting down the seconds, my phone started to ring.

"Hijo." (*son*) my father's deep voice came through on the line.

"Why is Roberto playing on the phone?" I asked making small talk.

"He just misses his hermano." My father chuckled as I sighed. That meant I would have to deal with his pestering ass my whole visit.

"I will be there mid evening. I'm wrapping up something tonight, so I won't be able to fly out this late." I picked up the picture frame of my mom and kissed it before sitting it back down. Because of my busy schedule, I hardly had time to see my mom. It had been three months too long, and when I got back, I planned on spending a weekend with her. I missed her cooking and all her shit talking.

"Si, it seems to be a small emmm, delay." His thick accent paused, and the line went silent for a couple of seconds before he continued. "Martinez, granddaughter will not be attending, so unfortunately the meeting will go on without her, for now." A huge part of me hoped that I didn't have to get married to whomever this granddaughter was. Marriage just seemed to be too far-fetched on my end. I chopped it up with my dad a little more and ended the call.

My heart never fluttered are skipped a beat when it came to a woman. My dick only stiffened and craved the hot and tight, silky tunnel of one. I just hoped whoever it was that I had to marry understood and respected that. I was going to make it clear that our union was nothing but a front and alliance. If she was pretty like the woman that I had in Hades locked away from the world until she agreed and got in line. Then I wouldn't mind fucking the brains out of a so-called wife. I had nothing but great fortune and exceptional dick to offer the opposite sex. Speaking of the Hades side of my house, the warm air covered my skin and the residue smell of something being burned hit my nostrils and calmed me all at once.

I entered my bedroom and walked straight to my walk-in closet. Removing the frame and then pushing my safe out the way, I unlocked the hidden door that would lead me down the steps of my chamber. Soon as the door opened, I braced myself for the feisty woman that had piqued my interest a little. She was a fighter and stood firm on all ten toes. I thought by the second day of being held in Hades she would surely cave in and fold, but she welcomed it. She fought me hard each time my hidden door opened. Although she was no match for me, I loved the hard effort she put up.

Her arms swung wildly as I stepped to the side and grabbed her by the base of her neck. I sunk my sharp pinky nail deep into her neck until it penetrated and put her in shock.

"Simmer the fuck down. If I let you go and you swing again, be prepared to tumble your ass down those flight of steps." Silence. The only thing that I heard was her heavy breathing.

"I can't breathe good down here, I need air." The only light that illuminated the top steps to my chamber was from my closet.

Her soft voice was replaced now with a slight rasp from all the ashes and dust that surrounded her. I was sure that her throat was burning, and she was in need of a shower and a hot meal. I wasn't all the way heartless. I had my guard bring her food and water and I knew the max number of days that she could be held captive in my chambers without collapsing or having major health problems.

"I'm going to let you come out, take a shower, eat and then we will talk business. I'm pretty sure now, you are ready to comply. Right?"

"Fuck you." She huffed as I squeezed her neck tighter. My dick stiffened against her stomach as I brought her closer. Leaning down so I could speak directly in her ear, I could feel her chest rising and falling and her once steady breathing became choppy and shallow breaths were now being taken.

"I would fuck you. I'd fuck you so good that you'd forget all about your title as a struggling Queen pin." I looked down and smiled at her clamping her thighs tight. The rebellion was locked into her eyes. I wouldn't press her any further.

"Try to run and the men outside my door have been

ordered to shoot first, then check in with me after," I warned as I stepped to the side to let her by. I had been careless with showing her Hades. No one entered this part of my house or even visited my room. Anytime Kenya came over she remained on the opposite wing. Sovereign stood in my walk-in closet as I locked the heavy door and moved everything back into place.

"Come." I moved past her and went to sit on the chaise in front of my bed.

"Strip down." I stared at her intently, I tried to read the tattoos that were scattered about on her smooth-looking toffee skin. The tattoo that stuck out the most was the one along her collarbone that said, "Man Eater." I stared into those deep hazel brown orbs of hers and also noted the tiny, shattered heart tattoo right on her high cheekbone that must have been easily covered with makeup. The two tear drops tatted on the opposite side of her face could have meant multiple things.

She had a story and she been through some heavy shit, it was the main reason why she didn't act like a damsel in distress being snatched up by me. She didn't have an ounce of fear within her. She didn't jump at the sound of my voice, and she was currently standing with her hands on her hips like she didn't just hear what the fuck I just ordered her to do.

"Strip, Sovereign." I hated repeating myself.

"You know if you let me out of this hell dungeon of yours, I'm going to kill you. Usually, when people learn my name, they meet their fate. So, what's yours?" all the blood rushed to the head of my dick. I looked at her dry plump lips and traced every curve that she had with my eyes. Even with her looking crazy and her wild curly hair all over her head, she was beautiful as fuck. Bolder than a nigga with a gun stuck to his head and talking shit. I was stuck on my own words for the first time ever. Sovereign was a bloodhound, she noticed me being stuck and continued her assault.

"You got some sexy ass lips and eyes, kind of remind me of my twins that I enjoy from time to time. Nah, your look is more exotic, it looks like you one of those freaky mothafuckas, that's why you want me to strip and shit." A look of amusement crossed her face and then her face was void of emotion. She was very good; she had the gift of gab and confidence reeked straight from her pores. She kept her eyes locked in with mine unwavering as she stripped out of her top and then skirt. She slid her panties down slowly until they formed into a puddle around her bare feet.

She turned around and bent over to pick up her clothes and I stood to teach her a fucking lesson. Sovereign was fuckin with the wrong nigga. I was the nigga that would bring her down to her knees and have her going to a shrink to be evaluated to make sure she was sane. I was the nigga that she would daydream about during the day while conducting business. I would be in her nightmares and wet dreams every single night when she closed her eyes. Her pussy lips glistened, and no foul smell permitted the air.

"Stay just like that and don't move Sovereign." My voice came out husky as I moved to my dresser to retrieve a condom. I pulled my dick out and protected myself. I eyed the rolls on her back and all the stretch marks that decorated her thighs like tiger strips and let out a grunt. I never expected my dick to react to a woman of her size, but I was about to find out what this feeling was all about.

I grabbed the top of her ass and let my dick guide it's way inside. There was no slow lovemaking or trying my very best to ease in slowly. Sovereign talked big shit so she should have been prepared to take a big dick with hard long strokes in her snug, shit! Just the tip was in, and my toes curled so tight that they started to cramp. Forcing my thoughts back on the lesson that I was teaching, I pushed all ten inches halfway in before she was falling to the floor on her knees howling like she was a virgin.

"What's wrong, Sovereign? You can't take dick?" I got down on my knees behind her and gripped her waist, pulling her back up and entering her again. Every time I got halfway in, she ran, and I couldn't hold back my chuckle. She smelled like fire mixed with burned ashes which made my dick even harder. I pictured me fucking her right in Hades while the flames crackled around us.

"Yea, you can't take dick baby girl. I ain't into teaching a woman how to take my dick. Next time, watch your fuckin' mouth and do as I say." I slapped her on the ass and stood to my feet. Snatching the condom off, I tossed it into the small trash bin. I left her right on the floor panting and trying to save face.

What she didn't understand and what I didn't understand was that she ignited some weird shit that I couldn't explain. I dropped it, that feeling was dangerous and something I couldn't be pondering on. I vowed to never stick my dick inside of her snug tunnel again. I thought about the smart remarks of her claiming to fuck twin brothers and a dark thought crossed my mind. This woman was not mine, she would soon be working under me and paying a percentage for the syndicate's protection. She wasn't even my type of woman, don't get me wrong, I've seen a couple of big girls that looked good and carried themselves even better. Sovereign took the whole cake of that; she looked damn good and dangerous. She knew how lethal she was and what drew me in to her was her ability to keep on fighting.

She wasn't some delicate bitch that caved in when it came to being pressured. When she looked at me, she had the same stare that I gave plenty of people. In a creepy way it felt like I was staring at the woman version of me. The wheels in my head started to spin, this woman could very well bring millions to the table.

I stood under the multiple jets and lathered my body with soap. When I got to my dick, I couldn't help but shake my head. My nigga was still hard as metal, the veins and blood pulsed. I grunted and squeezed the tip as I picked up the flick of my wrist and beat my shit down until what felt like gallons of nut spurted out and went down the drain.

When I stepped out the shower, Sovereign stood there with an amused look plastered on her face. I winked and snatched the towel that hung on the rack behind her and walked out the room. Fuck her thoughts, she should learn how to take dick. With the kind of mouth, she had on her, that was a big disappointment, just two minutes inside of her good ass snatch pissed me off. As grown as she was, the huge disappointment came from her not knowing how to relax the floors and walls of her pussy and receive me like a champ.

"The first is coming up." She said over the shower water.

"Yea." I picked up the toothbrush and started brushing my teeth.

"So, if you don't plan on killing me, you need to let me go. I have things to do and rent on some of my properties will be due." I spit the paste and water out my mouth and looked at her scrub her body. I took in every curve through the shower glass. There was no shame when she lifted her titties to scrub around and underneath properly. Next was her stomach, she lifted what most called a fupa and scrubbed for a while before she washed the cloth off and added more soap.

"You pay rent?" She got quiet and stared at me, maybe she was embarrassed, maybe she knew that I was thinking back to my remark earlier when I let her out of Hades. She was indeed a struggling Queen pin.

"What's your favorite color, Sovereign?" I changed the subject, since me and her would be doing business, I'd give her some free game on how to easily own all of the properties she rented.

"Why?" She placed her foot on the shower bench and opened her legs wide as she cleaned her pussy.

"Answer me." This was weird, here I was making conversation and thinking reckless at the same time. I already had my plan outlined; she was coming to Mexico with me. It was going to take more than just tonight to get her on board without a fight. A woman like her felt she was just as powerful as me. Which was cool until I brought her down to reality.

"Teal." She soaped the towel again and cleaned between her ass cheeks, when she was done doing that, she spun around to get the soap off of her. Sovereign turned her back to the water and bent forward. I looked on like I was being entertained. She squatted down as she leaned forward and reached behind her to spread those ass cheek to wash away the soap. The water cascaded between her asshole and pussy, cleansing her thoroughly.

I haven't eaten pussy in so long, but the way Sovereign was making sure she was clean thoroughly had me amused and on edge at the same time.

"What? You used to prissy ass bitches that look all sexy cleaning themselves." She laughed while adding more soap to the towel. "I'm a big girl baby, it might not look all sexy the way I clean this ass, but I gets the job done." She smirked and turned her back to me. I let out a chuckle and left her crazy ass in the bathroom alone. If it was left up to me, I'd have

Sovereigns thick ass thighs sitting comfortably on my shoulder, while I feasted on her pretty fat pussy.

When I got back in the room, I put on a pair of boxers. I eyed the dirty clothes that she threw in the small trash bin and wondered why she had thrown them away. She couldn't be that fucking bold. She didn't even know what the fuck I had planned for her ass. For all she knew, I could be ready to throw her ass back in Hades for the night.

I picked up her dirty clothes including her panties and looked at the sizes. I picked up my personal cell phone and put a text message into Kenya. She was my assistant and got paid well to do whatever it was I asked of her. I told her to get my guest a new wardrobe and let her know Sovereigns favorite color along with sizes. Money and power could get your favorite stores that were closed opened and cleared out no matter the time. I paid Kenya well, soon as she got the text, I was sure that she would be slipping on her heels and preparing to do what I said. Sovereign was going to Mexico with me. When we got back to the states, I was sure she would fall in line perfectly with the syndicate.

I paged my house maid, and she came up with my favorite massage oils. I sat on my chaise and enjoyed the work that Miss. Devriz was giving me. When she got down to my legs and feet, she took her time. Sovereign pranced in like she wasn't being held captive. Her body was dry, and she had no shame with all her curves out on display standing naked. Miss. Devriz looked up from massaging my feet and smiled at Sovereign who surprisingly smiled back.

Sovereign said nothing as she helped herself to some of the lotion and body oils that Miss. Devriz brought up. When she was down moisturizing her skin, she got in my bed. My whole body stiffened, Miss. Devriz stopped her foot massage and eyed me cautiously.

"Continue." I told her with my back turned to Sovereign. No woman not even Kenya ever got in my bed.

"Hope you didn't think I was going back in that chamber of yours. I smell too good for that shit. Oh, and I only like sleeping naked. Hope that don't bother you much." I didn't even bother answering her. This struggling ass Queen pin was trying her best to have me by the fucking balls.

QUEEN

*W*ho the fuck was this nigga Inferno? From the encounters that I had with him so far, I gathered up that he was really that nigga. One of a kind and that meant a lot coming from me. I knew a lot of niggas coming up, niggas that was rich and came up in the game. Based off what all I saw so far with Inferno; he didn't just have lots of money and riches. The man was wealthy and smart as hell. Crazy didn't describe him best, something was really off with him. I never been kidnapped or held against my will. I imagined how his greatest enemies were treated.

One place I refused to go back to was his dark smokey chamber. It smelled so strong and held so many fumes, that I started to hallucinate. I refused to cave in and give him what he wanted. I stayed in that room for far too long. There was absolutely nothing down there but burnt objects and skeletons. I didn't know if the skeletons were real or just for decoration, but the shit was creepy as hell.

The thing with me, is I was used to being in control. I was a certified man eater, I got what I wanted and made men bow down to me. I tried the same gift of gab with Inferno and that shit came back hard on me. When he entered me all of my senses and sane thinking left my body. It didn't return until he denied me. Denied me? That shit still fucked with me hard. I tossed and turned in his massive bed and every time I opened my eyes they landed on him, sitting comfortably on his plush black couch with his feet up scanning a magazine like what he was reading was interesting.

A crazy part of me wondered if he would join me in bed and finish what he started earlier. All he did was page his house maid and have her bring up some type of herbal tea that knocked me out. When I woke, Inferno had that sneer plastered on his face. Welcoming me to Mexico a place I was supposed to come to anyway to meet with my Abuela. I kept my cool, I didn't plan on kicking and screaming, I was smart but outnumbered. There was no point in wasting energy, clearly, he didn't plan on killing me so that was a plus. Maybe I could use all of this shit to my benefit.

I looked at my clothing and smiled, I had on a teal three-piece pantsuit. The top fit like a bra, the pants were high waist and left a little of my stomach out. I didn't know what the hell he put in that tea, but I felt well rested and calm. I had a Prada purse next to me, when I went to look in it my cellphone was there and all the belongings I came with. That's what confused me, I was for sure kidnapped, but he didn't take away my phone, I was still able to talk and communicate with my gang.

Once the jet landed, he stayed seated across from me. I heard him speaking Spanish and could make out a couple of words. I didn't speak fluently like my Abuela and father. I only knew a couple of basic words. I looked out the window and saw high mountain tops. The sun shined brightly, and flashbacks of my childhood came rushing back to me. My father always loved coming to his country. He took pride when he would tell me stories about being raised out here.

I watched Inferno stand and stifled my laugh. He rocked snakeskin cowboy boots, a Piteado belt with some tight ass jeans that had the bulge in his pants looking ridiculously big. The plaid black and white shirt he had on was unbuttoned showing off his fine ass abs. I just knew the bitches were crazy over him.

"Welcome to Culiacan' Sinaloa." He smirked and held his hand out. I stood without his help and made my way to the exit where a black Escalade truck was waiting. Soon as I hit the concrete, a flamboyant dressed man stepped out dressed similar to Inferno. He had a tight pink plaid shirt with suspenders, short shorts on with oil up and down his legs with pink cowboy boots on and a pink scarf wrapped around his neck. He was beautiful as hell with green eyes and long curly hair going down his back. You could tell from his extra plump lips he got lip injections done. Everything about him screamed dramatic down to the way he walked.

"Hola mami," he smiled and walked around me. When he got to my back side he started yelling "Ai Yai Yaaaiiiiii! Too much ass for you Malice." He slapped me on the top of my ass and hugged me from the back. "So pretty, so gangster looking. You his little chulo, chica?" He popped his lips and threw his arm around me. We started walking side by side. Usually, I would've pushed his ass off of me, but he smelled like my favorite perfume which was Chloe.

"Inferno, Roberto, don't let me remind you what to call me again. This is a business partner of mine." Inferno winked at me as I rolled my eyes hard at him. Still choosing not to speak. I was stuck on the fact that his name was Malice.

"Don't let my big brother scare you, Chica. He's so

uptight, such a bully." He fake pouted. Inferno climbed in the front seat and me and Roberto got in the back.

"Straight to the compound." He told the driver with no other pleasantries. We rolled listening to Roberto go on and on about how he didn't like the nail techs out in Mexico. He lived in Miami and was visiting out here for a couple of months to meet his new siblings. He asked Inferno a couple questions and most questions he asked was ignored. I made small talk with him; I liked his outgoing personality. He seemed like a sweetheart, besides him being over the top dramatic, I enjoyed his conversation.

We traveled through deep canyons until we entered a rain-forest, following the trail the ground underneath us seemed very rocky. My Abuela stayed more on the city side. I had no plans of telling them that I knew all about Mexico. Hell, it was a part of me and soon as I decided to agree with my Abuela, I too would be a powerful woman. Whenever Inferno decided to get off his power trip and let me free, I hope that was in a day or two, I would call my Abuela and meet with her since I was already out here.

Taking my phone out, I turned the camera facing me and took in my face. I was bare of any makeup. I felt naked, like the real me was exposed. I eyed the two tear drops that I constantly covered in remembrance of my parents. That was my greatest weak spot. The broken heart that sat on my opposite cheek was the definition of how I felt every day. I forced myself to be strong at a young age because I didn't have a choice. I didn't pick this life; it chose me, and I lived up to the shit with no regrets.

"Chica we're here." Roberto smiled and hopped out the car to jog around to my side. He opened the door and bowed a little. "I'm still somewhat of a gentleman, you see? That asshole is already up the heel ready to go find our Papa." I couldn't hold back the giggle that left my mouth. Roberto was truly a character. I looked up the long-slanted pathway and saw that Inferno was already at a great distance. "You and your brother close?" I decided not to be the reserved person that I'm used of being. I was used of keeping a blank expression on my face, I never really talked much around my gang because I really didn't have too much to say. If it wasn't about business are making money, I didn't concern myself with it. The only person that was able to get me opened and talking, even joking sometimes was my spoiled baby sister. Roberto just had a peaceful and good aura about himself. It seemed like we clicked the moment I stepped off of Inferno's private jet. You all that reading this book probably wondering how am I so fucking calm. How did I get kidnapped, kept in a chamber that was used to start fires with fake or real skeletons for days straight so calm? How can I just adapt to this fine ass stranger that dragged me to Mexico against my consent.

Survival and learning how to adapt to any situation without panicking is all I can tell you. When you have been forced to adapt and play things out until it reveal itself so many times in life you will understand why I was so calm. My intuition was telling me that this was the start of another crazy chapter in my life that I would have to adapt to. I was far from dumb, Inferno wasn't going anywhere no time soon, I envisioned him becoming a thorn in my side. We had some shit in common without him having to confess it to me. Without me knowing much about him, I knew that we both held dark and disturbing thoughts.

"I want to have a better relationship with my Hermano." (Brother) his beautiful green eyes shined with sadness. "We have a lot of siblings, and they don't treat him nice, but I try to. Malice is not easy to break through to, but I'll never give up. I love him and that's why I'm here." He perked up and smiled. He grabbed my hand; I relaxed when I felt how soft his hands felt enclosed with mine as we walked up the pathway. Roberto talked and talked about how big his father's compound was, and he promised to give me a tour later on in the night. I just nodded my head and smiled at everything he said, Roberto was green and didn't know much. I could tell, I also didn't expect him to realize that he was walking hand in hand with a certified shooter.

I took in the Spanish massive home from the foyer. The house was indeed big enough to get lost in something similar to my Abuela's house. Roberto left me in the front room to go find Inferno. I contemplated if it was too soon to text my Abeula and give her my location. If this was Inferno's father home, then his dad was someone very important. I noted everything from the time I arrived on the property. Security was swarming everywhere I didn't need assistance with putting pieces to the puzzle. This nigga father was a part of the cartel.

If it wasn't the cartel, then what else could his father be a part of to have so much fucking security. His front room looked like it was worth my whole fortune.

"You too far in your mind." Inferno had a cigar between his thick lips. His deep baritone voice did something to me every time he spoke. The outfit that I thought was comical on him was replaced with a custom-made fitting suit. Although his eyes were the most beautiful thing, I ever saw they didn't even twinkle nor look welcoming. His once wild beard was now tamed and neatly trimmed forming into a nice goat tee. Inferno was the type of man that looked good with or without hair. Right now, he tapered fade and short dry curls made him look sexy as hell. I thought my heart skipped a beat, but I shrugged it off. It had to be that stupid ass tea he let me drink the night before.

For the first time since I was that thirteen-year-old determined kid, I felt nervous and exposed to him. He didn't get the make up wearing, scar covering Queen. Right now, he was looking at the raw Sovereign. I was so used of people looking at me with nothing but respect and sometimes fear. Inferno stared at me and saw me for what I truly was. I couldn't even contain my small chuckle that escaped my lips. A struggling Queen pin is what he called me. When I really thought about it, and all the money I wasted on just revenge for Melvin, only to have it all backfire back in my face. It was true, I was indeed struggling, I made struggling look beautiful. I saved several lives and put food on a lot of men and women tables. Yet, I hadn't secured another million.

I fell off and almost hit rock bottom after Melvin. I still didn't even know how he was able to get away again and with a lot of my money and the daughter that I claimed as mine. It's like he put a curse on me, and I was struggling to get back to where I wanted to be. Staring at Inferno and feeling that fuzzy feeling when I didn't even know shit about this nigga had me vexed and upset with myself.

I looked at him as if I was trying to figure it all out. He stared back with absolutely no expression left on his face for me to read his mind on what he too was thinking. When he opened his mouth to speak, that's when it was confirmed that we both were thinking of two different things.

"Don't get caught up in your thoughts about me. If you wondering if your pussy good, the answer is yes. I personally like to feel it in my bones when I'm nutting. I can't get that from a woman that runs like a track star from the dick." He winked to fuck with me more. I didn't offer him an expression or words. I didn't need him to tell me if my pussy was good or not. I knew it to be a fact. Truth was, Inferno probably snatched his massive dick out of me the moment he discovered just how good my pussy truly was. It was lethal and dangerous for his well-being. I was indeed a man eater; I'd capture his body first and then his soul. Love wasn't for me, and it would never be for me. If he thought for one second, he had me spent and lost in my thoughts about him catching me off guard and sticking that dick where it didn't belong in the first place, then that was on him. I could always flip the script but for now I was playing things his way.

"I don't have time to show you to your room. As you know, you're in my neck of the woods so running won't be smart." That was a clear threat that had me laughing. His left thick brow rose, and I kept the shit eating grin plastered on my face. If only he knew that Mexico was my neck of the woods as well.

"You have an enchanting smile, it's viscous, laced with ill intent. Treacherous Queen you are. I love a fucking challenge." He walked close to me, so close my breathing switched gears on me and I hated that too. He was a sight for sore eyes, and he knew it. Everything on him was picture fucking perfect. His thick ass eyebrows, structured nose, and defined jawline. The masculinity in him was too powerful to inhale, even the masculine smell of him mixed with fire had my clit thumping hard. I was so caught up staring at him that I didn't realize that my hard nipples were up against his hard body. He looked down at me like a giant and smiled.

"I bet that pussy ready to bite a nigga." He winked as I stumbled back. I hated him and all this fucking winking of the eye shit he did. "Come, it's time for you to meet the man of the house." He turned and walked with his hands tucked in his suit pants pockets. The gesture alone showed that he didn't see me as a threat walking behind him.

The four-inch heels click clacked against the marble floors. We turned corners and walked down long hallways. This place was beautiful and very elegant looking. I didn't have time to marvel at all the unique paintings and family photos. What I did gather was that whoever was Inferno's dad, had a whole colony of kids. We made it to a set of double doors, the guards locked eyes with Inferno first and terror flashed in both of their eyes as they moved quick to open up the doors.

We entered his father's office and it seemed very rude of Inferno to impose when it looked like his father was holding a meeting. Champagne flutes sat on his desk; his hair was slicked back with a suit that looked similar to Inferno's. He never looked up, his eyes were locked in on the guest that sat in the chair with one big guard standing directly behind whoever occupied the seat.

When his father looked up, his eyes locked with Inferno and a big smile took over his face.

"Mi Hijo." (My son) Inferno nodded as his father's eyes landed on me and stayed put.

"Martinez? Is this tu Nieta?" My body went still as I waited to hear the voice.

"I told you, my men are looking for her but she will be on board." My Abuela voice almost startled me. This couldn't be a coincidence.

"From di pictures… it's her, turn around." I turned to walk out, reaching for the handle and turned it to realize that it was locked.

"What's going on dad?" Inferno voice boomed as panic started taking over me. No, the world couldn't be this fucking small.

"Nieta? What a pleasant surprise. Come sit down." She

pointed to the seat next to her as I tried my hardest to sort through my thoughts.

"Why is she with you Malice?" His father voice held skepticism. I could also feel my Abuela's eyes fixed on me.

"She will be on board with the syndicate that I have in the states soon. I was simply waiting on her answer." Inferno looked at me then back to his dad like he was waiting for his answer.

"Well, it's good you two are here, we were discussing the new Golden Triangle. You two will get married by next week and then we can pledge our new alliance with one more head of Mexico before things start flowing-"

"No!" Inferno and I spoke at the same time. He looked at me with a disgusted look that instantly ticked me off.

"Next week, I have birthday plans and business concerning my syndicate." Inferno explained.

"I have a couple of things back in the states to handle as well." Truth was, I needed more time to get the fuck out of the fucked-up position I was in. No way I was marrying this nigga standing before me.

"Three days to wrap your affairs up, this will take place by next week. No if ands or buts." My Abuela took the lead on speaking up.

"Find another wife dad, she's overweight and can't take dick." I looked at Inferno and stood to my feet, I was ready to take his fucking head off.

"She doesn't even know her place as a wife. Ghetto trash, struggling ass, wanna be Queen pin." He continued his verbal assault as I took a step towards him and was held back by my Abuela.

"She can lose weight, and she can be trained. She will be a great asset to the empire we are building." She reassured them, while yanking my arm. I took a seat and slowly

116

bounced my leg. I chewed on my bottom lip until it felt raw. A laugh was bubbling up inside of me and I fought hard to contain it. I wanted to laugh my anger off so badly to keep from spazzing. Instead, I zoned out and forced my thoughts on Aiden and Caiden taking turns devouring my center. I needed to get away from Mexico and figure some shit out and I needed to do it fast. They talked as if I wasn't sitting there making plans and setting dates for more meetings.

The more and more they talked the angrier I became. Once the meeting was over, I found the nearest exit and marched my ass to the busy street and hailed a cab to the airport.

SOULFUL HURTZ

*a*ka Teddy
    I hate when it was close to summer, people always started asking questions, like why I had on so many clothes. School was long and boring; I end up getting suspended for snapping and punching a nigga in the face for testing my gangsta. I let these hoes talk shit, they were females and emotional creatures. When it came to these niggas, I wasn't pussy, no nigga was gone disrespect me and get away with the shit. I was on edge and not because something was wrong.

Everything was actually going right. My mom was home more, she had her slip ups but was still trying and my sisters were ecstatic about the effort she was putting in. I finally turned eighteen the other day. That shit didn't matter much because I was heavy on my grind and trying to stay focus. I still had a family to provide for. I smoked a blunt and hustled from sun up to sun down. A couple of my niggas popped up at my house with blunts. Clapback and Murk'um dropped off shoes, I was thankful but didn't know if they were trying to be funny. It didn't matter because I was rocking fresh shoes finally. It felt good to have my feet in some kicks that weren't used and worn down.

I really didn't give a damn about image, all I cared about was taking care of my sisters and making sure we never starved again. My mom cooked a big birthday dinner and played music and reflected all day long about the special day she gave birth to me. Same night she disappeared for a couple of hours. I stayed up waiting for her and didn't say much of nothing when she came in stumbling. She apologized the next morning and things went back normal.

I sat on the raggedy steps in front of my house, smoking. I really didn't have shit to do since I was suspended, and it was still school hours. The block was dead, didn't hear nothing but birds chirping and older people laughing. A lot of people looked down on the projects, but we were a tight knit community. People talked shit but still looked out for you. We had so many charity events and the holidays were cheerful. Celebrities always came and dropped off loads of toys for kids. Free haircuts and hairstyles were giving as well. I didn't even want to look at my own damn haircut. I looked grimy as fuck; my hair had grown out into a mini fro.

I noticed two cars creeping on my street, I automatically reached for my .44. I relaxed when I saw Queen's Audi behind an all-black Chevy Impala. I stood up and couldn't hold back my cheesy smile. I was worried about Queen and niggas wasn't telling me much.

She hopped out of the Impala, looking beautiful and serious as hell.

"This a twenty sixteen, bitch fresh, ain't it?" She smiled wide. I nodded my head and thought that this was probably a whip that she planned on putting work in.

"It was only fifty-five hundred, can't beat that at all." She stepped away from the driver's side and walked around to the passenger door and leaned on it. Today she had on all white and I thought she was bold as hell leaning up against the car.

"This shit is fresh Queen." I smirked and walked up to her. We slapped hands three times for the gang and pulled each other in for a hug.

"I want you to drive me somewhere, Clapback gone take my car home."

"Alright, let me go tell my moms I'm leaving." Queen looked like she wanted to say more but she didn't. I ran in the house and to my surprise my mom was sitting up on the couch smoking a cigarette laughing at family feud.

"I'll be back a little later Ma. Can you make the girls dinner?" I really needed her to come through for me today. Queen was our bread and butter, and I was very anxious to ride with her.

"Soulful handle your business, I'm not doing anything today but lounging." She smiled up at me then ashed her cigarette. I went to kiss her on the forehead and said a silent prayer. I was trying to trust my mom more and so far; she had been doing better.

When I got back outside, Queen was sitting on the passenger side with her eyes glued to her phone. I knew how to drive thanks to her; she taught me a while ago. It still didn't take away the nervous feeling I had. Queen was a woman of few words; she showed you more with actions so I wouldn't question why she wanted me to do the driving. I got in on the driver's side and watched Clapback speed off. Buckling my seat belt, I pulled off slow.

"How did your birthday go?" She never looked up as she typed away on her phone. I had no clue where I was going, but I drove until we were on the busy street away from the projects.

"Same shit different, day. I smoked with a couple of

niggas and hustled the rest of the day." She nodded her head and told me to get on the freeway and head over towards her clinic.

"I see your mom is back home, were you putting the work?"

"The work secured and moms trying to get clean." I reassured her.

"I understand, just don't get your hopes to high Teddy. That's your mom, love and respect her no doubt. The people you love the most, always hurts you the worst. You dig? I live life not putting high expectations on people because sometimes they just can't help who they are." I didn't respond to that, she looked out the window like something was weighing heavy on her mind.

"Some shit bout to change, everybody ain't gone ride with me. They gon' pretend to but actions will be exposed." She sparked a blunt and rolled the window down halfway.

"I'm riding with you Queen." I spoke in confidence. I hadn't proved myself much to her, but I knew for a fact that I would never cross her.

"I know, and I promise all of this shit gone pay off. One day soon, all your troubles will be gone. I'm about to sacrifice some shit to make it happen for both of us. We both know the struggle. I just want you to pick your confidence up, you a boss ass nigga, a big steppa. You got to walk it like you talk it, Teddy." She passed me the blunt and I declined.

"I ain't tryna drive high and shit." We both started laughing at that.

"I respect it, this is your car, so if you damage it that's on you, nigga." My eyes got big as fuck.

"What?" I didn't think I heard her correct. A car would help me drastically.

"This yo shit, I'm giving you a month to get your L's."

She smiled and I swerved a little, ignoring the cars honking my eyes got blurry from tears of joy.

"Queen." Was all I could say at first.

"You really my nigga Teddy, I fucks with you tough. I'm getting ready to make an announcement, I called an emergency meeting so that's where we headed. Niggas gone hate but they gone respect whatever comes out of my mouth." I nodded my head in agreement, niggas knew not to test anything Queen said. She stood on every word she spoke, if she even sensed a challenge or a threat, she would nip it right there in the bud.

"Man, you know I don't like accepting gifts and handouts. I wouldn't dare disrespect you and turn it down. I really appreciate this shit, my sisters gone love it too. Thanks Queen." I pulled into the back of her clinic and killed the engine.

"I got you as long as you got me. I ask for nothing back but your loyalty. Be my ears, and eyes when I'm not around. I don't trust easily, but when I look in your eyes Teddy, I see a part of me in them." She smiled and a feeling came over me. It felt like this was a deep moment for Queen and I. Some shit just didn't have to be explained to be understood. Right now, I understood everything it was she was saying.

"Stay in the car for like ten minutes, enjoy your whip, then come join the meeting. You know how niggas get jealous if they think I'm paying one of y'all more attention than the other." We shared another laugh and Queen got out the car. She was a pro when it came to transforming back into that cold calculated boss. Her face was void of everything as she walked with confidence. Bundy stepped out the back door and eyed me first. A look of curiosity crossed his face. His eyes landed on Queen as he held the door opened wide for her. A blind man could see how deeply in love he was with her. His whole intimidating facial features turned soft each time he laid eyes on her.

Taking my eyes off them, I couldn't hold back the silly grin that was plastered on my face. I really had my own car now; this shit was real. When Queen got out the car, she left the pink slip in the seat. I picked it up and eyed my name in big bold letters. Putting the pink slip in the glove compartment, I looked into the backseat and noticed shopping bags. I envisioned my sisters sitting in the back seat big cheesing, I couldn't wait to pull up to my house and show them the car we now had.

I reached over and looked in the bags and noticed that Queen not only laced me with what looked like summer clothes. She hooked my sisters up too. I wouldn't even ask her how her crazy ass knew our sizes either. I wouldn't be surprised if she went to my house and found out on her own.

Tucking my happiness, I stepped out of my car and hit the locks. I walked into the back door with a new feeling. I felt more confident in myself, I didn't put the hoodie over my head or look down at the floor. I made eye contact with every nigga in the room as Queen words flowed through my head.

I just want you to pick your confidence up, you a boss ass nigga, a big steppa. You got to walk it like you talk it, Teddy.

Yea, that's what I was on from now on. I listened to her talk and when she got ready to announce the new lieutenant everyone seemed like they were on the edge of their seats.

"Teddy is a young ambitious nigga, he keeps his nose clean, and I can trust him with my life. I will be back out of town for a couple of weeks rearranging some things. He will lead the meetings and count the dough. If respect is not given, then he will also handle that accordingly too." I made sure to lock eyes with every nigga and female that sat around in folding chairs. Although my heart was thumping hard, I dared a muthafucka to step up and get bold.

Clapback had a look on her face like she wanted to protest but knew it wasn't in her best interest.

"Bundy will be the second Lieutenant, when I leave to go back to Mexico, I expect for shit to run the same but better." Queen gave Clapback a stern eye as she mumbled some shit under her breath.

"So, what we gone do about the syndicate shit. We just gone sit here and act like that nigga didn't kidnap you. Are we getting down with them niggas? Falling in line or what?" Clapback sounded like she was pissed off.

"It's more to it, deeper than what the naked eye can see, when I'm ready to explain that I will." Bundy handed her an already lit blunt. He looked like he was just happy to be right next to her.

"Everybody here is gang. You leaving us in the dark now Queen?" Clapback didn't know when to shut up and that was a major flaw of hers. Something about her didn't sit well with me, so I kept my distance from her. I never wanted to disrespect Queen's sister.

"I'm keeping you out of my personal business. If it pertains to the gang then I will make that shit known. Right now, its personal, it's not F.Y.F business. So, drop it… or you can figure out a way to stop dealing with that nigga Killa. It's bad for business." Clapback shut her mouth as we all sat in silence. I was thinking about the new position along with all the responsibilities it came with. I was ready for the challenge, ready to get this money by all means necessary.

"Let me make it clear, we don't bow down. If I see a big opportunity for us all, I will take it. We are small right now, very close knit. I love that for us, I just want you all to be prepared for something far greater. If I come back from

Mexico and call an emergency meeting, then just know we have expanded. Longer sleepless nights will occur. If I also decide to get down with the syndicate, nigga then best believe it will involve more money for us."

"It won't Queen, them niggas extorting people out of their dividends," Murk'um spoke up.

"That won't be the case with us if or when I do make my final decision. Now if any of you feel like I'm not making good decisions for us as a whole then any of you are free to walk away. Walk away before you attempt to do some shady shit. No matter how many years we got together, I won't hesitate to kill you."

I tuned out the conversation and start thinking of ways to step my own shit up. I had to move smarter. I definitely had more on me now and had to figure out just where I could relocate my stash.

Once the meeting was over, I walked out to the parking lot forgetting that I even had a car. Usually, I'd catch the bus back home or one of them would take me home. Instead, I was holding the keys to my own shit. Excitement flowed through me the closer I got to my Impala. Hopping in my car felt surreal as fuck, I turned up the radio and cruised all the way home. I wouldn't bitch up in front of Queen. I let the tears of joy fall from my eyes and didn't wipe them away until I pulled up in front of the projects. Looking at the time it was only about seven, deciding to detour from in front of my house, I drove past Jocelyn house and blew the horn.

I didn't care about her being outside with her trout mouth homegirls. Jocelyn brought peace into my life, and I wanted her bad. She rocked baggy gray sweats with a spaghetti strapped shirt. She had on some purple UGG sandals. When she noticed it was me, she smiled widely making me smile. I was so excited, I just wanted to show her my car first.

I got out the car and leaned on the hood waiting for her to approach me. I loved when Jocelyn wore contacts it gave me the perfect view of those big innocent eyes. Her caramel skin held a permanent glow.

"You got a car, Soulful." She smiled hard and hugged me tightly before I could confirm that it was indeed my car. I hesitated at first. This was the first time I felt her in my arms. She smelled good as fuck and felt like cotton in my arms. I slowly put my arms around her waist and pulled her in close. She was tall like me, just a little shorter so her head stopped at my chin. The wind blew making her sweet smell drift up my nose. I let her go when I felt my dick bricking up. I didn't want to disrespect her in that way.

"Shit looking up for a nigga." I smiled.

"I see, this is really dope as heck Soul. I guess I'm riding with you in the mornings and when we get out of school." I just nodded my head. With the way things was looking, I didn't know if school would be on my agenda. Then again, I didn't have a choice because Queen still paid my tuition and wanted me to keep going. I looked at Queen like a big sister, I didn't want to disappoint her, I actually liked making her proud.

"You got that Jah." An awkward silence passed, and we just stared at one another. Today, I really stepped out my shell, I never really approached Jocelyn, she always came to me and made it a point to talk to me. I liked that she didn't diss me like all the other broads did at school. I knew I was a dusty nigga and didn't have much, so I never defended myself. The goal was to take care of my family, I didn't give a fuck what others thought of me.

"I went to your class and got you the missing assignments, so it won't affect your grade." She smirked as I nodded and just stared at her getting lost in her beauty.

"Why you staring at me like that." She blushed.

"I like you Jah and I think…" What the fuck was I on? I was about to tell her that I thought I was in love with her. Nah, I'm tripping hard as fuck. I licked my lips and kept my mouth shut.

"You think what Soul?" Feeling nervous, I tucked my hands in my pockets. I didn't feel like it was the time to step to her. Jocelyn deserved a nigga that was paid, and I wasn't that. I could barely buy myself a meal and provide. I didn't know shit about relationships, but I know if I had it like that, I would treat Jocelyn right. I wasn't some horny teenage nigga. I wasn't a virgin either. I fucked a couple of older homegirls from around the way. What was crazy about it was they was all grown as fuck, in their mid-twenties. All the girls my age wasn't really feeling me like that. They were superficial and cared about what all a nigga had.

"I just think you beautiful as fuck when I get on and have more money. I want to make you mine." I was serious as fuck; I couldn't hold back any longer. "So, you can have fun with that nigga you claim as a boyfriend. Don't fuck that nigga Jocelyn, I want to be your first and last." I didn't give a fuck what her response was. I expected her to pop off, but I was willing to take that to the chin.

"How you know I'm a virgin." Her eyes went into slits and suddenly my mouth went dry. I couldn't feel no type of way but damn I could've sworn that she was. No rumors went around about her fucking on none of these project niggas. Niggas loved being in her face but that's as far as it went. Around here, if a nigga fucked on a bitch, they bragged and boasted about it. Jocelyn was pretty as fuck and she hung with other pretty popular girls.

"I'm just messing with you, Soul. To be honest, I think we soulmates." She giggled shyly and tucked some hair behind her ear. "I've liked you for a long time, but I'm not thirsty. I was waiting for you to say something. I'm ready to be yours now." She looked me directly in the eyes and I fell in love with her instantly.

"Come here." I talked lowly. I looked at her friends who was now staring and shooting daggers our way. I sat on the hood of the car and let her walk between my legs. I grabbed her by the ass and pulled her close, I tongued her ass down with my heart beating fast as hell. I got a car and the girl of my dreams. Jocelyn felt perfect in my arms. Some would try to judge and say some stupid shit like "Oh its young love." In my eyes it could be whatever kind of love because I stood there a hundred percent sure that Jocelyn was the one for me.

I promised Jocelyn that I would pick her up early in the morning for school. When I left from in front of her house it felt like a young nigga was floating.

EMPRESS AKA CLAPBACK

"**I** don't know why the fuck she gave Bundy and that dirty ass fat nigga the position over you!" I was pissed, I felt like my man deserved a chance. Murk'um stared at me like he was pissed but said nothing, so I continued my rant.

"Then what's going on with her and this nigga from the syndicate?" I looked over at him and admired his fine chocolate ass.

"If I wasn't fucking on you, then I would have that fuckin position, Empress." He spat and sat up, pulling his shirt over his head. "It ain't like the pussy mine, I told you this shit got to stop." I rolled my eyes hard, Murk'um tried to cut me off a million times. I never begged him to fuck with me or to continue fucking on me. Each time he did one of his little fake cut offs, he ended up blowing up my phone the following day. We were inseparable, we both had a good understanding. I was his main bitch, and he was my main nigga. We fucked around from time to time, well maybe all the time. In a weird way we just always understood each other.

"Nigga please, ain't nobody stopping you from coming over here or blowing up my damn phone. Here you go acting like a lil bitch go ahead and be fake mad for zero point five seconds." That was the truth, Murk'um was sprung off me, all these niggas were. Pussy ruled the entire world it's how my sister got into the boss-ass position she was in.

"Whatever Empress, you been holding back. I'm trying to see what all going on." I frowned at him.

"Why? You starting to make me feel like you trying to go against the grain."

"Bitch you stupid, you know how I'm giving it up over Queen. She just always secretive expecting us to go along with shit when she drops it in our laps. A nigga tryna be prepared for whatever." He eased my suspicions, my sister got on my nerves, but I loved her and wouldn't let the next nigga like Murk'um pull some stupid shit.

"She's going to take over our Abuela's cartel. That's why she keeps going back and forth saying she going to Mexico. When she does that, we all gone be sitting at the top of the food chain." I smiled.

"That's why we need to plan some shit to get you in position to take your rightful position as lieutenant. She like that little fat fucker too much. Bought him a car and all. She feels sorry for him because he don't got much." My sister was a cold-hearted bitch, once she had a soft spot for you. She would go above and beyond to make sure you were straight. I loved my sister but disliked a lot of her traits. We were two different people which was quite obvious.

"How the fuck we pose to do that?" I could tell Murk'um was on edge. I dragged him into a lot of my shit. He was my scapegoat, and he was always there to pick up all my shattered pieces.

"Wait for her to go to Mexico. We got to watch Teddy

when the time is right... we break into that nigga crib. I'm pretty sure he keeps all the dope in there. That will prove to Queen that he is in no fuckin position to be making plays for the gang." I smiled; I was smart as fuck.

"I can't risk shit going left Em. I mean you already ain't got your other fucked up situation under control. If Queen finds out, we are good as dead. Who you think your grandma gone side with?" That pissed me off, I hated when this nigga acted so scared of Sovereign's ass.

"Me! That's who!" Murk'um smiled because we both knew the real answer to that.

"If that's the case then you would be the head bitch in charge." He smirked then folded his muscular arms across his chest.

"I'm ladylike, Sovereign acts like a nigga. I don't want to run shit. I want to reap the benefits." I answered truthfully.

"Yea, I hear you." He pulled out a pack of cigarettes and took one out the pack and sparked it. "You just remember if anything, I do mean anything backfires, it's all on you." He walked to the door and stopped.

"Get rid of that baby." I cringed and remembered that I needed to set up an appointment to have this abortion.

Once Murk'um left, I ran some hot bath water. I still had Murk'ums nut oozing out of my pussy from earlier. Murk'um was a thugged out ass nigga that knew how to fuck bomb!

I loved Murk'um but I loved money more. I wanted to be filthy fucking rich with no worries at all. I wanted to be treated like a princess, traveling the world with unlimited money.

Easing down in the tub, I grabbed my phone and called Sovereign.

"You good?" I asked, it was normal for Queen not to

speak first when she answered the phone. Most of the time she answered and waited for you to get to the point.

"Yea." She sighed. "I'm with the twins, eating and drinking."

"Freaky asses." I teased and giggled, my sister was lucky as hell to have two fine doubles, fulfilling her sexual fantasies. Besides that, the twins were cool and brought in lots of money from Hollywood. If the three of them weren't fucking, then they were having a good time. I sometimes got jealous because my sister didn't have friends outside of me and the gang. The twins and her became close, I also noticed she spent a lot more time with them.

"What you want baby sis?" Her voice was calm. I smiled because this is the side of her that I loved. She played the mother and big sister role effortlessly.

"Just checking on you. Wanted to make sure you were good. Earlier you had this look in your eyes. I know the look all too well Sovereign, something is stressing you." Something had her worried, while she masked it well and kept a blank face most of the time. I knew her well and I knew it was something outside of the gang stressing her out.

"Your Abuela, is stressing me. We will talk soon about it. Just know, I'm sacrificing a lot again for us."

"Is there something that I can do?" I wanted to help if I could.

"No, I wouldn't put you in that position Clap. It's only temporary, I just need you focused with your eyes opened. All that questioning me in meetings needs to stop. I wouldn't leave you in the dark, but everything is not to be spoke on in front of the gang." I immediately felt bad for speaking out of term. My sister told me everything, I just got so caught up in the moment when I saw the disappointment on Murk'um face. I wanted him to know that I was riding hard for him too. He always had my back and made sure I was straight.

"It won't happen again." I promised.

"Alright, get some rest. Love you." She hung up. I laid back in the tub to relax a little before I started to bathe. I got my phone and went straight to Instagram for a while then handled my business in the tub. Drying off then covering my body with my favorite lotion. I pranced in my room, only to be knocked in the face, falling flat on my ass. I saw nothing but stars and didn't know what just hit me. When I heard his voice, I shivered and peed on myself.

"You been running from me bitch." I mindlessly scooted backwards until I felt my back hit the wall.

"I haven't, just been busy." I tried to force the fear out of my body but was failing miserably. I remember when the young me fell so deep in love with this devil. I fell for all the lies and thought I was making the right decision. My head started to pound hard, and I could feel blood leaking from my nose and could taste it in my mouth.

"Locks are changed and you still fucking on that nigga. You think you can duck and dodge me bitch, don't you? I don't give a fuck where you go or who you run to; I will always be near." I shut my mouth; I had been running. I barely stayed at home, if I didn't go to Murk'um house, I made excuses to stay at Sovereigns.

"You forget what the fuck I'm capable of Empress. If you don't run me some money very soon then I'll take you to Cuba and sell you to the highest bidder like I did my daughter. Since you more ran through the price would be low, then again, I'd still probably make good profit. You beautiful as fuck, got that exotic look too." He pulled his pants down and stepped out of them. I swallowed down the lump in my throat and prepared myself for what was to come. I tried to think of

Murk'um pleasing and licking all over me then fucking me good. My pussy was dry as hell and I knew that this nigga was getting ready to barge his way inside of me. The least I could do was try to enjoy the very rough sex that I was about to receive.

"Sovereign is about to take over the cartel soon. Real soon! When she does that, I'll always have a big amount of money to give you." He chuckled lowly, I hated myself a little. It felt like I had no control over this situation. Until I found a way to kill this nigga, I had no choice but to go along with whatever he wanted.

Have you ever done something so foolish in your life that you were ashamed. It came from the past but there was no way to make it disappear. All of this started for me when I was seventeen. I let this nigga get in my head and it was the first time in my life that I had done some disloyal shit to my sister that I wish I could take back. Once it was done it couldn't be reversed.

I loved Sovereign so much but back then; I was stupid as hell. My young body reacted to this man in a way it had never done before. I fell in love and was willing to do whatever it took to keep him. I didn't know shit about love, but I thought I had a clue. Melvin was handsome and smooth as hell. He got in my mind, and nobody could tell me that he didn't belong to me. When Queen found out about his wife and unborn child, I did too, and it crushed me even worse than it did her. I wanted him dead on the spot, but Sovereign had plans of torture.

I got scared, I didn't want him folding and telling my big sister that her little sister was deep in love with him. I had no one to confide in so I told Murk'um everything. Sovereign would visit with Melvin once a week to fuck with his brain. She swore up and down that Melvin's father had something to do with our parent's death, but I knew that wasn't the case. Each week she went to visit, I would become more afraid of Melvin saying something to Sovereign about our relationship.

Not only that before Queen got to the point of torture and capturing Melvin, but he somehow already knew that she was aware. Melvin knew the lengths Queen would go, so he got in my mind and already prepared me to help him with a plan of his own.

I spun the situation a million times; I couldn't go against Sovereign and just kill Melvin because that would raise her suspicions. I was caught in between the two because I loved them both so much. I couldn't see myself killing the love of my life. As more time went on, I fell into my scandalous role. I stole lots of money from my sister and helped kidnap his daughter then helped him escape.

Sovereign killed any man that was a part of F.Y.F. attached to Melvin. She had no clue that it was all me.

"Go clean your face, I want some pussy."

QUEEN

$\mathcal{I}$ stood in the mirror, staring at the raw me. When I looked at my reflection, I saw a fair mixture of my mom and dad which often pained me. Every time I looked myself in the mirror, I tried to search for something that I felt I was missing. Off top, I was beautiful as hell. I couldn't deny myself of that, I felt empty. A lot of shit in my life was unsettled and I desperately wanted to get to a point where I felt a hundred percent happy. I had my days where I felt satisfied. Happiness is what I felt when I had my parents here with me. It felt unreal and after all these years of being forced to live without them, I figured it would become easier, but it didn't.

It felt like each year that passed by the reality of not being able to look my mother and father directly in the eyes crushed me harder each time.

It was nearing two in the morning, my pussy pulsated with satisfaction. The twins took turns feasting on me until I had no choice but to tap out. We got so high and drunk, it felt so good to zone out and be out of touch with my actual reality. I ran my hands through my hair and flinched when my curly strands got caught into an object on my finger. Carefully untangling my hair, I held my hand out for close observation and jumped back when I stared at a ring that looked like it was worth more than my entire savings.

Goosebumps covered my body; my mouth went dry. I went from room to room checking to see if anyone was here with my gun secured in my hand. Bottles and take-out food from a couple hours ago littered the living room as evidence of me having a really good time.

It wasn't like Aiden and Caiden to just leave me in the room alone. Our routine would be to check out and get breakfast in the morning.

Picking up my cellphone, I took a seat on the couch and went right to the unknown text message. The time was now four o clock in the morning. The text made me cringe hard.

Fiancé, I will see you in a couple of hours to meet with my attorney to go over a few things because you seem confused.

Your Excellency.

I burst out laughing as I responded with a laughing emoji. I shot Bundy a text message and then locked my phone. Forgetting the ring was even on my finger, I showered and went to my duffel bag to throw on my joggers with a graphic shirt. All I wanted to do today was hide in the comforts of my home and think. I needed time to fucking think. I pulled all my wild curly hair into a high ponytail then rolled me up a blunt. A knock at the door sounded off, I knew it was Bundy, so I grabbed my belongings then opened the door to give my bag to him.

We said nothing to one another as we walked towards the back exit of the hotel. When we got in his car, I let the music do the talking. I smoked on my blunt and looked out the window. Never in my life have I ever encountered a man like Inferno. He made me feel like I had no fucking privacy. I wondered if he slid this ring on while I was sprawled out naked and snoring. The twins loved my big breast. So, I could only imagine them laying on each one sleeping good too. I hope Inferno didn't scare them off. They were my babies, and I enjoyed their company outside of making money.

I shot them both a text from the group messenger I created for us. It was still considered early morning. Nearing five o' clock, Aiden responded saying they both were good and that I had a crazy nigga on my hands. Caiden responded five minutes later saying Inferno wasn't normal, he claimed Inferno had a Flamethrower pointed at their heads and told them to leave calmly. I chuckled and locked my phone. What sane nigga walked around with a fucking Flamethrower?

Pulling up to my house, my neighborhood was quiet. I looked over at Bundy who looked like he was pissed about something. His jaws kept clenching as he held onto the stirring wheel tight.

"What's wrong with you?" I really didn't want to know. All I wanted to do was rest but I also cared about this nigga feelings. Bundy looked over at me with sadness in his eyes. How could a man be so damn fine, a cold killer but emotional at the same time. I could have fucked on Bundy and maybe we would've had something solid. I saw him for what he was and how he could possibly try to change the parts of me that I didn't want to change.

He was a man that wore his heart on his sleeve, a woman like me would run circles around Bundy. I nipped what we had before it could even get started. I didn't want to lead him on and play with his feelings. Men that got deep in their feelings did crazy shit to express just how bad you hurt them. I wasn't the one for all the extra shit, Bundy was a good dude. Who he was on the inside was selfless and very unique. I valued our friendship and wanted to keep it like that.

"If I was to quit working for you, would you be with me then?" I fixed my face before I spoke. I even remained quiet for some time before I even responded to him. I could have ripped the band aid off and said no. Instead, I was about to give him my real outlook. I didn't want a relationship at all.

"I don't want to ever be the chick that becomes mentally content with a man, just to say I have one." He went to move his mouth, but nothing came out. His eyes landed on the huge rock on my finger. I didn't care to explain just yet what was going on with the whole marriage situation. Talking about it made it real.

"What does that mean Queen?"

"It can mean a lot of things; I just know that women tend to force themselves and train their brains to become mentally content with a man. They overlook red flags just to feel secure with a man. I get it, nobody's perfect. I just will never brain wash myself again and overlook red flags." That was the truth, I made that mistake years ago with Melvin. I played with my own mind and ignored my intuition. I wanted the kind of love my parents shared. At the time I thought I could make that happen with Melvin. I ignored all the questions that would constantly pop up in my head. I kept telling myself that no one was perfect.

"It may sound like I'm talking in fuckin circles. I like you Bundy, I don't get the butterflies in my stomach when we close are alone like now. Don't feel fucked up about it because I don't get that with no man. I don't want a relationship; I'm trying to secure all of our future and that's with money. Let's say you quit, and I fuck with you, I can tell you now, I wouldn't get rid of the twins. I wouldn't be faithful to you; I wouldn't treat you good at all Bundy." He kept his eyes on my ring and I already knew what was about to come out of his mouth.

"You marrying this nigga. You know me, Queen. I keep quiet to please you, but I love you." I was cringing hard now, that's what turned me off with Bundy. He was very emotional and didn't know how to take the fucking hints. I was letting him down nicely when I could have ended this whole conversation minutes ago.

"That's the thing Bundy, I don't want a man to keep quiet because he's desperate for my acceptance. If I ever do get a man, I want that nigga to make noise. I got love for you too Bundy but this between us will be nothing but a friendship. Me getting married is not for love. It's business. I want you to find a woman that's normal, let her be your peace baby, I will never be your peace because I don't know what the fuck that is." I grabbed the side of his handsome face and rubbed it softly for a couple of seconds.

Hopping out of his car, he kept his eyes on me. I went to the back seat to get my duffle bag then tapped the door of his car. I hope he didn't make things awkward as fuck. I wish he never even conjured feelings for me to begin with. At the end of the day Bundy was a grown ass man and he knew the rules. Him asking to quit didn't mean shit to me either. It wouldn't make me want him or look at him like he was doing something big for me.

I made it inside and went straight to my bathroom to wash my hands and get in the bed. I probably slept for about an hour in a half before I was awakened.

"Sovereign." His Spanish thick accent stirred something in me. I had lied to Bundy about having butterflies. Inferno made me feel stupid butterflies without even trying.

This man was irresistibly fine, one hand in his black dress pants the other holding his lit cigar.

"Get up, my attorney is here. She will go over some papers with you. I have personal rules for you as well but that's not concerning our so-called marriage. Be professional and courteous." I just looked at him blankly and sat up.

"I thought I was too fat to be your wife. Oh, and I can't take dick."

"That's true, but you will be my wife and also be a part of my syndicate. I'm a very busy man Sovereign, the longer I stand here and talk to you about a bunch of nothing, the more time we waste." He had a look of irritation plastered on his face.

"I don't like wasting my time or my words. Get up, clean yourself, and meet us in the front."

"What if I don't want to fucking marry you? You can't force me to do shit that I don't want to do." He smiled and walked towards my dresser. Picking up his flamethrower he neared me.

"For some odd reason Sovereign, I wanted to melt your fucking face when I saw my soon to be wife laying up in the middle of the night with two men. I wanted to set that entire room on fire and get rid of you for good. It's quite obvious you don't respect yourself. You have no fucking class. You also don't give a fuck about your health either."

"I love my size and I'm in good health." I stood to my feet ready to go toe to toe with him. Until he squeezed the trigger to his flamethrower. The smell of gas permeated the air and then the flame came soaring out causing me to stumble and sit back down on the bed.

"I wasn't talking about your weight." He chuckled lowly. "I'm talking about your life. I don't give a fuck how you feel about yourself nor what you think. See, I don't have a choice right now but to marry you. So, you will get in line and start acting how a wife is supposed to act. You will not embarrass me, or I will kill you and then burn you. I'll send half of your ashes to your money hungry Abuela then piss on the rest." He snarled, then focused on the flames.

"I'm not going to argue with you. Miss Mason is waiting, and she gets paid by the hour. The quicker you sign the papers the faster we can get all of this shit over with. We will get married tomorrow and head to Mexico the following day. A small ceremony will be held there and then your Abuela will inform you of the rest." I shook my head no, anger started to rise high inside of me.

"Let me know if you disagree, I can get rid of you now."

"Okay," I sighed. I might as well get it over with. Since he felt like he had the upper hand in this, I would let him think that for now.

"Okay?" He frowned.

"Yes, let's do this. I have things to do. Now can you turn that shit off and move." He smirked and let the clutch go. Dropping the flamethrower to his side he walked towards the door.

"Good choice."

I kept on what I already had on from earlier. I wasn't trying to impress him. What he didn't know was that he was slowly waking up my crazy. I had been chilling before him and my Abuela came into the picture. Now they were pulling me in the direction of pure evilness. When I walked into my living room, Inferno sat in the corner of my living room. He had a book in his hand and never looked up to acknowledge me. That stupid flamethrower rested on the side of the black love seat.

"Hello, I am Miss. Mason, Malice Ruiz attorney. I have some documents to go over regarding you two union. It will take about an hour to go over." A pretty chocolate woman spoke with a upbeat voice. I wondered how she managed to work with a nigga like Inferno. Speaking of nicknames since he refused to refer to me as Queen. I planned on calling him by his first name to fuck with him.

I took a seat across from Miss. Mason and let her talk her ass off. I didn't really listen to shit she said because I really didn't give a fuck.

"This paper is a list of things that Mr. Ruiz have in place for you to abide by. He calls it Terms of Service. If any of these are not followed, then a penalty will follow. If you look over here on the paper you will see that there are fees that will be paid within twenty-four hours, if you are in violation. My apologies this is the way Mr. Ruiz told me to word it." I looked over at him, he licked his index finger and turned the page. Acting like he was so fucking invested in what he was reading.

"These are a list of rules, specifications, and requirements of this contract." She handed me the paperwork and I scanned it. My eyes bulged as my leg bounced slowly then fast.

In bold letters it mentioned that I couldn't have any sexual relations outside of him. The penalty was a three hundred-thousand-dollar fee. As she read all the ridiculous rules aloud, I kept looking over at him until he looked up from his stupid book.

"You should see what I do to people that refuse to pay me." He smirked and closed the book.

"This marriage isn't real, why do you care about who I sleep with Malice?" I raised my brow and gave him all of my attention. I glanced over at Miss. Mason, and she had a look of worry. I could tell she was very uncomfortable with what was taking place.

"Terms of Service states that you will be my wife for ten years. You will beg for the dick, and I might give it to you. I love to fuck raw, so you will be tested and once I really fuck you... the pussy will be mine exclusively." He stood there with not an ounce of shame. He didn't blink and he kept his beautiful orbs locked in with mine.

"I don't want to fuck you." I laughed, "So don't get your hopes up."

"Then you will be celibate, continue on." He sneered and looked at Miss. Mason and she continued to speak. I cut her off in the middle of her talking by standing up and marching over to where Inferno stood.

"I'm treating this shit like an affair, that I'm not supposed to even have." I smiled up at him.

"Oh yea?" His brow raised as he stepped even closer to me. I could smell cigar and mint on his breath. He stuffed his hand between my thighs and moved each finger applying a little bit of pressure.

"Let the affair start. Sit yo hot pussy ass down, and listen to the Terms of Service, Sovereign." He sat back down with amusement dancing in his eyes, placing those big prominent eyes back on Miss. Mason he nodded his head, and she continued speaking as I just stood there in front of him for a couple of seconds. I was trying to figure him out but couldn't. I think that's what irked me the most. I didn't like the sound of Terms of Service because I wasn't servicing this man of shit. I planned on doing me and not paying shit for the penalty.

"The Golden Triangle expects you two to have a strong union and lots of stability. Cartel or syndicate business will not be discussed to any outsiders on your behalf Ms. Martinez. Also, you two will procreate within two years of union." A lump formed in my throat and suddenly it felt like I couldn't breathe. I knew I couldn't conceive but that bit of information was personal. I never been back to the doctor to check on my uterus to see if I could even bare another baby in my womb.

"My father must have added that to the paperwork, that will not be necessary." Inferno chimed in breaking my train of thought.

"It is necessary, Mr. Ruiz wants to ensure that a heir to the cartel shoes will be filled if something was to happen to you or Sovereign." He scoffed and said nothing, there wouldn't be any baby making. I was sure of that. The first time, I felt Malice inside of me had me speechless and scared shitless. I never had a man fill me up the way he did, that scared me and had me literally running away from the dick. Heat shot throughout my body thinking about how big and wide Malice felt inside of me. I shifted my legs and squeezed my thighs tight. Hearing a chuckle, Inferno looked at me and winked.

"Is there anything you will like to add to the Terms of Service?" Miss. Mason looked directly at me, and I shook my head no.

"If I think of anything, I will let Mr. Fireman know and he will call you." I smirked.

"It will have to be added now, your union starts tomorrow." I remained quiet until I thought of something and spoke.

"Let the records state at the bottom, that I will do me regardless of a Term of Service." I eyed her as she wrote in cursive.

"The rules stand, Sovereign. Miss. Mason do not add that. This isn't for her to add to, I pay you. Pick up the pen and sign the fucking papers."

There was no point in arguing, I picked up the pen and signed the papers and stood to my feet. Inferno stood tall as well with a look of satisfaction plastered on his face.

"Like Jagged Edge say, let's get married."

MALICE

*O*ne week after marriage
I eyed Mi'elle with seriousness, I should have never flown her out to Mexico but the mere thought of the way her pussy gripped my dick had been on my mind a lot lately. After she played stupid games, lying trying to keep me for herself. She admitted to faking the pregnancy just to make me commit. If a man wasn't careful, they would have fallen for Mi'elles antics. I was not some regular man, so I played along allowing her to play herself.

I often looked at Mi'elle and wondered how such a beautiful woman could be so caught up into a dangerous man like myself. I didn't lead women on, but they always led their own feelings creating delusions of having something more with me. Kenya would have been here, I just decided to give her a break until she could put her focus back on the friendship that we had together and our business.

I had Kenya currently wrapped up in charity events and scouting new business ventures to clean more of my money. By the time, I paid her a visit the closeness and attachment issues that she was having should be gone. I have been in

Mexico with my hell-bent stubborn wife for a whole week and was happy that she went with her Abuela to be groomed. Sovereign was a tough cookie that was very hard to break. The day after our marriage she disappeared and called herself being laid up once again with those fucking twins. Disrespecting me wasn't an option so I taught them all a lesson by setting that hotel on fire. I caught them stumbling out the back of the hotel and had my security hold each twin down. I set their hair on fire and sent my final warning; they were to stir clear of my wife if they loved their lives.

What woman enjoyed two men at the same time of the same blood? Sovereign that's who, she was a huge mystery that was hard to figure out. I couldn't deny her beauty, what intrigued me was, she would be the first woman that I ever encountered who seemed to hate my guts. Whenever I eyed her, that plump sexy lip of hers would turn up with disgust.

"Happy Birthday Papi." Mi'elle spoke in her thick sexy Spanish accent. She had curves in place for a million years. She was beautiful as hell with those deep seductive eyes that enticed the hell out of me. She had on red lace with white stockings.

"Where's my gift?" My tone was now husky, my dick was ready to break out of my boxers. I sat up in bed and looked at her standing in the middle of my room. My father gave me his contractors and I had them build me a house in Rosarito. It had been empty for over a year and some change but now that I was here, I loved the place. My room had ocean views the mini palace sat high in the mountains just like my father's compound.

Mi'elle smiled and disappeared from in front of me. While she went to get my gift, I went to hop in the shower. Last night she fucked and sucked me dry. I planned on breaking her off one more time than sending her back to the states.

My father probably planned a huge dinner for me, a dinner that I didn't want to be a part of. Killa and Big B had already texted me and let me know that they had arrived last night and was staying at a hotel. Before hopping in the shower, I looked over my text messages and emails. I had tons of Happy birthdays and cash deposits from lots of my associates. I stopped at Kenya's long ass text message and closed it out. No way in hell did I plan on wasting time reading all of that. The best birthday wish came from my mom, we talked on the phone for hours last night before Mi'elle came over. I missed her so much; it was starting to pain me. I put my mom at the top of my list of things to do when I got back to Cali.

I was now thirty-three and was sitting on top of the fucking world. I wouldn't stopped not now or ever. I still had so many goals and things to achieve, I would remain focused.

Walking back into my master bedroom I stood with a towel wrapped around my waist. Mi'elle laid back on my California king bed with her vanilla thighs spread wide. Her fat pink pussy was being devoured by a chocolate beauty that moaned each time she licked up and down her swollen slit. They looked so fucking sexy and nasty, their moans had me dropping the towel and gripping my dick tight. They switched positions until they were in a scissor position. All you could hear was wet pussy slapping against one another.

Mi'elle grabbed the chocolate beauty C cup breast and bit down on her thick hard nipples then sucked slowly while her eyes remained on mine. She rotated her hips slowly as I stepped closer. The sight before me was so fucking sexy pre cum started to leak from the tip of my dick. Thick pussy lips entwined close together, each lip separating the other as their swollen clits rubbed against each other. So much wetness between the two women, my dick jumped.

I hurriedly walked off and snatched a condom off my dresser and slid it on. Climbing on the bed, I broke the two up. Laying on my back with my dick saluting the both of them. I winked at the chocolate beauty. She wasted no time, sitting up and climbing right on top. She eased down on my dick, and I wasn't impressed. Her walls barely clinched my dick. Mi'elle grabbed her waist and licked up and down her spine as the chocolate beauty leaned her head back and moaned. Mi'elle creeped around to the front and sloppily kissed the chick while toying with her clit. Finally, the chick riding my dick, pussy muscles contracted and applied some form of suction on my shit.

"Get off my dick, both of ya'll suck it." I just wanted to nut so I could get my dick started. The show was nice but since the chick pussy was loose, I lost interest.

Mi'elle knew that I meant business, she gave the chick a look and she eased right off my shit. They both got on their knees and tongued each other down and took turns going up and down my dick. They licked and sucked my balls and deep throated me good. I felt someone else presence in the room and looked towards the entrance of my bedroom.

Sovereign stood there with a scowl on her pretty round face, those hazel brown eyes were full of fire. I smiled and winked at her, grabbing a handful of Mi'elle's curly hair, I forced her to take all ten inches of me. She gagged and moaned while the chocolate chick tickled my balls.

Sovereign was so fucking pretty she had my dick twitching inside of Mi'elle's mouth. She turned around giving me a nice view of her round ass and I imagined busting my nut all over it. Snatching Mi'elle head back, I grabbed my dick and drenched them both with my nut until I was left on empty. Out of breath, feeling good, I looked over at both chicks and sneered.

"Mi'elle, don't ever bring a loose pussy bitch to my bedroom again."

"Sorry, Inferno." She instantly looked sad, I shrugged my shoulders and got out the bed to shower again.

"Thanks for the effort regarding the birthday gift. I will be in touch soon." I ignored their stifling conversation and closed the bathroom door. I stayed in the shower for an hour wetting my wild curls to tame them more. I put some leave in conditioner and stepped out the shower. I went through phases, letting my hair grow then wanting it cut with waves. When I walked back into my bedroom, I heard noise. That wasn't normal because my estate was always quiet. I shrugged it off because my security would have alerted me if something was going on. Opening up my room window to let the stench of pussy out, I paused and took a deep sniff of the air.

I welcomed the smell; shit I missed hades in my chambers. I could smell fire from miles away. It was my favorite smell next to a woman's pussy. Banging on my room door made me realize that maybe… no that couldn't be. No fires should have been going on unless I started one.

"Excellency! Sir!" I could hear the muffled screams followed by hard knocking. Snatching the door open with my flamethrower secured in my hand, I eyed my security. He was a short Hispanic guy that looked nervous every time he encountered me.

"Your wife… umm she has a gift for you downstairs. It's umm… a burning gift." I made a mental note to fire this nigga. I couldn't have someone protecting my life that was constantly nervous. I smiled at him anyway and told him I would be downstairs once I got myself dressed. I took my time and applied lotion to my skin. After my boxers were on, I stepped into a pair of black jeans. I still heard loud commotion and decided against putting on a shirt. My wife was putting on a show and I couldn't wait to be entertained. I grabbed my Cuban cigar and hit the stairs with a light jog.

When I made it to the front of the house, my walking slowed down. The adrenaline came over me. I didn't even have to open the door, my floor to ceiling windows gave me the perfect view of outside. My Rolls Royce Sweptail was on fire while Sovereign leaned on the statue that was located in the middle of my long driveway.

A car that was special and dear to me sat burning and she nonchalantly stood smoking a blunt watching it like she was amused. I had my car shipped out days prior to me returning to Mexico.

The guards that stood on the inside of my house by my two double doors opened it and stepped away. It felt like my whole body was on fire.

When I got outside, Sovereign spread her arms with a demonic look on her face.

"Happy birthday hubby." She flicked her blunt into the flames.

"I figured since you like to burn shit and pop up on me unannounced fucking with my company. I'd pay you a visit."

For the first time, I saw my wife for what the fuck she was. I couldn't speak because I was indeed infatuated with the grand fire before me. Anger thumped through my veins, and I didn't know if I wanted to strangle or fuck the shit out of her.

Sovereign was bat shit crazy, no one ever had big enough balls to do what she had just done. She looked so innocent, so fucking sexy and thick. Her chubby feet looked good in a pair of Christian Dior flat sandals. Her thick thighs were out, it looked like her jean shorts were basically painted onto her. The crop top shirt was big and loose, showing half of her stomach.

I was utterly speechless; I couldn't move or say a word.

"You keep fucking with me, Malice." She pointed her pretty little index finger my way. "This multimillion-dollar home is next on my fuckin' list. Now, if you will excuse me... I have two niggas back in Cali that needs my attention."

She walked down the driveway with her own personal guards flanking her sides. I assumed her Abuela laced her with guards since she was out here.

"Come here Sovereign." I broke the trance I was in and stepped off the steps near the fire. She held the middle finger up.

Sovereign flipped her long curly hair behind her back, she waited for the guard to open up the back door. Once she slid in, she turned and winked at me, then slid her Gucci frames on her face.

My car exploded, the force of explosion had glass particles flying all in my face and scraping my arms as I hit the ground.

I eyed my favorite car and cursed under my breath.

"Maldita Perra." *(Fucking bitch)* I got off the ground and told my guards to get the extinguisher to put the fire out. I limped back into my home to get my phone. I needed to call my father and cancel whatever birthday plans he had in place.

This union between Sovereign and I was just getting started. I was more than ready to put her ass in check. Teach her a fucking lesson. She was a wild card, untamable, I accepted the challenge now and was ready to tame her.

SOVEREIGN

$\mathcal{S}$ tanding in my Abuela's garden felt like some kind of fairytale. She had wildflowers that stood tall all around. Like we were in the middle of a big maze. I let her dress me today and couldn't help but to enjoy the feeling of the teal silk slip that hugged my body. The slip was short, it drifted up to my mid-thigh and stopped. My hair was curly and flowing past my ass with a teal colored rose next to my ear. I felt sexy and rich while I held on to my champagne flute letting the flavors of the imported wine tease my taste buds.

My Abuela rocked a similar pink slip that fell pass her ankles. She sat in a folding chair with her legs crossed. I stood close to the folding table and her guards. The big bricks of cocaine stacked into a mountain looked so unreal. One end of the table had at least sixty bricks of pure cocaine. I could step on it five times and it would still be as potent. In the middle of the table were big bags of pills. They looked like ecstasy, but she said they were way better than that and it hadn't touched the states just yet. On the other end was Herion. I never seen so many drugs in my life.

"Expanding your empire in California would call for extra muscle. You need to talk to your husband about his syndicate protecting you all. I expect you to sit in every meeting for my cartel. You are the new face and new leader. Until I step down fully you will sit in and get to know all these people that serve us willingly. That gives you enough time to get business in California going good and smooth." She picked up her napkin and dabbed around her mouth.

"Abuela, I can't express how much gratitude I have at this very moment. Thank you." I walked over to her and squatted in front of her while embracing her fragile wrinkled hands. I stared at the locket that held my father's ashes in it and fought back emotions that was rushing fast inside of me. My mother's locket was inside of my safe. I still felt bitter that a ceremony was not held for the both of them. My Abuela, searched high and low for their bodies. That's what she told me. By the time she found them it was too late for a traditional ceremony, so she had them cremated. A part of me felt like they never left and that it was a sick joke.

"What's on your mind Mijo?" I cast my eyes downward.

"I still have an enemy. My intuition tells me he's closer than I think." I thought of Melvin, he had been crossing my mind a lot. I didn't have the resources to find him or his family. After my parents disappeared so did his parents. I was only able to get a little information out of his wife. She was loyal to that nigga and refused to talk.

"Don't worry about Melvin. That will be handled." She eyed me seriously.

"It's personal, I want to be the one to end him when you do find him." I was getting super excited because my Abuela's reach stretched far, so far that she would have all the answers within a week or two.

"Thank you, Abuela." I stood up and stretched a little.

"Si, now back to di product." She dabbed her face again and I wish I had a towel too. It was burning up in Mexico today. My Abuela's mansion was old and there were no vents inside. She had ceiling fans all throughout the house, but it blew hot air. So, it was no point in trying to go back inside at all.

"You will take my private jet and take this to the house I written down on the piece a paper that Juan is holding. No one except your husband can know about this house. Inside of the master bedroom will be a big picture frame of your dad, behind that is a safe that's built into the wall. That's were all the product and money will go to stay protected. In the back yard, there's beautiful orchards. They look real but they are not. Tap the space with your foot three times and it will open. That's your savings a gift from me since you're now official. I will show you when you come back out here the graves that I have dug with my money underground all around Mexico." She spoke proudly and talked like it was nothing big.

Juan her close bodyguard handed me an envelope that was pretty heavy.

"The jet is yours; you will need it to fly back and forth. I have another one. In that envelope are keys and pictures." Her smile wiped off her face.

"Pictures of who you will kill with no questions asked. They live in a small city called Pueblos ma'gicos. It's very colorful and looks magical so don't get caught up in sight seeing. Those people look down on us over there. Which is why that's the next place that the Martinez cartel will take over. The keys is to the house that you will live in in California. You have a million dollars' worth of product. I have to ensure your safety now. Which brings me back to your husband. His syndicate will protect your gang in California."

"My gang has nothing to do with cartel business." I

155

placed my hands on my hips. I didn't want to do any business with Malice.

"The drugs mijo, it's cartel drugs that will move in the states so the syndicate and Ruiz cartel will protect and be involved." I simply nodded my head. Hating the fact that I had to go ahead and get on board with Malice syndicate.

"Who are the people I'm killing?" I held the envelope up.

"Husband and wife, enemies. That's all you need to know." Just like that it was dropped. I didn't have no problem with killing, I could do that with my eyes closed. I sat down and drunk more wine and smoked two blunts with my Abuela. Once she yawned, I knew it was time for her to take her mid-day nap. I had Juan and my guard take the product out of the garden and load it into the town car. We had it stored on the jet in suitcases. I couldn't wait to get back to Cali and thrive hard as hell.

Today was the start of something new and different. My savings was secured, and it felt good to finally reach a point in my life to be able to say I was officially winning. My stomach clutched tight, and I knew it was my gut telling me, that this was the beginning of a storm. Money changed people lives for better or worse. True colors would show soon but I didn't know from who.

I took a long bubble bath reciting how the meeting would go in a couple of days with my gang. I looked at the pictures of the couple I was supposed to kill and just stared longer because they looked familiar as hell. After getting out the tub, I oiled my skin down and walked into my massive bedroom. My Abeula had it decorated elegantly. I had a large room with a big private bedroom. It was serene and sophisticated. I had a space for lounging and a fireplace, a small office space that had a door to close off my bedroom with a walk-in closet the size of my entire room back home. The room was teal blue and tan. I was supposed to be staying with Malice but after watching his freak show, I decided against it.

I drifted off to sleep and dreamed about myself in a long mink coat with my feet covered in snow. It was definitely a dream because I had the twins on their knees with dog leeches on them. The dream quickly turned into a nightmare when Inferno melted the snow with a huge flamethrower. He burnt the twins while they were still on dog leeches. The twins magically disappeared, and Inferno stood in front of me looking like the perfect sculpted Greek God. He held handcuffs in his right hand and cuffed my hands behind my back. Pushing me down in the snow, I moaned lowly when his warm tongue attacked my center.

I was so turned on and terrified, I begin to toss and turn trying to force myself to wake up out of this crazy ass dream. When I woke up, the room was dark, the fireplace had sweat trickling down my skin as I inhaled the stuffy hot room. My face was in the pillow and my hands were cuffed resting on top of my ass.

"Malice?" I whispered in shock trying to move my body but couldn't. It felt like I was locked in place.

"In the flesh, Sovereign. You thought you was going to just burn my foreign whip and get away with the shit?" It was so hot in the room I could feel the sweat dripping off of me. His tongue swiped my pussy lips, and I jolted forward a little. Inferno was underneath me between my thighs. I was dripping wet and was sure that my essence was leaking right onto his perfect face.

"You have a problem, Sovereign." His deep dark voice penetrated me deeply. Goosebumps covered my sweaty skin as he took my swollen clit into his mouth and hummed lowly. "A problem that I have to solve, since I'm your husband. You know?" He dragged his tongue to my asshole then back to my thumping clit. He was teasing me, and it drove me insane. Tears welled into my eyes when he sucked on my clit hard then soft.

"I'm the only nigga, that can eat this pussy like this." He flicked his tongue hard, a stream of my liquids rushed out and I dropped my head further into the pillow when I heard him gulp it down like I was giving him a waterfall.

"I have to tame you, baby." Whap! He smacked my ass so hard I spasmed and released all over his face. "Good fucking girl." The bed shifted from his weight. I didn't know what he was up to, but I was too spent to even talk. I felt his thick mushroom head at my opening and tried to brace myself.

He pushed all the way in, I wanted to move my arms but couldn't because the cuffs. I grabbed the top of my ass and squeezed.

"That's right baby, spread them meaty cheeks and let me in this tight ass pussy." His voice was husky and sexy all in one. It sounded like he was on edge and in need. I noted that and tried my hardest to cut the fuck up on his dick. I grabbed my ass cheeks and closed my eyes tight, trying to adjust to his dick knocking my walls out. I wanted to prove to this man that I wasn't no punk bitch, I could take dick. It was hard just trying to take all the dick he had.

"Make that pussy bite this dick, Sovereign." He hit the bottom of my pussy making waves of pleasure take over me. I couldn't hold back my moan as he smacked my ass and hit a certain spot inside of me that had my legs trembling.

"Make that pussy bite this shit!" He groaned and grabbed the sides of my ass and squeezed. I simpered lowly and contracted my pussy on his shaft.

"Like that, each time I stroke down and pull up, you squeeze that fat ass pussy tight on this dick." He coached while spitting between my ass cheeks. He stuck his thick thumb in my ass and kept his strokes short. My eyes were rolling back, and I was lost in complete euphoria. I never felt this feeling in the pits of my guts. My stomach cramped and tightened my knees burned from the friction. The cuffs were so tight, my arms stretched far behind my back. The pain and pleasure of it all had my tears soaking the silk pillowcase beneath me.

"Fuck, I got to take my time in this pussy." I shook and howled again, releasing everything pent up inside of me. He stopped stroking, I felt him fumbling around with the cuffs. Releasing my sore wrist from captivity, I rested them on my sides as he slid out of me.

"Turn around." This is the part where I should've declined. I felt weak and vulnerable as hell and didn't know how I would feel facing him.

"You ain't no man eater baby. I'm sitting here eating yo ass up. Stop acting like you scared of me Queen. Turn yo ass around and fuck me back like a wife supposed to do." He noticed my man eater tattoo and right now he was making me look like a fool. I usually controlled my sex life, any nigga I took to bed, I had the upper hand. Right now, my legs felt shaky my insides tingled. I was still visibly trembling from the back-to-back orgasms that Malice pulled out of me.

I turned around slowly, and he wasted no time pulling my legs far apart and sliding back in.

"Fuck!" I screamed, he placed the palms of his hands flat on my inner thighs and angled his dick downwards as he did push-ups in my pussy. Using his thumb to stimulate my clit, I shook my head from side to side because my insides and clit was still so sensitive. The pleasure was insane. Our bodies were slip and sliding from the sweat and heat trapped inside the room.

"Look at me Sovereign." That deep husky voice had my

pussy putting his dick in a deadly grip. My eyes fluttered and landed on his as he said nothing and kept penetrating me deep. Those prominent big blue eyes penetrated my soul, he didn't blink he just stared with a look of determination.

"That shit you pulled earlier, made my dick hard as fuck. I wanted to lay you on top of my foreign car, strangle and fuck the shit out of you."

That made my pussy gush out even more. He felt it too because he pulled back and looked down at my pussy like it was spitting fire.

"You want me to strangle you Sovereign." His thick, rough hands crept up my stomach until he was pinching both nipples. I foolishly nodded my head yes and he grabbed my throat. My eyes got big as his strokes got harder.

"Look how that pussy biting my shit." He squeezed my throat tighter almost cutting off my air supply. Panic rushed through me as I grabbed his wrist. Using my neck as leverage all you could hear was his pelvis smacking up against me. His groaning and grunting was sending me, between him pounding the lining out of my pussy and choking me tight. I couldn't do anything but cry out with full blown tears of bliss.

"This dick to die for, ain't it." He sneered using his free hand to reach down and pinch my clit. That's what did it, the pain and pleasure sent waves down to my core and I exploded hard, clamping my legs around his waist. My eyes burned my neck throbbed, it felt like I was having an intense explosion.

"You haven't been wearing your wedding ring." He nibbled and whispered in my ear. "You got to wear that shit night and day." He started stroking again. My body jumped from each stroke.

"Malice… I can't take anymore." I shocked myself with that. I never tapped out; sex usually never lasted this long. I was hot and sweating, I wanted to close my eyes and go to sleep.

"Yea you can." He sat up and pulled me up until my breast was against his chest. He looked down in my eyes and something weird transpired between us that had me nervous. When he lowered his head to connect his lips against mine, I allowed his lips to brush past my lips but when they stayed in place, I moved my head.

"I don't... I can't kiss you." The last man I kissed broke my heart. I couldn't allow anything close to what reminded me of Melvin.

"In due time you will." In one swift motion he turned over on his back and had me on top of him.

"Work your hips and fuck my dick." He slapped my ass. "You a man eater remember? Make that pussy eat my dick up." I sighed hard because this was not what I had expected at all from Malice. I slid down on his dick and stopped midway. This man was too fucking big for my tunnel. Sitting on top felt excruciating.

"That running shit making me mad, Sovereign. Sit and take all this dick." When I hesitated, he grabbed my waist and pushed me all the way down. My head fell forward, hands on his chest. I stayed still and was thankful for his patience. Slowly I worked my pussy by grinding up and down, contracting my walls each time he thrusted upwards. His hand practically glided and slipped down my wet slippery body. The room temperature had to be over a hundred degrees.

Sitting upward, he captured both breast and squeezed them together. Sucking and biting on each nipple making me shutter.

"Oh fuck, Malice." I whimpered and sniveled not giving a damn about the snot coming out my nose. He eyed me intensely like he was searching for something in my eyes. Sensing that the moment was too much for even him, he turned us back over until his frame caged mine. Tiny moans flew out my mouth as he grips my wrist tight. He brings his mouth back close to mine, sticking his tongue out, he grazes my lips and again I retreat from kissing him.

I'm so damn tempted to let his lips crash into mine with the way he feels buried deep inside of me, but I try my hardest to ignore that feeling. Malice grunts and frowns then starts pounding into me, my pussy starts to clamp around his shaft. Now he's doing a sexy growl as I breathe hard as hell squeezing my eyes shut trying to take all of him and hold back from another orgasm. It feels like if I cum again it will all be over for me.

The control he's exerting is driving me crazy, the things he's making my body do is starting to scare me. Burying his head in the crook of my neck, he licks with his whole tongue tasting my sweat. He clamps down and bite down where his pinky nail penetrated me when he choked me back in his chambers. I shuttered and moaned feeling my explosion reaching its peak. Short stroking then long stroking me while he applies pressure to my clit got me shaking. He leaves my neck alone then attacks my lips and this time I don't refuse.

The deeper he kisses me the harder I cum and now I can feel him convulsing inside of me with force. I felt his dominance as much as I felt myself giving in. My butterflies started to roam in my stomach again, I tried to ignore them, but it was insane. I felt weak and fully satisfied as I fell back and closed my eyes.

I woke up the next morning in a different room. My body felt like it was on top of clouds as I blinked my eyes and looked around. This was the same room that sent me into a rage when I walked in seeing Malice in a fuck fest with two women. The sheets were now red instead of white. At least he changed the sheets I thought as I tried to stand but couldn't. The ache between my thighs was a reminder of what went down between us.

Happy that he wasn't around, I took in his room. It had a dark theme to it. A huge fireplace that was way bigger than the one I had at my Abuela's house. Red and black had to be this man's favorite color. Looking down at my naked body, I had bite marks and purple bruises all over. I thought back to the kiss we shared and shook my head. I had to gain control over this situation. Forcing myself to stand, I stumbled a little. I needed to shower and dress to go back to my Abuela's to get some of my things.

Going into Malice huge bathroom, I noticed my personal hygiene items on the other side of the sink. I walked right out the bathroom and went to his walk-in closet. All my clothes were there as well hanging nicely with my shoe boxes stacked on the top shelf. I hope like hell he didn't think that I would live here with him. That's what husband and wife did, but this was business.

After showering, I put on some leggings and a Christian Dior top with matching sandals. I noticed my makeup bag was missing and had to calm myself down. I didn't just freely walk around with the tattoos on my face showing they were intimate to me. I didn't like people asking questions.

I walked around the big empty house for about ten minutes until I heard voices outside. The kitchen leading to the huge backyard. I stood at the sliding glass watching a couple of chicks dip in and out the pool chasing each other and laughing. Malice stood shirtless with Gucci swim trunks riding low on his waist. He looked like he was in pure amazement by the fire he started on the BBQ grill. I watched the dude that I learned was Killa stand and smoke while he chopped it up with a scary looking big dude that kept a straight face. He sat in front of a glass table that had a container of meat with a lid on top.

As if he sensed me from across the yard. Malice turned and looked directly at me winking.

"What you waiting on chica?" I turned around and Roberto stood behind me with a bikini pink bottom on. I admired his eight pack as he fanned his face with his hands like he was burning up. The house was way cooler than my Abuela's. Malice had the Ac on, which I greatly appreciated.

"Just woke up." I kept it short as I turned and continued to scan the backyard. I didn't know these people, and this wasn't my crew.

"I'm going outside with my girls, and to catch a tan. It's a nice hot day, I'm just happy my hermano invited me." I wanted to ask if his brother would be pissed by him coming outside with a damn thong on but held my question and decided to ask something else.

"You and Inferno aren't that close?" I asked as I stepped to the side leaving space for him to exit if he wanted to.

"Not really, I try to build a bond, but Malice thinks all my father's' children hate him. Most of those Perra's do but not me. I admire my hermano. He's smart and besides his crazy demeanor, I know he has a good heart." A look of sadness crossed his face before he smiled and continued. "No matter what, I want him to know I love him, you know. Him and my father the only people that accept me for me, instead of judging. Now come outside, so I can tell you everything you need to know about your husband." He smiled making me roll my eyes.

"I'll be out soon. I'm going to find something to snack on."

"Si, don't take forever. Put on a swimsuit, I want to see

how that booty looks without clothes." We both giggled. I wasn't that opened to doing anything of the sort. I didn't even know how to swim and would panic if the water came up to my neck.

Opening up the pantry in the kitchen I went straight for the instant cinnamon oatmeal. Next, I opened up the refrigerator and grabbed the uncured bacon. Since a kid I loved eating oatmeal with bacon. I was surprised that Malice stuck up rich ass had basic meals in his kitchen. I imagined him having a chef and food already being prepared.

I heard the sliding glass door opening and didn't look up, I already imagined it being Roberto coming back in to check on me. After seconds passing by and me smelling the stench of BBQ, I knew it was him. The small hairs on my skin stood up and my stomach started fluttering.

"Burna boy, what's good?" I chuckled turning the fire low on the stove. My water was boiling and ready to put inside the bowl of oatmeal.

"Your ring, you will wear it." I could hear his footsteps drawing near. Flipping my bacon, ignoring his statement, I remained quiet until I thought of something to say.

"This is just business between us." I reminded.

"Last night, was passion, your tears, and the feel of that gushy ass pussy on my dick. I bet that pussy talking right now. They always do when their excellency is near." I could hear the cockiness in his voice.

"You need something?" He pressed up against my ass, I could feel him rocking up.

"I think you need something else from me. Then we can talk about all the drugs you're flying into the states. I don't think that's a good move." I turned around facing him.

"That's my business with my gang, it has nothing to do

with you." I snipped, eyeing him, daring him to challenge me.

"It's cartel drugs. My father and your Abuela got the same stamp now on all drugs. She should have told you to ask me. I could have your shit transported through caskets and delivered to a mortuary in two days. You can't move drugs that recklessly just because you have a hand me down jet."

A look of annoyance took over his face as I shrugged.

"I guess I'm willing to take my chances." I tried to turn around, but he placed his large hand on my shoulder.

"You won't, now I'm telling you how the drugs will be transported. My syndicate is now protecting your petty gang. Free of charge since this is a union. If you don't want to listen, then I will enjoy burning that fucking jet right on the runway. He released my shoulder, I turned away from him and took my bacon out the skillet placing it on a paper towel to dry up the grease.

"You just need to remember that this is business, Malice."

"And you need to remember that we work as a team rather we like each other or not. That pussy thinks otherwise." He smacked me on the ass and that was all it took for my clit to start back thumping. I decided to fuck with him since he constantly fucked with me. I knew my pussy was good and it had him feigning for more. I turned around and slid my hand along his length. Power rippled through me as I stared into those magical eyes of his.

He reached down and grabbed both ass cheeks and squeezed tight.

"Careful, Sovereign." He warned me but I ignored him. I planned on having some fun. Reaching into his shorts my hand slid on slick hard skin. I could feel his dick veins on the palm of my hand. I got lost to the feel of him, vaguely aware that we were in the kitchen, people could easily walk in here and I think the thrill of that was sending me into overdrive.

The scent of him invaded my nose, I closed my eyes briefly and allowed myself to breathe. His thick lips pressed against my neck as his hands roamed all over my body. Yanking my leggings down until they hit the tile floor. I didn't have time to stop and think on what I was doing because I didn't know. Our sexual chemistry was strong. I wanted to see for a second time was it even real because this marriage wasn't.

It felt like I was melting right in front of him. The feel of his rough hard fingertips grabbing my soft fluffy breast underneath my shirt had me in a zone. A low murmur escaped my lips as he captured them into his hot mouth and explored with his tongue.

Wounding my arms around his strong neck, he lifted me effortlessly and moved us from in front of the stove. I enjoyed the way his long-muscled body flexed under me as he moved. Malice lips found my shoulder and he bit down hard then sucked.

"You need to pace yourself with the dick you receive from me. You keep this shit up and that pretty ass pussy gone hurt all the time." He traced his tongue up my neck. I didn't even know when he pulled his dick out, but it was sitting right between my hot silk opening. I wrapped my legs tightly around him.

"Fuck me Malice." I didn't care how thirsty I sounded. His eyes flickered with lust as he thrusted inside of me. Planting his feet against the tiled floor, he bounced me slowly up and down his dick. Gripping my ass, he angled my hips down as he drove deep inside to the hilt.

He growled and a moan ripped free from me. It felt like he belonged right here inside of me and a crazy part of me felt like I would want this feeling forever. Sex clouded the brain; I could control and handle myself without getting lost in this situation. Dick like this made women do crazy shit. I already had power at the tips of my fingers and money so in my mind it wouldn't hurt to get some good dick on the side. In the back of my mind though, I knew something more complicated was brewing between Malice and me.

KENYA MONROE

I missed his smell, his touch, those big, beautiful eyes, and the way his dick felt pulsing deep inside of me. We were friends before lovers. Or maybe he was my lover, and I was just a friend that he enjoyed having sex with. Everything at this moment felt like it was strictly business. Why couldn't he see that he was really killing me softly? Why couldn't I stop the way I felt about him? Getting him out of my system and making money, was something I was set on doing from the very beginning.

Was he in love with me? I knew the answer was no, it was sometimes hard to tell with the way he reacted to some of the things that I did. He loved the way my mouth suctioned his big juicy dick and swallowed every drop. He watched my feet cramp up and loved the way I squirted all over his dick, promising him that my pussy belonged to him and only him. We shopped together, ate breakfast, lunch, and dinner. I had my very own room in his house. Yet I still wondered why he kept me at bay, refusing to see and know how I felt about him.

Inferno loved all the things I contributed to the syndicate.

During the day he loved to watch me work and handle his business and at night he admired the way my back curved and arched like the crescent moon on a beautiful night. He only loved parts of me, I wanted him to love all of me. Something was different and it started to bother my soul. He had been gone for a week and barely called me. The longest I have gone without him near was close to a month but even then, he called to check on me every day.

What was happening? I didn't know but I needed to find out. I was willing to accept how we already were if only he would get back into the old groove of things and treat me how he was treating me before he admitted to marrying some strange bitch for his father's cartel.

I stood in the restroom, nervous and excited. Excited to see my man after a long week of him barely checking in. I couldn't call Inferno if it wasn't on business, he wasn't really the type to talk as much on the phone. If he did call me, it meant he needed me to handle something, or it would be a simple hurry over. He gave me a list of things to do when he left to Mexico and so far, I executed all of them and even had a new business proposal for him.

Usually, I had excuses to call him and chat about different things regarding the syndicate. After the conversation with that ran dry, I would make light jokes keeping him on the phone longer and he would accept it before other business of his came up and he would excuse himself.

I was nervous of seeing him because lately it had been hard for me to tuck and bury all of my emotions. Just the sight of him had me yearning to be close, to touch and feel him all over me.

"You got to stop worrying about that nigga so much, Kenya. Make your money and find you another nigga to be caught up on, one that feels the same fuckin way." My cousin

Janessa snapped me out of my thoughts. I hadn't realized how tight I was holding on to the restroom sink until she came out of the stall. Janessa was my assistant and she helped me tremendously with keeping up with all of Malice extreme task. Whatever I couldn't get to, Janessa did. The only thing that Inferno refused for her to know about, and handle were the multiple deposits that I took care of daily. He was really funny about who handled his money. Legal money for that matter. He was making lots of legal money, as far as his dirty illegal money, I had no clue of how much of that he had. I assumed it was a lot because even the money he cleaned had to be disguised under multiple businesses.

"I'm not thinking about him, I'm just very sleepy and you know how crazy and random he can get in these meetings. I think in a week or two I'm going to ask for a small vacation to catch up on rest." Although I didn't owe Janessa an explanation, I loved her like a sister. She was the only friend I had and could really trust. She gave me an unsure look turning the faucet on to wash her hands.

"Good, I think you do need some rest. You're starting to get bags under your eyes. Plus, you have to make time for yourself as well Kenya." She gave me a sympathetic look and I almost caved in and let out a sob. I was miserable and felt so weak as a woman. My mother wouldn't stand for it if she knew how bad I was letting a man control the strings of my own happiness. I wasn't raised this way, I just loved Inferno so much and it happened so fast that I truly couldn't help myself.

Janessa told me she would see me in the meeting room, and I plastered a fake forced smile. When she walked out, I released my breath and let a couple of tears fall before dabbing them away. I stepped back closer to the mirror and checked out my makeup. It was still picture perfect. I ran my hands over my now honey blonde hair, tucking away any flyaways. My hair is wrapped tightly in a perfect bun, making my eyes look more chinky. I slide my black blazer back on, over my white silk blouse and adjusted my pencil form fitting skirt.

I looked very classy with an edge of sexiness. Applying more nude lip gloss I puckered my lips and smiled. I gave myself a reassuring pep talk. Maybe Inferno was too busy and hadn't had time for me, it was my fault that I got too deep into my own feelings and mind.

I constantly had to remind myself that Malice Ashonti Ruiz was no ordinary man. He didn't have all the time in the world like most men did. His main focus was making money and then more money after that. *But if a man really loves and wants you, he will make the time*, my mom's words echoed in my brain.

Shaking that off I exited the restroom and looked down the empty hallway. I took pride being at the syndicate head-quarters. It was a two-level furniture store with expensive luxury home décor and furniture imported from out of the country. It was my idea, and I found the perfect building on Melrose boulevard to set up shop. It was one of Inferno's gold mines and it brought in lots of cash monthly.

The third level was made for staff only, the syndicate used the third level for our meetings that we had monthly. I caught the elevator to the third floor and walked a couple steps to our meeting room which had glass soundproof glass. I noticed a couple of new faces and frowned when my eyes followed Malice's line of vision. He eyed a chick who was full figured rocking a two-piece black suit with a blouse that showed too much cleavage. She was beautiful, I couldn't lie about that, but she couldn't have been Malice type. I eyed her for a very long time, she seemed to be in her own world as she talked to the men that stood behind her chair. She sat in my seat, directly across from Malice.

I saw a big diamond ring on her finger and sighed in relief, the bitch was married. So why was Malice practically eye fucking her like he did me during meetings? Making my presence known, I opened the glass door and just like the queen I was, all attention was on me. Everyone spoke and greeted me properly except the mystery bitch that never stopped talking to the men that she brought with her.

Inferno cleared his throat and all talking seized as all attention was now directed towards him. I quietly took my seat next to Janessa, she sat properly with her notebook and iPad ready to take notes.

"Before, I allow Killa to take the floor and start our meeting." He stood and my mouth watered at the sight of him. Every time I saw Inferno, he was dressed impeccably nice. He had on a Prada Re-Nylon black, short-sleeve shirt that zipped up showing a little of his chest. His Prada shorts was the same material as his shirt stopping past his knees. He only wore his iced-out Jesus piece chain with a diamond watch that probably blinded everyone in the room. One pinky ring sparkled on his hand, and I froze at the sight of a white gold wedding band encrusted with diamonds.

He got married? As if he could read my thoughts and feel my pain, he looked over and winked at me then continued to roam the room with his eyes.

"I would like to introduce a new member to the syndicate. Her name is Queen, she is my wife. Her street gang will have the syndicates protection, I want you all to get familiar with her because a lot of big things will be taking place within the next couple of months. Killa go ahead." He took a seat, picked up his phone and started texting like he hadn't just broke my fucking heart. When I took my eyes off of him, I looked across the table and made eye contact with Queen. Her stare down was lethal and cold, she no longer looked pretty to me. She had a dark aura about her and the look that was plastered on her face was a powerful one. I smiled at her, trying to be a little welcoming. I would never stop fucking Malice so she should open up and get used to her husband being shared.

Instead of smiling back at me, she kept a blank face and winked at me. Something Inferno would do. Had she been around my man for so long that she copied what the fuck he did.

"Excuse me Killa, I hate to interrupt." She cleared her throat, never taking her eyes off of me. I suddenly felt like the room had gotten stuffy when the AC worked just fine.

"What's your name sweetheart?" I looked around to see if she was really talking to me.

"Yes, you... You have been staring at me since you walked up, outside the glass door. Tell me your name. First and last." She finally broke her stone-cold expression and smiled.

"Kenya Monroe, Inferno's assistant," I added and looked over at Inferno to see if he was paying attention and if he would back me up. Inferno was still typing on his phone, he paused from one phone, put it down then picked up his second phone.

"I didn't ask you what you were to my husband. It's obvious what all you do for him." She chuckled. "Kenya Monroe don't stare at me too long. I get uncomfortable when people stare at me pass ten seconds. My trigger finger too happy for that type of fuckery. Its nice meeting you." She took her eyes off of me and looked at Killa who wore a smirk plastered on his bitch ass face. I shifted in my seat as I listened to Killa ramble on and on about guns and new potential gangs that he felt the syndicate would profit over.

Killa was excellent at all the street shit, he aligned things properly and had become Inferno's supplier easily making sure any drugs or guns that even touched the streets was solid. He was also a math genius and cold count up all money fast and be able to detect when someone was short just by holding a duffle bag of cash in his hand. Big B was the scary enforcer. If Malice or Killa sent Big B your way, you knew that you would be taking your last couple of breaths. Big B was as cold as they came, he looked and acted the part. I never really heard him say much, he always stood behind Inferno watching everyone closely. He was like Inferno's second pair of eyes.

Thirty minutes of talking, it always took Killa that long to update and tell us everything that had been going on for the month. I didn't give a damn, but a lot of other syndicate members that was into illegal dealings looked forward to hearing every word he spoke. Inferno basically sat in the meetings as the head over it all to agree or disagree. When he didn't say anything that meant he was on board. Killa sat down with a satisfied look on his face. He picked up his blunt and sparked it. I got nervous because I knew my turn was coming up.

I waited for Inferno to give me the floor in which he did by simply saying my name, never looking up from his phone.

"I set up a clothing drive which is charitable, it's also a way to give back to the communities. The event will be held next month around two p.m. I would like if everyone could attend to see the pleasant faces and appreciation that the community has."

"Kenya, we ain't tryna see no fuckin faces during the day. You know how much business we gots to handle?" Killa looked at me like I was stupid, and I was ready to curse his ass out.

"A fucking clothing drive, it's like you pull shit out of that fake ass of yours each month." My bottom lip dropped as I looked at Inferno.

"Careful Killa, let Monroe finish." I released the breath I was holding.

"I started a funding account for the clothing drive, I also wanted to start another anonymous shelter for the homeless downtown L.A. which is also in the making but its taking time trying to find the perfect contractors. This will serve as a perfect tax write off." I paused as Janessa nudged me; my hands were getting clammy. I was nervous, I loved helping people of the community just like Inferno did as well. He never spoke about the joy he had in doing it but deep down, I knew he liked giving back like I did to the unfortunate.

Now was the time to present this opportunity that I had been pondering on for months and I hoped he didn't shut my idea down.

"I, umm, wanted to have a special host for a gala fundraising event. Maybe a known celebrity to bring more celebrities out. The syndicate could make loads of money from that and…" Inferno finally looked up and focused on me.

"The clothing drive is a go; I like the sound of the shelters too. I will get back to you on the gala thing. If anybody else would like to add anything to the meeting, you can if not you all can leave." I stayed seated but everybody else seemed over the meeting and ready to go. Queen and her men stood and walked towards the exit. She stopped right next to me and leaned down.

"I have a clinic, ask Malice about the info. Underneath all that makeup, I would love to give you a facial." She smirked and kept walking. I wanted to throw my water bottle at the back of her head.

"Queen." Inferno called her name and she stopped at the exit and waited saying nothing.

"My place ten p.m. sharp." She mumbled something under her breath and left out leaving her fragrance behind. Once the room was empty, Inferno sat quietly with his elbows now on the table. He was focused still on his phone, and I wondered if he could hear my heart breaking.

I wasn't stupid, I could feel their chemistry without them having to say much. I cleared my throat so my voice wouldn't sound choppy from wanting to cry and decided to press him for information.

"Your wife is pretty." I started out.

"She is, and very deadly." He put his phone down.

"Seems like you two are falling into your roles perfectly, Inferno. Where does that leave us?" I timidly ask.

"It leaves us how we been Kenya. She is my wife you are my assistant. I am the boss you are the worker. I say that to stop you from asking me any further questions. I have a meeting in another hour and don't have time for pointless conversation." I quickly nodded my head and stood up fast. I couldn't wait to get to my car and do my favorite thing, which was cry.

"Kenya?" He stopped me from walking out the room, his deep baritone voice did it for me all the time.

"I've been busy, you know that. I ain't trying to hurt your feelings. You know I got mad love for you, and I appreciate everything you do for my organization. You the key to this shit." I nodded my head and offered him a weak smile.

"Come sit in my lap, Kenya. Show me, how much you miss me." I hated the foolish grin that appeared on my face. I tried to play it cool, but Inferno had me ready to run and leap into his arms. Pulling out his wallet, he opened it and removed a condom. That made me frown but I refused to complain. Inferno and I never really used condoms, so I felt a little offended. The sight of his big dick had me forgetting about his wife, the condom and everything else.

As I straddled his lap, he slid my panties to the side. I simpered and tried to adjust to his size as a little more hope entered me. He filled me to the brim and satisfaction immediately took over. Malice was my man, and I was for certain that one day he would choose only me.

EMPRESS

"*You hurt her and me, Melvin." I cried looking into his dark eyes trying to read them the best that I could. I hated seeing my sister cry but what made it all fucked up was how I had to hide my true feelings. I think he hurt me worse, and I wanted to make that clear before my sister sent the gang after him.*

"*Baby, Queen won't believe me, but you have got to believe me. Yes, she is my wife and a couple of years back she gave me the okay to do me. She is fighting cancer, that's why I got to find her. We haven't been together for a long time; she doesn't deserve to die brutally. You know that is what Queen will do to her.*" *I knew what my sister was all about, and I stood behind her a hundred percent when it came to her punishing those who crossed the gang.*

"*She doesn't look sick Melvin! She's pregnant with your baby and she looks healthy.*" *I argued while thinking back of the pictures Queen had shown me.*

"*She wants her family to have a piece of her when she leaves. What the fuck? Empress, you really sitting here not believing me? Your man? The person you claim you want to be with?" My mind felt confused, I wanted to believe him to make the hurt go away. I kept thinking about different shit like, what if what he was saying were true? I loved Melvin more than my young self and anyone around me which was wrong on so many levels. He listened to my fears and how I truly felt about a lot of shit. Things that Sovereign didn't take the time out to listen to because she was always busy trying to sacrifice her own life for the both of us.*

I felt like shit, but I couldn't stop the love that I had for Melvin. How would I even be able to be with this man without my sister killing us. The more I sat and listened to him plead his case with me before he plead his case with my sister the more, I became worried and scared. I couldn't imagine my life without this man. I was willing to sacrifice it all just to be with him even if it meant keeping our relationship a secret and away from the world.

Nobody had the right to judge me. Everything happens for a reason and Melvin reasoning for liking me and I liking him couldn't be explained properly. I guess sometimes the very thing that's forbidden becomes enjoyable to sinful souls.

"You listening to me Empress?" I looked into his eyes as his callous hands engulfed my soft trembling hands.

"I don't even know what to do Mel, I don't want you getting hurt or killed. We both know Sovereign is powerful as hell and she has the money to move shit around." My breathing was constricted like I was being smothered. I saw my sister in action, she could be very treacherous. I saw the evil in her eyes and watched her kill men without even blinking. I watched her track down each man that ever violated her as a young teen. She tortured them with a vengeance until their souls begged out for mercy.

Half the shit she did that I saw, would keep me up at night replaying in my head. Sovereign acted like she was the Most High. It was like the more money we made the more power driven she became.

"I'm willing to sacrifice my life, Empress, I will never flip on you though; I love you too much. I know I fucked up, but I can't leave this earth with you thinking that I betrayed you and lied about how I feel." He squeezed my hands, and I could feel the truth revealing itself.

"Do you love Sovereign?" It was a question I always asked, and it was a sick one too. I expected him to love my sister as well, she deserved someone to love her just as much. I was willing to come in second to her with Melvin. Sovereign endured things from a teenager that I wouldn't wish on adults.

"Yes, I love Sovereign. You know how she is Empress; she will never believe my side of the story." That was true, once Sovereign came up with her own understanding of things, nobody could change her line of thinking.

"We have to plan something, Mel. I swear I would die if something was to happen to you." He released my hand and wiped the tears from my face that I couldn't stop from falling.

"I want you to be the one to take me to her. Sovereign is very vindictive when she feels like she has been crossed. In her mind, I have done the unthinkable. She won't kill me right away; she got enough money to torture me for a couple of days and then end me once she feel like her revenge has been fulfilled. In the time of me being captured, we need to put a huge dent in her pockets then move fast to help me escape." I immediately shook my head no.

"I can't steal from my sister, Melvin! How the hell will I help you escape?" I questioned giving him a confused look.

"We have to, right now she worth a whole lot of money. Money moves mountains Em, just listen! We break down her pockets, so I can have enough money to survive when you help set me free. I know in my heart that Sovereign will torture me and try to hold me captive. You don't know that dark side of Queen. I watched her hold niggas for weeks until they were begging her to take their lives. I watched niggas end themselves in front of her just to be put out of misery. It's so much to your sister that you don't know. Just hear a nigga out, ok?" I nodded my head then crossed my legs Indian style. I had to put my feelings to the side and really listen because if it meant his survival then I was down to do whatever to help him.

"Queen is going to play shit cool; I have to keep going around her and you for maybe a week or two before she sends one of y'all. She might lie and say she wants me to make a drop to the warehouse that we store product and guns. Up until she make her move on me, we will be able to move shit around like the most of the money that she keeps in her safe." He paused and lit his cigarette. I shook my head because I always told Queen to open up a bank account. She had a lot of hidden places for cash. She claimed she didn't want the feds watching her, so she didn't trust banks. I had a bank account and I saved money up constantly just to have for whatever I needed.

"I can handle the money part and I got a couple loyal niggas on the team. Most of them niggas is gone have to sacrifice their lives for me once this shit blow up. What I need from you, is to get in good with that nigga Murk'um. Don't look like that, Empress. This shit important! I need you to get closer with that nigga. I see how he looks at you, he a weak ass nigga and pussy will convince him to do whatever it is that you want him to do. He will play a major

role in helping you." I had a bad feeling in the pit of my stomach.

I felt like if we thoroughly planned this out properly with no hiccups that everything would work out and be done with. I also had another feeling that told me that I should have just picked up the gun that I had on my nightstand and just ended Melvin. I couldn't do that; I just knew like hell that somehow some way this shit would all come back and bite me in the ass. For Melvin, I was willing to chance that.

He was my first love and although it was wrong on so many levels. Love didn't disappear in thin air just because it wasn't traditional. I loved my sister without a doubt, I would lay down and die for her. When our parents left, we were all we had. Sovereign stepped up when most kids her age wouldn't have.

"It's really dangerous, I just know in my heart that it will work. I need you and I need for my wife to have that baby. The least I can do is fulfil her wishes before she dies, Empress. You do understand right baby?" He stared deep into my eyes; I remained silent before I nodded my head up and down without giving him a verbal yes. My stomach started to ache; fear started rising inside of me. My loyalty felt torn between two people.

Melvin wasn't blood but he was considered my first love.

I wish back then I could change that entire conversation, I wish that I could have picked my gun up and killed Melvin myself. I followed everything this nigga told me to do. The only thing that he did for me was flip the script and black male me a year later. I still couldn't get over the fact that he took his daughter and sold her for more money. It didn't hurt me at first when I kidnapped her. It bothered me hearing my sister cry over that little girl. The last time I heard Queen cry was when our parents left.

I bonded with Princess; I considered her my daughter too. It didn't bother me because I just knew I would still be able to sneak off and be with her since her dad would finally have her. Melvin didn't see the shit that way, he got rid of her fast confusing me more and showing me how evil he truly was. At first, he lied and said she was with family, but when I refused to steal more money, he crushed me by saying that he would sell Princess and make a killing off of her.

I didn't know what the hell this nigga was using all the money that he had stolen from Sovereign. I didn't even know where the man really stayed. Each time we met was on the outskirts of the city. He would leave the state and pop back up demanding. Melvin was more obsessed with Sovereign then anything. He would ask me questions about Queen, ask for pictures then get mad when he would find out that she was fucking multiple different niggas.

As more time passed, I finally fell out of love with him and saw him for who he truly was. Murk'um and I got closer than close, and I kept trying to find ways to end Melvin. Each time I had the opportunity I froze up. I couldn't explain why I froze up; I just did. The fear of doing it just had me stuck. Now I let things get out of hand, it felt like I was running out of time. It was only a matter of time when all of this shit backfired on me and knocked me down hard.

I was tired of kicking money out to this nigga and going through the troubles of keeping him at bay. It felt like I was constantly looking over my shoulders, living in fear. Which wasn't cool at all. I looked over at Murk'um and felt secure in his bed. Picking up my phone, I went to Queen's number and just stared at her contact name. I often contemplated making that call to her for us to meet and for me to confess. I always backed out of that because it was too late.

I knew Sovereign loved me but was it enough to keep her

from killing me once she found out all the shit that I had done. I was a part of the reason to a lot of her troubles. Down to her taking a big loss on the money she had before me, and Melvin plotted hard against her.

"Lay down Clapback, I hate when you do that shit. It's our off day and you up fighting with your thoughts and shit. Let shit be what it is until it changes and faces you." Murk'um pulled me down next to him and spooned me. My sleep was always chopped up. I could sleep for a hour or two but would wake up battling my own thoughts. I stayed spinning shit a hundred times and my head trying to reason with myself.

That's how it felt when you had demons riding your back all day. I would pray but I've done so many foul things along with Sovereign that I knew for a fact God would not be listening to us. When you made your bed, you had to lay in it.

"I got to make some shit right before it's too late, what stresses me the most is I don't know how." My brows knitted together; I was trying my hardest to fight back the tears that somehow already escaped.

"Look at me." I turned slowly until I was laying on my side looking at Murk'um. His eyes bored into mine. His hands gliding up and down my body slowly, I shut my eyes and tried to relax my scattered nerves.

"It's too late to double back now, let that shit go. On the real Empress, you got to let it go. I done asked you several times did you want to plan a way to kill that nigga and each time you say some bullshit. So, it confuses me how you be around here most days acting like a fuckin' zombie. I'm not trying to be mean or no shit like that. I'm just being real, if you not trying to plot a way to kill this nigga then stopped stressing yourself over him. We got bigger shit to focus on, you feel me?"

I nodded my head because I couldn't reveal my whole hand without revealing the next person dear to me hand. If I revealed more of what I knew about the whole situation, then bloodshed would spread, and my life would not only be threatened by my sister but my Abuela too.

MALICE AKA INFERNO

I was in a bad ass mood; I knew what the problem was but refused to see it that way. There was no way a woman that I was practically forced to marry for my father's sanity and protection could possibly be on my mind so tough. I bit my bottom lip thinking about the way Sovereign pussy clenched my dick. The hesitation and rejection of her kissing me. It had been two weeks since I laid eyes on her, my men watched her, but she threw them off of her in just one day. I almost wanted to kill them niggas because they got paid well just to follow a woman and keep tabs on her but failed at doing just that. Sparing their lives, I ended their jobs and hired new men, then told Big B to find her. I didn't know if she was in Cali or in Mexico, her whole demeanor changed after the meeting I had in place for the syndicate.

I sat in the backseat of my business car, ashing my blunt out the window looking at the outside of my mother's house. This was my real home, the only woman that truly understood me and wanted nothing but the best for her only son. I smirked at all the flowers and plants my mom had planted over the years to keep her busy. She didn't have to work because I took care of all her needs, but she loved to create projects around the house. She traveled a lot and explored the world to keep her mind off of me and the things that I was up to.

I didn't even know if she was home now because I hadn't called. There was no indication of her being here, she always parked her car in the garage. She would probably lose her cool if she had known that I up and got married without informing her. If she knew it was because of my father, she'd fly back to Mexico and shoot his ass herself. My mom was a strong beautiful black woman that didn't take no shit from anyone. I could understand why my father was so smitten and still in love with her.

For some reason, us men took to women that was hard to obtain and control. I had to start looking at things that way because before Sovereign I didn't want a woman to be just mine fully. Even still with her, I didn't want to commit or to be expected to carry on in a way as an average man. I had too much money to be worried about the next person feelings. I couldn't deny the feeling of being ghosted from Sovereign; she changed her number like I wouldn't be able to obtain the new set of digits in seconds.

I just had a lot on my plate and tracking her down and coming after her wasn't the number one thing on my to do list. It's why I had Big B to handle that.

"Something tells me, your outside of my house, after acting like you don't have a mother for two months." I closed my eyes and inhaled the good kush that filled my lungs and released it. Holding my phone up, I tilted my head to the side smirking.

"What's up ma?" it felt good just hearing her voice. I missed my mom so much that sitting in front of her house made me feel close enough to her.

"Malice Ashonti Ruiz! I wish I was home so that I could slap the fire from you." I chuckled lowly and remained quiet. I let the breeze hit my face as my head rest on the seat, the smell of my mother's freshly mowed grass hit my nostrils with a small scent of flowers. I missed being here the most. It was peaceful and quiet in San Clemente, a good distance from Los Angeles.

"What's on your mind son?" I could already hear the worry in her voice.

"A lot, Ma, always a lot. It's a new girl in my life as well, that's complicated. I will have to explain that to you in person. Where are you?" I quickly changed the subject before she could even start her motherly interrogation. I could have easily called the security that I kept attached to her and find her location, but I didn't invade in her privacy like that.

"Thailand, with a friend." I raised my eyebrow at that, I hope this friend wasn't someone that I would later have to burn to the ground. I tapped the petition letting my driver know to drive off to my next location.

"What friend? Have I met this friend?"

"No and you don't have to. I don't need you scaring him, he is really nice Malice and I like him." I shook my head at that.

"Ma, if he is scared of me, then he's not man enough at all. How do you expect this man to protect you? I will have to look into him, send me his full name." I wanted my mother to comply but also knew that she wouldn't which was fine with me. I had already fished for my business phone and started texting her security detail, getting all the information that she wouldn't give. If I didn't kill the nigga first, then my dad would whenever he found out that my mother was dating. My dad just couldn't let my mom go.

He'd let her have fun but soon as he was informed that

she had become too familiar with a guy. A freak accident would happen, and the guy would disappear. My mother never had proof and I thought it was absurd at first, that my father had men watching her all the way from Mexico. After time passed, I realized that it was my father. He watched my mom very close, almost better than I did. He still had that hope that before he died, they would somehow get back together.

"Did you hear me Malice?" I didn't hear a word that she said because I was busy typing away on my business phone.

"My apologies Ma, had to respond to a message." I halfway lied.

"I said Alexander is a good man, he has his own money. He's a big-time lawyer with no kids, so if we were to get married you wouldn't have to deal with step-siblings." She giggled and I stared at the phone blankly.

"There will be no marriage." I didn't know what my mom was thinking. I couldn't see her marrying just a regular ass nigga. Something wasn't right with this nigga already, I already gathered that he was lying and hiding something. I texted my security asking for a picture of this new guy. What older nigga that was supposed to be some lawyer making good money didn't have a family somewhere tucked.

"Don't start that stuff your daddy do." My mom scoffed into the phone, I could imagine her lips curled and tight like she would do when I was kid before she smacked me in the back of my head.

"Okay Ms. Stella got her groove back, have your fun for now. I'll be in touch later. I was popping up on you since I miss you. I'll be back by your house in two weeks, I expect my favorite meal awaiting me." I smirked, already prepared to take her brutal tongue lashing.

"Nigga please! Don't go running off demands like you do

those people in your organization better yet your whores Ashonti. I'll see you soon and don't get all in my business, let me live my life. I did my part by raising you now it's time to live for me."

"Oh yea?" I reasoned.

"Bye son." She hung up just as my driver merged onto the freeway. We were immediately greeted with heavy ass traffic. I saw that my security wasted no time sending me a picture of the gentlemen that my mom was out with having the time of her life. Soon as I zoomed in on the picture my stomach summersaulted. He looked like he came straight from Mexico, what type of games was my momma playing? This nigga resembled my dad and if I wasn't tripping, he looked like the same nigga that the cartel was having problems with.

I forwarded the picture to my dad and counted down to sixty. When I got to forty, my burner phone sounded off.

"Who is he?" Was all I wanted to know.

"Nueva is a dangerous man son." I could hear the warning behind my father's thick accent, but it pissed me off more. We still didn't know if Nueva was the one that put the hit out on my dad since the Ruiz cartel lost his alliance.

"You say that, like you don't know who your son is. I think you also forget who was in that picture big cheesing, we know the great lengths that I will go for the woman who birthed me." I calmly stated trying to keep my respect intact for my father.

"He's sending out a message since we took over the docks. You know how big the docks are hermano. We have a meeting with Nueva in five days, I expect you and your wife back in Mexico in three days." I didn't even want to fuck with Sovereign right now, I didn't like the feeling she gave me at all. The magic she worked on my dick and the feel of

191

her was dangerous and could weaken a powerful man like me.

"I don't need her with me for that." I spat, ready to hang up now.

"Ju forget son. She is a Martinez turned into a Ruiz. However, the Martinez cartel still stands as long as her Abuela breathes. She is your wife and her not showing by your side is a bad look to the other cartel heads." He hung up and this time, I tossed the phone and told my driver to make a detour. I was done handling business for the day. I needed to relax my mind and then locate my wife to get her stubborn ass on board for this important meeting. If Nueva wanted to send a message, then I would too, starting with his hidden family.

I strategized the whole way over to Kenya's house. Right now, I wanted a home-cooked meal and my shoulder blades massaged by her delicate hands. I had a feeling that some shit was about to spark and I was well ready for that and whatever else it brought on.

Once I made it to Kenya's house, I waited in the backseat. My men in the car behind me got out first and did their normal routine of checking the permeator and getting in place to secure and guard her house. I let my driver know to be back here at five in the morning sharp. Harris my driver and whoever else on my payroll got paid really hefty to do their job and turn a blind eye to whatever they might come across or see. Rather it was illegal or legal, they kept their mouths shut and worked exceptionally well.

It was very rare that I had to fire someone, if I did have to fire somebody and they got the chance to live it was because they didn't know too much of shit. However, if they knew just a small ounce of how my syndicate operated then death would be the only answer for their extermination.

I let myself inside of Kenya's house and was satisfied with the sweet smell that came from her living room. Kenya made sure that her nice cozy home was decked out in nothing but high-end luxury furniture. It was really girlie and soft as hell, no man touch added to this shit. You could also tell she lived alone with the setup of her living room. I slipped off my Versace loafers. Kenya's living room was decorated light pink and white, easy to dirty up. I walked to her kitchen first because I knew that's where she spent most of her time. Sure enough, she sat at her kitchen island with a glass of red wine poured high to the brim of her cup. Her laptop was opened as she pulled her reading glasses up the bridge of her pointy nose. I never understood why she wore fucking glasses when she still squinted while reading the emails that she had opened up.

"I ordered take out tonight, I got behind on a lot of your emails so I'm catching up." she said without acknowledging me. I leaned down and pecked her on the forehead and walked out the kitchen. I didn't fuck with Kenya when she was working because she took her job very seriously. Its why I kept her pockets fat, she did a damn good job with my budget and making sure everything was in place. I never had to double back and check if what she was thorough enough. She proved timelessly that she was fit to be in her position. Each year she had gotten even better at what she did. Out of Mi'elle and Kenya, I spoiled Kenya with gifts and trips and did more with her. Since she carried her weight and didn't just wait around for me like a lost puppy.

To me she earned that right, plus it wasn't until this year that she started exposing more and more of her feelings. If it was any other female, I would've cut her off but not Kenya Monroe. She was just too damn good at what she did, I just hate she had to fall in love with me. I was comfortable with the friendship that we had. I liked chilling with her and talking about expanding and making my syndicate bigger. When she talked about feelings and expecting more from me, it fucked up the whole mood.

After I shower and ate, I laid in Kenya's bed to get a few hours of rest. That was another thing that was cool about Kenya. She knew how to separate work from pleasure, if it was any other chick, they would already be in this room trying to suck the skin off my dick. Kenya knew when I came over for pussy and she also knew when I just simply needed rest. Between juggling the cartel and my syndicate and this new marriage shit, I was becoming a little tired, but I'd never give in to that. A couple of hours of rest was needed to reset myself.

I woke up around two in the morning hearing Kenya's light snores. With my eyes still closed I squeezed my dick and thought about blessing Kenya with some powerful strokes until I woke back up around four to shower again and leave back out since my driver would be arriving at five. Knowing my mom was out with a nigga across the country trying to send a message out to the cartel had me alert with a million thoughts circulating through my brain.

I could feel another person presence before my brain could register the signature perfume she rocked. I reached for my 44. That I kept underneath the fluffy pillow and heard her clicking her teeth. I watched her silhouette reach for the lamp and once it clicked on my eyes adjusted to my wife sitting on the chaise that I often lounged on to read my books when I came over here.

"How fucking cute." She stroked her nine-millimeter that sat in her lap, like an overprotective owner stroked the back of their cat... I took her in, and she looked so fucking dark and sexy. Her round chubby face held a glow, her face was bare of any make up just how I liked it, it gave her a rough but sexy look seeing the tattoos that sat in awkward places on her face. She had a crazed look in her eyes like she had been up all day and night putting in major work. I had to chuckle lowly at her sophisticated gang banging looking ass.

Her hair wasn't loose and curly, she had that shit parted down the middle braided in two Indian braids. Her hazel eyes made the room light the fuck up and I swear this bitch threw my heartbeat off. I didn't like that shit one bit.

"I see you haven't learned a damn thing from that expensive car of yours getting burned down to the ground." She licked her clear glossed up lips. She wore all black from head to toe like a thief in the night, she even had black leather gloves on.

"I'm starting to love your crazy side, Sovereign. Shit makes my dick hard, wifey... its good seeing you. We are expected in Mexico for cartel business." I sat up in bed letting the covers fall off of me. Kenya moved a little in her sleep, she shifted so much the cover fell off her body exposing the fact that she was naked.

"I guess we just gone keep finding each other in somebody else's bed." Her brows raised.

"Not us, Sovereign. Maybe me, but not us." I looked her right in the eye to let her know how serious I was.

"Let me make some shit clear to you, hubby... This shit between you and I." She paused and pointed the gun between the both of us as I stood on the other side of the bed with my dick bricking up.

"This shit ain't got no real substance. You ain't shit to me but a nigga with a nice long dick and thick tongue. You know how to work it, I even got to admit, you know what you doing and you do that shit very well. I can see why weak ass bitches like her, work so hard to gain and keep your favor.

But a bitch like me ain't that impressed, see I got to have my own wings and spread them, can't no nigga on the face of this earth but my biological dad say they put me on to a damn thing because I worked hard as fuck on my own to gain the status and power. This between us is nothing but business, you might have more money and power, but you will respect me as your fake ass wife. You going along with shit concerning cartel business just like I am. You can never have me by the balls Malice. Just like you have access to pop up on me and throw fake temper tantrums, so do I. So, this is just a lesson being taught to your playing with fire ass." She stood up and laughed at the sight of Kenya sitting up looking on with wide confused eyes.

"Everybody else might fear you or walk on eggshells with your pretty eye having ass. See me? I'll eat you for breakfast, lunch, and dinner. I'm a fuckin' man eater baby, watch your fucking moves with me." She walked out the room, I eyed her curvy ass until she disappeared. Sovereign had me so fuckin hard pre cum oozed out tip of my dick. Sovereign didn't know how bad I wanted her now. She turned the fire all the way up and I was ready for whatever challenge she had up her sleeves.

"Why the fuck was she in my house Inferno?" Kenya slid out of bed with her arms folded across her perky breast. My eyes traveled to her bald pussy, and I wished it was Sovereign standing in her spot. I said nothing as I walked away and went to the bathroom to throw water on my face. Ignoring Kenya was the best thing to do right now. I didn't want to hurt her feelings.

Kenya just couldn't mind her business though; she stood by the bathroom door watching me intently.

"Did you hear me Inferno? Why the fuck was she here?"

"Lower your voice and stop asking me questions where I

pay bills at. She is my wife; she doesn't need a reason to pop up. I'm about to get ready to go. Do you need something from me or are you going to keep asking stupid questions Kenya?" I turned the water off and eyed her. She turned around and I shook my head at her. If she wanted some dick now was her chance to make that shit, clear while my dick was still rock hard from Sovereign. I repeated myself one last time.

"You want something Kenya?"

"Yes, I do Malice! I want something that will last forever." She wiped at some of the big crocodile tears that came down her pretty face. Maybe Kenya Monroe should have been that girl for me. The one I should have married and placed high on a pedestal. She was smart, always ready, and willing. Kenya didn't talk back; she went hard for me and my syndicate. If it wasn't for her a lot of shit wouldn't have been as smooth as it was. I couldn't force myself to fall in love with her and give her something that I didn't want with her. The spark that I had with Sovereign in just a short time frame was never there for me with Kenya. I don't think a woman has ever held my attention like Sovereign did. It was something about Sovereign that made me want to keep her very close to me.

I constantly tried to keep fucking on Kenya whenever I had the opportunity as well as Mi'elle. They were of my connivence, and I was a busy man that still had sexual needs. Never have I ever tried to readjust my business to create time for a woman. Time to spy and pop up on a woman that I didn't know too much about besides the stupid background check I did on her. I knew it was more to Sovereign's life to make her the cold standoffish female she was, but I wanted her to open up to me on her own timing. When I was handling business, I thought of Sovereign wishing I could be a fly on the wall to see what the fuck she was doing when I wasn't with her. Sovereign was very intriguing, sexy as fuck and she matched me well.

Sovereign was a power driven, ten toes down hustler and I loved that shit about her. A woman that wasn't a damsel in distress. Sovereign didn't mind getting her hands dirty and placing her feet down to the dirt to put in that real street work. I was so used to sensing fear from people being intimidated by me, when the first encounter from Sovereign showed me that I indeed made her break out and sweat. The fear was nonexistent within her, and I couldn't do shit but respect that shit.

"We do everything together already. I won't smother you. I just want to be the girl for you Inferno."

"All I can give you is nothing. Because nothing last forever Kenya. If you can't accept the nothing that I have then you are always free to find a man that can give you that something. I have a wife; my duty is to remain with her. I'll see you at next month's meeting." I walked away from her because I did care for her. I hated to see her so caught up on me. I was definitely not the man for Kenya Monroe. The best thing she could do for herself from here on out was to find another man to become obsessed over.

I knew what it felt like now to like someone and not be sure if they liked you the same. To lay in bed thinking of that special person wishing you can get them to act right. Becoming so selfish that it was sickening. In my dark ass mind, I didn't want anyone touching Sovereign. I wanted to be the only man to feel, touch, taste and hear her. I wanted to make her smile, cry, be happy and angry. I wanted all of that shit. Rather she wanted it or not. She didn't have a choice. I made up my mind that this marriage shit could work in both of our favor. I was still selfish thinking that maybe I could still keep all the women I was fucking satisfied. Kenya and Mi'elle were free to do them, I didn't care what or who they did as long as they stayed clean and wrapped the shit up. Sovereign I wanted to keep to myself, I knew I couldn't just tuck her away because she was on the same power trip that I was on. The only challenge would be getting Sovereign to see and understand that shit.

A random thought of killing Kenya came to mind. I quickly shook it off, but it still lingered. A broken-hearted woman would eventually become bitter and start plotting. I cared for Kenya but not enough to keep her alive to fuck with my cartel or syndicate. Decisions, decisions.

SOULFUL HURTZ

A slight grin spread across my face as I sat across from Jocelyn watching her look at the menu. We sat in a five-star steak house about to eat some good ass food. I couldn't believe how things turned from shit to sugar for me in a short period of time. My mom had been proving herself more and more each day. She stepped up with the girls and did her motherly thing with them. It left me a lot of time on my hands to step up with the gang and run things how it was supposed to be ran.

When Queen popped up with all of those drugs, we sat around the plastic folding table with crab legs and lobster tails, along with glasses of champagne celebrating new wealth to come. We had several new stash houses, so I didn't have to worry about hiding work in the same place that I laid my head at. I called a lot of shots and was still able to focus on school. I couldn't lie and say that I didn't want to be a part of school anymore. The way I saw it, in a couple of months things would be set straight for me. We would only make more money as time went on.

I stayed in school because it was my obligation to. I

didn't want to disappoint Queen by dropping out and getting cocky. I was no dumb nigga, I wanted to still go to college and make something of myself. It just became hard to live a double life. I rubbed my hands down my fresh fade and looked at Jocelyn, she looked so pretty and perfect. Her posture was perfect like a model. Today was Saturday and all I wanted to do was spend time with my girlfriend.

It felt like bitches knew I was on the come up, ever since I pulled up to school with my car and Jocelyn big cheesing in my passenger seat. I wasn't worried about none of them hoes because they weren't worried about this fat dusty nigga when I was really down bad. All the girls at school did was tear me down when I was already having it hard at home. Jocelyn never did me like that so for that reason alone a nigga was humble.

"We can share a Tomahawk steak and order some sides to share as well." Jocelyn closed the menu and looked up at me smiling. She was like a fresh breath of air; it made me happy just knowing she was happy with me.

"We ain't got to share shit Jah. Order what you want, I told you I was treating you today for your birthday." I got excited with the thought of her finally turning eighteen. I planned on leaving this restaurant and going home to get a change of clothes then taking her fine ass to a nice hotel and laying her down. I wasn't no virgin nigga; I had been fucking grown bitches since I was fifteen. Grown bitches were different, they didn't care about how I looked. They didn't see the bumps on my face and laugh. Their eyes traveled right down to my raggedy gray sweatpants and the big ass print that I had. I was packing and had a lot of dick to break a bitch down if I wanted to.

A lot of times the older bitches I fucked on was a means to me and my siblings having a home cooked meal. Thanks to

Queen and all the facials and pimple popping she did my face was starting to clear up. I still didn't feel a hundred percent confident with myself, but I liked the fact that I was now dressed better and all them ugly ass bumps was slowly but surely disappearing.

"I like the new you." She picked up her strawberry lemonade and smiled bashfully.

"What was the old me like?" I wanted to know her viewpoint on how she felt about me, I knew she always looked my way but could never determine her thoughts about me. I assumed that she too thought I was a bum fat nigga with bad ass acne.

"The old you was shy, quiet... letting people treat you wrong. I saw pain every time your eyes met mine. The weight of the world on your shoulders. You really lived up to your last name, you were hurting bad." She reached across the table timidly and grabbed my hands. Picking my left hand up she pecked the rough side of my hand with her soft succulent lips. That shit did something to me, I didn't know what it felt like to receive affection and adoration, but Jocelyn was the female that had me experiencing a lot of things for the first time.

I remained quiet until the waitress came to the table to take our orders. We made small talk until our food arrived. After we ate and joked around, I found myself locked into my thoughts worried about taking my time with Jocelyn as far as laying her sexy body down and taking her down. I ain't never broke a girl virginity, wasn't a soft bone in my body. I didn't know shit about making love, I didn't eat pussy because I wouldn't dare put my mouth on a random bitch.

All I did was hardcore fucking, enjoying the feeling of nutting in a condom then keep it pushing. With Jocelyn things had to be different. She was delicate and too beautiful to be treated like a slut.

"What you thinking about?" She asked as I pulled out a knot of cash and peeled a couple back to place into the small fob.

"You." I kept it short. I took in her diamond shaped face loving the way her curly natural lashes looked without her glasses on. I downed the rest of my drink, I wasn't broke, but I wasn't rich and wasting food and juice still wasn't an option for me. I knew what it felt like to not even have anything or nothing at all.

We left out the restaurant and I opened Jocelyn door like the gentleman I tried too always be with her. Before she got into the car, I pulled her close to me. She placed her hand on my stomach and rubbed my round belly. That shit right there had me blushing and looking away from her.

"I can't wait to cuddle with you all night long." She tilted her head up and puckered her lips. This shit still felt too good to be true with this girl. She was just too damn good looking for a nigga like me. I bent down a little and aligned my lips with hers. I pecked her three times then just stared in her eyes.

"I hope you don't break a nigga's heart Jocelyn. I don't know how I'd react to that shit." I grabbed a handful of ass watching her blush and turn red in the cheeks.

"I hope you don't break mine either Soulful Hurtz. I know that dope boys got a lot of hoes." I put my nose in the crook of her neck enjoying the smell that came from her body.

"I ain't ya average dope boy, as long as I got you, I ain't worried bout no other bitch. I won me a trophy." I didn't know if it was corny as hell but soon as we got in the car, I connected my phone to the Bluetooth and played Future ft Kanye "Trophy". We vibed on the freeway with my hand holding hers as I controlled the stirring wheel with one hand navigating to my house. I was so ready to get her to the hotel that I almost was about to say fuck going home.

I was a clean nigga and had to wash my ass every night so getting a change of clothes was a must. We pulled up to the projects, I parked close to the curb then helped Jocelyn out. The hood was jumping at seven p.m it was the weekend, so shit was gone be popping all night.

"I ain't gone be long." I let Jocelyn know as I stuck my key in my door and let us in. I didn't mind her coming in the house, I rearranged some shit in the living room and had it looking way better. I opened the door and frowned when I didn't smell a home cooked meal. Luv sat on the new sectional couch that I had just bought watching the new fifty-inch TV that I got from Walmart.

"Luv, what I tell yo lil ass bout watching love in hip hop? It ain't for kids, put some other shit on." She smacked her lips then looked past me and smiled brightly at Jocelyn. She got up and hugged her as I surveyed the front of the house.

"Where Passion?" I asked Luv, Passion always ran into the living room from our room to greet me and tell me about her day.

"She went with momma to McDonald's, momma said she don't feel like cooking. We ate ice cream and hot Cheetos; they should be back in a minute." She flopped her little frail self back on the couch and flipped through the channels. I watched Jocelyn take a seat next to Luv on the couch. The both of them started talking, while I debated with myself. A part of me wanted to go back outside and hop in my whip to go find my mom and Passion. I didn't really like them walking around the projects. McDonald's was a ten-minute walk from the house. I shrugged it off thinking that it was good for my moms and Passion to spend some alone time.

"How long they been gone?" I yelled over my shoulder, opening the door to my room.

"I don't know but they should be coming back." Luv yelled back. I opened the top drawer to my dresser and dug out a fresh pair of boxers along with a white beater. I went to the closet and got a fresh outfit for the next day. I planned on taking Jocelyn out to the Court Cafe in the morning. Tomorrow was a slow day since it was Sunday. I wanted all of us including my momma to go to the Pier and play games and walk the beach.

Soon as I bent down to pick up my Nike backpack, I heard a loud boom. My heart immediately started to speed, I wanted to panic but I went right into protection mode. Throwing my backpack on the ground I heard muffled voices. I couldn't really make the voices out, but I could hear Jocelyn telling them that she didn't have no money. Frowning at her words, I snatched my gun from the top of the closet. I practically tip toed towards my room door.

Right now, I could hear the intruders fucking up the front of the house. They didn't come to harm nobody because I didn't hear them popping off at Jocelyn and Luv.

Hearing their footsteps come down the hallway, I pumped myself up. I was killing somebody today. I ain't have no drugs or no major cash here at this house no more. These project niggas probably thought I had money now since I was pushing a car. They thought they were bout to catch me slipping but that wasn't fenna be the case here tonight. Queen gave me my own personal stash spot since we had more dope to move.

No longer able to waste any more time for the sake of my sister and Jocelyn safety I popped out in the hallway shooting first watching two bodies drop. I delivered a head shot to the first tall body that was bulky. The second person turned their back in the middle of me shooting them, they collapsed hard onto the carpet.

"F.Y.F mutha fuccas." I moved towards them and kicked their guns away from their hands. Snatching the ski mask off the first nigga, I squatted down stunned as fuck.

"I knew this nigga was moving foul." I shook my head. Hawking up spit, it landed on his face. The second body caught my attention, it was the voice that stalled me.

"Murk'um." She simpered and struggled with turning over.

"Jah take my sister and go to your house!" I yelled; Luv was probably traumatized enough from them busting up in here.

"You fat muthafucka!" Her voice sounded like she was gargling mouth wash. Coughing up blood, I moved towards her and turned her over, removing the ski mask.

"What the fuck you on Clapback?" I felt betrayed and confused as fuck. Her eyes were starting to roll back as her body convulsed. Panic surged through me. I never had problems with Clapback, I always thought she was weird for fucking on Murk'um but didn't judge her for that shit. It wasn't my place to insert myself in nobody's business if it didn't concern my money.

"Fuck!" I stood up and fished for my phone in my pockets. I dialed Queen because I truly didn't know what to do. She answered on the second ring and said nothing as usual.

"Queen, I killed Murk'um and umm your sister Clapback, I shot in the back or somewhere I don't really know man! Fuck! Her body convulsing and it ain't looking to good. They broke into my apartment with ski mask on, I don't know what this shit about Queen and I don't know what to do."

"You must be drunk." She chuckled nervously. "I'm gone send someone to check on you, take your medicine and go lay down. Rest Teddy, stop talking so crazy." She hung up leaving me standing there confused as fuck. I sat down on my couch; I didn't even bother to look at the bodies in the hallway. It felt like I was stuck in a bad dream. Shit just went left fast as fuck. My nerves were rattled bad, if I killed Queen sister then I didn't know where that would leave us. Queen changed my life; I just didn't know what to make of all of this at this very moment.

After sitting there for fifteen minutes, I heard cars pulling up. I still didn't move, I just stayed seated wondering what the fuck my fate was gone be. I didn't feel defeated, so I kept my chin up. I was protecting my girl and little sister. I didn't know what the fuck Murk'um and Clapback was on. Queen taught me to always shoot first and ask questions later.

A crew of five men in all black with gloves and masks walked in first. They said nothing and walked right towards the hallway. After a couple of seconds three more men walked in, two of them had menacing scowls on their faces. The one in the front didn't look bothered at all, he held a flamethrower in his right hand. In his left hand was a thick Cuban cigar. He looked like he was a mixed nigga. Something about him was dark, his eyes looked icy as fuck.

"I'm Inferno, Queens husband. While my men work, I'll take a seat and explain somethings to you." One of his men followed him to the couch, the other nigga walked to where the men were working, one picked up Murk'um's body.

"Fuck, tell me do the bitch got a pulse. Pussy too good to be dead man." The dude that walked in with Inferno stood over Clapback like he was pissed.

"There's a faint pulse." One of the workers said.

"Good, get her to our doctors, make sure you tell them she has to survive. My wife wouldn't know what to do

without this treacherous bitch. I will let her decide her fate."
He looked at me as a long stream of ashes hit the carpet.

"Killa get over here, we are in the middle of conducting business." Inferno's voice was flat void of any emotion.

"First body?" He raised a brow; I shook my head yes still unable to speak. He sat up in the love seat across from me and smirked but that shit looked like he was sneering at me.

"Understandable, Queen wanted to be here. She's in Mexico, I was getting ready to head there too. Until she called." He never broke eye contact as he took a deep pull from his cigar and then released the smoke.

"You made a big mistake tonight, well, actually two mistakes Teddy. One mistake was not delivering two head shots to your intruders. Second mistake was calling on an unprotected phone line admitting to the crime you did."

"I'm sorry, I wasn't thinking." He pointed to the phone still sitting in my hand, I passed it to him and watched him squeeze it with one hand until the screen shattered in his hands. He tossed it on the floor and held his free hand out as the big nigga behind him handed him a clear bottle that looked like it had water inside.

"I'll be moving your location; this spot will be burned down to the ground." He popped the cap off and poured the clear liquid onto the already broken phone.

"No need to worry, my men moving all of the important things that your household needs." He picked up his flamethrower and squeezed what looked like a trigger. Flame shot out and caught on to the phone as it began to burn slowly. Inferno started to talk again but he looked like he was stuck in a trance watching the small fire before us.

"Big B is the big nigga behind me, he will give you the address of where you will be staying. Queen will not return until three to four days and she will break the news to your crew on what happened and decide what explanation to give. When I caught my first body, I burned them until it was nothing, but bones left. I didn't sleep for a whole week until I went and bought some sleeping pills. Not saying that it's going to make it better. When you catch your first body it stick with you more than the bodies that comes afterwards. It's like the soul of the first body you take follows you around in life taunting you like you can't or won't kill again. I proved that first soul wrong every single time I killed a person. It's kind of like training your conscience to believe in what you feel is right. Don't fret the situation to hard young man, you did what you was supposed to. Only next time, you learn from this and never miss your mark."

He stood up as I let his words sink in, something inside of me felt weird as hell. It felt like I wasn't even breathing normal. By the time they had the suburban truck loaded up with all of our personal belongings. I walked out the house slowly turning around to see Big B walking out the house with lighter fluid leaking from the bottle. He drenched the three steps that led to the front door as Inferno took his flamethrower and placed it down on the front doorstep. Security stood around us blocking us from the nosey ass neighbors that was most likely watching.

The cold breeze made the fire travel faster until the whole project unit set ablaze. Inferno watched for a couple of minutes and shook his head.

"I wish I could stay and watch the fire take this place all the way down, but I have to move out. Get your family and go to the address Big B gives you." He turned and walked off with one hand stuffed in his pocket, his free handheld on to his flamethrower. The nigga was insane, his calm nonchalant presence was evident as he waved bye from the back window.

It hit me then that my mom and Passion hadn't made it home just yet.

"Fuck!" I shook my head in defeat, I couldn't stay stagnant. I was going to have to go looking for my mom and sister. There was no way she up and went to fucking McDonald's it had been over an hour now and I knew that Luv and Jocelyn were now worried. I got the keys and address from Big B then jumped in my car to go find my mom and Passion first.

In the pits of my stomach, I felt something wasn't right. Fear soared throughout my body, and I found it ironic how I was saying a silent prayer to God after I just killed a nigga. I just hope that God would listen to me because I would lose my cool if something happened to my little sister or momma.

I drove block after block stopping to ask a couple of people that I saw hanging out if they saw my mom. Each person said no, I was losing hope wondering where the fuck could she possibly be. I knew like hell that my mom wouldn't ever possibly think to go get high while she was out with my sister. Something inside of me forced me to face the facts. The raw truth of who my mom was. Sure, she got her act together over the past couple of weeks and did the motherly thing. Antoinette still had her nights where she would stumble in reeking of alcohol and pass out on the couch mumbling but I didn't think she was still using due to the next morning. She would wake up and get the girls ready for school.

I didn't ask her questions because she was grown as hell. I was already blaming myself for everything. I got so caught up in hustling and trying to provide that I didn't pay closer attention. I felt overwhelmed and out of control of what was probably going on. After praying again, a thought popped up in my head. When my mom would disappear for days and I would get worried for her, I would go searching for her at a particular park.

Senseta Park had nothing but junkies and homeless people. It was located on the outside of the projects. Up and coming dope boys would hang out there and make the most money because junkies kept coming up to them to get high. Their crack was stepped on a million times making the junkies want more and more product. Junkies would run out of money and perform sinful acts like stealing from their loved ones and even pimping out their fucking kids to the perverted dope boys just to get high for ten minutes. I didn't want to go to Senseta because I knew if I went there and saw my sister in such a fucked-up environment. I would never be able to forgive my mom.

I pulled right into the parks parking lot and grabbed my gun from the glove compartment. Trash littered the grass the air smelled like drugs, piss, and shit. I started from the front of the park and worked my way through. Checking the park restrooms, I came up empty handed. Feeling hopeless I turned to walk back to my car until I heard a loud scream. That scream belonged to Passion. It was the same scream she had when she saw a rat during wintertime in our apartment.

It was so dark that the only light that helped my vision was the streetlights. Pulling up my jeans, I picked my pace up until I reached the park's gym. I could hear a bunch of talking and laughing followed by my sister crying. My adrenaline was on a hundred as I pulled my gun from my waist. Making my way to the back of the gym, I ran to my sister that was being held down by two fiends and snatched her up while pointing my gun.

"Their hurting her Soulful! She's dead! Mommy is dead!" She held onto my neck so tight it felt like she was choking me. I stood tall with her and pushed a couple of fiends out my way so I could see what their attention was on.

My eyes had to be deceiving me, my heart instantly broke for the second time out of my life as I watched my mother's limp body get pounded from the back. The dope boy held the top of her forehead as he thrusted in and out of her, the grunting noises had me nauseated. I couldn't think straight as I picked my gun up and blew his fucking brains out. Passion screamed again, bringing me back to reality as all the fiends scattered away like roaches. My mom laid on the concrete looking lifeless as Passion cried her little heart out in my arms. Just within two hours, I caught another body. Only this time, I didn't give a fuck about the body I just dropped. I placed Passion to her feet and checked my moms for a pulse. Once I felt one, I picked her up and carried her to my car. After tonight, I didn't want shit to do with her. I planned on taking my sisters far the fuck away and providing for them the best way I knew how.

I couldn't focus on school or Jocelyn; I was here to grind hard and provide for my sisters. I couldn't be wishing on a fucking star trying to pray for my momma to get clean, when she constantly made stupid ass decisions like the choice she made tonight. Once I got Passion and my mom in the car, I stopped by a pay phone to call Jocelyn. I needed her to bring Luv on the next block so I could take her to the address that Big B provided. I didn't want to take the chances of hitting the projects and running into the police when I still didn't have a driver's license.

"You, okay?" Jocelyn asked me as she tried to search my eyes. I struggled with looking into her beautiful eyes because I knew that I was about to hurt her. It was never my intentions to do so though.

"Yea, I'm straight. Thanks for looking out for Luv." I

looked back at the car and could still see my mom knocked out. Passion had a haunted look in her eyes that pained my soul.

"I still can come with you; my mom is gone with her boo for the weekend." She smiled and placed her hand on my arm. It amazed me how calm she was after she heard and saw what went on back at my house. Then again if you lived in the projects, you became immune to certain shit. Like niggas robbing you and watching a few bodies drop around you. Jocelyn's brother was a hitta so she knew how shit went.

"Nah, but listened Jah, you free to move on. I got some heavy shit I'm dealing with and you probably ain't gone see a nigga for a while." She shook her head no and I let out a breath that I had been holding. Licking my dry lips, all I could see was the bodies I dropped tonight. Just like that, I forgot all about the good time I had with Jocelyn. I forgot about how she calmed me and felt good to my soul.

"Let me be there for you Soulful, please?" I wanted to say yes but I couldn't put that type of burden on her. I stepped back, preparing to turn away from her. I had been standing here too long and my mom needed medical attention. I didn't know what tomorrow would be like or how things would be with Queen and I since Clapback was now on her deathbed. Although I had every right to shoot her sister, that was still her flesh and blood. I knew the great measures that I would take for my little sisters right or wrong. I could only hope that I still had a chance to be on Queen's team.

"I got to go Jah." I turned to walk away, and she grabbed my hand, pulling me to her she grabbed a hold of my shirt and tried to pull me closer to her. She stood on her tippy toes struggling to reach my lips. I finally gave in and moved down to her lips and kissed her passionately before releasing her. She had tears welled up in her eyes and I had tears pouring from my soul. I often wondered why my life was so fucked up. Every time shit looked up to a nigga some bad shit had to happen that would pull me back down into that deep depression that I had to fight with just to stay sane for my sisters that fully depended on me.

"Promise me that you will come and see about me, when you straight. If you ever need me Soulful, I will be right here for you." I nodded my head and turned to walk away from her. Each step that I took felt heavier than the last. I got in the car and embraced the silence. I drove twenty miles to a good hospital and carried my mom in through the entrance. I laid her down in the chair and took a good long look at her.

Backhanding the tears that had fallen down my face, I barely could recognize her. I saw her in the light and got mad all over again. She had knots all over her forehead and her lips were swollen as well. It looked like her nose was broken; her brown body had bruises all over. The purple maxi dress she had on was ripped and exposing some of her lady parts. Niggas had violated my momma bad but not how she violated Passion by putting her in that predicament.

Yelling out for the concierge to come help her and send my momma a doctor. I walked out of the hospital with blurry eyes and a heavy heart. I remembered what Jocelyn told me and agreed a hundred percent. My mom knew what she was doing naming me Soulful Hurtz. I had a permanent feeling of hurt embedded inside of me. I didn't see that shit going away no time soon.

INFERNO

$\mathcal{I}$ don't know when I took a liking to my wife. If I dug into my thick skull, it would probably show me the first time I entered her. The pussy felt like it was made just for me. If I dug a little deeper then I think what made me infatuated with her was when she gave me a birthday present. Setting my favorite car on fire, had my dick rock hard every single time I thought about the flames tearing my multimillion-dollar car apart.

I sat on the edge of my bed reading one of my favorite books, "The Power of Mental Discipline." I couldn't focus good on the book because my eyes kept drifting off to Sovereign. The sun kissed her brown skin in the right places as she stood out on the balcony looking out at the waves crashing against the rocks underneath us. She hadn't said anything since I arrived last night. Lots of phone calls she made, excusing herself from me plenty of times throughout the night. Her head was in a different space, her focus was off. I could see the pain evident in her eyes every-time she turned and looked at me, even if it was for seconds.

She was far away from the drama, and I could see the

confliction and turmoil she was in. I watched her curvy frame toss and turn; she mumbled curse words in her sleep like somebody was haunting her down.

Today was the meeting with Nueva, and I needed her on point as my wife. She needed to appear strong, I lacked sympathy in certain areas, especially when it came to this side of the business. People constantly made their beds in the game. Didn't matter to me if they were family or not, if they weren't living by the code then they were as good as dead. Sitting my book next to me, I stood and made my way to the balcony. It was time we addressed the elephant in the room.

Her hair was wild and curly, it smelled like sweet fresh fruits. Each time the wind blew, the smell of her hair and body hit my nose drawing me in more. I stood behind her, enjoying the feel of her curvy soft ass against my semi hard erection.

"What you want from me, Malice?" Her voice was low and very delicate. This was the side of her, I thought I would never see. She was vulnerable, caught up thinking about her treacherous sister.

"You know, being Queen comes with a lot. Weakness is a form of being unfit to rule. This is a big reason why women should stay in their lanes. Unless your something like your Abuela, void of any emotions. Her only desire is money and power. I don't see that in you." I stopped talking and moved some of her hair to the side to lean in close to her ear.

"I'm not weak." She hissed, bracing the rails. "You're crowding my space." I smiled at the irritation laced in each word she spoke.

"You're not weak, but right now that's what I see. A decision of ending your sister's life could have been made last night." I reminded her. I didn't give a fuck how bad it hurt. A decision had to be made, she was now tied into my syndicate.

216

Dishonor and moving funny was not acceptable. Right now, no one knew what happened. The kid Teddy knew because he was the shooter. If that got out and around town that Queen let her sister still be a part of what we had going, then people would start to test deadly waters.

She moved from in front of me and walked into the room. I stood in the same place, calming my own anger. In order to deal with a woman like Sovereign, you needed lots of patience. Once I walked back in, she was already seated on my expensive tufted two-arm chaise lounge that only I would sit on. A lit blunt permeated the air. I picked up my lighter torch and flicked it on and off, staring at the fire.

"A decision has to be made Sovereign. Just so you know, I don't give a fuck how dear the bitch is to you."

"Well, I do! That's my baby sister! Empress has to have a good explanation."

"There is none!" I finally raised my voice, marching to where she sat so comfortably. "It's a lot you need to know about that selfish bitch, the only reason she is still living is because I want you to learn a valuable lesson in this. What I will tell you is that nigga that Teddy killed was her man... even after you told them not to mess around. She was pregnant with his baby. She didn't like the fact that you gave Teddy a higher position than her man and she took matters into her own hands. Trying to frame your lieutenant." She shook her head no; I could see her swallowing whatever salvia she had left in her mouth before she spoke.

"How do you know that?" I ignored her and continued to push her into her tipping point.

"What if her plan went through? If she robbed Teddy of all the new drugs and money that our cartels have provided for your gang? You would have killed an innocent man, right? You wouldn't be sitting here looking like a dumb weak bitch." I smirked; she stood so fast she stumbled on her own two feet. Picking her hand up to slap me, I caught it, and grabbed her up by the throat feeling her buck against me. Fury was locked into her eyes, but I didn't give a damn about that. I squeezed her neck tight until I felt and saw her gasping for air. I looked down at the black silk gown that rested mid-thigh and started to rise higher.

"You have got to learn how to stay in a woman's place. Especially when it comes to me, Sovereign. I'm not these weak horny ass niggas that will bow down and listen to whatever the fuck your filthy mouth spits." I gritted; I wasn't about to ease up on her. I didn't care how big her eyes had gotten; Sovereign was going to learn things the hard way. I wasn't the nigga that she could raise her hand to or get slick out the mouth with.

"You can't fuck me baby, I fuck you. I tell you what it's going to be and then you rely the message when it's time to do so. You will follow my fucking lead, or I'll burn your tender ass until you comply with what the fuck, I'm telling you." I took steps backwards with her clawing at my hand that held her neck in a death grip. Each time she hit me, I squeezed tighter until she realized that there was no escaping.

My dick was hard, and I hated how bad she turned me the fuck on with her nasty attitude. Kicking her legs apart with my foot, I pushed her back on the bed, making her silk gown rise up around her waist. I grunted at the sight of her fat pussy, shaking my head at the sight of how wet she was for me. I released a chuckle that had her frowning as she massaged her neck.

"Your sister is out; she will not be a part of your gang. She will have no dealings with you at all. If you don't kill her, you better outcast her." I placed my knee on the bed and made my way between her thick shiny thighs. Her breast already spilled out the top of her gown. The closer I got the faster her chest rose up and fell.

"Fuck you, Malice." She attempted to knee me in the balls, but I caught and squeezed her knee, until she screamed from me knocking her kneecap out of place then moving it back to its rightful place.

"Okay, Sovereign... I'll fuck you, long and hard. The next time you try to cause me pain, I will double yours." I pushed deeply inside of her to the hilt. Grabbing the top of her shoulders since she called herself running from the dick. I pushed out of her a little then pushed all the way in.

"Ohhh!" She yelped, lifting those pretty legs around me, until they locked behind my muscular buttocks.

"Yea ohhh, make that pussy bite this dick and shut the fuck up." I pummeled her pussy until she was shaking on my dick.

Nut number one was out the way, now it was time for me to talk shit. Easing up, fondling her sensitive bud, the sight was comical. Sovereign tried to leap off the bed as she pleaded for mercy.

"My wife can't be no weak ass bitch. You wanted the power baby, it's at your fingertips. You not just making decisions for yourself." I stopped torturing her and picked my movement back up. Stretching her walls felt like I was fighting them. No matter the size of my dick, her pussy squeezed and choked my shit making me twitch inside of her.

"Empress is a treacherous bitch. She will make everything you worked hard for crumble. Take care of that situation and make sure it never leaks into cartel business. Are we clear, Sovereign?" I positioned my dick downwards and pulverized her center. She shook her head side to side refusing to answer me. I guess Sovereign needed a little more motivation.

Spreading her thighs further apart until she was practically doing the splits. I spread her ass cheeks and spit between them. Easing my dick into her tight asshole she looked at me as if I lost my mind. I could feel her body tense up under me. Taking her sensitive clit between my thumb and index finger I offered her stimulation to keep her mind off my initial penetration.

"You the type, that love shit the hard way." I mumbled, keeping eye contact with her. I inched in painfully slow; I hated going slow but to keep from splitting her ass in half I had to proceed with caution. I didn't even plan on going all the way in.

"Pleeeeaaassseee!" She begged and that made it worse.

"Oh, now you can talk?" I formed circles on her clit and moved my dick back then pushed forward loving the way her tight ass clenched me.

"You gone listen to me from now on?" I popped her clit twice, her eyes rolled back. She quickly nodded her head up and down but that wasn't good enough for me. Easing out of her ass, I pushed back into her contracting center and thrashed her shit until she started screaming and speaking in tongues.

"Yes, oh fuck! I swear, I will, I'll do it! Malice please! Wait!!!!!" I chuckled, wrapping my hands underneath her. She simpered and sniveled, while her soft breast rubbed up against my stomach and chest.

"Fuck you feel so good, Sovereign." Her pussy was so slippery and wet. I kept forcing myself to focus and not close my eyes like a bitch.

"I'll never stir you wrong. Just listen to me, I'm king you

Queen, you understand?" I laid back and slapped her ass, making her ride me.

"Yes!" Her body and face were drenched, her hair glued to parts of her body and face. She was beautiful and thick; I could really get used to this shit. With more grooming and coaching, Sovereign was gone end up being a match made from the pits of hell for me.

Her body shook, I growled and gripped her ass tight. We came together as she collapsed right on top of me breathing hard. The smell of sex and sweat added with her intoxicating smell had me closing my eyes as I listened to her light snores. I hoped this was good enough to get her stubborn ass to act right in this meeting. This cartel shit was nothing like shit in the states. One sign of weakness would be used against you. Sovereign probably thought she knew a lot, which she did. I just knew more and would have to help her catch up.

Three hours later.

"How did you know all of that about Empress? What all do you know?"

I looked Sovereign over and licked my lips. She had on a two-piece business suit. My favorite part about it was the color, which was red. Her make up was light and her lips burned with red lipstick. She had on big diamond earrings with her wild curly hair tamed better than earlier. A red rose was tucked on the side of her ear. As usual she smelled good as hell. Right now, she was looking like a boss-ass bitch.

"I wired all of your people houses. It's best to stay ten steps ahead of any future problems. The rest of what you should know, you will find out in due time." I cut the tip of my cigar then placed it in my mouth. Holding my hand out for her to grab. We walked towards the front of the house we're my guards stood holding the door open.

"I've provided for my sister since we were little." Her eyes looked off like she was in deep thought.

"I sacrificed myself in the literal sense. I've done things that people like you would never understand. When my parents died and disappeared, I stepped up with no clue of which way to go but I made things happen and I provided like I should have. That's why I know my sister has a good explanation." She slid into the back seat of the town car as I got in behind her.

"Then your sister bit the hand that fed her," I concluded. It was hard for her to accept the cold facts, but she had to accept and understand it.

"I can't kill Empress." She looked at me, those hazel brown eyes telling a story.

"I never said you had to." I looked out the window briefly, then back into her fiery eyes. I was always unbothered by the way she looked at me when she thought she was getting a point across. I can see how convincing and menacing she probably looked to her team of weak-ass niggas. That shit only made my dick hard, I loved the challenge that she always presented.

"You can't kill her either." I chuckled this time at her choice of words. There wasn't a soul on this planet that could direct me and tell me what the fuck I couldn't do.

"I won't make any promises." I kept it short.

"If you do something to my sister, I will stop at nothing to —"

"Shut the fuck up, before you say some shit you will regret. That's the reason why I am willing to wait and let you find out everything you need to know the hard way." Silence took over the car, my phone chimed alerting me of a new text message. Kenya sent me a picture of her wearing a yellow thong with heart yellow stickers covering her nipples. She took a couple of poses that would normally have me ready to send the private jet to have her bust that shit open. Right now, I didn't give a damn, so I locked my phone.

Anxiousness surged through me, business in the cartel worked a little differently. I couldn't go in this meeting drawing my flamethrower and melting this nigga's face off. He sent a message by courting my mom, I received that message and was ready to make things clear to him.

"This meeting, follow my lead. All you have to do is look how you look and keep your mouth shut." The car came to a stop. My driver Luca came around to my side of the door to open it. I could see that our guest already arrived.

Three Cadillac Escalade trucks were parked right in front of my father's estate. I eyed the two guards that held guns in their hands like they were guarding the president.

"I've done my own research. I know how to handle myself." I turned in my seat to face Sovereign just as Luca opened the door. This woman made me want to choke the living shit out of her. What research had she done, I wouldn't be surprised if she had her Abuela pull information for Sovereign's advantage.

Miguella, her Abuela was a different kind of breed. She truly didn't give a fuck about no one or nothing but herself. It was very crazy to me how the Ruiz and Martinez cartel united. A lot of men stayed out of Miguella's way, not wanting to do business with her at all. Miguella didn't move off morals at all. She moved off of greed and hunger for power and more money.

"Do what the fuck I told you Sovereign. You forget your sister is only alive because my top paid doctor is keeping her that way in the states. Don't fuck with me." I mushed her in the head as she cursed behind my back. Big B and Killa stood on the first set of steps. If only my mom knew who she was overseas with. I hoped like hell she didn't fuck Nueva. No matter how much peace the Ruiz cartel would try to keep. My father would bend that peace and seek blood if this man fucked my mom.

Snatching Sovereign hand, I gave a light squeeze and this crazy bitch tried to squeeze tighter. I chuckled at the effort and gave her another squeeze that made her suck in air. Her eyes welled with tears I turned all the way towards her and yanked her by the hand. She slammed right into my hard body.

Leaning down, I inhaled her scent then nipped her ear with my teeth.

"Keep fucking with me Sovereign, I'll postpone this meeting and punish that fat, pretty pussy of yours while I'm texting my people in the states to dope up that treacherous bitch with so much morphine that will make her flat line right on the fucking spot. Wipe your fucking face, fix your fucking face, and carry yourself like a fucking boss bitch and the wife of a cartel king." My mouth hovered above her ear as she snatched the cloth from the top of my suit jacket and dabbed at her eyes. She placed her soft hands on my neck then turned my face until my ear was touching her plump lips.

"When this is over, you will never touch, taste, or smell me. You better hope like hell you can locate me." She grabbed the outside of my crotch and squeezed. My dick stiffened from the tight grip she had. "One day, very soon… you will see just how tight of a grip that I got you by these big balls of yours. You will beg and beg hard for me to release these bitches." She released her grip and quickly walked away from me, leaving me breathing hard and pissed with a hard ass dick. Her curvy ass backside didn't make matters any better.

Soon as we walked in, my father's butler held a tray with

champagne flutes. We all declined except Sovereign who downed the first glass with a couple of gulps. She held her French tip index finger up to have the butler wait. When she finished her flute, she placed the empty one on the tray and downed another. Sitting that one down, I pinched the tip of my nose to stop myself from torching her ass.

She picked up the third flute, just as I grabbed her free hand. I led her all the way to the left wing of my father's estate where he held all his important meetings. As the guards opened the double doors, Sovereign burped and hiccupped loud as fuck. Killa couldn't hold back his laugh, Big B looked like he was struggling to keep a straight fucking face. Sovereign laughed lowly and shrugged as she took a small sip from her flute. I gave her a warning glare for the last warning I had to offer. If she fucked up and made me look bad in this meeting, I planned on killing everything attached to her that she gave a fuck about.

I kept a neutral face and observed the many men that accompanied the rectangular cherry wood table. Nodding my head and making eye contact with every man that sat in this room. I made my way to Sovereign's Abuela first to show respect, I kissed each side of her cheek as Sovereign did the same to my father to show the unity that we all had. The Golden triangle was in place, no matter how we felt about each other. In front of outsiders, we had to appear as one.

I pulled Sovereign seat out and eyed her with adoration to prove to every man at this table that she was mine. Once I pulled out her seat and made sure she was seated, Killa took a seat away from the table to the far-right corner as Big B stood behind me with my flamethrower in his hand. My father nodded to me, and I winked back at him. That was my cue to begin the meeting.

"Thanks, Nueva for joining the Golden Triangle, meeting

new members as well as alliances." Out the corner of my eyes, I could see Sovereign's Abuela pass her a white envelope. She picked up her champagne glass and took a small sip from it, sitting it back down quietly.

"I do not wish to make an alliance, perhaps we can make peace amongst each other." I smiled at him, I decided to jump into the real reason this meeting was called.

"Peace? You speak of peace as if it is easily given. I know that you are very intelligent Nueva... very calculated in everything it is that you do. So, when a powerful man like yourself takes it upon yourself and out of your busy schedule to find yourself in my neck of the woods, courting my mother. The Ruiz cartel will answer to the hidden messages that you are sending." My father cracked his neck, running his hands down his hair that had pounds of gel in it. His face was turning red. Tension in the room was so thick that you could slice through it.

"I would love peace, you see... we are about making money peacefully with no hiccups involved. We stand on that." The look on my father's face wasn't peaceful at all. I could always sense when he was about to explode. I was surprised he hadn't spoken just yet. He couldn't sit still, every couple of seconds, he shifted in his seat. His jaws kept clenching; this meeting would probably turn into a blood bath in a matter of seconds. My father loved my mom with everything inside of him. Nueva could have picked any other wife to play around with. He went after my mom because he knew the effect it would have on my father.

"What can a half breed like yourself tell me about a fucking hiccup." Nueva slammed his hands on the table. I snatched my eyes from him as my father leaned forward. I shook my head no. My father could never stand back and watch someone disrespect me. We all knew how much other cartel heads talked about me. How I wasn't fit to run a cartel being a half breed. They didn't respect me and right now Nueva was trying to press buttons to get a reaction. I was a businessman first and a cold-blooded killer second. Our cartel was just rebranding itself. We didn't have the time for a stupid war, but Nueva kept pushing for one, his wish would be granted. My patience was starting to run out. The urge that I was feeling to have Big B drown him in lighter fluid was starting to rise.

"I will tell you a lot about a hiccup." Sovereign stood allowing the bottom of her seat to scrape against the floor. "See, my husband is Muy lindo (*very nice*), but me? I'm into sending messages right back to the muthafucka that thought they could try to fondle my pussy with no fucking condom." I bit my bottom lip and concealed my anger that was about to spill out over the entire room. Sovereign was stepping out her place.

"What can a perra negra do to me!" He stood up and I could hear guns being drawn.

"Sit the fuck down and let this black bitch give you the only warning you will ever receive before I have your men viewing you like the perra you truly are!" Her voice elevated, bouncing off the walls. I could see fire blazing behind those pretty, hazel eyes. She picked up the white envelope and slid it across the table.

"Before you open that envelope, and I start talking fucking freely. I'll advise you to make your men leave. What you are about to pull out of that envelope is very personal and I'm willing to bet my life that you do not want any of your men to see." She smirked and picked up her champagne flute. A couple of seconds passed before Nueva waved his hand. I was so stunned that I had to take a seat myself and let Sovereign work the room. She was looking even sexier from how well posed she stood. I looked over at my father and he had an amused look plastered on his face. Killa looked like he was super excited to see what had unfolded.

When all of Nueva's men cleared out the room. Sovereign laughed loud like the villains do in those marvel movies.

"Open that fucking envelope, I got shit to do and I'm ready for this problem to be wrapped up in five minutes." Nueva carefully opened the envelope as pictures spilled out. So, no one could see, he hurriedly picked them up and gripped them tightly. His tan colored face started to turn pale. His hands trembled as he looked up at only Sovereign with fear in his eyes.

"You love trannies Nueva?" She raised her brow and smirked. "I have nothing against what a man likes, but what will all the other cartel members that you have strong alliances with think of that? I mean not only do you pay to fuck, but you also visit brothels like the one you visited in Thailand. Ain't no telling what you told my mom in law to break free from her to go slut that small snappin' turtle dick of yours. You went to the cheapest brothel in Thailand to go fuck on underage boys. I have that on tape to by the way." She let out a small laugh, Nueva had a haunted look on his face.

"Here in Mexico, they'd cut your fucking dick off for such acts. Good thing my father-in-law has nothing to worry about when it comes to you fucking the love of his life." She picked imaginary dirt from underneath her nails and looked up at me and winked.

"What do you want from me?" His voice cracked, he sounded like he was on edge of breaking down and crying.

"I would prefer your life, but I don't have the final say. See men have a way of making things harder. I'm not into having piss contest nor seeing whose balls are bigger. For the troubles and the expensive time of mine that you have wasted. I demand fifteen percent from your cartel each month that will be paid upfront in cash. Don't try to fuck me because I know how much your cartel makes by the week." That evil sneer of a smile covered Sovereign's angelic face as she took a small sip of her champagne then continued.

"The Ruiz and Martinez cartel will receive twenty percent cash profit that will be split down the middle. If I even think your plotting some bullshit, I will end you, were you stand. I actually would start with your legacy first. I'd enjoy watching your sick ass suffer first, then ending your misery last. You do understand what I'm saying right?" She taunted him by walking behind him and placing the top of her hands on top of his shoulders.

"Yes." He bowed his head not even able to look any of us in the eyes.

"Great! Now if you all excuse me, I have other shit to tend to." She walked past me and directly up to her Abuela who smiled a proud smile. Kissing her on the cheek she opened the double doors and left me sitting in the same spot wondering how the fuck did she think to get her own research in such short time. I thought she was so consumed with her sister's mess that she hadn't even thought to dig deep and find out what all the meeting was about. Once again, she proved me wrong and my liking for this woman rose a little more.

SOVEREIGN

$\mathcal{I}$ sat at the dinner table ignoring all the praise that I had been receiving from the meeting. Everyone seemed pleased with my actions except my bitch ass husband. Malice was really starting to become a nightmare for me. This whole marriage had me feeling like I was living in some twilight zone. It felt like he was trying to force cuffs on me and keep me as his personal prisoner. One thing I couldn't deny was how each time he eyed me, he caressed every part of my body. Sexually he was the best I ever had, he overpowered my body and had the magic key to make me say and do crazy shit in bed. My body caved in and bowed down to him every time. My mind always wanted the opposite.

"Eat your food, Sovereign." He looked at me from across the table, sitting his fork down. His rough deep voice sent tremors down my spine. Always demanding, always telling me what to do like I was a child of his. I was tired of Mexican food. It's all we ever ate day and night. I was ready to get back to the city. I needed to desperately get back to my sister. I needed to look her in the eyes and get some understanding. She was a part of me, if this was betrayal then she would be the third person to step all over my heart. A painful lump formed in my throat just thinking about my Empress. I was falling into a deep pit of depression, and I didn't know how to stop it.

I tried to force my armor of being strong to hide how I was feeling. Slowly but surely, I felt myself cracking into small pieces. Picking up my spoon I scooped up some rice and beans and placed the combination in my mouth. I tuned them out until Roberto looked at me and smiled. His aura seemed to lighten my mood, so I smiled back.

"You want kids with my hermano, chica?" He put the taquito between his index finger and thumb like it was a blunt and fake puffed from it before taking a bite.

"No, I don't. Kids will get in the way of business." I followed up, not wanting to reveal that I couldn't have kids. At least I thought I couldn't. If I could have kids, I'd never have them with a crazy muthafucca like his brother. I was plotting a way to get away from him when I made it back to the states. Once I saw Empress condition, I would take over and take her away from Malice people.

"Kids can be taken care of by di grandparents." My Abuela smiled as she picked up her cup and sipped. I ignored her and played around with my food. I could feel Malice eyes on me, and I ignored his stare. For years, I felt numb when it came to the opposite sex. The only thing I used a nigga for was sex and half the time that wasn't satisfying enough. The twins definitely pleased me by licking and sucking all over me, but they didn't compare to Inferno. Not even their average size dicks compared. Inferno dick was bigger than both of their dicks put together. The length and size, the way he stroked inside of me and touched me had me wet every time he was near.

I never gave a damn about who a nigga was laying pipe

too either until I stumbled on this dick head. He was to intense, too cocky, he knew how he operated in the bedroom. I hated him for trying to wake something up inside of me that I buried a long time ago with Melvin.

"Hermano." Roberto smiled and popped his cherry red lips. He stood up from the table and moved his imaginary bang from in front of his face. Roberto was so damn random, but I loved his randomness, while we sat at a table full of serious individuals Roberto was the one to lighten up the mood.

"Not now, Roberto. The adults are talking." He winked making me roll my eyes hard at him.

"I just want to say something really important since everybody's so serrrriiiooussss." He stood up and put his hand on his hip.

"I'm not gay no more...I am DELIVERT! I likes women." He dropped down low and popped his ass before standing back up. "I saiiiiddddd! I'm not gay no more! I like womenssss! Women! Women! Women!" He switched his hips and cat walked around the huge dinner table until he was standing behind me.

"Like Andrew Caldwell said. I am delivveeerttttt!" He kissed me on the forehead then cheek, placing his arms around my neck he hugged me from behind. I couldn't hold my laugh; I started cracking up. The look on Malice's face was comical. His brown skin turned red, even their father started to chuckle.

"Wheeewww, I saw that on TikTok honey. Y'all was starting to suffocate me with all this masculine dead energy." He fanned himself then stuffed his mouth with food. I found myself relaxing a tad bit. I still had a mission to go on at midnight. Murder was on my mind; I didn't give a damn about anything else but handling what my Abuela sent me to go do so then I could check up on my sister.

Excusing myself from the table, I went to Inferno's private study room where he was starting a new book collection. Pulling out my phone, I called the only person that I knew to keep it real with me.

"How are you, Queen?" His deep voice held skepticism in it. If anybody stay worried for me, it was Bundy.

"I'm worried, Bundy. How is she?" I took a seat behind the oak wood desk and placed Bundy on speaker.

"She's fine, not talking or making eye contact with anyone but she's fine. She has asked for you, said she needs to speak to you about somethings."

"I understand." I got quiet wishing I had a blunt and a glass of Dusse. I desperately needed something to calm down my anxiety.

"Teddy has been moving the same. I can see the worry in his eyes. You do understand that the kid was just protecting his household, right?" I could hear Bundy's heavy breathing; I nodded my head instinctively like he could see me. I had to pay Teddy a visit. I didn't want him to think that I was now against him. I understood that Empress was on some sneaky weird shit. Teddy killing Murk'um and shooting Empress was what Teddy was supposed to do. I was only human and couldn't help but to worry about Empress. It had been me and her when there was nobody else.

"I understand, let him know that it's all love and I'll see him soon." I tapped my fingers against the desk.

"Got you, Queen. I miss you, want you to be safe. Who been rolling up your blunts since you not around me?" I bowed my head and smiled, licking my lips I softly laughed. Bundy got on my nerves because he never hid the way he felt about me. He was a good friend and always made sure my needs were met, even if they were the smallest things.

"She has been rolling them herself, because she chooses to." Inferno stepped into the small dimly lit room. Flicking his lighter torch on and off. I pressed the end button on the call and looked into his eyes.

"Seems like he might be a problem that my flamethrower will solve." He walked around the desk right into my space. Taking a seat at the edge of the desk, he kept his eyes locked in with mine.

"Bundy is my business." I didn't blink, I just kept my gaze locked in with his.

"My wife business is my business." He smiled, leaning forward to stroke my left cheek. I hated the instant goosebumps that covered my skin just from one simple touch from him.

"You're sadly mistaken Malice, now if you will excuse me. I have to prepare for a late-night mission." I stood to my feet and prepared myself to walk away, until he grabbed me firmly by the wrist.

"I don't think you understand, Sovereign. The pussy is remarkable as fuck, it proceeds itself and speaks loud as fuck to me. It's so good that from now on, if I even think a nigga is fondling it or even fantasizing about feeling you then his flesh will burn slowly, until I have a nigga's skeleton bones in Hades." He yanked me between his legs and grabbed a handful of my ass, giving a tight firm squeeze, I simpered and closed my eyes briefly.

"You got a good mouthpiece on you; I can't wait to see the way these soft pretty, plump lips feel like on the tip of my dick. That tongue spit fire and I know when it strokes that sensitive vein on the shaft of my dick, I'll release down your virgin feeling throat. You're all mine Sovereign, you're a Ruiz. A Queen pin, you will learn your rightful place as my wife and the respect will follow." He released the grip he had on my ass and smacked my ass hard; the sting had my clit thumping hard.

"Now run along…. Do this last mission for your Abuella, so all of her skeletons can fall out of her closet. Daddy will be here to clean up another mess of yours." He stood off the desk, forcing me to take a couple of steps back from him. Grabbing my chin, Malice leaned down to kiss me and I turned my head letting the kiss land on my cheek. Squeezing my chin tight, he chuckled and walked away.

"Four men will accompany you tonight. My men, not your Abuella's. Enjoy tonight, this will be the last time you get your hands dirty. We are too wealthy for such things. It is an insult to me, to have my wife doing peasant kind of work." Closing the door behind him, I stood in the same spot for ten minutes straight. Shaking off the weird eerie feeling that formed into the pit of my stomach. I walked out of the room to go to our master suite to suit up for tonight's events.

"Remember, Sovereign… give them headshots. Nothing to be explained, in and out." My Abuela sat up in bed with her nightly glass of wine. I don't know why I traveled here first; she insisted that I came to see her before carrying out the hit she put me on.

"I hear you, Abuela." I gave a small smile. I hadn't told her about what all was going on back in the states. Tomorrow, I planned on explaining to her what all took place with her favorite grandchild.

"You make me so proud, El amado *(Beloved)*." She smiled and coughed a little. "I just wish, you Papa could see what all he could have been. Surely, he lives through you."

My heart ached at her revelation. I learned a long time ago to just let my Abuela talk. Elders were stuck in their own beliefs. I didn't like wasting time and energy trying to convince her of my own beliefs. I hated when she mentioned my father. She never acknowledged my mother unless she had something bad to say.

"When you see me tomorrow, we will talk about this Melvin... and his whereabouts." That brought me joy. I was ready to carry out this hit just to get a step closer to my own revenge. I leaned forward and placed a kiss to my Abuela's cheek. There was nothing left to say.

The city of Mexico seemed to never sleep. I loved the architecture of the entire country. Some parts were dirty and gritty. While other parts seemed magical. I thought back to how my father use to reminisce of being here and I remembered the pride he took in his country.

"I always know I'm home Mijo by the smell of fresh tortillas. It's all about life's simple pleasures." My father was a simple man; it never took too much to make him happy. I loved my mother the same but because of me being a daddy's girl, I missed him more.

Just like my Abuela said the city Pueblos Ma'gicos was lit up and looked very magical. Instead of trash being littered around on the streets, it was clean. No kids out roaming the streets. Everyone seemed to be in their homes sleep. This was like the Beverly Hills of Mexico. It was one way in and one way out making the escape more dangerous.

"Park around back, I don't need you all going in with me. I want to be in and out, no hiccups." I didn't like doing dirt with people. I didn't have time to be worried about the moves the other men made. Plus, I didn't feel comfortable with them. I didn't trust these niggas with my life.

"Don't get out this car, I don't need attention on us either." We were about an hour in a half away from Malice place. I had no plans of even going right back to his house either. I was going to spend the night at my Abuela's and then take the private jet back to Cali in the morning.

Hopping out so I wouldn't hear they're protesting to me making them stay in the car. The cold crisp air hit my face first, I threw my black hoodie over my head and glanced down at my rose gold Patek. It was nearing one in the morning. This couple was old, so I was sure that they had to be sleep. Checking my surroundings, I saw nothing out of the ordinary. My Maxim Nine Mili gun cost a grip. It was the world's first integrally suppressed nine-millimeter handgun. I didn't need to connect a silencer to it. I imagined the cost but didn't know because my Abuela gave it to me as a gift.

Walking through the backyard, I admired the rose-bed the married couple had leading up to the back door. My conscience told me something wasn't right when the back door unlocked and opened with no problem. The smell of fresh tortillas hit my nose first along with spices. The house was traditionally crafted out of stone walls and archways with low ceilings. I walked so softly, that I couldn't hear my own footsteps. The palms of my hands started to sweat from anticipation. It was different killing someone that had wronged me. I never killed for others especially not knowing why the fuck I was even killing.

My Abuela wanted me to shoot on sight. Hopefully they were tucked in bed sleep. The front room was dark, but the moonlight shone through.

"I've waited for you for over a decade. I purposely leave the front and back door open for Ju. Turn the light on and show me your pretty face Sovereign." That weakened voice came from a rocking chair that faced the window. His dry vocal cords sounded stringy and strained. I had the perfect opportunity to kill him now and find his wife. I couldn't do that because this old ass man called me by my government and not too many people had the pleasure of knowing that. Curiosity coursed through me as I squinted to find the light switch.

Once the light came on, I quickly walked around until I came face to face with a wrinkly old man that looked like he was in his late eighties.

"We don't have much time Sovereign." My hands started to shake as I licked my lips.

"Time for what?" I gritted placing my index finger on the trigger.

"My execution. My little sister is very powerful and persistent. She sent you here to kill me and my wife." My stomach tightened and a million questions roamed through my mind. If Abuela would kill her own brother, who else would she kill.

"Tio (*Uncle*)?" That voice instantly brought tears to my eyes. My skin became clammy, and I started to sweat profusely even though the house was cold. I hadn't seen that face since a kid, but I'd never forget that thick accent and deep voice. "Who are you in here talking to?" My breathing became shallow as I attempted to speak but nothing came out. I was starting to become overwhelmed with a million emotions as the footsteps down the dark hallway came closer.

I saw his face first, and we both remained stuck in place as if time stood still.

"We don't have much time, Mijo." I heard this crazy old man talking but my eyes were currently locked in with my....

"Papa?" I said a little above a whisper before everything started to spin around me. My vision blurry, I felt myself hitting the cold tile floor before darkness consumed me.

To be continued......

CONTACT THE AUTHOR

Leave a Review! Tell me what you think! ~ Masterpiece

CONTACT THE AUTHOR

Contact the author!

Hey Pieces! It means so much to me to get your honest feedback. Please feel free to join my private readers group on Facebook! **Masterpiece Readers**

Join my mailing list by texting **Masterpiecebooks** altogether to the number 22828!

Contact me on any of my social media handles as well!

Facebook- Authoress Masterpiece & Masterpiece Reads

Facebook private group for updates- Masterpiece Readers

Instagram- authoress_masterpiece & masterpiece_lgee

Email – masterpiece3541@outlook.com

Made in United States
Orlando, FL
02 May 2023

32710045R00139

JAMES FENIMORE COOPER:
New Critical Essays

JAMES FENIMORE COOPER:
New Critical Essays

edited by
Robert Clark

VISION
and
BARNES & NOBLE

Vision Press Limited
Fulham Wharf
Townmead Road
London SW6 2SB

and

Barnes & Noble Books
81 Adams Drive
Totowa, NJ 07512

ISBN (UK) 0 85478 086 6
ISBN (US) 0 389 20592 3

Printed and bound in Great Britain by
Unwin Brothers Ltd.,
Old Woking, Surrey.
Phototypeset by Galleon Photosetting,
Ipswich, Suffolk.
MCMLXXXV

Contents

Introduction

When I began seeking contributions to this book I had three aims: I wanted to broaden our view of Cooper beyond the Leatherstocking tales, I wanted to develop our understanding of the relationship of Cooper's work to its historical moment, and I wanted to demonstrate how recent advances in critical method now made it possible to discuss aspects of Cooper's writing that had been held in oblivion by previous orthodoxies. I also hoped to publish work by established Cooper scholars, by relative newcomers to Cooper studies, and by critics who had not written on Cooper but whose critical approaches I wanted to see applied to his work.

It is a rare future that corresponds exactly to our initial desire, especially when that future depends upon such seemingly contingent yet deeply significant factors as who is interested in what at the moment your letter arrives. Thus, the historians I wanted to write about Cooper's influence on his society were preoccupied with other concerns, but three critics were developing perspectives on *The Pioneers* each of which in its own way seemed too good to miss. We therefore have a volume that departs slightly from one of my aims in order to satisfy the other two, and a range of thinking about a central Cooper text which by virtue of publication within the same volume highlights the complementary nature of individual critical acts—and the irreducibility of the text to one single and correct reading. While on the negative side we can be sure that some critical readings are wrong, on the positive we can only agree on the kinds of discourse that are productive of significance, and perhaps on the social factors that determine their power.

It is a matter of curiosity to me sitting down to introduce these essays that whilst Richard Godden in Keele was opening a perspective on *The Pioneers* by reading the literal figuratively

7

and the figurative literally, Eric Cheyfitz in Washington was linking Aristotle's distinctions between these same terms to Cooper's representation of Indian language and his sense of the 'frontier'. The approach is highly germane to Cooper, arguments between Natty and Dr. Batt about the figurative and the literal having filled many of the lulls in *The Prairie*, but it is one that has been neglected by Cooper scholars who have generally followed Cooper's contemporaries in taking a common-sense view of language. Another nexus of concern that links these essays is Cooper's attempt to legitimize his own position, and that of his class, with respect to the national destiny and the lower orders: a theme which surfaces in Heinz Ickstadt's thinking in Berlin, Charles Swann's in Keele, and my own in East Anglia. Yet another nexus, one linking the work of Cheyfitz to that of Brotherston and McWilliams, is the construction of Cooper's Indians out of literary and imaginative materials that function to deny or obscure an actual history Cooper seems to have understood more profoundly than any of his white contemporaries. Linking all these essays is a shared concern to explore the 'madeness' of Cooper's writing, a rejection of the still potent old new critical assumption that the critic's task is to reveal the coherence (for even ambiguity is but contradiction made coherent), mastery and univocality of the text. Equally rejected is the assumption of the once-popular myth-and-symbol school that the critic is free to offer his or her interpretation of the text as an uncovering of actual and universally held attitudes towards gender, the land, the function of the individual within the nation's history. In place of such assumptions, the contributors to this volume assume that literature is a complex mediation of historical experience, offer scholarly research into Cooper's conditions of production, and also bring to bear an interest in the problematic, the inconsistent, that haunts his writing.

It is this last aspect, one frequently noticed by early reviewers but scarcely studied by the critical institution, that seems to me most in need of further analysis, not just at the level of physical implausibility so hilariously anathematized by Twain, but also at the levels that Eric Cheyfitz points out—the fact (also picked up by Twain and used to preface *Huckleberry Finn*) that characters do not appear to be talking to

8

each other, rather lost in a private language; or, as in Richard Godden's reading, that *The Pioneers* contains not one plot but many, some of which are subversive of others, some of which are manifest, others repressed; or in Gordon Brotherston's long-needed (158 years) dissection of what is and is not said about the Indians in *The Prairie.* Cooper, after all, is an historian who consistently got his history wrong, a narrator given to the trite, the hackneyed, the obvious, the absurd, the utterly incredible. He is also the author of at least several books which have been rarely out of print in most languages of the world during the last century and a half, a man far more widely read in historical terms than any American novelist before Hemingway, Fitzgerald and Faulkner. His works also remain in many ways the most profound testament to one of history's most determining events, the destruction of the Amerindian peoples and the concomitant loss of their way of life, the conquest of 3,000,000 square miles of land and the political establishment of the present world's dominant nation state.

I would contend that Cooper's historical significance does not come about *in spite of* his literary failings, as it is usually thought to do, but rather *because of* them: put another way, that the ideological and historical complexity of the experiences he relates cannot be expressed in a fiction that protects itself from absurdity. To exemplify the point, let me rehearse two moments from *Oak Openings* that Heinz Ickstadt's and Gordon Brotherston's essays call to mind. One concerns the Bee-Hunter's dog Hive, a large mastiff not likely to be missed yet somehow not mentioned in the apparently full description of the Bee-Hunter's life which opens the novel. Hive is only introduced much later on when Cooper feels the need for a tracker-dog to search out the Indians. We are then treated to a description of Hive's very large kennel standing a small distance from the Bee-Hunter's *chienté*, and a retrospective description of how when Boden (the Bee-Hunter) returned home in the opening chapters he had attentively fed and cosseted his dog. From the reader's point of view this can only seem odd since a large mastiff is usually the first thing to strike one's attention when returning home from a long trip. It does not come as an afterthought.

Shortly after Hive has entered the narrative Boden and Whiskey Centre spend three days voyaging down the Kalamazoo and then several more skirmishing with a party of Powattamies at the entrance to Lake Michigan. During all this time there is no mention of Hive, but several days later again there he is, bounding along the bank, as Bourdon makes his way homeward. The dog pops in and out of the narrative in this way until he is finally left locked in the palisaded *chienté* when the Powattamies burn it down. Although the Indians sift the ashes for the bones of Boden and his friends, no dog bones are mentioned. Nor, come to think of it, did the dog howl or even whimper as he was burned to death. Perhaps Cooper simply forgot about him. Certainly he does not reappear.

The second instance concerns the nourishment of Boden, Whiskey Centre, Blossom and Margery for three days when they are in hiding after the *chienté* has been burned down. They are hiding under a fallen tree very near the smouldering ruins, surrounded by hundreds of Indians who are searching everywhere for them. Because Cooper shares with Poe and Melville a fascination with 'how-to' pragmatism, a fascination which is central to pioneering capitalism and, as Poe constantly reveals, a way of granting local plausibility to general absurdities, he is impelled to tell us how the party fed during this period. Their diet consisted of 'a dozen large squirrels' (420)[1] and some fish, an explanation which might lead the careful reader to suspect that the party, ladies included, had been chewing raw flesh during this period. Certainly such a thought seems to occur to Cooper for seven pages later he is at pains to point out that as it was far too dangerous to light a fire in the day-time, 'the cooking of the party had been done at night, the utmost caution having been used to prevent the fire itself from having been seen.' Such a remark, while closing off the problem of the raw and the cooked, makes the narrative even less plausible; what has become of those renowned faculties, the Indian sense of smell, the acuteness of their hearing? And can we really believe that a fire can be better hid in the night than during the day?

These are small instances of the illogical logic of any Cooper text. What is of interest is that the reader reads on, usually unperturbed, and Cooper writes on, seemingly confident that

10

Introduction

out there beyond the frontier such minor flaws (and such larger ones as the question of which tribes lived where and when) can be left behind, swallowed up in the *tabula rasa* of the white men's maps which, having obliterated all antithetical history, tell no tales. Perhaps Cooper is just concerned to write a saleable adventure and this only requires a sufficient diet of death, fear, conflict, heroism, treachery, escape, romance. Cooper's narratives, like the Westward movement, are object lessons in how to keep making money by moving on, no matter the obstacles, no matter the mental cost.

I think it important to recognize the dominant pragmatism in the writing because this is what unifies texts otherwise at risk of breaking under their own contradictions. It is what, in effect, makes them readable by Cooper's culture; it is the law of its verisimilitude. Again *Oak Openings* can furnish example; in it Cooper offers some of his most forthright condemnations of white expansionism, even going so far as to have Margery pronounce that the Indians 'have a better right to the land than the Whites' (312) and offering some exposés of Christian hypocrisy that rival those of Melville in their devastating implications for the ideology of continental settlement. This said, however, Cooper-as-author speaks wholeheartedly in favour of the need for Christian morality as an essential supplement to Reason, and of his faith in God's providential design for the progress of (North American) Man towards perfection (319, 413). Cooper's authorial voice thus siding with an ideology that his heroine's voice has exploded, one could hypothesize an author who intends to ironize his own agreement with the attitudes of a conformist readership. My own interpretation is rather that the author's voice and those of his characters articulate a series of contradictions that Cooper seeks to resolve by continuous displacement, a pragmatic solution of the kind that was used to resolve the conflict over slave labour, free labour and most other tensions in the ante-bellum years.

To take the point further, in *Oak Openings* as in all his novels after *Home as Found*, Cooper offers several set-piece attacks on the power of the demagogue to mislead the multitude. These passages express the alarm of the Democratic gentry at their marginalization by 'Mobocracy', at the growth of the urban political machine and at the power of the press. Against the oratorical demagogue and the growing power of mass society, Cooper implicitly offers the book as an inherently rational and democratic form, one that speaks from one man to another, that allows close examination of its arguments and that demands thought in production and reception. Samuel Johnson and other eighteenth-century enlighteners would have agreed, but there is a marked class bias to this belief, access to print requiring literacy and social connections whereas speaking to one's fellows requires only a larynx. Cooper's position in effect amounts to no more than an argument for gentlemanly rather than popular means of exchange. Now if, as we have seen above, gentlemanly narrative authority practises its own deceptions on the credulity of readers, its ability to criticize demagoguery is fatally undermined. Cooper's formal and narrative strategies can thus be discussed in terms of both political rhetoric (the act of persuasion), and as attempts to provide imaginary resolution to the contradictions of his ideological and class positions.

The snug fit between Cooper's pragmatism on the one hand and the Enlightenment ideology of the book on the other has tended to ensure that the implausible and inconsistent be passed over in order to allow the real business of discussing Cooper's characters and events. In a common-sensical world it violates the paradigm of good taste, and threatens the iconic value of the text from whose power the critic in turn derives his social significance, to point out that the master is not masterful. The speedy consequence of such thinking is to question whether anyone is, more especially those who claim such status, and radical deconstruction ensues. Yet surely this is what those of us who believe in a progressive and improving history should now be doing, for to analyse the content of a Cooper text without analysing its form is at least to do only half a job, at worst to repeat unconsciously the paradigm: discuss, for example, 'the frontier' in Cooper's work, as many essays have done, without expressing the arbitrary and mythological form of this concept, and the myth is thereby given a new lease of life, critically reinscribed in the consciousness of another generation. Criticism in this sense comes dangerously close to losing its function as a demystifier and becomes the reverse: the way a rational and sceptical age has of rejuvenating decrepit myths. Cooper's work has been all too useful in this respect. I hope this volume will lead readers in an alternative direction and help us understand the radical uncertainties that gave birth to his writing.

NOTES

1. Page references are to the Mohawk Edition (London and New York: G. P. Putnam's Sons, 1896).

13

1

Instructing the American Democrat: Cooper and the Concept of Popular Fiction in Jacksonian America

by HEINZ ICKSTADT

In American nineteenth-century literature there is partially submerged tradition of bourgeois fiction which is linked, in theory and practice, to an idea of democracy, an idea of the People. It derives from the Enlightenment, and those figures in American literary history who most fully, almost tragically represent it, though central to their time and culture, were inevitably left behind when continuities broke down and history entered a new phase of accelerated changes. William Dean Howells, who recorded the symptoms of his growing obsolescence long before he died, was such a figure—as was James Fenimore Cooper, Howells's senior by half a century.[1] Their careers and, with certain qualifications, also their literary theories resemble one another to the point of duplication. Both shared the universalist assumptions of eighteenth-century Humanism and the Enlightenment, both were deeply committed to an idea of the 'Old Republic' and struggled to recognize its image in the turmoil of new or still evolving socio-economic orders; both conceived of their literary profession as a business and as a quasi-public office and defined the novel in terms not only of its aesthetic but also of its social and political functions, i.e. as a specifically democratic and thus popular art.

I shall enquire into some of Cooper's ideological assumptions; analyse the thematic and structural tensions and ambiguities in several of his novels within a context of intense national debate on the meaning and direction of American democracy; compare Cooper's concept of the People with that of his fellow-Jacksonian George Lippard; and finally discuss the changes that were going on within the system of the novel by the time of Cooper's death.

1

Literature—still understood in the broader sense of 'Letters' —for Cooper was a means of social influence and power, an occupation worthy of a gentleman whose father had once hoped to see him in high office—the highest, in fact. 'Books'— Cooper wrote in his very first novel—'are the instruments of controlling the opinion of a nation like ours. They are engines alike powerful to save or to destroy.'[2] Accordingly, he believed that there was 'perhaps no class of men' more effective in the general interest of humanity than 'popular writers of high character'.[3] One should note that Cooper explicitly links the importance of literature to its popularity and that he sees the manipulatory misuse of that power as being checked by the author's moral sense and his awareness of his public function.[4] If the writer followed moral principles he was above party and self-interest, on 'neutral ground'[5]; if he voiced what everybody was able, yet perhaps not always willing, to recognize as true and just, he could not help but act and write in the name and interest of the general public.

In his *Notions of the Americans* (1828)—which he wrote during the first years of his voluntary exile in Paris—Cooper projected American society as an ideal republic of responsible and sober citizens where classes were existent yet 'separated by less impassable barriers' than in Europe,[6] where 'common instruction' was widely diffused, and incentive for individual achievement balanced by considerations of social solidarity. Cooper admitted to a certain impoverishment of the aesthetic sense but felt it was amply compensated for by 'a simple dignity in moral truths, that dims the lustre of all the meretricious gloss which art and elegance can confer on life' (127). In America, unlike in any other nation, common sense had been established 'as the sovereign guide to public will' (228). To be sure, not

> every man . . . was wise enough to discriminate between the substance and the shadow of things, but so many are as to have given a tone to the general deportment of the whole. (236f.)

This rule of common sense and the certainty that 'in the tossings and agitations of . . . public opinion, the fine and precious grains of truth gradually get winnowed from the chaff of empiricism and interestedness' (230), was, for Cooper, founded on America's political institutions. These, he believed with many Democrats, were the embodiment of Reason in social relations and established a just, if complex, balance between individual freedom and collective interest. Literature, within that context, became a public institution, a secular church,[7] whose function had to be at once affirmative, critical and exhortatory: affirmative, because in its commitment to the democratic doctrine it accepted the existing social order in recognition of its latent ideality; critical and exhortatory, because the public had to be reminded of, or yet instructed in, the moral virtues and the civic consciousness required to maintain its institutions.

In his fictions, therefore, Cooper pursued a twofold purpose. They were to instruct the American democrat in what it meant to be American: that is, to make him understand the past and yet to be completed struggle to transform a state of wilderness into a state of civilization as the true meaning of American history. At the same time, by providing models of right conduct and by dramatizing the 'simple dignity of moral truths', they themselves were thought to function as moralizing and civilizing agents that helped fulfil the project Cooper ostensibly enacted on the thematic level of his novels.

Cooper acted out his public rôle as man of letters in the guise of novelist, historian, political essayist and pamphleteer; and even though he regarded his literary endeavours as related yet different modes of discourse, he often enough—especially in the novels of his later phase—blurred distinctions, crossed border-lines. The didactic, however, from the beginning, is encoded in

17

his fictions as an aspect of their public function. Since fiction was to be above public opinion and yet instrumental in the shaping of it, the different processes by which 'truth emanates from the collisions of minds'[8] form an essential part of his narrative structure. Speech-making, sermonizing, debate, court or trial, and tribal council are, therefore, recurring elements in an overall formal design that displays the novel's commitment to a republican idea of justice as well as its affinity to republican institutions. As one might expect, a fictional mode which is so clearly meant for communication, and in which communication and its forms themselves become topical, follows, stylistically as well as structurally, an ideal of simplicity. In a famous authorial digression, directed in all likelihood against the gothic darkness of Charles Brockden Brown, Cooper insisted on merely wanting to treat

> of man and this fair scene on which he acts . . . , not in his subtleties and metaphysical contradictions, but in his palpable nature, that all may understand our meaning as well as our-selves—whereby we manifestly reject the prodigious advantage of being thought a genius. . . .[9]

Such writing may considerably vary established narrative conventions but its innovations—and Cooper considered himself, with some justification, an innovative writer—are predominantly in the area of subject matter. For his fictive traveller in *Notions of the Americans*, 'the only peculiarity that can, or ought to be expected in their literature, is that which is connected with their distinctive political opinions.'[10] Cooper, who once confessed to a friend that he would gladly go to his grave if he had succeeded in contributing anything to America's mental independence,[11] defined that independence exclusively in terms of republican consciousness. Apart from it, individual or national peculiarities were to be measured and controlled by universal standards of 'refined simplicity and considerate humanity'.[12]

I have sketched Cooper's conception of the public dimension of his literary project and of his rôle as man of letters because its latent contradictions affected especially his later work as well as his career. He could not convincingly maintain his rôle of disinterested gentleman who spoke in the interest of the

'People'—not at least in a society which defined 'People' more and more in terms of either individual and mass, or honest poor and idle rich. Nor could he balance a cultural particularity rooted in nature with his belief in a cosmopolitan culture of style and manners. Most of all, his formal and thematic pursuit of justice began to jarr with the ideological assumption of his project that justice and reason were inherent in the idea and institutional form of the republic, and that conflict of opinion was therefore bound to issue in consensus. In his various endeavours he tried to centre a dynamic expansionist-capitalist society on eighteenth-century principles in order to symbolically control change and secure continuity. In the end, he was forced to either resign the 'Myth of the Republic'[13] altogether, or to modify it in Jacksonian terms, that is in terms of westward expansion and the common man. Eventually, he chose the latter. But his increasing difficulty in holding together the public and the private, in identifying gentry interest with the commonweal and thus in maintaining a vision of American history that was at once progressive, just and above party, points to changes and disruptions not only in the society but within the system of letters as well.

2

In his study of the American historical imagination Harry Henderson perceived in Cooper's work a fundamental tension between an awareness of historical process and a vision of cultural wholeness.[14] With the latter Henderson meant an ideal of social life realized in the customs and manners of a community or group, in Cooper's case that of the American landed gentry. It could either be conceived of as utopian image of a higher civilization which history was progressively fulfilling, or as a nostalgically remembered image of a past which history was in the process of destroying. One can say—with some simplification—that during the first part of Cooper's literary career (which, for all practical purposes, was cut in half by his seven years in Europe from 1826 till 1833) the dominant structure of his fiction is progressive, clearly showing his intention to 'unite the country around its past' and in the promise of its future. The novels of his later phase, however, are pervaded with a sense of loss and of decline; here historic process is thrown into doubt, if not seen altogether as a destructive agent.

Of the two topics Cooper exclusively dealt with in his earlier phase—the history of the American Revolution and the history of settlement and Indian warfare in upper New York State—I shall concern myself, however briefly, with the second. In dealing with the removal of the Indians and with the rightful ownership of the land, he very toughly chose issues which were not only of traumatic relevance for himself[15] but touched directly on the legitimacy of the republic. Furthermore—as Robert Clark has argued persuasively—Cooper was dealing with a past (already become legend in the East) which was repeated as contemporary history all along the frontier and, in Jackson's programme of Indian removal, was to become the very core of an official policy of economic and territorial expansion.[16] Even though *The Pioneers, The Last of the Mohicans* and *The Prairie* were written before Jackson came to power, and even though they represent a republic which was centred in the villages and pastoral landscape of the East and whose western expansion had reached its final limit at the Mississippi, they established a pattern of historical interpretation that satisfied an increasing need for collective justification, consolation and atonement.

In all three novels—most clearly in *The Pioneers*—the states of nature and of civilization are set against each other in radical opposition. At the same time, they are connected in an ascending scale of hierarchy as successive stages of a progressive history. Each stage has its own 'ideal of social life' (Henderson)—Indians, hunters, squatters, settlers and the gentry—deriving identity from its specific relation to the land; and the competing claims of these various groups to use or own the land according to their different rights and habits make for the most important conflicts of these books. The novel, in all of these cases, has some resemblance to a court where the claimants argue their case and justice is spoken in accordance with the highest law—that is, the law sanctioned by the upward movement of history. The ascendence of the gentry—confirmed, in the end, by marriage, inheritance and re-established genealogy—is linked inevitably to the decline of its opponents, and fiction justifies and at the same time absolves the victors by giving dignity to the defeated; Chingachgook's melancholy and his apocalyptic death by fire, as well as the apotheosis of the dying Natty Bumppo, are glorifications of what is known to be irretrievably lost to history's upward movement.

The world of these earlier Leatherstocking Tales is neatly ordered into sequences of semantic oppositions and analogies; on all levels of hierarchy the forces of good confront those of evil (the lines are not quite so sharply drawn in *The Pioneers*). And since the different stages of hierarchy are separated and connected in a great chain of being which rises from nature and culminates in civilization, there is a clear line of succession by which virtue and legitimate ownership is handed on from Chingachgook to Natty via Judge Temple to Oliver Effingham (the line of virtue and order), just as there is a line of negative succession (a line of selfishness and anarchy) which runs with a diminishing degree of moral aberration from Magua to Ishmael Bush to the ecologically wasteful settlers of *The Pioneers*. No doubt there is the tension—early noticed by Sainte-Beuve—between alternative social visions ('The two dreams of Rousseau: the man of nature, and a social contract unanimously agreed upon'),[17] but the novels are firmly anchored in hierarchy, and the gloom and final apotheosis of the vanishing order is part of a ritual of legitimation and emotional purgation arranged from the perspective and for the benefit of the victor. However, the tension that Sainte-Beuve had pointed out was bound to increase when the hierarchy itself came into doubt and the price paid for civilization did not seem equal to the value received from it. This feeling of malaise, hinted at in *The Pioneers*, deepened over the following years, not only with Cooper but in the culture itself which exulted as much in the triumphs of progress as it observed them with anxiety. 'The ravages of the axe are daily increasing—the most noble scenes are made desolate, and oftentimes with a wantonness and barbarism scarcely creditable in a civilized nation', wrote Cooper's friend, the painter Thomas Cole. 'Such is the road society has to travel; it may lead to refinement in the end, but the traveller who sees the place of rest close at hand, dislikes the road that has so many unnecessary windings.'[18] In the case of

Cooper, this aesthetic and moral anxiety was ultimately connected with the question of whether history was indeed about to by-pass the gentry, the only guarantors of true civilization, and thus to destroy 'Nature's beauty without substituting that of Art'.[19]

3

Cooper left the United States in 1826 when John Quincy Adams, the last president of the old political and social élite, was still in office; and he returned in 1833 under Jackson, a president whose republican-agrarian rhetoric he shared and whose fight against Congress and the Mother-Monster Bank he had supported from abroad. If anything, Cooper's commitment to the idea of the republic had increased while in Europe and he tended to link the American institutions to the happiness of all mankind.[20] He had witnessed the revolution of 1830 in Paris; his house had been a centre of republican sympathies and open to European—especially Polish—refugees from feudalism. He had written three explicitly political novels—*The Bravo* (1831), *The Heidenmauer* (1832) and *The Headsman* (1833)—which, as he wrote, applied republican (i.e. American) principles to European facts.[21] And although he was highly irritated by the adverse criticism these books had received by an American press he knew was in the hands of his political enemies, he believed that the order of the Old Republic was, in fact, strengthening. After the revolution, the American gentry had made the mistake of putting themselves in opposition to the mass: 'they fancied there were irreconcilable interests to separate the rich man from the poor man, and that they had nothing to expect from the latter class should it get into the ascendant. . . . The error', he continued, 'has been discovered and . . . the nation shows all proper deference to education and character.'[22] However, this hoped-for alliance between the people and its intellectual and social élite never came about—as he found out when he tried to rouse his constituency, the reading public, with a grandiosely titled 'Letter to His Countrymen' (1834) in which he related his own mistreatment by the American press to Jackson's mistreatment by Congress and both to the American public's willingness to let itself be manipulated by foreign opinion and a financial oligarchy of *nouveaux riches*.[23] Therefore, he concluded, since his country evidently did not need his service as a novelist, it was time for him to resign the office and to end his literary career as author of public-minded fictions. (He resumed it after four years of abstinence.) But if he had expected to shock his readers into more political awareness, he was disappointed—instead of loyalty, he received ridicule.

However, since it was in the character of a true democrat to compete in the market of opinions, and a gentleman's duty to be the guardian of the principles of his community,[24] he engaged in public controversy with even more and grimmer determination. The stubbornness and occasional gusto with which he took Horace Greeley and several other editors of the Whig press to court on charges of slander were less a matter of personal vindictiveness than an effort to make his private grievance a test case of public (and republican) rights and institutions.[25]

Cooper had started his defence of principles with an attack on the new financial élite whom he suspected of trying to use Congress and its legislative power to establish a quasi-oligarchic rule.[26] The more he became entangled in lawsuits and public altercations, however, the more it seemed to him that it was the larger public which was corrupt or easily corruptible—without knowledge of, nor care for, the institutions, without heart, taste or discrimination, its only interest money and fast success. So much did he in fact identify his literary production, indeed his whole existence, with the political traditions of his country that he blamed his diminishing literary reputation on readers who 'in their hearts, are deadly opposed to the[se] institutions'.[27]

Therefore he rarely made use of the dominant political rhetoric of the period which set the People (the mass of honest producers) against the Aristocrats (the moneyed and idle few)—a rhetoric which could be used by almost anybody and to all purposes, as the Democrats found out in the election of 1840 when the Whigs out-Jacksonianed the Jacksonians in populist appeal.[28] But by giving in to his growing irritation with public opinion and the mass, and by seeking the dangers of a system only in the particularities of the system itself, he sidestepped the issue of power which was implied in Jacksonian rhetoric and of which he had been conscious before. In formulations that anticipate the later fears of intellectual élites of mass society, he identified the unprincipled leadership of the mass media and the unprincipled opinions of the majority as sources of a political corruption peculiar to democracies: 'In Democracies there is a besetting disposition to make publick opinion stronger than the law. This is the particular form in which tyranny exhibits itself in a popular government'[29]; and: 'I resist the tyranny I find in the country: not that which exists in distant lands.'[30]

In his primer of American democracy, *The American Democrat* (1838), the social claims of an élite of enlightened and propertied few are set against those of an unenlightened mass which in its eagerness to place opinion over law, self-interest over public interest, endangers the life of the republic. And yet, Cooper had not given up the People—he denounced them in terms of mass and mass opinion but he felt also tied to them, even when in violent disagreement, by virtue of his faith in the republic. His effort at public 'censure and correction' was part of his public rôle as man of letters and an investment in 'the counteracting influence of reason, which, in the end, seldom, perhaps never, fails to assert its power'.[31]

However, there can be no question that he regarded the People as enlightened only when they recognized a natural social hierarchy which distributed social and political responsibilities according to talent, and whose cornerstone was private property. There were abuses, to be sure:

> [C]ivilization has established various and in some cases, arbitrary and unjust distinctions, as pertaining to the rights of property. . . . Still, most of the ordinances of civilized society, that are connected with that interest, are founded in reason, and ought to be rigidly maintained.[32]

If rights were equal, nature was not—but the consolations of religion were equally available to all.

Cooper's toughly argued position is essentially a reworking of Jeffersonian doctrine and as such more or less in line with the laissez-faire convictions of Jacksonian democracy. What separated him from his more radical, more egalitarian fellow-Jacksonians was his insistence on defending rights on the basis

24

of existing hierarchies—whereas they regarded these and the laws protecting them as artificial barriers to a free economy of nature and to the natural right of equal opportunity. Cooper's rigid defence of property rights during the 1840s was therefore bound to exasperate some of his admirers who, like George Lippard, found his conduct during the so-called Anti-Rent-War inexplicable in a 'novelist writing for the People'.[33] Obviously for Cooper and Lippard the term 'People' referred to something very different, as was inevitable in a society in which the language and the ideals of the Fathers were applied to new social and cultural conditions, and appropriated by different groups to legitimize or camouflage their particular interests; in which continuity was promised in the survival of republican rhetoric, and change evident in conflicting re-interpretations of original meanings.

To move from Cooper to one of Cooper's literary children is therefore perhaps less questionable than it might at first appear. Responding to the period's egalitarian rhetoric as well as to its experience of social and economic crisis—his family had severely suffered in the economic depression of 1837—George Lippard extended the concepts of the literary Enlightenment downward to include the poor people and the working class, thereby committing the novel more than Cooper had done to conditions of the market and of a specific mode of publication (its serialization in the newspaper). Like Cooper, Lippard walked the borderline between literature and politics, and in his rôles as novelist, journalist, editor and labour leader he pursued an early form of Christian Socialism. Inspired by the European revolutions of 1848, he founded a working-men's organization in Philadelphia in 1850 (the influential Brotherhood of the Union, predecessor of the Knights of Labour) which outlived him and his uncertain literary reputation long into the twentieth century. We do not know whether Cooper ever read Lippard (or answered the letters Lippard addressed to him); yet we do know that Lippard not only grew up on Cooper but absorbed him a second time via the fiction of Eugène Sue who, in his *Les Mystères de Paris*, had transplanted Cooper's hunters and Indians from the American wilderness to the urban jungle of the French metropolis.[34] Ironically, Cooper, in some of his later novels, inverted the procedure and used his own familiar formulas of Indian warfare to deal with contemporary social and political conflict.

4

Such is the case in *Oak Openings* (1848), the last of Cooper's Indian romances and, in a sense, a revision of the Leatherstocking cycle from a position of renewed confidence in the course of American history. Seven years before, in *The Deerslayer*, Cooper had apparently lost that confidence altogether; there is no indicated line of succession that would symbolically assure the continuity of tradition and of hierarchy. Deerslayer seems locked into a mythic past before the arrival of civilization—the embodiment of a dream of natural man (at once free *and* virtuous), proved impossible by history and therefore transfigured into myth. Terrence Martin and more recently William P. Kelly have argued that *Deerslayer*, rather than being a flight into myth and phantasy, was Cooper's debunking of a mythic history of progress that he had projected in the earlier Leatherstocking tales.[35] However, it seems to me that Cooper never completely resigned his faith. If, in enacting 'the end of pre-history', *The Deerslayer* anticipates, in cyclical closure, the end of civilized history itself, it also counteracts such closure through strategies of admonition and example. Like much liberal and reformist fiction up to Howells's *A Hazard of New Fortunes* it contains elements of a morality play in which the virtuous simplicity of Natty Bumppo and the sacrificial spirit of the simple-minded Hetty hold promise of spiritual redemption in a world dominated by the meretricious and the rapacious.[36] The final vision, combining the hortatory with the apocalyptic, shows nature growing over the ruins of a rudimentary civilization which had brought on its own destruction by violence and the sins of economic man. It is an image reminiscent of the last painting of Thomas Cole's sycle 'The Course of Empire', and it anticipates *The Crater* (1847), Cooper's symbolic foundation and subsequent destruction of an ideal Jeffersonian republic which incurred God's and Nature's wrath by succumbing to 'the enemy within'—the forces of greed and selfishness.[37]

Such elements of apocalyptic prophecy are absent from *Oak Openings*, even though it was published just one year after Cooper's classic jeremiad. On the contrary, all warnings against the 'enemy within' are integrated into a pervasive rhetoric of national aggrandizement. After so many years of bitterness and alienation it is Cooper's first novel of acceptance, and it is significant that his affirmation should be projected once again in the pattern of progressive history. Correspondingly, the question of the rightful ownership of the land and the idea of the just republic again become the central themes. However, in order to hold on to an ideal of 'justice in a republic' (the phrase is John McWilliams's), Cooper had to re-design his earlier project to a considerable extent, and the clash between the novel's ideological purpose and its formal strategies of reasoned discourse make for sudden inversions and breakdowns in narrative as well as argumentative logic. First of all, there are no gentry figures; the real cultural hero is the hunter who—in the manner of Jacksonian self-made men—rises to become settler and the political leader of the province. In *The Deerslayer* Cooper had modelled an ideal frontiersman quite distinct from the killer-hero as he was projected in Montgomery Bird's Nathan Slaughter, for instance, who is a Quaker by day and a raving savage by night.[38] However, if Deerslayer kills ceremoniously and with great reluctance and subsequent sorrow, Le Bourdon, Cooper's hero in *Oak Openings*, is removed from violence altogether. As a bee-hunter who combines careful observation of nature with an artistic sense of craft, he is already part of civilization. Therefore, the transition from one state of being to another (from the 'savage' to the 'civilised') which was accompanied by friction and mourning in the earlier novels, is allowed to happen much more smoothly here. The price paid for such easy triumph, is, of course, a loss in intellectual honesty.

The setting of the story is Michigan, the time 1812 at the beginning of the British-American war when England had incited its Canadian Indians to attack several American forts in that area. Le Bourdon and a small group of white people and loyal Reds try to escape from hostile tribes down the Kalamazoo River toward Lake Michigan. They realize too late that their most fearful enemy is in their midst—an

27

imposing and charismatic figure, Onoah or Scalping Peter, who acts as their scout. Cooper indeed re-uses an old formula with Onoah as Magua, Le Bourdon as Natty and Pigeonswing as Chingachgook under another name. However, the differences, not only in the conception of the hunter but in the portrayal of the Indian, are important. Scalping Peter is modelled after Tecumseh and described in the idealizing manner of Catlin's Indian paintings. He is at once noble and deceiving, an eloquent spokesman for the Indians' cause, and a leader above tribe who plans to unite all Indians in an uprising against white dominance. In the most impressive chapters of the book Indian chiefs and white men come together in a tribal council to argue out their different ideas of justice. Onoah, a powerful orator, is allowed to present in very concrete terms the grievances of the dispossessed. It is at this point, when it is clear that the history of white conquest cannot be reconciled with either Reason or the idea of Justice, that argument gives way to faith in Providence and to strategies of consolation.[39] The Indians kill two of the whites one of whom, a Methodist preacher, forgives his murderers as he dies. Whereupon Scalping Peter, overwhelmed by this example of Christian conduct, experiences conversion. He, the imposing figure of savage authority, becomes meek and helpless like a child, gladly submitting to the superior paternal wisdom (not power!) of the whites: 'I now *love* Yankees . . . Now I feel like a child' (408–9).[40] In the last chapter—which is told by an authorial narrator visiting Michigan thirty years after the narrated events—Le Bourdon (or General Boden[41] as he is now called) is married and has become the political and cultural leader of a blooming settlement. We are back—or so it seems—at the beginning of *The Pioneers* with its quasi-utopian promise of fulfilment, and the book appropriately ends with Scalping Peter accepting his fate and blessing white civilization.

That a writer of Cooper's intelligence could be driven to such blatant violations of narrative plausibility points to a latent conflict between willed belief and suppressed knowledge, between his determination to legitimate national history and his literary method of reasoned discourse which inadvertently forces such legitimation to reveal its ideological character. Not only are the whites made the blameless victims of Indian aggression ('Ah! Peter, why is it that you redmen wish so much to take our lives?' 433), it is their very peacefulness that ranks them higher on an ascending scale of civilization. The ideological nature of this image of Christian community becomes even more apparent when placed within the context of the Mexican War whose outcome very clearly is the cause of Cooper's almost jingoistic optimism. Similar ironies come from his effort to integrate into the symbolic pattern of his novel as much contemporary history as possible (mostly by editorializing comments and long authorial digressions). The war with Mexico, the European revolutions of 1848, social unrest are frequent contemporary points of reference. In fact, not only are the Indians compared to revolutionaries, they also argue like the labour leaders and the social visionaries of the period; they represent, in intended ambiguity, the voice of those dealt short by history—the voice of the disinherited and dispossessed.[42] Onoah's conversion thus implies not only reconciliation with (and atonement for) the past but is a ritual of consensus which solves conflict between opposing social groups in a Christian spirit of mercy and submission—the classic formula· of nineteenth-century middle-class fiction dealing with the 'social question'.[43] But on yet another level, Onoah—the noble redman, nature's gentleman with a grudge to bear—also resembles a representative of Cooper's own social group, the gentry. (Cooper had explicitly used that analogy once before in *The Redskins*.) In submitting to the historically inevitable, Onoah also seems to resign the gentry's claim to national leadership. With unity achieved on so many different levels of social and cultural conflict, progressive history is possible once again. For the moment, at least, under the impact of the Mexican War, Cooper was willing to make his peace with contemporary America and to rephrase the old myth of the Republic in the new and broader terms of Manifest Destiny and the Common Man.

George Lippard shares with Cooper a longing for the restoration of the pastoral order but with an even greater awareness of a paradise forever lost. Aggressively nostalgic and violently anti-urban, he is yet fascinated by the new experience of cities as no other American author before him.[44] Lippard explores an urban underground of labyrinths, trap doors, secret passages where virtue is endlessly pursued (yet hardly ever rescued), and where the glitter of metropolis is exposed as the false splendour of an essentially fallen world. It is a world in which the greed for money knows no limits and respects no sanctuaries, and in which innocence only provokes conspiracies that aim at its corruption. Consequently, even the most sacred personal relationships are broken up or drawn into doubt; parents betray their children, husbands their wives (or vice versa), brother is set against brother—so that next to the greed for acquisition and possession (sexual or other) the craving for revenge turns out to be the prime motive for action.

> The cant . . . about the amelioration of society, etc. . . . is but a very usual trick among authors, whereby they hope to add such a tone of dignity or utilitarianism to their pages as shall gild the pill of their licentiousness

—thus Poe on Eugène Sue and his *Les Mystères de Paris*.[45] No doubt Lippard's clever mixture of crime, protest and pornography was an equally lucrative way of speculating with the People—but that is certainly not the whole story. In a period of radical change in which economic relationships were becoming increasingly abstract, Lippard created a fictional world in which events could be strictly accounted for, and in which concrete effects had concrete causes. For a mass audience that felt left behind while fortunes were being made everywhere, he translated the 'invisible Empire' of anonymous economic forces back into a visible network of action and plotting. The injustice implied in the system's very processes could thus be dramatized and made concrete in actions immediately available to moral judgement. The confrontation of victim and victimizer is therefore a standard scene. Lippard insists on showing elegant hands blood-stained from money-making; on the speculator actually driving impoverished fathers into suicide and their pure daughters into prostitution. In two of his most popular novels, *The Quaker City* (1844) and *New York: Its Upper Ten and Lower Million* (1853), the bordello functions as the symbolic centre of the city's inferno; it is here where the privileged—bankers, clergymen, lawyers, politicians—not only take off their masks of respectability but

where, in their various perversions, they actually re-enact their
everyday corruption.

Lippard's fictions deal, almost exclusively, with the
weakness of fathers, the victimization of children, the
uncertainty of inheritance and of succession. (That some of
these are also Cooper's concerns seems to point to a cultural
anxiety they shared.) All these elements, however, are only
different aspects of the one central question which Lippard
pursues in emblematic images of rape, and in plots as
labyrinthine as Cooper's forests or as the city itself: who shall
have possession of the body of the maiden republic?

> Could Washington and his hero-band [thus Lippard's motto to
> *The Quaker City*], could the immortal throng of signers, once
> more assemble . . . what would be their emotions, as they gazed
> upon the fruits, which the republican tree has borne? We left
> you pure, they would say, we left you happy, and now we find
> Bribery on the Bench of Justice. . . . Are these the fruits for
> which we fought and bled? Was it for this we dared the rebel's
> gibbet, the traitor's doom?[46]

It is this imagery of violated pastoral, evident here as almost
anywhere else in Lippard's fiction that metaphorically connects
pornography and politics. Accordingly, the seduction of the
innocent, the rape of the maiden are dramatized in terms of
pastoral collapse and ecological catastrophe:

> A new world has broken upon her soul, not a world of green
> trees, silver streams and pleasant flowers; but a chaos of ashes,
> and mouldering flames, a lurid sky above, a blasted soil below,
> and one immense horizon of leaden clouds, hemming in a
> universe of desolation. (124)

Rape, pollution, penetration are part of a vocabulary of
transgression that, as Carol Smith-Rosenberg has pointed
out,[47] constitutes the symbolic language of social change.[48]
Indeed, in the fate of his women Lippard symbolically re-enacts
the violation of the body politic, of the old agrarian order, by
new social forces of disruption. The desolate home, the broken
family, the lost dignity of work, the humiliation of the Father are
elements of a melodramatic version of American history whose
victims are The People and the Garden Republic, and whose
villains The City and Industrial Capitalism.

31

It is a theme with some variations but only tentative happy endings. In one case, the hero, a Saviour-figure in the manner of Dumas's Count of Monte Christo, leads a group of working-men away from the 'savage civilization of the Atlantic cities' to found a 'free home beyond the Rocky Mountains'. As an attempt to start the American experiment all over again, this 'exodus' is symbolic of an intense, and intensely ambivalent, awareness of change inside the culture which counterbalanced a growing sense of doom and closure with a confidence in possibilities and new beginnings. For Lippard and, as Michael Rogin has shown,[49] for many of Lippard's Jacksonian contemporaries the city was a closed space in which economic equality and thus personal liberty were no longer possible. And yet, the final symbolic gesture of radical pastoralism which seemingly reaffirms a version of the agrarian past as a viable alternative to an urban present, is offset by a number of authorial statements proclaiming faith in civilization and progressive history:

> Ah, this enterprise which forms the impulse and the motto of modern civilization, will doubtless in the future ripen into good for all men, for there is a God,—but the path of its present progress is littered with human skulls. It weaves, it spins, it builds, it spreads forth on all sides its iron arms—and it has a good capital,—the blood of human hearts. (207)

Each refusal, each rebellion is thus channelled back into eventual affirmation by a deeply rooted trust in Providence. Even though the historic moment might be intensely rejected, and destruction seem imminent or even longed for, confidence in God's (or History's) mysterious Plan functioned as a veritable ideological fountain of youth in which anxiety over social change could be submerged and social vision pragmatically readjusted. Not unlike Cooper, Lippard was deeply troubled by the disruptions of, and the pain inflicted by, industrial expansion, grieved by the apparent loss of Republican virtues and traditions, the fate of the Old Republic, the price paid for civilization. And not unlike Cooper (though from a less paternalistic, more radical perspective from below) he reaffirmed faith in Providence and in the just republic of the future by giving voice to those—not the Indians and the gentry but The People—

whom progressive civilization, 'like a locomotive, rolling on an iron track',[50] had left behind.

5

In summing up, let me return to questions raised at the beginning: what had happened to the concept of a republican or democratic novel by the time of Cooper's death in 1851? It had failed to develop into a public institution, into a medium of enlightened discourse in which the People individually and collectively defined and redefined themselves, yet it had stayed political and national in ambition and in scope. It had been forced by the dynamics of Jacksonian society to open its definition of The People 'downwards' according to principles of Christian brotherhood and social justice (Beecher Stowe would have been another good example), and it had responded to the formation of class in a society that was egalitarian more in its rhetoric than in its social practice.

At the same time, the novel was being redefined in other ways as well. Edgar Allan Poe, who was a friend of Lippard's and therefore dealt with his novels only indirectly by critically demolishing those of Eugène Sue, also took on Cooper. In his famous review of *Wyandotté*,[51] he distinguished between two kinds of literature, the immortal and the merely popular, and he called Cooper, with unmistakable condescension, the best of the popular writers. If we keep in mind that Poe was dealing with the leading American novelist of the period, this degradation to the rank of the second-rate is indeed an indication that the concepts of art and literature were changing. Poe objected to the popular because it was, almost by definition, repetitious in its formulas, eminently marketable, made for use. In a similar manner, Melville claimed autonomy for the literary imagination by refusing to adjust his novels, in form and substance, to the conditions of the market. Neither Cooper nor Lippard had had any trouble with the usefulness of literature. Lippard's dictum that 'Literature merely considered as art is a despicable thing', Cooper would have readily assented to. He had refused to publish his novels in the fashion of the *roman de feuilleton*, yet more for economic than for aesthetic reasons.[52] Neither one of them minded producing marketable wares or complying with the wishes of readers and publishers alike (if, in the case of Cooper, within certain limits). Melville's insistence on not wanting to be used (as dramatized in 'Bartleby, the Scrivener'), his deep distrust of a public existence, is a long way from Cooper's determination to define his rôle as writer and as gentleman exclusively in public terms. Melville's reluctance turned his radicalism from social and political engagement into a cultural iconoclasm that made him eventually cut the epistemological rope which had tied the novel to the stable and ordered world of reason. In a radical fulfilment of Jacksonian democratic ideals he moved inward, toward the 'innermost self'. He used the rhetoric and imagery of political Democracy[53] only to get beyond and out of it. And yet transcending the public by way of metaphor also implied that one was still metaphorically tied to it.[54] The symbolic purgation of the private self (as acted out in *Moby-Dick*), projecting the rebellion and eventual taming of an 'enemy within', seems strangely related to the rituals of consensus central to Lippard's and especially to Cooper's novels. That the meaning of the harmony achieved (just as the meaning of the enemy subdued) is a highly ambivalent one, hardly matters in this context. Even in transcending the public (and the conventions of a public mode of fiction), Melville yet acknowledged the pressure of its continuing demands in symbolic structures of destruction, reconciliation, and renewal.

NOTES

1. On the concept of radical bourgeois fiction see J. Schulte-Sasse, 'Literarischer Markt und ästhetische Denkform', *Lili*, 2 (1972), 11–31 and Peter Bürger (ed.), *Zum Funktionswandel der Literatur* (Frankfurt: Suhrkamp, 1983), also my 'The Novel and the People: Aspects of Democratic Fiction in late 19th Century American Literature', in M. Sienicka (ed.), *Symposium on American Literature* (Poznan, 1979), pp. 89–106. On Cooper as gentleman, literary businessman and man of letters see William Charvat, *The Profession of Authorship in America, 1800–1870* (Ohio State University Press, 1968), pp. 68–83 and especially John P. McWilliams, *Justice in a Republic* (Berkeley, 1972) and J. F. Beard (ed.), *The Letters and Journals of James Fenimore Cooper* (Harvard University Press, 1960–68), 'Introduction' to Vol. I.

2. Quoted in Beard, *The Letters* . . . , Vol. I, p. xxii.
3. Op. cit., loc. cit.
4. On public virtue see Gordon S. Wood, 'Republicanism as a Revolutionary Ideology', in John R. Howe, Jr. (ed.), *The Rôle of Ideology in the American Revolution* (New York, 1970), p. 85, also J. F. Beard, 'Cooper and the Revolutionary Mythos', *Early American Literature*, XI (1976), 84–104.
5. 'In all enlightened times and countries, this matter of possessing a national literature has been regarded by sagacious statesmen as the one thing needful to cement the jarring and discordant elements, which constitute a people, by a feeling which all could share—a feeling of national pride in the productions of its own citizens forming a kind of neutral ground, on which conflicting sects and parties, casting aside their differences, might meet in friendship, as the tribes of Greece were wont to assemble at their Olympia.' Anonymous, 'Cheap Literature: Its Character and Tendencies,' *Southern Literary Messenger*, X (1844), 35—a concise definition of the democratic fiction (and its public function) that Cooper had in mind.
6. *Notions of the Americans* (New York, 1828), Vol. I, p. 108.
7. Cp. Karlheinrich Biermann, 'Zwischen Bürger und "Volk": Zum gesellschaftlichen Rollenverständnis des Schriftstellers nach der Julirevolution von 1830 (Victor Hugo)', in Bürger, op. cit., pp. 127–46.
8. *Oak Openings* (New York & London: Putnam's, Iroquois Edition, n.d.), p. 182.
9. *The Pilot* (Iroquois Edition, n.d.), p. 90.
10. *Notions of the Americans*, Vol. II, p. 131f.
11. Beard, *Letters* . . ., II, p. 84.
12. *Notions* . . ., I, p. 127f.
13. Cp. William Hedges, 'The Myth of the Republic and the Theory of American Literature', *Prospects*, IV (1979), pp. 101–20.
14. Harry B. Henderson III, *Versions of the Past* (New York: Oxford University Press, 1974), p. 88f.
15. Robert Clark, *History, Ideology and Myth in American Fiction, 1823–1852* (London: Macmillan, 1984). Clark convincingly shows that Cooper's obsession with the question of rightful ownership was central to the period. George Lippard's novels are another case in point.
16. 'Liberal America was not a static social system, and the transformation it underwent during Jackson's lifetime found the Indians at center stage. Indian dispossession is part of the history of American capitalism. Jackson and other political figures, freeing Indian land for the commodity economy, initiated a market revolution. They cleared the obstacles to free market relations, politically and by force, before the market could act on its own.' Michael Rogin, *Fathers and Children: Andrew Jackson and the Subjugation of the American Indian* (New York: Knopf, 1975), p. 12f.
17. In George Dekker/John P. McWilliams (eds), *Fenimore Cooper, The Critical Heritage* (London: Routledge & Kegan, 1973), p. 134.
18. Thomas Cole, 'American Scenery', *American Monthly Magazine*, January 1836, p. 12.

19. Op. cit., loc. cit.
20. Beard, *Letters* . . . , II, pp. 76, 126 and 295.
21. '. . . the Bravo is perhaps, *in spirit, the most American book I ever wrote . . .*' (the emphasis is Cooper's). Beard, *Letters* . . . , IV, p. 461.
22. To Samuel Rogers, 19 January 1832. Beard, *Letters* . . . , II, p. 180.
23. Cp. his letter to Horatio Greenough, 9 August 1836. Beard, III, p. 233.
24. *The American Democrat* (New York, 1838; Penguin, 1969), p. 147.
25. Cp. McWilliams, *Justice in a Republic* and Dorothy Waples, *The Whig Myth of James Fenimore Cooper* (Yale University Press, 1938).
26. 'A minority may be right, certainly, but a minority under this form of government, that wishes to substitute its peculiar views for the fundamental law, is attempting to subvert the institutions.' To William Cullen Bryant and William Leggett, for *The Evening Post*, February 1835. Beard, III, p. 103.
27. To Horatio Greenough. Beard, III, p. 330 (cp. also ibid., p. 247).
28. Rush Welter, *The Mind of America* (New York & London: Columbia University Press, 1975).
29. *The American Democrat*, p. 142f.
30. To Cornelius Mathews and Evert A. Duyckinck, 6 December 1841. Beard, IV, p. 202; for an earlier and decidedly different interpretation see his letter to Richard Bentley, 6 April 1835. Beard, III, p. 143.
31. *The American Democrat*, p. 130.
32. Ibid., p. 188.
33. Quoted in David S. Reynolds, *George Lippard* (Boston: Twayne, 1982), p. 98f.
34. Leslie Fiedler, 'The Male Novel', *Partisan Review*, 37 (1970), 89.
35. 'For the ending of the series is a celebratory beginning that prefigures the death of a hero who longs for beginnings.' Terence Martin, 'Beginnings and Endings in the Leatherstocking Tales', *Nineteenth Century Fiction*, 33 (1978–79), 87; also William P. Kelly, *Plotting America's Past* (Carbondale: Southern Illinois Press), esp. pp. 159–88.
36. The pattern is constant in liberal fiction and evident as much in Beecher Stowe's *Uncle Tom's Cabin* as in Howells's *A Hazard of New Fortunes* where Conrad Dryfoos's quasi-sacrificial death prefigures the possible redemption of the body politic.
37. Cp. Allan M. Axelrad's excellent *History and Utopia: A Study of the World View of James F. Cooper* (Norwood, Pa.: Norwood Editions, 1978). However, Axelrad underestimates the progressive underlining of Cooper's apocalyptic vision. The prophecy of impending doom is part of a basically optimistic trust in history as Providence, as Sacvan Bercovitch has convincingly pointed out in his *The American Jeremiad* (University of Wisconsin Press, 1978).
38. Montgomery Bird, *Nick of the Woods, or The Jibbenainosay* (1837, New York, 1939); cp. Martin Green, 'Cooper, Nationalism and Imperialism', *Journal of American Studies*, 12 (1979), 161–68. And yet one should note that although Deerslayer is virtuous in the individual act of killing, he merges with the English in their final massacre of the Indians. Cooper is reluctant to show but honest enough not to completely hide the link

between Christian spirit and civilizing conquest. In a similar vein Hetty's death diverts attention from the real victims at the same time that it symbolically atones for a collective crime in which Deerslayer also participates. In this sense, the final massacre can indeed be called 'the product of a composite social will'. See Phil Fisher, 'Killing a Man', in *Hard Facts* (New York: Oxford University Press, 1985), pp. 22–86, esp. p. 72. In thus admitting guilt and complicity in a painful yet necessary process of conquest, Cooper, according to Fisher, psychologically and symbolically clears the ground, marks 'the end of pre-history' which makes history and civilization possible. The end of the book would make such an optimistic reading doubtful.

39. *Oak Openings*, p. 312.
40. Scalping Peter's 'progress' thus symbolizes what Michael Rogin has analysed as the 'infantilization' of the Indian which justified Jacksonian policies of Indian removal as well as Indian reeducation. *Fathers and Children*, pp. 208ff.
41. Perhaps it is not too far-fetched to point out that Boden means 'soil' in German (a language Cooper was at least familiar with). General Boden, especially in the last chapter, seems an embodiment of Jacksonian agrarian Democracy.
42. *Oak Openings*, p. 257.
43. A typical example of such fiction is Charles Sheldon's *In His Steps* (1896).
44. With the possible exception of Charles Brockden Brown whom Lippard greatly admired and to whom he dedicated *Quaker City*.
45. 'Marginalia', *Complete Works of Egar Allan Poe* (New York: Putnam's, 1902), Vol. IX, p. 262ff.
46. *Quaker City; or, The Monks of Monk-Hall* (Philadelphia: Petersen and Brothers, 1845), title leaf.
47. 'Sex as Symbol in Victorian Purity: An Ethnological Analysis of Jacksonian America', *American Journal of Sociology*, 84 Suppl. (1978), 213–47.
48. One should note that Cooper also uses a rhetoric of transgression—of scalping, murder and the death of the innocent—in *The Deerslayer*.
49. 'Nature and Politics as Romance in America', *Political Theory*, 5 (1977), 5–30.
50. *New York: Its Upper Ten and Lower Million* (Cincinnati, 1853), p. 207.
51. 'Marginalia', p. 389ff.
52. Beard, IV, p. 110.
53. Alan Heimert has demonstrated this extensively in his influential '*Moby-Dick* and American Political Symbolism', *American Quarterly*, 15 (1963), 498–534.
54. The political implications of Melville's work have been explored especially by Michael Rogin in 'The Romance of the Self in Jacksonian America', *Partisan Review*, 44 (1977) and *Subversive Genealogy* (1984); also by Sacvan Bercovitch in *The American Jeremiad*; Myra Jehlen, 'New World Epics', *Salmagundi*, 1977, 49–68; and Robert Clark, *History, Ideology and Myth*.

2

Cultivating an Audience: from *Precaution* to *The Spy*

by JAMES D. WALLACE

> When I arrived for the first time at New York, by that part of
> the Atlantic Ocean which is called the East River, I was
> surprised to perceive along the shore, at some distance from the
> city, a number of little palaces of white marble, several of which
> were of classic architecture. When I went the next day to
> inspect more closely one which had particularly attracted my
> notice, I found that its walls were of whitewashed brick, and its
> columns of painted wood. All the edifices that I had admired
> the night before were of the same kind.[1]

In those trivial and futile imitations of classic architecture,
Tocqueville believed he had found the essence of democratic
art. Despite half a century of increasingly anxious attempts to
fulfil the promise of a new Golden Age in the flowering of
democratic culture, those accomplishments to which Americans could point were riddled with the same contradictions as
Tocqueville's temples; Jefferson's Monticello, Barlow's epics,
Tyler's drama, William Hill Brown's novel—all aspired to be
temples but were after all only warehouses made not from
marble but from whitewashed native brick and wood.
Emerson was only the most famous of the dozens of critics,
foreign and domestic, who deplored the imitative qualities of
American art and hoped for the day 'when the sluggard
intellect of this continent will look from under its iron lids, and
fill the postponed expectation of the world with something

38

better than the exertions of mechanical skill'.[2]

And yet originality was only a part of the lack. As original a creative genius as Charles Brockden Brown had traced his brief career virtually unnoticed, because American readers found in his novels nothing to match their established expectations and tastes. Democratic political institutions had not automatically produced an audience for indigenous American art, and whoever would invent an American novel would also have to invent a reader for it.

After completing *Precaution* in June of 1820, Cooper immediately began work on *The Spy*. He expected to write his second novel as rapidly as the first, but he soon discovered that he could not. On 28 June 1820 he wrote to Andrew Thompson Goodrich, his publisher: 'The task of making American Manners and American scenes interesting to an American reader is an arduous one—I am unable to say whether I shall succeed or not.'[3] Two weeks later he again wrote: 'The "Spy" goes on slowly and will not be finished until late in the fall—I take more pains with it—as it is to be an American novel professedly.'[4]

The making of an American novel proved even more difficult than Cooper had anticipated. For *Precaution* he had had a thousand models; the writing had been a simple exercise in the imitation of the British novels that flooded the American market, and Cooper had been assured of success when one of his early readers thought she recognized the story:

> There was a Miss McDonald, a friend of the Jays, staying with them at the time; she declared the book quite interesting, but it was not new; 'I am sure I have read it before,' she declared— this the author considered as a complimentary remark, as he had aimed at a close imitation of the Opie School of English novels.[5]

For an 'American novel professedly', there were no models. Of course there were some three or four score 'novels' produced by American writers, but these were so ill-conceived, conceptually confused, and badly written as to render them useless for Cooper's ambitions.[6] Even Brown, the most noteworthy of his predecessors, had clearly failed.[7] The early attempts at American fiction had repeatedly foundered on the two obstacles to an American literature that Cooper later identified in *Notions of the Americans*: the lack of adequate financial reward to encourage authors and publishers to risk an indigenous fiction, and what was conceived as a poverty of materials for American settings and characters.[8]

His formulating the task as that of 'making American Manners and American scenes interesting to an American reader' was the key to Cooper's success. *Precaution* was originally intended for a small, private audience (Mrs. Cooper and a few close friends) but in the writing Cooper discovered that his mimicry could appeal as well to a large, established audience for moral fiction—the Miss McDonalds of America. To ensure an audience for *The Spy*, Cooper had to cultivate the sensibilities of those readers he already knew. Through a careful modification of the generic norms of the 'novel of purpose', through a brilliant Americanization of the setting and the characters of *Precaution*, and through a profound insight into the essential American hero, Cooper at once retained his original audience and transformed it, inventing simultaneously the American novel and the American reader.

It has long been acknowledged that one important source for Cooper's first novel was Jane Austen's *Persuasion*; characters, incidents, and the whole development of the plot of *Persuasion* recur in *Precaution*, and Cooper's first novel concerns the problem of marriage for the three daughters of an English baronet.[9] Yet in adopting Austen's characters and plot, Cooper was not aiming at her audience. Rather, he 'aimed at a close imitation of the Opie school of English novels'. Mrs. Opie's tales had an established audience, one accustomed to the aggressive didacticism of Mrs. Opie's fiction:

> Sometimes she shows the calamities resulting from lying, from temper, from improper education, and again the happy results of doing one's duty, controlling one's temper, and honouring one's parents. It is seldom that Mrs. Opie leaves her readers to draw the moral themselves. . . . Usually there are numerous signposts.[10]

The moral fervour of the Opie school was one of the targets of Austen's characteristic irony. Austen's Anne Elliot can discuss

Scott and Byron with a young man, caution him against the moral erosion that reading poetry causes, and leave the party amused that 'like many other great moralists and preachers, she had been eloquent on a point in which her own conduct would ill bear examination.'[11] Mrs. Opie's heroines are never so duplicitous. In *Temper, or Domestic Scenes* (1812), Emma reflects on poetry and adultery after seeing the tomb of Abelard and Eloisa:

> When Mr. Egerton first read aloud to me the poem whence Mr. Varley quoted those fine lines, I was charmed by the beauty of the verse, and interested for the sorrow that it expressed. But when I found that it was the sorrow of unlawful love . . . I lost the deep interest I originally felt for the eloquent nun. . . .[12]

The seductive power of beautiful language must always be stoutly resisted in Mrs. Opie's moral tales, and this is the attitude Cooper's tone reveals as well. Of his own heroine he writes, 'It might be said that Emily Moseley had never read a book that contained a sentiment or inculcated an opinion improper for her sex or dangerous to her morals.'[13] Emily's sister Jane, who has not had the benefit of their aunt's careful guidance in reading, enjoys the poetry of Thomas Moore until an evening when a woman she detests praises it. Then Jane casts Moore's poetry into the fire:

> 'Oh!' cried Jane, 'I can't abide the book, since that vulgar Miss Jarvis speaks of it with so much interest. I really believe Aunt Wilson is right in not suffering Emily to read such things.' And Jane, who had often devoured the treacherous lines with ardor, shrank with fastidious delicacy from the indulgence of a perverted taste, when it became exposed, coupled with the vulgarity of unblushing audacity.[14]

Cooper himself not only read Moore's poetry but enjoyed it enough to use it often as a source for epigraphs in his later works, but *Precaution* embodies the attitude Mrs. Opie's audience expected.

In addition to the high moral tone of the Opie school, Cooper also adopted the characteristic theme of the novel of purpose. All of Mrs. Opie's tales illustrate the effects of proper or improper education on young women. The essential business of the Opie school is the dissemination of Lockean principles of education. In the typical Opie tale an ineffectual father, stripped of the authority of patriarchal institutions, struggles to inculcate in his daughters some moral quality or idea—truthfulness, temperance, obedience—that will insulate them from the seductive evils of the social world. His success or failure depends on the consistency and rationality of his efforts rather than on his authority as a parent. Often an aunt will take one daughter in hand and raise her in a manner that creates the desired principle, while the father impotently struggles with the other daughters. The novel of purpose isolates and formalizes one of the central anxieties of eighteenth-century British culture: the apparent threat to traditional social institutions is represented by the erosion of parental authority. In *Precaution* Cooper presents an ineffectual father, a superficial mother, and an exemplary aunt. The mother's ambitions for rank and wealth leave one daughter susceptible to seduction; the aunt's good sense arms the youngest daughter with 'precaution'. With its family as a microcosm of the social body, *Precaution* belongs to the efforts to redefine Protestant culture in the wake of the political and economic revolutions that were transforming England, France and the United States.[15]

Still, *Precaution* is not merely an Opie novel. It contains traces of a suppressed violence that is alien to the frail sensibilities of the novel of purpose. The violence haunts George Denbigh, the incognito Earl of Pendennyss. Denbigh's father dies in church, melodramatically interrupting a sermon on 'the hope, the resignation, the felicity of a Christian's deathbed'; later, Denbigh is wounded while protecting Emily from her brother's 'unloaded' gun; finally, during a thunderstorm, Denbigh encounters his uncle, who has been driven mad by grief and unrequited love. Each of these episodes marks a stage in Denbigh's self-transformation from an anonymous gentleman to a powerful nobleman. Denbigh is the first in a long line of orphaned sons in Cooper's fiction. Cut off from the social definition of his character by his father's death and by his own choice to conceal his peerage, Denbigh proceeds to create his own character in his wooing of Emily Moseley, his acts of heroism, and his display of sensibility. For Mrs. Opie, violence (abandoning seducers or intemperate liars) is a consequence of inadequate parental guidance. For

Cooper, violence is a mode of creating and defining character. Because Denbigh is in fact the Earl of Pendennyss, all of Emily Moseley's precaution is wasted. The novel is not 'about' the consequences of improper training; rather, it is about Denbigh's ability to create himself in the violent transitions to which his author subjects him.[16]

The violence in *Precaution* remains an undercurrent, barely disturbing the surface of the Opie tone, and Cooper was generally satisfied with his attempt to capture the interest of the Opie audience. Though he published anonymously, the only important American review identified *Precaution* as an American production and favourably contrasted its 'solidity and healthful spirit' with the 'chimeras dire' and 'feverish imaginations' of *Melmoth the Wanderer*.[17] British reviewers were more temperate in their praise but still found that *Precaution* claimed 'a distinguished place amid this species of publication'.[18] Though it sold poorly in the United States, it was actually rather popular in England, where it had twice the sale of *The Spy* and had by 1851 gone through five British editions.[19]

The reservations about *Precaution* that limited his American audience were suggested to Cooper by his friends:

> that he, an American in heart as in birth, should give to the world a work which aided . . . to feed the imaginations of the young and unpractised among his own countrymen, by pictures drawn from a state of society so different from that to which he belonged.

Thus Cooper determined to write his 'American novel professedly' and to make it as American as possible: 'He chose patriotism as his theme. . . .'[20] The same moral impulse that structured his first novel motivated the second and dictated the choice of theme, but it could not provide him with the social density of the British setting. In his effort to make American scenes and manners interesting to American readers, Cooper salvaged what he could from his British imitation. The family of *Precaution* becomes the Wharton family, and the inquiry into the breakdown of patriarchal authority becomes a

43

vehicle for exploring the moral status of the American Revolution and American patriotism. The latent violence surrounding George Denbigh, carefully contained in *Precaution* by British social structures and cultural forms, is manifested as the violent landscape of *The Spy* and becomes the external container of small residual loci of British social structures.

The opening of *The Spy* demonstrates the economy of means by which Cooper achieved this transformation. Landscape and atmosphere become important for the first time in his writing as Harper/Washington seeks shelter from a gathering storm. The storm is a convenient way to get Washington to the Wharton house and to set in motion the plot, but it also serves as an emblem of the Revolutionary War, of which Washington is also the victim. The emblem is made specific later, as Washington contemplates the Westchester countryside after the clearing of the storm:

> 'What a magnificent scene!' said Harper, in a low tone; 'how grand! how awfully sublime!—may such a quiet speedily await the struggle in which my country is engaged, and such a glorious evening follow the day of her adversity!'[21]

Landscape is an agent of the Revolutionary Mythos in *The Spy*; it adumbrates the anxiety of war and the hope for peace.[22] It is the 'neutral ground' where the armies clash by day and the Cow-boys and Skinners roam by night. As such, landscape is the externalized manifestation of the latent violence in *Precaution*; the residual Americanness of the earlier novel becomes America itself in the successor.

At the centre of this initial landscape stands the Wharton house, which contrasts with the 'very humble exterior' of Harvey Birch's dwelling. Although the secret of Mr. Wharton's Tory leanings is long withheld from us, his house itself, with its superior appearance, 'extremely neat parlour', Madeira-drinking host and formal dinners, is a repository of British values, and within its walls the genteel minor plot of *The Spy* will be played. The very name of Wharton's estate, 'The Locusts', suggests through a pun that Wharton's luxury and pastoral repose are a kind of plague on the new nation.

The Wharton house in the middle of the neutral ground is a synechdoche for life in America during the Revolution: British troops huddle behind their pickets in New York and foray into Westchester; American troops camp at Four Corners and sally forth to engage the British. The Wharton house is the first in a long line of fortresses in Cooper's fiction; the romantic moated castle of the British sentimental tradition becomes the realistic stronghold of a new American tradition. There is a spectrum of such fortresses in *The Spy*, ranging from the Wharton's elegant house to Harvey Birch's cave-like hut in the Hudson Highlands. To venture from one fortress to another is to enter a world of real and fancied danger. Lawton and Dr. Sitgreaves ride from Four Corners to The Locusts and receive a warning from the invisible Harvey Birch that they are risking their lives; Caesar flees the ghost of Johnny Birch; Harvey Birch, whose calling demands that he continually roam the landscape, is captured repeatedly. The true denizens of the landscape, the Skinners, occasionally overcome a fortress, remove anything of value, and put it to the torch. Harvey Birch's hut, composed of logs, bark, mud and leaves, contains almost nothing from the civilized world except a glass window, and when he learns that the light reflected from the glass has betrayed his hut's location to Frances, he smashes the window. All comforts, possessions, and wealth must be sacrificed to the exigencies of survival in the violent American landscape. The characters who have been able to make this sacrifice—Birch and Washington—are the seminal forces of the Revolution. Those who are incapable of such sacrifice lose everything, including their integrity.

Cooper effected the Americanization of scene by a simple reversal. The latent violence of *Precaution* was contained by the formal class structures of British society, while in *The Spy* the structures of society are contained by the landscape of violence. Cooper achieved the Americanization of his characters by a variety of means. Some are essentially unchanged from *Precaution*, some are derived by an isolation of personality traits, and some are invented altogether in order to explicate the meaning of his proclaimed theme, patriotism.

As Cooper pointed out in his 1849 Preface to *The Spy*, 'The dispute between England and the United States of America, though not strictly a family quarrel, had many of the features of a civil war' (p. vi). His central family, then, could represent

45

the larger conflict. Rather than summarizing the course of the Revolutionary War or entering circumstantially into its political, social and economic origins, Cooper could ground his presentation of the War in the personal reasoning and passions of individuals.[23] The mildly comic English baronet becomes a Tory sympathizer who attempts to conceal his true interests behind the appearance of neutrality. Wharton wants merely to preserve his property from 'my kind neighbors . . . who hoped, by getting my estate confiscated, to purchase good farms, at low prices' (p. 35). In a revolution, however, as in any family crisis, such vacillation has terrible consequences. In the microcosm of his family, Mr. Wharton's 'natural imbecility of character' contributes to the disastrous engagement of his elder daughter, Sarah, to the flashy Colonel Wellmere; in the macrocosm of the war it leads to the burning of the Locusts by Skinners. The combination of Sarah's aborted wedding and the Skinners' attack reduces Wharton to his essential condition: 'Mr. Wharton sat in a state of perfect imbecility, listening to, but not profiting by, the unmeaning words of comfort that fell from the lips of the clergyman' (p. 296). In this state he is borne away by an ironic emblem of his character—a clumsy carriage, faded and tarnished, with a coat of arms:

> 'The "lion couchant" of the Wharton arms was reposing on the reviving splendour of a blazonry that told the armorial bearings of a prince of the church; and the mitre, that already began to shine through its American mask, was a symbol of the rank of its original owner'. (p. 311)

This mottled picture is all that remains of Sir Edward Moseley's rank in *Precaution*.

Sarah is avowedly pro-British. As the elder daughter, she has been subject for some time to the flattery of the British soldiers who had frequented the Wharton house in New York City. 'It was much the fashion then for the British officers to speak slightingly of their enemies; and Sarah took all the idle vapouring of her danglers to be truths' (p. 30). The words 'fashion', 'idle vapourings' and 'danglers' fix the moral status of both the British officers and Sarah. It is this consistent under-estimation of American will and ability that will cost the British their colonies, in Cooper's judgement.[24] By sharing it, Sarah exposes herself as susceptible to superficial appearances and vain boasting.

Sarah's engagement to Wellmere is a brilliant metonymy for America's colonial connection to Great Britain; the colourful Englishman courts the unsuspecting daughter of America despite his wife at home. British occupation, like bigamy, is a violation of natural law—that same natural law which is the basis for the Revolutionary Mythos. It is no accident that, waiting for Caesar to fetch the wedding ring, Dr. Sitgreaves should begin meditating on the 'natural' status of monogamy:

> Marriage, madam, is pronounced to be honourable in the sight of God and man: and it may be said to be reduced, in the present age, to the laws of nature and reason. The ancients, in sanctioning polygamy, lost sight of the provisions of nature, and condemned thousands to misery, but with the increase of science have grown the wise ordinances of society, which ordain that man should be the husband of one woman. (p. 289)

Frances, to whom these remarks are addressed, answers, 'as if fearful of touching on forbidden subjects', that she had thought the teachings of Christianity were the basis of monogamy. Sitgreaves replies,

> True, madam, it is somewhere provided in the prescriptions of the apostles, that the sexes should henceforth be on an equality in this particular. But in what degree could polygamy affect holiness of life? It was probably a wise arrangement of Paul, who was much of a scholar, and probably had frequent conferences, on this important subject, with Luke, whom we all know to have been bred to the practice of medicine—(p. 290)

Sitgreave's comic banter raises an issue of great importance: it is not revealed religion, but rational deductions of natural law that provide the basis for monogamy, whether in marriages or among nations. Revelation or enthusiasm are too often merely the glossing of selfish motives, as the Skinners amply demonstrate through their parroting of Revolutionary rhetoric. Sarah has been seduced, both politically and emotionally, by Wellmere, just as her father has been seduced by British wine, tobacco, and gilded chariots.

The political implications of Wellmere's crime are further

developed when Lawton asks him what the punishment for bigamy is: ' "Death!—as such an offense merits," he said. "Death and dissection," continued the operator [Sitgreaves]. . . . Bigamy, in a man, is a heinous offense!' (p. 290). Sitgreaves adds 'dissection' in the interest of accuracy and from his professional bias, but it is as well a forecast of the dismemberment of the British empire—dissection as the penalty for British colonial policy.

The wedding of Sarah and Wellmere precipitates a crisis on many narrative levels: Birch, the ubiquitous servant of the Revolution, reveals that Wellmere has an English wife; the Skinners attack and burn The Locusts; Sarah falls senseless and lapses into insanity. Sitgreaves speaks as if Sarah's sanity were the price of American independence:

> 'This is a melancholy termination to so joyful a commencement of the night, madam,' he observed in a soothing manner; 'but war must bring its attendant miseries; though doubtless it often supports the cause of liberty, and improves the knowledge of surgical science.' (p. 309)

Once the ties of Sarah's mental dependence have been removed, she, like her father, has no support; the two of them represent the fate of American Tories, dispossessed and stupefied by the defeat of the British.

Frances, the younger daughter, manifests first mental independence, then support for the Revolution, viewing the 'idle vapourings' of the British officers with scepticism and then resentment. Of course, Frances is Emily Moseley in American dress, but instead of 'precaution' Frances takes as her guiding principle 'patriotism'. Two circumstances exemplify Frances's patriotism: her love for Peyton Dunwoodie, and her adoption of Washington as a surrogate father. The love of a Tory's daughter for a patriot hero, a theme that was to become a cliché of the Revolutionary War novel,[25] contrasts with the bigamous marriage Wellmere proposes; Dunwoodie is one-dimensional in all things, as his passionate friendship with the significantly-named George Singleton suggests.[26] While the course of their true love is ruffled by misunderstanding, ultimately the marriage of Frances and Peyton is never in doubt. When the aged Birch meets Wharton

Dunwoodie during the War of 1812, the United States and the child of the marriage merge into one: ' 'Tis like our native land! . . . improving with time;—God has blessed both' (p. 458). The Dunwoodies are the legitimate, fertile parents of the new nation.

The imbecility of her father leaves an absence at the centre of Frances's family life—an absence that Washington unmistakably fills. The first time the disguised Washington speaks to her, he gives her a 'smile of almost paternal softness' (p. 20), and in Birch's hideout he specifies the character of his mythological rôle:

> God has denied to me children, young lady; but if it had been his blessed will that my marriage should not have been childless, such a treasure as yourself would I have asked from his mercy. But you are my child: all who dwell in this broad land are my children, and my care; and take the blessing of one who hopes yet to meet you in happier days. (p. 412)

George Dekker has criticized Cooper's treatment of the Wharton sisters as 'excessively neat' and 'stereotyped',[27] but the paternal image is not simply the literalization of Washington as 'the father of his country'. It connects to a complex pattern of paternity and familial relations in *The Spy*, and this pattern in turn is Cooper's exploration of the meaning of his original insight into the Revolution as a civil war, the portrayal of what Jay Fliegelman has called 'the American revolution against patriarchal authority', a comprehensive re-orientation of American culture in the interest of justifying the rebellion against the patriarchal authority of the British monarch. Throughout the eighteenth century the relation of the colonies to the crown was conceptualized as that of children to a father, and the gathering impetus for revolution can be traced in the changes in the rhetoric of family comity beginning in the early 1760s.[28] As Fliegelman has shown, the rhetoric of patriarchal authority was transformed by the educational theory of John Locke; in the course of the eighteenth century the image of the stern, autocratic father was usurped by a new father whose authority derived from his capacity to nurture his children and to prepare them for a life of virtue. The hagiography of Washington, the childless father of his country, precipitated in

Parson Weem's *Life of Washington* (1800), legitimized Washington's rôle as the adoptive 'good father', the antithesis to the authoritarian yet curiously weak extremes of George III:

> The new understanding of greatness as goodness reflected an essential theme of the antipatriarchal revolution that would replace patriarch with benefactor, precept with example, the authority of position with the authority of character, deference and dependence with moral self-sufficiency, and static dichotomies with principles of growth: Sovereignty and power were no longer glorious in and of themselves. Rather, they were glorious, as Washington had demonstrated, only as opportunities to do good.[29]

Thus Cooper, by a series of minor adjustments, brilliantly transformed his British comedy of familial relations into a drama of revolutionary aspirations, creating a pattern of familial and political conflict, a pattern which was indisputably American and yet which would be familiar and accessible to an audience accustomed to British fiction.

Around this central core Cooper wove his theme of patriotism. His primary means for dramatizing this theme was also his most radical and enduring act in the making of an American novel: the invention of Harvey Birch. Birch was created as a socially marginal character; certainly none of the genteel characters who frequent the Wharton house would be willing or able to act as a spy, and Washington must blush when, from the purest of motives, he must go under a false name. It is precisely his marginality that makes Birch an effective spy. Cooper underlines this point by presenting another spy in his narrative: Caesar, the Wharton's black servant, 'had established a regular system of espionage, with a view to the safety of his young master' (p. 57), and members of the household are given to remarking, with an indulgent chuckle, 'Really, Caesar, I find I have never given you credit for half the observation that you deserve . . .' (p. 281). Absolute loyalty, a kind of familial patriotism, characterizes Caesar's place in the household, and his bearing is a rebuke to succeeding generations, just as Birch's is.

Corollary to his social marginality is Birch's capacity to create a personality for himself, to invent himself anew at need. He is a master of the impenetrable disguise; in fact, Washington alone knows who or what he really is. More significantly, he recreates himself in moral terms in the course of the novel. Initially his acquisitiveness and his pot of gold are stressed. Birch's progress through the novel entails the gradual loss of everything associated with the avaricious side of his personality: his pot of gold, his house, his freedom of movement, his reputation as a peddler. In addition he suffers these losses at the hands of American agents—the Skinners and Dunwoodie's troops. The effect of this process is to emphasize the choices Birch must make between self-interest and patriotism. With each such choice he recreates himself in the form of a perfect patriot. In this respect Birch is the descendant of George Denbigh; the two heroes of *The Spy*, Birch and Dunwoodie, are the product of a bifurcation of Denbigh's character into its genteel and its self-creating components. Just as Denbigh's father dies at the beginning of *Precaution* and leaves him free to abandon his property and title, to invent himself as a gentleman, so Birch's father dies early in *The Spy* and leaves him free to serve the interests of the Revolution under our general father, Washington. Birch thus becomes what one critic has called a 'renegade' archetype, his character formed 'by his perpetual striving for self-definition in a fictive world in which the self can scarcely be conceived to exist outside of a stable social matrix'.[30] Yet Birch is less a renegade than an emanation of Washington's will, the embodiment of those pure qualities of infertility, sacrifice and freedom at the heart of the Washington mythos.

Still another aspect of Cooper's representation of Birch has been pointed out by Barton Levi St. Armand. St. Armand relates Birch to legendary and mythic prototypes: Birch's pack and his father's remark that 'you will be a pilgrim through life' (p. 147) clearly suggest *Pilgrim's Progress*; his homelessness, mysterious appearances and escapes, and alienation suggest the Wandering Jew; his rôle as Washington's agent echoes Christ's rôle in the Trinity. For St. Armand these prototypes mean that Cooper participated in the 'Literary Calvinism' which was to shape the symbolic romances of Hawthorne and Melville; whatever the status of that conclusion, St. Armand is correct in regarding Birch as 'the domestication of an international Romantic archetype'.[31] Cooper incorporated, without insisting upon, features from mythic prototypes in precisely the way that American architects and sculptors incorporated classical forms as an affirmation of a Golden Age in the New World. While Mr. Wharton's Tory sympathies are represented through his tarnished coach and through the gilded tablet that 'proclaimed the virtues of his deceased parents' until Trinity Church was burned, Birch's essential Americanism is proclaimed in his relation to living legend.

After the success of *The Spy*, the patterns of Cooper's creative activity were firmly established. His exploration of the cultural life of his nation, his adaptation of popular subliterary forms to the purposes of his romances, his novelistic core of genteel characters animating an ideological or metaphysical theme, his presentation of a socially marginal hero as the essential American—all these were permanent features of Cooper's career. Having discovered a means for cultivating his readers, for leading them by easy steps away from the popular fiction of British origin into an indigenous fiction, Cooper made that means a virtual formula to which he could return after the failed experiments of the 1830s for an assured success. The importance of Cooper's protracted grappling with the problem of readership cannot be over-estimated. Cooper created the community of readers whose taste would dominate the market for fiction in America (and for American fiction abroad) throughout the nineteenth century. Most of the fiction we recognize as most characteristic and valuable in the period was designed for Cooper's readership and is unthinkable outside the horizon of expectations Cooper had established.

NOTES

1. Alexis de Tocqueville, *Democracy in America*, trans. Phillips Bradley *et al.*, 2 vols. (New York: Knopf, 1946), II, 52.
2. Ralph Waldo Emerson, 'The American Scholar', in Larzer Ziff (ed.), *Selected Essays* (New York: Penguin, 1982), p. 83.
3. *The Letters and Journals of James Fenimore Cooper*, ed. James Franklin Beard, 6 vols. (Cambridge, Mass.: Harvard University Press, 1960–68), I, 44.
4. *Letters and Journals*, I, 49.

5. Susan Cooper, 'Small Family Memories', dated 25 January 1883 and published as an introduction to *Correspondence of James Fenimore Cooper*, ed. by his grandson, James Fenimore Cooper, 2 vols. (New Haven: Yale University Press, 1922), I, 39–40.

6. See Terence Martin, 'Social Institutions in the Early American Novel', *American Quarterly*, 9 (1957), 72–84.

7. Brown's fiction appealed to Cooper in its 'power and comprehensiveness of thought', but Cooper felt that Brown had 'curbed his talents by as few allusions as possible to actual society'. *Notions of the Americans, Picked Up by a Travelling Bachelor*, 2 vols. (1828; rpt. New York: Frederick Ungar Publishing Co., 1963), II, 111.

8. *Notions of the Americans*, II, 108.

9. See George E. Hastings's meticulous study, 'How Cooper Became a Novelist', *American Literature*, 12 (1940), 20–51.

10. Margaret Eliot Macgregor, *Amelia Alderson Opie: Worldling and Friend* (Menasha, Wis.: The Collegiate Press, n.d.), p. xi. For a summary of Cooper's career as a writer of moral tales, see James Franklin Beard, 'Introduction', in Cooper's *Tales for Fifteen* (Gainesville, Fla.: Scholars' Facsimiles & Reprints, 1955).

11. Jane Austen, *Persuasion* (London: Oxford University Press, n.d.), pp. 113–15.

12. *The Works of Mrs. Amelia Opie*, 3 vols. (Philadelphia: James Crissy, 1843), III, 139–40. *Temper* seems to have been Cooper's favourite among Opie's works. He met Opie in 1830 through Pierre Jeanne David, who wrote to her that Cooper had said, 'Let us go see the author of *Temper*, I have a profound admiration for her works' (Macgregor, p. 110).

13. *Precaution: A Novel* (New York: W. A. Townsend and Company, 1861), p. 137.

14. *Precaution*, p. 87.

15. On changes in English society, see Harold Perkin, *The Origins of Modern English Society 1780–1880* (London: Routledge & Kegan Paul, 1969) and E. P. Thompson, *The Making of the English Working Class* (1963; rpt. New York: Randon House, 1966). For a survey of the changes in ideal family structure and the use of the nuclear family as synechdoche for British and American culture, see Edwin G. Burrows and Michael Wallace, 'The American Revolution: the Ideology and Psychology of National Liberation', *Perspectives in American History*, 6 (1972), 165–306.

16. This transforming violence in Cooper's fiction is the 'immortal serpent who writhes and writhes like a snake that is long in the sloughing', as D. H. Lawrence calls it in *Studies in Classic American Literature* (New York: The Viking Press, 1961), p. 53. See also Richard Slotkin, *Regeneration Through Violence: The Mythology of the American Frontier, 1600–1860* (Middletown, Conn.: Wesleyan University Press, 1973), p. 557.

17. The unsigned review appeared in *The Literary and Scientific Repository, and Critical Review*, 2 (1821), 364–75.

18. *The Gentleman's Magazine: And Historical Chronicle*, 91 (1821), 345. Another British review appeared in *The New Monthly Magazine and Literary Journal*, 3 (1821), 132.

19. William Charvat, *The Profession of Authorship in America, 1800–1870* (Columbus: Ohio State University Press, 1968), p. 73.
20. James Fenimore Cooper, 'Introduction', in *The Spy: A Tale of the Neutral Ground* (New York: W. A. Townsend and Co., 1859), pp. ix–x.
21. *The Spy*, p. 58. Further references will be cited parenthetically.
22. James Franklin Beard defines Revolutionary Mythos as 'that elusive but distinctively coherent cluster of ideas, values and attitudes (more a *Weltanschauung* than an ideology) that enabled reflective citizens of the early Republic to comprehend the awesome circumstances that brought them to their independence and guided their thinking about themselves into the nineteenth century.' 'Cooper and the Revolutionary Mythos', *Early American Literature*, 11 (1976), 85.
23. In his review of Catherine Sedgewick's *A New-England Tale*, Cooper would argue that the 'true historians' of society are not the recorders of statutes but Henry Fielding's describers of society as it exists and men as they are. *Early Critical Essays (1820–1822)*, ed. James Franklin Beard (Gainesville, Fla.: Scholars' Facsimiles & Reprints, 1955), pp. 97–8.
24. In *Lionel Lincoln* (1825) Cooper is particularly careful to present the indolence of the British generals who occupy Boston as the cause for the failure of their campaign.
25. See Donald A. Ringe, 'The American Revolution in American Romance', *American Literature*, 49 (1977), 352–65.
26. Observing the care Dunwoodie bestows on the wounded Singleton, one character remarks, 'You speak of him as if he were your mistress.' Dunwoodie replies, 'I love him as one' (p. 118).
27. *James Fenimore Cooper the Novelist* (London: Routledge & Kegan Paul, 1967), p. 35.
28. Burrows and Wallace, 'The American Revolution'.
29. Jay Fliegelman, *Prodigals and Pilgrims: The American Revolution against Patriarchal Authority, 1750–1800* (New York: Cambridge University Press, 1982), 210–11.
30. Harry B. Henderson, III, *Versions of the Past: The Historical Imagination in American Fiction* (New York: Oxford University Press, 1974), pp. 51–2.
31. 'Harvey Birch as the Wandering Jew: Literary Calvinism in James Fenimore Cooper's *The Spy*', *American Literature*, 50 (1978), 348–68.

3

Literally White, Figuratively Red: The Frontier of Translation in *The Pioneers*

by ERIC CHEYFITZ

1

It's far easier to call names, than to shoot a buck on the spring. . . .

—*The Pioneers*

L'ethnocentrisme n'est-il pas toujours trahi par la précipitation avex laquelle il se satisfait de certaines traductions ou de certaines équivalents domestiques [Is not ethnocentrism always betrayed by the haste with which it is satisfied by certain translations or certain domestic equivalents?]

—*De la grammatologie* [*Of Grammatology*]

In the beginning of 1900, the federal government of Mexico sent out a decree to get rid of all the Yaquis in the state of Sonora. By reason of this order, the governor of the state started persecution and execution of the race, and in many cases even Yoris (Mexicans) were taken just because they spoke Yaqui.

—Refugio Savala

In a scene from *The Pioneers* (1823), in which Cooper seems particularly concerned with orchestrating the various languages, both domestic (dialects and jargons) and foreign, that compose the tale, his narrator steps forward at a particular

55

moment of conversation between Natty Bumppo and
Chingachgook to strike a pose that will reappear regularly
throughout the Leatherstocking Tales (1823–41): 'The hunter
now raised his head again, and addressed the old warrior,
warmly, in the Delaware language, which, for the benefit of our
readers, we shall render freely into English.'[1] The pose that
Cooper's narrator assumes is that of a translator of Indian
languages. I use the word *pose* because, as we know, Cooper was
essentially ignorant of Indian tongues (what little he knew he
knew through his reading of the Reverend John Heckewelder,
of which more later). Yet the evidence suggests that he believed
the pose (thus dissolving it from his perspective), not literally, of
course, but figuratively.[2] That is, if Cooper could not actually
speak any Indian languages (and he could not), he still believed
he was representing the Indians in some truthful way by
allowing them to speak in a language equivalent to their own
(and here the boundaries between the literal and the figurative
begin to blur): the language of metaphor, which in the
eighteenth and first half of the nineteenth centuries represented
the essence of 'primitive' languages in a certain strain of
Western linguistic philosophy, articulated by names such as
Vico, Warburton, Condillac, Rousseau, and Emerson. Implicit
in the conceptions, the fantasies, of this ur-language is its
universality, its transcendence of any particular language, and
hence its virtual transparency to, or representability by, all
languages. In this sense, the language of metaphor was
conceived of as truly original, possessing an identity with either
an essential human nature (metaphor is the language of primal
passion in Rousseau's 'Essay on the Origin of Languages . . .')
or with physical nature (metaphor is the language of natural
facts in Emerson's *Nature*). '[T]his is plain English enough,
though spoken in Iroquois'—a comment made by Natty
Bumppo to his adversary Rivenoak in *The Deerslayer* (1841)[3]—
could serve as Cooper's credo in this case. And as we will see,
this credo, which assumes a transparency of Indian languages
to Western ones, has political causes and consequences that
operate within the territory of a question: what does it mean to
give voice to those whom one is depriving of a voice in this act of
representation?

In what follows I want to point to the ways in which

Cooper's pose of understanding is the subject of *The Pioneers*; and in doing this, I want to suggest some specific ways in which this pose typified Cooper's culture, which was in the process of translating the American Indians and their cultures, in two senses of the word *translate* that I will explore.

The first sense is, no doubt, the one that comes most immediately to mind: 'to turn from one language into another' (*O.E.D.*). However, the second meaning with which I am concerned—'to use in a metaphorical or transferred sense' (*O.E.D.*)—is inseparable in its history from the first, as our first theory of metaphor, that of Aristotle in the *Poetics*, shows: 'Metaphor [*metaphora*] is the application of an alien [*allotriou*] name by transference [*epithora*] either from genus to species, or from species to genus, or from species to species, or by analogy, that is, proportion.'[4] *Metaphora* comes from the verb *metathero* (literally, 'to carry across'), which, as Liddell's and Scott's *Greek-English Lexicon* notes, contains among its other meanings the sense of translation from one language into another. Yet that the same word, *metathero*, can refer to either the translation of one language into another or the transference of sense within a language is not simply what brings the idea of metaphor within the context of translation or the idea of translation within the context of metaphor. For as Aristotle's definition of metaphor suggests with its notion of the 'transference' of an 'alien name' into a familiar context, the very idea of metaphor seems to find its ground in a kind of territorial imperative, in a division, that is, between the domestic and the foreign.

Indeed, if we read Chapters XXI and XXII of the *Poetics*, where Aristotle develops his definition of metaphor, we find that this definition rests upon a division of language into 'current or proper words' (*kurion onomaton*), those 'in general use among a people'; and 'unusual words' (*tois xenikois*), under which, among others, Aristotle places 'strange (or rare) words' (*glottan*) and those that are 'metaphorical' (*metaphoran*). What I want to note immediately is that the word S. H. Butcher translates as 'unusual' is *xenikos*, which means *strange* or *foreign*. Thus, while at the beginning of his discussion Aristotle appears to distinguish between the 'metaphorical' and the 'foreign', when in Chapter XXI he defines a 'strange' word as

57

any word 'which is in use in another country', at a subsequent moment he also makes the metaphorical a species of the foreign, as the terminology of his definition suggests and as he makes clear when in the language of Chapter XXII just cited he classifies metaphor under 'unusual words'.[5]

So, as Roland Barthes points out in his essay 'L'ancienne rhétorique', Aristotle's theory of metaphor 'rests [*repose*] on the idea that there exist two languages [*deux langages*], one proper and one figurative [*un propre et un figuré*]'. And, Barthes continues, this division into a proper and a figurative language cannot be separated from the division 'national/foreign' (*national/étranger*) and 'familiar/strange' (*normal/étrange*).[6] Within Aristotle's theory of metaphor, then, a theory that has exerted and continues to exert, whether explicitly or implicitly, a controlling force on the way Westerners think about language, the figurative becomes the foreign, or strange; the literal becomes the national, or normal. Thus, within this context a language becomes foreign to itself (see footnote 5). At the same time, as I have tried to suggest in my brief exploration of the relationship between translation and metaphor, the division between the proper and the figurative can govern the division between foreign languages, with the national becoming the literal; and the figurative, the foreign. And here it is worth remarking that the word, *kuria*, which Butcher translates as 'current or proper', that is, literal, has among its most immediate senses those of *authority and legitimacy*.

In exploring through a reading of *The Pioneers* what I referred to as Cooper's and his culture's pose of translation, I want to suggest within the context of colonization that informs the novel some specific ways in which the rhetorical alienation of a language from itself (in this case English) and the rhetorical division of two foreign languages (in this case certain Western and Indian languages) significantly interact. I want to argue, then, that the pose of Cooper's narrator is not simply a convention of the novel, a matter of *vraisemblance* (of a certain kind of aesthetics), but a matter of politics.[7]

Like Cooper's narrator, Cooper's hero, Natty Bumppo, or Leatherstocking, also plays the part of a translator, 'forever finding it necessary to explain the savage man to the civilized and the civilized man to the savage', as Roy Harvey Pearce puts it in *Savagism and Civilization*.[8] Indeed the illiterate Leatherstocking's skill with what he calls 'the speech of "Kill-deer" '[9] (his gun) is equalled by his skill as a translator—'. . . the grayhead has many [tongues]. . . . He can talk to the Pawnee, and the Konza, and the Omaha, and he can talk to his own people', Mahtoree, Natty's Sioux antagonist in *The Prairie* (1827), reminds both the old trapper and Cooper's readers.[10] And both in the Leatherstocking Tales and the culture of which they are a part, this language of violence—the speech of 'Kill-deer'—is translated by and is a translation of a violence of language that we will explore in *The Pioneers* as a violence of translation, practised by white cultures on red ones and within white culture itself, when Cooper's characters try to communicate with each other. *The Pioneers*, which Edwin Fussell calls in part 'a tragedy of misunderstanding',[11] is nothing but a complex of scenes of such translation.

By way of entering this frontier of translation, I want to focus on a scene, near the middle of *The Pioneers*, where Judge Marmaduke Temple (the founder and presiding authority of Templeton, the 1793–94 frontier community that is the setting of Cooper's novel) and a group of other characters, whom we will meet along the way, are taking a leisurely ride on horseback through the Judge's domain.

Richard Jones (the Judge's cousin and Sheriff of the county) has organized the excursion we are following; and one of his purposes in doing so is to show his cousin Elizabeth (the Judge's only child, who has returned home to stay after four years away at school) 'the "sugar bush" of Billy Kirby' (219), who on the day of the outing is tapping maple trees and making maple sugar on the spot. As the party on horseback steers toward the outdoor factory of Kirby, Jones, in a manner typical of his pompous authority, begins to lecture Judge Temple on how the latter might 'introduce a little more science into the manufacture of sugar, among . . . [his] tenants' in order that 'instead of making loaves of the size of a lump of candy', they might make 'them as big as a hay-cock' (221).[12]

Immediately, Elizabeth, who has a ready charge of wit, which she is quick to use, comes to her father's defence: first, with an apparently good-natured parody of her cousin's hyperbole, in which she conjures up a tea party where 'potash-

59

kettles' are 'tea-cups' and 'the scows on the lake' are 'saucers';
then, in a fiercely sarcastic tone that attempts to explode the
Sheriff's grandiose 'projects of genius' (221–22). But the
Sheriff remains untouched by Elizabeth's volley. Indeed, he
sees his hay-cock-sized loaves of sugar not as an exaggeration,
a backwoodsman's tall tale, but as an 'appeal' that a lawyer or
scientist might make 'to common sense, good sense, or, what is
of more importance than either, to the sense of taste, which is
one of the five natural senses.' '[I]s not', Jones continues, '["a
big loaf of sugar"] likely to contain a better illustration of a
proposition, than such a lump as one of your Dutch women
puts under her tongue when she drinks her tea[?]' Finally,
after having profoundly conflated the physical and psychological senses of *sense*, and within the realm of his own logic
equated the taste of something with its size, the Sheriff
proceeds to state his 'proposition', now boiled down to the
most general terms, after he has illustrated it:

> There are two ways of doing every thing; the right way, and the
> wrong way. You make sugar now, I will admit, and you may,
> possibly, make loaf-sugar; but I take the question to be,
> whether you make the best possible sugar, and in the best
> possible loaves. (222)

What we have here is the beginning of one of those scenes of
verbal slapstick of which Cooper is so fond (and that have cost
him dearly in the estimation of his critics, who find such scenes
neither funny nor relevant to the action of the Leatherstocking
Tales). In this instance it is Richard Jones, who, violating
common sense in the name of common sense, carves out a
territory of nonsense, which the other characters legitimize
either through their silence or through responding to this
silence as if it made sense. Judge Temple immediately offers this
kind of response: first, acknowledging the 'useful[ness]' of
Jones's 'inquiry' into the quantity of sugar made and the means
of making it; and then, envisioning a future 'when farms and
plantations shall be devoted' to sugar-maple cultivation, which,
hopefully, 'may be improved . . . by the use of the hoe and
plough' (222). Perhaps Judge Temple is only attempting to
keep the verbal peace by responding sensibly to the nonsensical
Sheriff. But Richard, who is obsessed throughout *The Pioneers*

with achieving in private argument the authority over the Judge that he lacks in public, immediately calls into question Marmaduke's notion that maple trees can be cultivated by 'the use of the hoe and plough':

> 'Hoe and plough!' roared the Sheriff;—'would you set a man hoeing round the root of a maple like this. . . . Hoeing trees! are you mad, 'duke? . . . Poh! poh! my dear cousin, hear reason, and leave the management of the sugar-bush to me. Here is Mr. Le Quoi, he has been in the West-Indies, and has seen sugar made. Let him give an account of how it is made there, and you will hear the philosophy of the thing.—Well, Monsieur, how is it that you make sugar in the West-Indies; any thing in Judge Temple's fashion?' (222)

We will turn to Monsieur Le Quoi's response to Richard Jones's question, but first let us scrutinize Jones's response to Judge Temple; for if the frontier of Templeton is a violent place—a place where, to cite only two examples, settlers exuberantly slaughter game and hack down forests and where a dispossessed Indian, the Delaware Chingachgook (Natty's red counterpart, who is also known in the tale as Mohegan, John Mohegan, and Indian John[13]), commits a kind of suicide rather than endure his dispossession—we might begin to see in Jones's comic response the ways in which this violence of action is related to a violence of language.

We have just witnessed Judge Temple, then, trying to settle a dispute between cousins. In this attempt, however, with his reference to hoe and plough as a possible means of cultivating maple trees, he only succeeds in unsettling Richard Jones, who was beginning to feel quite at home in his argument about the 'best possible' way of making sugar loaves. While we must admit that the Judge's reference to the hoe and plough as a means of improving maple tree cultivation appears incongruous, given either eighteenth- or nineteenth-century methods of working sugar maples (in fact, hoe and plough were tools used to cultivate sugar cane), we must also admit that it appears to be Richard Jones's intention to silence the Judge rather than to engage him in legitimate argument (argument in which the two sides, agreeing on a stable set of terms, actually listen to each other). The Sheriff roars at his cousin—

literally assaulting him with the sound of his words—while constructing a comic picture of a man set by the (it is implied) ignorant Judge to muddle around the root of a great maple with a tiny hoe; and then, drawing the inevitable conclusions from his parodic construct, Jones questions Marmaduke's sanity, claiming for himself 'reason' and the authoritative right to 'the management of the sugar-bush' that reason confers.

To support his attack on the Judge, which proceeds under the name of reason, the Sheriff, as I have noted, summons the testimony of M. Le Quoi, who, because he has owned a sugar plantation in the West Indies and 'seen sugar made' can tell Judge Temple 'the philosophy of the thing' (in the context of the preceding quote, Jones is using 'made' in the sense of 'cultivate'). But what must strike us immediately is that *the* philosophy of the thing is in fact *two* philosophies and that these two philosophies have nothing in common except the term *sugar*; that is, neither we, nor the Judge, nor Richard (nor anyone for that matter) can learn anything about the philosophy of cultivating sugar-maple trees by studying the philosophy of cultivating sugar cane.[14] The two cases are as unrelated as are the two climates, those of northeastern America and the West Indies, where the respective plants grow. The Sheriff's reasoning is once again absurd, which seems to be Cooper's point (although as usual Cooper keeps everyone else in the party, including the Judge, silent on this point, so that only the reader is left to recognize Jones's nonsense). Still, there seems to be more of a point than the display of absurdity in Jones's violent verbal strategy. This something more is a point about the conflict of contexts, a conflict we hear again and again as we listen to the arguments between the figures of *The Pioneers*. And violent argument, as Thomas Philbrick has pointed out, is the principal form of linguistic exchange between the figures in Cooper's novel.[15] But my word *exchange*, with its insistence on some sort of reciprocity, is the wrong word to describe what is going on between the Judge and the Sheriff in the present case. For while the Judge speaks within the context of New York sugar maples, the Sheriff responds within a wholly different, or unrelated, context, that of West Indian sugar cane. The Sheriff's response, then, suggests that he does not really hear the Judge, that, in fact, as I have suggested, his purpose, however unconscious, is not to give the Judge a legitimate hearing, but only to condemn him to silence, which we must admit is best done by not hearing him, for then, even if he speaks, he is still silent from the position of his auditor. And, indeed, Richard's 'strategy' seems effective, for the Judge makes no further response to his cousin.

Whatever the reason for the Judge's silence—whether it is simply to keep the peace with his ceaselessly argumentative cousin or because the Judge does not really hear Richard's words (so long has he been listening to Jones's cant that we might excuse a 'deaf-ear' policy)—the effect of the silence articulates the fact that what might have appeared as dialogue is no more than two monologues, related only by the term *sugar*, which is common to both, but only in terms of its sound, not its sense. For all the apparent communication that goes on, each man might as well be speaking within the literal context that his words invoke: the Judge within the confines of New York, and the Sheriff within those of the West Indies. Indeed, in terms of a philosophy of cultivation the word *sugar* in the Judge's context is foreign to the word *sugar* in Jones's context.

Keeping in mind both the foreignness of the contexts—New York and the West Indies—that the Judge and the Sheriff refer to in their 'dialogue' and the way in which this foreignness suggests the two cousins as foreign to, or estranged from, each other, which they are in so many ways throughout the novel, we might hear Richard's response to Marmaduke as an attempt at translation. The Sheriff's translation, however, is not faithful to the context of the Judge's words; rather, the translation freely imposes its own context on them, settling an argument, which it also manufactures, by subduing the Judge to silence. We can also describe this act of free translation, this settlement of an argument, in terms of settling or colonizing territory; for we could say that what the Sheriff attempts with his absurd translation is the imposition of West Indian manners on the inhabitants of New York. In Richard Jones's words an obliteration of boundaries occurs. The Sheriff's violent translation fabricates a fantastic frontier where temperate zone becomes tropics (sugar maples become sugar cane), while the steaming Jones over-runs the mild-tempered Judge.

As I noted previously, following the Sheriff's attack, the Judge is silent and the next voice we hear is that of M. Le Quoi, which, like an echo of the Sheriff's translation of the Judge, mixes two contexts—English and French: 'Sucre! dey do make sucre in Martinique: mais—mais ce n'est pas, one tree; —ah—ah—vat you call—Je voudrois que ces chemins fussent au diable—vat you call—steeck pour le promenade' (223). In his response to the Sheriff's call for authoritative support against the Judge, M. Le Quoi, while speaking what I think can fairly be described as a half-breed tongue, also implicitly marks the radically different contexts of the two cousins by noting that while sugar is manufactured in the West Indies, it is not made from a tree. The Frenchman, however, preoccupied with negotiating the 'steep and slippery' (223) mountain trail, which he curses ('au diable'), cannot come up with the English term for the West Indian sugar plant but can only manage a free translation of it into a wholly different context, that of strolling ('steeck pour le promenade'). Immediately, though, he finds his faithful translator in Elizabeth, who recognizes Le Quoi's polyglot attempt to arrive at a pun: 'steeck pour le promenade' = walking stick = ' "Cane," said Elizabeth, smiling at the imprecation which the wary Frenchman supposed was understood only by himself. "Oui, Mam'selle, cane" ' (223). But before the Frenchman can articulate the philosophy of cultivating cane, as Richard Jones asked him to do, the Sheriff himself, who 'seldom . . . suffered any conversation to continue, for a great length of time, without his participation' (237), once again leaps vocally forward to command the talk with a translation: ' "Yes, Yes," cried Richard, "cane is the vulgar name for it, but the real term is saccharum officinarum; and what we call the sugar, or hard maple, is acer saccharinum. These are the learned names, Monsieur, and are such as, doubtless, you well understand" ' (223).

As we learn at a later point in *The Pioneers*, in a conversation between the Sheriff and the Judge, Richard Jones's father 'could speak. . . . Greek and Latin'. Indeed, at that point, the Judge, weary once again with his cousin's talk, will concede to the Sheriff 'the qualifications of your family in tongues' (317). In the case under scrutiny, we might note, then, that the Sheriff's Latin is correct (his translation of *cane* is faithful). We might also remark that the purpose of his translation appears to be not the furtherance of the 'argument' about the philosophy of making sugar (and how could it be, since there never was such an argument in the first place), but simply the assertion of his qualifications, his authority, no matter how irrelevant this authority might be to the context on which it is imposed. And, as we might expect, following Jones's own translation, M. Le Quoi, whom Jones initially invited to speak in his (Jones's) defence, is silent.

Elizabeth Temple, however, does not let this matter of tongues drop; rather, in a whispered conversation with Edward Oliver Effingham (alias, as we see him now, Oliver Edwards, whom the community suspects of being a half-breed and who is the companion of Natty and Chingachgook), she uses this matter to coyly interrogate the mysterious young man about his identity:

'Is this Greek or Latin, Mr. Edwards?' whispered the heiress to the youth, who was opening a passage for herself and her companions through the bushes—'perhaps it is a still more learned language, for an interpretation of which we must look to you.'

The dark eye of the young man glanced towards the maiden, with a keenness bordering on ferocity; but its expression changed, in a moment, to the smiling playfulness of her own face, as he answered—

'I shall remember your doubts, Miss Temple, when next I visit my old friend Mohegan, and either his skill, or that of Leather-stocking shall solve them.'

'And are you then, really ignorant of their language?' asked Elizabeth, with an impetuosity that spoke a lively interest in the reply.

'Not absolutely; but the deep learning of Mr. Jones is more familiar to me, or even the polite masquerade of Monsieur Le Quoi.'

'Do you speak French?' said the lady, with a quickness that equalled her former interest.

'It is a common language with the Iroquois, and through the Canadas,' he answered with an equivocal smile.

65

'Ah, but they are Mingoes, and your enemies.'

'It will be well for me, if I have no worse,' said the youth, dashing ahead with his horse, and thus putting an end to the evasive dialogue.[16] (223–24)

As Oliver Edwards opens a passage through the forest for Judge Temple's party, Elizabeth Temple, with an apparently playful interrogation of Edwards about his linguistic skills, attempts to open a passage into the young man's identity, which remains, until the very end of the novel, a secret, kept from everyone, including the reader, except Leatherstocking and Indian John; and which, as we will see, interests Elizabeth beyond any simple playfulness. Pursuing the figure of translation, we should note that this attempted passage into Oliver's identity begins in a confusion, a tangle, of tongues; for Elizabeth's opening question exposes her ignorance, whether feigned or real, of the difference between Latin, Greek, and the 'more learned language' of the Delaware. Whether or not Elizabeth is posing as ignorant of the differences between these tongues, we are never told. But clearly she is using her ignorance or her pose of ignorance to pose questions that show she *is* ignorant of Oliver Edward's identity, questions that are themselves posed in terms of determining the differences between certain white and red tongues.

A confusion of identity, then, is posed in terms of a confusion of tongues. This configuration, I propose, is the tangle that marks our passage into *The Pioneers*, our passage, we could say, into a passage of passages. But having found this passage, which way are we to take it? Since we are in Natty Bumppo's territory—however disputed this territory is, by Judge Temple and the other settlers, who by the end of the novel will force Natty from it—and since Natty is such a superb pathfinder, a consummate 'reader' of passages as he describes himself in *The Last of the Mohicans*,[17] only surpassed at times by the red men whose interpretative methods he has adopted, let us try his 'red' methods of finding the way. Let us locate, that is, an exceptional, or readable sign, something that appears unnatural in what might otherwise appear to be the natural course of things, something like a bent twig or a footprint hidden by the passage of a stream.

66

Returning, then, to the tangle at the beginning of our passage to look for a sign, we can find nothing exceptional in Elizabeth Temple's confusion of Latin and Greek; that is, we can imagine without difficulty Cooper intending his readers to take this confusion literally. For women of Cooper's time, which is also in part the fictional time of *The Pioneers*, did not ordinarily receive a classical education. And so while a woman of Elizabeth's social class might have learned some Latin and Greek from the male members of her family and so might recognize the two languages in their written form, it is quite possible that *hearing* two brief Latin phrases (*saccharum officinarum* and *acer saccarinum*) spoken in a distracting situation—the key words of which *saccharum* and *saccarinum* sound very close to the Greek from which they come (*sakharon*)—she might confuse the Latin and the Greek. However, that Elizabeth would confuse these languages with that of the Delaware might very well seem exceptional to Cooper's readers, but not, I think, for linguistic reasons. For even though scholarship on Indian languages was a growing field at the time of the publication of *The Pioneers*, how many of Cooper's readers can we expect read the learned journals where the findings of this scholarship appeared and thus would have been able to identify any of these languages if they had either heard them or seen them transcribed? I can only speculate here, but my guess is not many, beyond the 'experts', some of whose work we will look at momentarily, who contributed to these journals.

If, then, as I am proposing, a 'typical' reader of *The Pioneers* were struck by Elizabeth's confusion of Delaware with Latin and Greek, it would be for ideological reasons (however unconscious, however sublimated into the purely linguistic); that is, it would be because such a confusion appeared to violate the cultural paradigm that prescribed a distinct boundary between the *savage* and the *civilized*. Indeed, Elizabeth Temple's reference to the Delaware language as 'more learned' than either Latin or Greek might not only appear to violate the paradigm in the mind of Cooper's reader, but might even appear to take a decisive step toward reversing the hierarchy that structures the paradigm. Perhaps, then, in order to defend against the idea of such a transgression, this

67

reader might take Elizabeth's reference to Delaware as 'a still more learned language' than either Latin or Greek as simply ironic, a smilingly playful expression of white contempt for the poverty of Indian tongues, when compared to the richness of Western civilization's two great classical languages, although perhaps this reader might translate 'learned' to mean only 'obscure' or 'difficult' in this case, which would avoid the transgression just as effectively. But perhaps Cooper's reader, not requiring the defenses that I have just proposed, would take 'learned' to mean what it says, while still finding Elizabeth's reference exceptional, because it violated a cultural norm. If the reader were to insist on this literal reading or that such a reading was as possible as the other two, and if this reader then happened upon Part II of Heckewelder's *History . . . of the Indian Nations . . .* (1819), which, as far as we know, was the prime source of Cooper's notions of the Delaware and Iroquois, then the reader would find support for a literal reading, although, as we will see (and Cooper's reader might have seen as well) in following certain passages in Heckewelder, the boundary between the literal and the figurative, or ironic, reading of 'learned' is not at all clearly marked.

2

Part II of Heckewelder's *History* is 'A Correspondence' between Heckewelder and Peter S. Duponceau, corresponding secretary of the Historical and Literary Committee of the American Philosophical Society, 'Respecting the Languages of the American Indians'. In 'Letter XII', from Duponceau to Heckewelder, we find the following questions: 'But who cares for the poor American Indians? They are savages and barbarians and live in the woods; must not their languages be savage and barbarous like them?' Throughout the correspondence, Duponceau's answer to this last question, and Heckewelder enthusiastically supports him in this answer, is an emphatic 'No.' Indeed, far from being 'savage and barbarous like them' (a phrase I will return to shortly), Indian languages, as Duponceau understands them with Hecke-welder's help, are at least as learned (as complex, as rich) and at times more so than Latin and Greek, to which Duponceau is constantly comparing the language of the Delaware, or *Lenni Lenape*, the tribe that for Heckewelder, who was a missionary among them, represented the height of savage civilization (a paradoxical assessment that Cooper assumes in his work). In 'Letter XVI' Duponceau, sketching a classification of all languages, groups Latin and Greek into the category of the '*synthetic*', 'in which several ideas are frequently expressed by one word'. And, like Latin and Greek, 'Indian languages . . . are "*synthetic*" in their forms, but to such a degree as is not equaled by any of the idioms which I have so denominated. . . .' Indian tongues, then, 'deserve to make a class by themselves'; for

> [t]hey are the very opposite of the Chinese, of all languages the poorest in words, as well as in grammatical forms [Duponceau does tell us that he is 'no Sinologist'] while [Indian tongues] are the richest in both. . . . In the Chinese much is understood or guessed at, little is expressed; in the Indian, on the contrary, the mind is awakened to each idea meant to be conveyed, by some one or other of the component parts of the word spoken. These two languages, therefore, as far as relates to their organisation, stand in direct opposition to each other; they are the top and bottom of the idiomatic scale, and as I have given to the Chinese, and its kindred dialects, the name of *asyntactic*, the opposite name, *syntactic*, appears to me that which is best suited to the languages of the American Indians.[18]

Having placed Indian languages at 'the top' of the 'idiomatic scale', richer 'in words' and 'grammatical forms' than even Latin and Greek, Duponceau confirms this hierarchy with a rhetorical question in 'Letter XX': 'The Greek is admired for its compounds; but what are they to those of the Indians?' And in the same letter, in a similar vein, he grows positively ecstatic, when considering the Delaware compound '*Wulamalessohalian*! THOU WHO MAKEST ME HAPPY!':

> I will not proceed further; but permit me to ask you, my dear sir, what would Tibullus or Sappho have given to have had at their command a word at once so tender and so expressive? How delighted would be Moore, the poet of the loves and graces, if his language, instead of five or six tedious words slowly following in the rear of each other, had furnished him

with an expression like this, in which the lover, the object beloved, and the delicious sentiment which their mutual passion inspires, are blended, are fused together in one comprehensive appellative term? And it is in the languages of savages that these beautiful forms are found! What a subject for reflection, and how little do we know, as yet, of the astonishing things that the world contains![19]

We have before us a scene of translation in several senses of the word. As 'Letter XX' tells us, Duponceau, at the time he is corresponding with Heckewelder, is 'busily employed in studying and translating [from German to English] the excellent Delaware Grammar of [David] Zeisberger',[20] who, until his death in 1808, was a colleague of Heckewelder. Further, of course, Duponceau's comparison of Indian tongues to Latin and Greek implies the activity of translation, which can only proceed on the basis of such comparisons. In addition, there is another sense of the word 'translation' that seems operative here; for in the *O.E.D.* we find that to *translate* can mean 'to transport with the strength of some feeling; to enrapture, [or] entrance.' And so, we might translate the translation of *Wulamalessohalian*, THOU WHO MAKEST ME HAPPY!, as THOU WHO TRANSLATEST ME, noticing that in Duponceau's description of the compound its very action on what it represents is one of translation, for it 'fuse[s] together in one comprehensive appellative term' 'the lover, the object beloved, and the delicious sentiment which their mutual passion inspires'; fuses them together, indeed, as Duponceau in his ecstasy seems fused with the word and the language he is so lovingly translating. *Wulamalessohalian*, Lewis Cass notes in taking exception to Duponceau's orthographical transcription, and translation of the word, 'has such power to kindle his [Duponceau's] enthusiasm'.[21]

This act of translation, however, is not simply an act of pure ecstatic empathy with, or faithful representation of, 'the poor American Indians'. Let us grant that Duponceau's translation seems intent on rescuing the Indians from translations like those of Lewis Cass, who, in the course of attacking Cooper, Heckewelder and Duponceau over a two-year span in the pages of the *North American Review*, finds Indian tongues 'harsh in the utterance, inartificial in their construction, indeterminate in their application, and incapable of expressing a vast variety of ideas, particularly those which relate to invisible objects'; tongues, Cass continues, that conform 'to the complaint of Cicero' about Latin, 'that it was unfit for metaphysical investigations'.[22] Let us grant Duponceau's opposition to this stance, and even appreciate it, but let us also notice that Duponceau's translation, while attempting to rescue Indian languages from the clutches of experts like Cass,[23] also appropriates these languages in this romantic rescue mission in ways that dispossess the Indians of their tongues, leaving them, to borrow Lewis Henry Morgan's words, 'passive and silent spectators'[24] of an act of colonization from which they are removed. We can see this act of translation as colonization in a passage cited earlier, where, preparing to eulogize Indian languages, Duponceau implicitly separates the languages from the people who speak them: '[M]ust not their languages be savage and barbarous *like them?*' Duponceau asks Heckewelder. And the form of the question initiates the ironic rescue of the languages from their native speakers. Duponceau leaves the Indians in a state of silent 'savagery' while he translates their languages into the 'civilized' territory of the classics. 'If', Duponceau writes, the '[Delaware] language was cultivated and polished as those of Europe have been, and if the Delawares had a Homer or Virgil among them, it is impossible to say with such an instrument how far the art could be carried.'[25]

With motives apparently opposite to those of Lewis Cass, Duponceau's translation enacts a similar dispossession, the removal of Indian tongues into the mouths of white poets and scholars, where (and it is only here that Duponceau's vision differs from that of Cass) these tongues can be 'cultivated and polished' in order to realize what the passage suggests is their virtually unlimited 'civilized' potential. Duponceau does not tell us if, having been cultivated in white mouths, these tongues will then be given back to the Indians.

Duponceau's removal of Indian tongues might figure for us another form of Indian removal that was already taking place during the time of his correspondence with Heckewelder (1816), and would continue to do so with increasing intensity, becoming official government policy, during the quarter-

71

century following, when Cooper was publishing his Leatherstocking Tales. The removal I refer to is the quite literal
translation of the Indians by the American government from
their homelands in the east to lands reserved for them west of
the Mississippi. Michael Paul Rogin reminds us that 'from
Jefferson's Presidency to the Mexican War, expansion across
the continent was the central fact of American politics.' And
this expansion was acccompanied by, indeed based upon, the
dispossession of the Indians through what Rogin quite rightly
terms 'acts of force and fraud'. '125,000 Indians lived east of
the Mississippi in 1820,' Rogin continues. 'Seventy-five
percent of these came under government removal programs in
the next two decades. By 1844 less than 30,000 Indians
remained in the east, mainly in the undeveloped Lake
Superior region.'[26]

By the 1790s, when Cooper was a boy, growing up by the
shore of Lake Otsego in New York, the territory he would
figure forth as Judge Temple's domain in *The Pioneers*, the
Iroquois, who appear as the villainous Mingoes in three of
Cooper's Leatherstocking Tales, had virtually vanished from
their former homes, treated, tricked, or simply forced out of
their land after the Revolution. And the Delaware, whom,
following Heckewelder, Cooper would convert into his good
Indians, enemies of the Mingoes in the same three tales, and
who were occupying New Jersey, Cooper's birthplace, when
the first settlers arrived in the New World, had been pushed
west of the Alleghenies into the Ohio wilderness by the force of
white settlement. 'You have had the advantage of me,' Cooper
is reported to have said to an acquaintance, 'for I was never
among the Indians. All I know is from reading and from
hearing my father speak of them.'[27] Although he was never
among the Indians, with the exception, perhaps, of brief
contact with 'some small party of the Oneidas, or other
representatives of the Five Nations' and 'deputations to
Washington from the Western tribes',[28] Cooper grew up on a
vast tract of land conveyed by the Indians to George Croghan
in 1768. In 1769 Croghan obtained a royal patent to the land,
which was later bought by Cooper's father, Judge William
Cooper, at a mortgage sale. Questions remain, pertaining to
the rights of Croghan's heirs, about the legality of Judge

Cooper's settlement of and on the 20,000-acre Croghan patent, land that Cooper and his brothers were legally dispossessed of by creditors, during the time that he was writing *The Pioneers* (1821–22). And most recently, in a psychoanalytic reading of Cooper's novel, Stephen Railton has reintroduced parallels between the Croghan and Effingham families, and between Cooper's father and Judge Temple.[29] But, perhaps, in any exploration of the historical contexts of *The Pioneers*, questions of dispossession and legality should focus first neither on the Croghans nor the Coopers but on the Indians, whose initial cession of the land, both in and outside of the novel, sets these legal conflicts in motion.

I am not suggesting that George Croghan's Indian deed was illegal. On the contrary, the evidence points to its legality,[30] just as within *The Pioneers*, as we will see, the Indians willingly cede their land to the Effinghams. What I am suggesting is that the very word *legal*—a word that much of the criticism of *The Pioneers* has focused on—when applied to white dealings with Indians, marks a violent problem in translation. That is, we must question whether this white term, historically inseparable as it is from the notion of land as private property, has any meaningful equivalent in cultures where land is not *owned* (at least not, apparently, in our sense of the term) but held in common.[31] And if the term *legal* cannot be translated into Indian tongues with any significant degree of faithfulness, in what sense is it 'legitimate' to use this term as a mark that differentiates between acts of force and fraud and acts *we* term 'legal'? But even if we were to insist on the possibility of such a translation (and this possibility needs to be more rigorously pursued than I have the space for here[32]), we would still have to consider the position of the term *legal* in the violent history of white and red contact. Wilcomb E. Washburn comments on the ironically legal beginnings of that history:

> The status of the American Indian was locked into Catholic doctrine and Spanish legalism almost from the moment of discovery [of the New World]. The relationship was not to be merely that of conquerer and conquered. The Indian was condemned by a preexisting theory to a status by which he served as a material resource to be exploited and as a spiritual object to be saved. His dependence was fore-ordained by his

attacker. His status as a member of an independent community or nation could be formally denied even when he was able to maintain that independence against his oppressors.

The most direct and naïve expression of the Europeans' assumption of preexisting status in the New World is contained in the Spanish 'Requirement' (*Requerimiento*) which was ordered to be read to the Indians by a notary before hostilities could legally be commenced. The Requirement was [and in the following Washburn quotes from Lewis U. Hankel] 'read to trees and empty huts when no Indians were to be found. Captains muttered its theological phrases into their beards on the edge of sleeping Indian settlements, or even a league away before starting the formal attack, and at times some leather-lunged Spanish notary hurled its sonorous phrases after the Indians as they fled into the mountains. . . . Ship captains would sometimes have the document read from the deck as they approached an island. . . .'[33]

What Washburn's and Hanke's comments suggest is that the conquering of the New World, which is synonymous with the dispossession of the Indians, begins with the conversion of the Indian into a religious and legal fiction: 'a material resource to be exploited and . . . a spiritual object to be saved' (and the thrust of material exploitation and spiritual salvation cannot be separated here). In the beginning, then, in the white mind, the Indian becomes a pure figure, his/her 'independent', or literal, 'status' 'formally denied' in foreign language documents in which this figure is bound to prescribed paths and which, projected on the literal Indians, are then taken for the literal. In the beginning, before literal colonization begins or, rather, as an activity that is inseparable from the act of actual dispossession, we find the activity of colonization as translation, both in the meaning of the word as conversion from one language into another and as use in a metaphorical or transferred sense. In this case, however, the sense of translation means precisely not to understand the other that is the original (inhabitant), or to understand that other all too easily, that is, as if there were no question of translation, solely in terms of one's own language, where the other becomes a useable fiction.

The kind of translation that Washburn and Hanke describe for us and that we have seen Duponceau practice—at least in part—recalls Richard Jones's violent translation of Judge Temple's discourse on sugar maples, which forged what I termed a 'fantastic frontier'. It is, then, within this context that I want to return now to Elizabeth Temple's smilingly playful interrogation of Oliver Edwards; for, as I have tried to suggest in beginning to link the interrogation to Duponceau's translation and the policy of Indian removal, I think that if we can translate this interrogation, which is itself a scene of translation, it can speak to us both about the fantastic frontier of *The Pioneers* and about the fantastic frontier of America that *The Pioneers* plays a part in generating.

3

In referring to Elizabeth Temple's interrogation of Oliver Edwards as a scene of translation, I am initially calling attention to its most obvious aspect: Elizabeth's apparent confusion of classical and Indian tongues and her strategic appeal to Oliver as a possible translator of these tongues, that is, as someone who might distinguish between them. That Judge Temple's daughter appears less interested in making these distinctions than she does in distinguishing the identity of Oliver Edwards is no more than an effect of *The Pioneers'* plot, which is determined by the movement of answering the question of Oliver's identity. Yet as I want to suggest, the question and the answer to this question, which resolves Cooper's plot, cannot be separated from the problems of translation that I have been raising: problems that have to do with the violent relation between the literal and the metaphoric as this relation figures the question of white and red identity and makes Cooper's plot inseparable from the plot into which white history weaves the Indians.

As I have noted, the community of Templeton suspects young Edwards of being half-breed (part Delaware, part white) for reasons that I will turn to shortly. Since, however, Judge Temple's daughter is falling in love with Edwards (the plot of the novel culminates with their marriage), she has a strong interest in proving whether he is white or red. For whatever egalitarian notions Elizabeth may share with her father, these notions are subsumed in *The Pioneers*, as well as in the rest of the Leatherstocking Tales, by the taboo against racial *amalgamation* (the term *miscegenation* was not coined until 1864), a taboo reflected throughout the tales both in Natty Bumppo's obsessive concern with proclaiming his own whiteness, which from the perspective of the white settlers is always in doubt, and in the difficulty in certain of the tales that the marriage proposals of red men to their white female captives have in getting translated.[34] One of the strong messages of the Leatherstocking Tales is quite clearly that a white, particularly a white female, is 'better dead than red' or, more accurately put, better dead than married to a red, which seems to amount to the same thing. So while Judge Temple does take Oliver Edwards into his home (in apparent atonement for shooting the strange young man in a hunting accident that opens the novel and that I will explore shortly) and while he argues with Richard Jones's prejudice against half-breeds that 'all are equal who know how to conduct themselves with propriety' (205), we realize as *The Pioneers* progresses and within the context of the Leatherstocking Tales, that the marriage of white and red automatically violates the propriety that is the basis for this equality.

When Elizabeth Temple, then, begins her smilingly playful interrogation of Oliver Edwards with the implication that he speaks the 'more learned language' of the Delaware (and thus *is* a Delaware, an apparent equation of language and identity that I will return to), we should not be surprised that Oliver's response, which suggests to Elizabeth that he may be 'ignorant of their language', seems to provoke such a 'lively interest' in her. But the first part of Oliver's response to Elizabeth's second question—'And are you then, really ignorant of their language?'—only confuses the hope she seems to be momentarily entertaining about the possibility of his white identity; for he replies, '*Not absolutely*; but the deep learning of Mr. Jones is more familiar to me, or even the polite masquerade of Monsieur Le Quoi.' Having moved away from and now back toward an identification with the Delaware tongue, Edwards, in the second part of his response, by referring, ironically perhaps, to 'the deep learning of Mr. Jones', implicitly separates Delaware and the Latin and Greek that Elizabeth apparently confuses. Elizabeth, however, does not comment on this implicit declaration of distinction (perhaps because it does nothing to settle Oliver Edwards's identification with the Delaware); but 'with a quickness that equalled her former interest' asks the young man if he speaks French, as if his knowledge of this most civilized of tongues might prove that he is not a 'demi-savage' (206). In his response, however, Edwards, 'with an equivocal smile' that confuses Elizabeth Temple's hope once again, identifies French not with the so-called 'civilized' but with the so-called 'savage': 'It is a common language with the Iroquois, and through the Canadas', he tells Elizabeth; and her response to Oliver's association of French and Iroquois suggests that her hopes for the possibility of his whiteness are not simply confused but completely frustrated, at least momentarily: 'Ah, but they are Mingoes, and *your* enemies,' she exclaims, in reference to the traditional rivalry between the Delaware and the Iroquois (a complex political relation that Heckewelder and Cooper, following him, simplify terribly[35]). The reference, which again raises the problem of language and identity by suggesting that opposites should not or could not speak the same language, translates Oliver Edwards back into the identity of an Indian; and his response, which 'put[s] an end to the evasive dialogue', does nothing to correct Elizabeth's translation: ' "It will be well for me, if I have no worse [enemies]," said the youth, dashing ahead with his horse. . . .'

The passage I have been analysing, in which a white woman attempts to track down the racial identity of a racially ambiguous figure, who continually escapes the pursuit by identifying with a mixture of tongues, raises the problem of the relationship between language and identity to which I have been alluding. This concern also appears forcefully in the social ciriticism Cooper collected under the title of *The American Democrat* (1838), and it is there that I want to explore this concern briefly, as a way of turning back to *The Pioneers*.

In *The American Democrat* Cooper tells us that among 'the common faults of American language' is an 'ambiguity of expression' (a complaint that Tocqueville, at the same time, voices as well) and that one of the effects of this ambiguity is to lead 'society' into 'mistaking names for things'. But, Cooper continues, 'the effort to subvert things by names' is ultimately 'inefficien[t]'. For however ambiguous or volatile names may be, Cooper suggests, they still remain extrinsic to things; and so things, no matter what names may do, retain their proper identities.[36]

In his chapter 'On Language' in *The American Democrat*, Cooper's prime example of the attempted subversion of things by names and the defence of things against this subversion is the use and the misuse of the word 'gentleman'. And as we read this example, what we find Cooper objecting violently to is the *extension* of this name past the limits of *propriety*, until what he imagines as its 'especial signification' is lost in the translation of the name, which he sees in his worst imaginings becoming 'synonymous with man'.[37] What Cooper is describing here, whatever he may intend, is *not* the subversion of things by names, at least not literally; rather, he is describing the movement we call 'metaphor' (the extension of a word beyond its conventional, or 'proper', boundaries to include other significations) and expressing his anxiety that this movement will become altogether too democratic, that is, go too far, finally obliterating the boundaries between the traditional (gentleman) and the new (man, that is, all men). We might recognize, then, that Cooper's opposition, things/names, is a figure for the opposition literal/metaphoric; and that the boundary Cooper asserts between the territory of language and the territory beyond language is actually a boundary dividing two territories of language. To put it another way: whatever desires the name 'things' expresses for a territory beyond names, a territory of pure nature, there is no such 'beyond' in Cooper's 'On Language'; rather, this territory is a political fiction intent on containing the spread of democracy, which Cooper figures here as the subversion of things by names.

Let us drop this fiction (things/names) for a moment, then, and talk in terms of the opposition that structures it, that between the literal and the metaphoric (although when we reach the end of *The Pioneers*, we will find that this opposition is a political fiction as well). As Cooper's example of this opposition—the use and misuse of the term 'gentleman'—might suggest, the distinction between the literal and the metaphoric is inseparable for Cooper from a notion of the 'civilized': 'A just, clear and simple expression of our ideas [one that uses names properly, or unambiguously] is a necessary accomplishment for all who aspire to be classed with gentlemen and ladies.' And 'no civilized society can exist without these social differences.'[38] Cooper's notion of civilization as that state which distinguishes between the literal and the metaphoric repeats precisely Rousseau's notion of civilization in *The Essay on the Origin of Languages* and implies what Rousseau makes explicit: the savage is that which blurs, or destroys, such a distinction.[39] This notion should have the force of reminding us that, like the opposition names/things, the opposition savage/civilized is a division that figures a division *within* the language where these terms, or translations of them, like names/things, occur, but that this division within is projected as a division between an outside and an inside, which is typically seen as natural rather than conventional (such is the case with the oppositions names/things and savage/civilized). What makes such a projection possible, however, appears to be the fact that the initial division within is already perceived as natural itself, that is, as a division between an absolute outside and an absolute inside. Thus, to recall my discussion of Aristotle's theory of metaphor, the division between the literal and the metaphoric implicitly *naturalizes* the literal by equating it with the national and opposing it to that outside termed the figurative, or foreign.

That such absolute distinctions cannot, finally, be argued we are, no doubt, aware. But that they continue to be made is, of course, another matter, a matter of foreign policy, let us say, where the projection of an absolute other (some kind of savage) has played and continues to play such a destructively significant part. As we will see now, the plot of *The Pioneers* is written within such a foreign policy distinction, that between the literal and the metaphoric, a distinction the plot tries to naturalize, even as the movement of the plot calls this naturalization process into question.

4

We first meet Oliver Edwards at the beginning of *The Pioneers*, when, as noted, Judge Temple wounds him in a hunting accident. It is Christmas Eve and the Judge is returning to Templeton with Elizabeth, after her four-year sojourn at school. He stops their sleigh when he hears the barking of Natty's hound, Hector, whose 'bay', the Judge announces, 'I should know . . . among ten thousand' (19). Immediately the Judge spots a 'deer-track' and 'extricat[es] a double-barrelled fowling piece' from the baggage in the sleigh. Directly, 'a fine buck dart[s] into the path.' The Judge fires twice, but '[n]either discharge . . . seem[s] to . . . take [. . .] effect.' Two shots, coming from the forest, follow. The buck leaps 'to a great height in the air' with the first, and falls to the earth with the second, which is accompanied by the 'loud Shout' of an 'unseen marksman' (20).

Instantly Natty Bumppo and his companion, Oliver Edwards, appear from the forest. And there ensues an argument, first between Natty and the Judge, and then between Oliver and the Judge, over who killed the deer. The form of this argument is that of legal proceedings, each side presenting evidence, based on the number of shots in the buck, to enforce its claim of ownership. But as Stephen Railton notes, 'Leather-stocking's repl[ies to the Judge] seem [. . .] slightly out of context'[40]; for the Judge wants to stick to the immediate case in hand, while Natty takes the occasion first to lecture the Judge on the Judge's incongruous choice of a fowling piece to shoot deer, next on his (Natty's) 'lawful dues in a free country', and then on the general scarcity of game brought about by the Judge's settlement (21–2). These lectures, which Natty formulates in a characteristic dialect that distinguishes him from the Judge who speaks the literary English of Cooper's aristocrats, are also interwoven with nostalgic anecdotes of the good old days before settlement. And these nostalgic anecdotes may make Natty's 'arguments' seem even more 'out of context'.

But what we should note is that when Railton says that Natty's responses to the Judge seem out of context, what he means or should mean is that they seem out of the *Judge's* context; that is, in dropping the Judge's name as the possessive adjective of context, Railton appears to take the Judge's context as the only context, the 'natural', or absolute, ground of the argument. However, the Judge's context is only the literal one, in the conventional, or legal, sense that he possesses the literal ground (the land) on which the argument is being conducted. Just as we heard Richard Jones and the Judge using the word *sugar* in contexts that make the word foreign to itself, untranslatable into itself except in the most violent way, so in the argument over the deer, the word *legal*, or *lawful*, which is used explicitly by Natty and is implied in the very figure of the Judge, is alienated from itself. For as this opening scene suggests and the rest of the novel demonstrates, Natty's use of 'lawful' opposes the Judge's use of it, which is structured by the right of the individual to own land, a right, a concept, that does not translate into Natty's world. Within the Judge's context, then, Natty, is using or, rather, misusing the term *law* by using it in a transferred, or metaphorical, sense (not in its proper sense); while within Natty's context, the Judge is using the term, or misusing it, in the same way. What is literal ground for Judge Temple (ground that can be owned by an individual) is from Natty's perspective fictional, or figurative, ground, while what is literal ground for Bumppo (ground open continually to the free use of all) is from the Judge's point of view fictional, or figurative, ground. While throughout *The Pioneers* Natty Bumppo and Judge Temple stand upon the same ground and ground their opposing arguments in the same term, *legal*, the alienation of the term from itself—its state of being in translation between what we usually term the literal and the metaphoric—calls into question the absolute literalness of all ground, the literalness of the literal, by suggesting the alienation of any term from itself, inasmuch as a term can never settle completely in a single context, but necessarily inhabiting a number of contexts simultaneously, comes to unsettle itself with its own foreignness when these contexts conflict, forging the activity we call politics.

In the middle of the argument between Natty and the Judge, Leatherstocking suggests to Judge Temple that it was neither he nor the Judge who killed the buck, but Oliver Edwards. The Judge offers to buy the deer from the young man, but the youth insists on '[f]irst ... determin[ing] the question of right [to the animal] to the satisfaction of us both', and 'with a pronunciation and language vastly superior to his appearance' asks the Judge: '[W]ith how many shot did you load your gun?' The Judge answers 'five', and Oliver, operating deftly, like a 'young advocate', proves to the Judge that he, Oliver, must have killed the deer, which has two shots in it; for there are, he points out, four bullets in the tree from behind which he appeared and in which direction the Judge shot, and the fifth, far from being one of the two in the buck, is in his own body (24). The Judge seems truly appalled at what Stephen Railton calls this 'legalistic revelation'[41] of his own carelessness, and in what can only be seen as an over-determined response offers not only to take Oliver home, pay his doctor's fees, and let the young man live there until he is healed, but also 'for ever afterwards' (25). As we will see, the Judge's unlimited generosity will appear to have been, from the vantage point of the end of the novel, an unconscious recognition that Edwards is no stranger at all, but has legal claims to the Judge's property. At the time of this first meeting this unconscious recognition seems marked by the fact that the youth's face is 'very familiar' to the Judge; yet Marmaduke cannot 'tell [his] name' (38), and, as we have read, in Cooper's work names, whatever the desire to do so, cannot be separated from the question of identity. (Oliver Edwards has not yet offered his pseudonym to the Judge and when he does, the Judge will not recognize that it is a transference of the first names of two people who are known to him, Oliver and Edward Effingham, Oliver Edwards's grandfather and father respectively.)

After some pleading on behalf of her father by Elizabeth, Oliver does agree to accompany the Temples home to have his wound cared for, and eventually stays on as the Judge's secretary, although his decisions are marked by a sharp reluctance and he displays at times an open, though apparently unfounded, hostility toward his host. Since the source of this hostility is the key to Edwards's identity, Cooper must find a way of justifying it in a masked form until the plot of the novel has run its course. The device he chooses is to make Oliver Edwards appear to be part Indian. And Edwards is allowed to slip into his mask by a speech of Indian John, made to the Anglican minister, Mr. Grant, and heard by Grant's daughter, Louisa, and Oliver, both of whom are accompanying the

minister and Mohegan back to the Grant's house after a
Christmas Eve church service, in which the minister has been
preaching a sermon on the dangerous 'obscurities of [biblical]
language' that, 'abounding in metaphors and loaded with
figures', have led to 'heresies' and 'schisms' (129, 127, 129).
Mr. Grant, who on the way home has been querying Oliver
about 'which of the states' the young man is a 'native'
of—something that he is 'at a loss to conjecture, from
[Oliver's] dialect' (137)—remarks on Oliver's 'resentment' 'to
Judge Temple' and proceeds to lecture the young man 'on
[this,] one of the worst of human passions': 'It was wrong, my
dear sir, very wrong, to suffer such feelings to rise, under any
circumstances, and especially in the present, where the evil
was not intended'—the 'evil' referred to being Oliver's
accidental wound. Oliver does not immediately respond to
this short sermon on Christian forgiveness, but Mohegan does:

> 'There is good in the talk of my father,' said Mohegan, stopping
> short, and causing those who were behind him to pause also; 'It
> is the talk of Miquon. The white man may do as his fathers
> have told him; but the "Young Eagle" has the blood of a
> Delaware chief in his veins: it is red, and the stain it makes, can
> only be washed out with the blood of a Mingo.' (138)

James Grossman's comment that 'Cooper delighted in con-
founding the ignorant with the mystification of jargon' bears
repeating here; for although Grossman intended this comment
to refer to the sea jargon of *The Pilot*, which to 'the unaided
reader' is 'a foreign language dimly understood',[42] we might
also apply it to the metaphorical language of Cooper's
Indians, which can also be mystifying to the extent that this
language often interrupts the steady progress of one's reading
and requires translation into the literal so that plot and action
can be followed. The speech of Mohegan, just cited, is a case
in point; and so we might begin to translate its metaphors into
the literal terms of Cooper's plot, as a way of continuing our
progress toward the revelation of Oliver Edwards's identity at
the end of the novel.

When Indian John tells Mr. Grant that '[t]here is good in
the talk of my father', he endorses to a certain extent the
Christian forgiveness that the minister has been preaching.

And this endorsement, if we need reminding, reminds us that John has been converted to Christianity by the Moravians, that he is, like his 'brother', Natty Bumppo, 'a mixture of the civilized and savage states, though there was certainly a strong preponderance in favour of the latter' in both Mohegan and Natty, whose 'habits', we are told, are 'so nearly assimilated to those of the savages' (85). This preponderance in Mohegan appears in the rest of his speech. Chingachgook tells Mr. Grant that the minister's talk is 'the talk of Miquon' (the Delaware name of William Penn, which Cooper has previously translated for us (84)), a figurative reference, it seems, to the talk of white peace-makers in general and specifically, perhaps, to that of Judge Temple, a Quaker in origin, who in his official position is also the prime keeper of the peace in Templeton. Mohegan emphasizes his suggestion that forgiveness is an exclusively white habit in the following sentence:

> The white man may do as his fathers have told him; but the 'Young Eagle' has the blood of a Delaware chief in his veins: it is red, and the stain it makes can only be washed out with the blood of a Mingo.

If we do not recognize immediately that 'Young Eagle' is a reference to Oliver Edwards (and we may not for this is the first time the name has been mentioned and its reference is therefore obscure), five paragraphs later, Louisa Grant pins the epithet on Oliver for us when, taking Indian John at his word, she remarks to the young man that 'by [Mohegan's] language' she recognizes that the Indian 'may be [Oliver's] relative' (139). There remains, then, only one sentence for us to translate, Mohegan's remark that 'the blood of a Delaware chief . . . is red, and the stain it makes, can only be washed out with the blood of a Mingo.' In a footnote Cooper himself translates 'Mingo' (the Delaware name for the Iroquois), telling us that we are to take it figuratively, as meaning 'enemy' in general. And we, unless we think that Indian John is simply being redundant when he says the blood of a Delaware chief is 'red', recognize that he is using red figuratively, by using it literally. The sentence, then, translated by Oliver for us and Louisa Grant a few paragraphs later, reads: '. . . revenge is a virtue with an Indian. They are taught, from infancy upward, to believe it a duty, never to allow an injury to pass unrevenged . . .' (140).

Oliver's reference to the Indians as 'they', along with his insistence to Louisa that he has 'been taught deep and practical lessons of forgiveness' (140), seems to distance him from Chingachgook's identification of him as a 'Delaware chief', but it only distances him partially. And so until the end of the story, he is taken by all the characters, except for Indian John and Natty Bumppo who know the secret of his identity, and presumably by Cooper's readers (who, no doubt, must assert their naïveté here), as a half-breed. Oliver accepts this identity and so in the course of the story we, along with the characters in *The Pioneers*, hear him make speeches that, in referring to himself as a dispossessed Indian, apparently refer to the red man's dispossession by the white.

Our belief in Oliver Edwards' mixed identity and thus in his advocacy of the land rights of his apparently proper people (for it seems that in this case a half-breed winds up functioning as a whole Indian) depends on our taking Chingachgook's identifying speech and all subsequent references to Oliver as a Delaware literally, as Louisa Grant and the other settlers in the novel do. And if we take Chingachgook at his word, then along with the settlers of Templeton we will be surprised at the end of the novel when we discover that we have been reading Chingachgook, and Oliver and Natty, who also speaks of Oliver in Chingachgook's terms, wrongly, according to the conventions of the white community in *The Pioneers*. For within these conventions, which Chingachgook's speech appears to question by using the metaphoric literally, Oliver is not a literal Indian, but a figurative one.

As it turns out, Oliver Edwards is Edward Oliver Effingham, grandson of Major Oliver Effingham and son of Colonel Edward Effingham. The latter, we find, was a business associate of the Judge before the Revolutionary War. But during the conflict the two took opposite sides (the Judge siding with the colonists, Edward Effingham with the crown); and by various twists and turns, which the plot reveals to us, the Judge, who at the outbreak of the war had become the trustee of Edwards's 'valuable effects and papers' (36), also became, after the war, 'the lawful purchaser' of his 'real estates', estates 'that old Mohegan (whose life . . . [Oliver's] grandfather once saved) induced the Delawares to grant . . . [the grandfather], when they admitted him as an honorary member of their tribe' (440, 441). Oliver, his father dead, has come to the Judge's patent, seeking his grandfather, who, reduced to senility, is under the care of Chingachgook and Natty (the latter, who grew up in the Major's household and became his 'servant', is repaying a continuous debt to his 'master' with this care). Oliver's hostility to the Judge, we find then, is a product not of his advocacy of Indian rights (at least not of literal Indian rights) but of his belief that the Judge has dispossessed the Effinghams of their land, land to which Oliver was the sole heir. The Judge, however, is no 'Mingo' and to prove this he will show Oliver his will, in which the young man has always been included by (his white) name as the equal heir of the Judge's estates along with Elizabeth. But before this 'legalistic revelation' of the Judge's 'whiteness', Oliver reveals to the Judge that he is also white, that Mohegan's reference to his blood as 'red' was absolutely figurative, or to put it another way, absolutely literal.

Upon hearing Oliver Edwards's tale of his whiteness, Judge Temple responds with what seems a rhetorical question: 'This, then, is thy Indian blood?' But Oliver, lest there be the slightest confusion between the literal and the metaphoric, answers the question:

> 'I have no other,' said Edwards, smiling;—'Major Effingham was adopted as the son of Mohegan, who at that time was the greatest man in his nation; and my father, who visited those people when a boy, received the name of the Eagle from them, on account of the shape of his face, as I understand. They have extended his title to me. I have no other Indian blood or breeding; though I have seen the hour, Judge Temple, when I could wish that such had been my lineage and education.' (441)

But the hour is different now. And as Edward Oliver Effingham reminds us with his smile, this proof of his whiteness is the real happy ending of *The Pioneers*—his marriage to Elizabeth and his acquiring of his lost land being contingent on this proof. Oliver, joyfully, is an Indian in name only. And in this case, as opposed to the ambiguous case of

86

Literally White, Figuratively Red

Natty Bumppo, whose white and Indian names mix indiscriminately throughout the Leatherstocking Tales, suggesting the ambiguity of Natty's identity, Indian names do not 'subvert' white nature, which remains safe from the incursions of amalgamation by settling in the territory of legal 'things'. Cooper's plot insists on this safety by insisting on an absolute distinction between the literal and the metaphoric, which, as I have argued, is another way of equating the literal with the natural, a way that settles those unsettling questions of identity that until the very end of the novel disturb the identity of Oliver Young Eagle Edwards. And in this settlement, in which Edward Oliver (Edwards) 'Young Eagle' Effingham is literal white man and figurative red man, we should note that the Indian half of Effingham ends by being freely translated into that territory of pure figurativeness, which, as we have seen, marks the white man's dispossession of the red. The white man, of course, remains to occupy the territory of the literal, the legal territory of real names: Edward Oliver Effingham, *contractually*, gets the girl and the land.

And what of Young Eagle? His fate, we might suspect, is that of Chingachgook, who, literally dead at the end of the novel (having passively, or is it stoically, accepted his death in a forest fire), must nevertheless undergo one final translation into white tongues, a translation pronounced by Young Eagle himself within a scene of naming, where we find Effingham and Elizabeth, married now, standing with Natty before the graves of Major Oliver Effingham and Chingachgook. Since Natty is illiterate, he depends on his young friend to read the inscriptions on the tombstones, and is overjoyed when he finds that his own name is 'cut in the stone, by the side of his master's', so overjoyed that he has 'Effingham guide [. . .] his finger to the spot', where he [Natty] 'follow[s] the windings of the letters to the end'. Having reached the end of this literal path, Natty asks his guide to read the inscription 'over the Red-skin', and Effingham begins the passage:

> 'This stone is raised to the memory of an Indian chief, of the Delaware tribe, who was known by the several names of John Mohegan; Mohican'—
> 'Mo-hee-can, lad [Natty interrupts]; they call theirselves! 'hee-can.'

87

'Mohican; and Chingagook'—
'Gach, boy;—'gach-gook; Chingachgook; which, intarpreted, means Big-sarpent. The name should be set down right, for an Indian's name has always some meaning in it.'
'I will see it altered. "He was the last of his people who continued to inhabit this country; and it may be said of him, that his faults were those of an Indian, and his virtues those of a man."'

Finally, the Indian is translated out of the world of 'man' to become in the logic of this passage of butchered red names, another species altogether. What is left after this last removal is indeed a fantastic frontier, the white male world figured as all that is human. From Elizabeth Temple Effingham, who has been listening, along with Natty Bumppo, to her husband's eulogy of Chingachgook, we hear nothing. But from Natty, that faithful translator of Indian tongues, we hear: 'You never said truer word, Mr. Oliver . . .' (451, 452).

NOTES

1. James Fenimore Cooper, *The Pioneers, or the Sources of the Susquehanna: A Descriptive Tale* (1823; rpt. Albany: State University of New York Press, 1980), p. 165. Except in one instance, which I note, all subsequent citations from *The Pioneers* are taken from this edition, with page numbers appearing in parentheses after the citation.

2. A particularly good example of what I take to be Cooper's belief in his pose is his 1850 introduction to *The Last of the Mohicans*, where he speaks with the authority of an expert about Indian character and languages. My contention that he believed in the authority he is assuming here rests on two points: first, his scrupulosity in matters of representation, discussed in footnote 7; second (and this point strengthens the first), his concern for researching Indian life by reading the first-hand accounts of Heckewelder and others, a concern that has been documented for us by a number of scholars, beginning with Gregory Lansing Paine (1926). That the accuracy of Cooper's representations and their sources has been a matter of debate (even among those who, like Paine, have taken care to document Cooper's research, as far as it can be documented), since Lewis Cass attacked Cooper and Heckewelder in 1826, suggests that Cooper's readers have perceived Cooper as believing himself to be speaking with some authority in the matter of Indian life (even if that authority is only the authority of others whom Cooper believed), rather than simply spinning fictions.

3. James Fenimore Cooper, *The Deerslayer, or the First Warpath* (1841; rpt. New York: New American Library, 1980), p. 283.

4. *Poetics*, XXI. 4 (1457b 7–9). I am using S. H. Butcher's translation. The numbers outside parentheses refer to the English text; those inside refer to the Greek. I am grateful to Professor Victoria Pedrick of the Georgetown University Classics Department for helping me find my way through the Greek, while at the same time I accept all responsibility for the variant translations and the interpretations based on them.

5. Ibid. XXII. 1 (1458a 19), XXI. 3 (1457b 4), XXII. 1 (1458a 21–22), XXII. 1 (1458a 22–23), XXI. 3 (1457b 4–5). In Chapters XXI and XXII of the *Poetics* Aristotle appears to be working with two notions of the foreign—metaphor becoming a third by analogy with the other two. The first notion appears when Aristotle defines a 'strange word, [as] one . . . in use in another country'. For the example he gives is not from a 'barbarous' language (anyone who was *barbaros* was a non-Greek-speaking person), but from the Cyprian dialect of Greek (XXI. 3 [1457b 6–7]). Here we become aware of how a language can be alienated from itself, both linguistically (in terms of dialect) and politically (from the perspective of one *polis* versus another). And in this case linguistics and politics are intricately interwoven. But this first notion of the foreign extends its boundaries into the notion of the barbarous, when in Chapter XXII Aristotle tells us that 'a style wholly composed of' 'strange (or rare) words' is a 'jargon' (XXII. 2 [1458a 23–25]). For the Greek word that Butcher translates as 'jargon' is *barbariomos*, which could not help but evoke in the Greek ear 'people who make [unintelligible] noises like "bar bar" instead of talking Greek', that is, *foreigners* in the way we typically understand the term (the quote is from H. D. F. Kitto, *The Greeks* (1951; rpt. Baltimore: Penguin Books, 1963), p. 7). It is at this point in the text that Aristotle once again makes a distinction between the metaphorical and the strange; for while a style wholly composed of strange words is a jargon, one wholly composed of metaphors is 'a riddle' (*atnigma*) (XXII. 2 [1458a 24]). But, indeed, because the boundaries between the metaphorical and the strange have already been blurred in the term 'foreign' (*xenikos*) and because we along with Aristotle are already operating within a territory where metaphor by analogy is being pursued, it is not difficult for us to talk of a riddle, which, after all, first presents itself under the guise of unintelligibility, as a kind of jargon, or barbarism.

6. Roland Barthes, 'L'ancienne rhétorique', *Communications*, 16 (1970), 220, 221. The translations are mine.

7. I take the term *vraisemblance* from Cooper, who, in his 1850 'Preface to the Leather-Stocking Tales', speaks of 'preserv[ing] the *vraisemblable*' in respect to his 'picture' of Natty Bumppo. That Cooper was also concerned with the accuracy of his Indian portraits is evident in this preface as well; for he takes time to respond to Lewis Cass's 'objection', made twenty-four years earlier in the *North American Review* (XXII [1826], 67), that these portraits were of ' "Indians of the school of Heckewelder, rather than of the school of nature." ' Cooper's response

to Cass is somewhat contradictory or ambivalent; for while Cooper claims 'the privelege of all writers of fiction, more particularly when their works aspire to the elevation of romances, to present the *beau-idéal* of their characters to the reader', he is also quick to imply in the same context that Heckewelder's Indians and therefore his (Cooper's) own are no less real than Cass's, but only seen from a different perspective. I mention all this to suggest that Cooper was scrupulous about problems of representation and that these problems were not merely questions of convention for him—of making his fictions appear real—but of 'moral nature and conscience' (the words are Cooper's in an 1822 book review), that is, of a fiction writer's responsibility both to his/her subject matter and readers. James Franklin Beard's 'Historical Introduction' to the S.U.N.Y. edition of *The Pioneers*, on which I base this brief discussion and from which I take the quote from the book review just mentioned (p. xxii), makes Cooper's moral scrupulosity in matters of representation clear. That Cooper was also very much concerned with the relationship between politics (where he insisted on raising questions of morals) and language we know from *The American Democrat* (1838), about which I will have more to say later on in this essay. We might suppose, then, that Cooper was sensitive to the fact that *representation* is both a political and a literary term. The thrust of my essay is to suggest how Cooper's representations of the Indians are both political and literary at once; how, in this case at least, the two uses of the term are inseparable.

8. Roy Harvey Pearce, *Savagism and Civilization: A Study of the Indian and the American Mind*, Johns Hopkins Paperbacks edition (Baltimore: The Johns Hopkins University Press, 1967), p. 205.

9. James Fenimore Cooper, *The Last of the Mohicans: A Narrative of 1757* (1826; rpt. New York: New American Library, 1962), p. 383. '[T]he speech of "Kill-deer" ' is Natty's own description of his gun. Elsewhere in *The Last of the Mohicans* Natty tells us that he 'know[s the] crack' of Uncas's rifle 'as well as a father knows the language of his child' (p. 230) and speaks of shooting at Hurons as 'let[ting] "Kill-deer" take a part in the conversation' (p. 247).

10. James Fenimore Cooper, *The Prairie: A Tale* (1827; rpt. New York: New American Library, 1964), p. 293.

11. Edwin Fussell, *Frontier: American Literature and the American West* (Princeton: Princeton University Press, 1965), p. 35.

12. For an interesting historical parallel to the discussion between Richard Jones and Judge Temple on sugar maples, see: 'An account of the Sugar Maple-tree of the United States, and of the methods of obtaining Sugar from it. . . . In a letter to Thomas Jefferson . . . by Benjamin Rush. . . .', *Transactions of the American Philosophical Society*, III (1793), 64–81. Rush, in arguing none too logically, for the development of an indigenous maple sugar industry, which he sees as potentially more than competitive with West Indian production, cites, as part of the proof of his argument, a receipt, made out to Cooper's father, Judge William Cooper, and published in the *Albany Gazette*, for £16 in payment for 640 lbs. of sugar made single-handedly 'in less than four weeks besides

attending to the other business of my farm' (p. 71) by one John Nicholls. In an 1897 introduction to Judge Cooper's *A Guide in the Wilderness* (1810; rpt. Freeport, New York: Books for Libraries Press, 1970), we find the following comment by a later James Fenimore Cooper (the novelist's grandson): 'Great profits were anticipated from the manufacture of maple sugar, and among Cooper's papers is a copy of a letter to the President of the United States (George Washington) which accompanied a present of "sugar and spirits produced from the maple tree" sent by Arthur Noble . . . and Judge Cooper' (p. ii). Neither the *Guide* nor Cooper's (the novelist's) *The Chronicles of Cooperstown* (1838) mention any such profits.

13. For an explanation of the historical confusions (between the Delaware, the Mahican, and the Mohegan Indians) involved in Cooper's naming of 'Mohegan', see: Gregory Lansing Paine, 'The Indians of the Leather Stocking Tales', *Studies in Philology*, 23 (1926), 33–5. In view of Natty's scrupulosity about Mohegan's name, which I take up at the end of this essay, Cooper's confusions, which he picks up from Heckewelder, are ironic.

14. In his article on the economy of sugar maples (see note 12 for full reference), Benjamin Rush points out that the process of rendering the extracted and boiled sugar is 'nearly the same' (p. 70) for both cane and maple sugar; but, of course, the plants must be cultivated and the sugar extracted from them before this point, and in these respects the two economies have nothing whatsoever in common.

15. In 'Cooper's *The Pioneers*: Origins and Structure', *P.M.L.A.*, 79 (1964), Thomas Philbrick discusses the novel as 'infused with a spirit of angry contention' (p. 588).

16. In this instance I am citing from the edition of *The Pioneers* described by the S.U.N.Y. editors as 'The Pioneers. New York: Wiley, 1823. [Clayton Printing]. First State.' My citation is taken from the reprint of this edition found in *The Pioneers* (New York: Holt, Rinehart and Winston, 1959), p. 224. The numbers in parentheses following the citation in the body of my text are from the S.U.N.Y. edition. In the edition that I use Cooper employs some descriptive phrases that make the tone of the passage more explicit. Were I to retain in this case the S.U.N.Y. text, which is based on an 1832 London edition, my reading of the passage would remain substantially unchanged.

17. In *The Last of the Mohicans*, in an exchange with David Gamut over the question of salvation and the authority of the Bible, we find Natty saying: 'Do you take me for a whimpering boy at the apron string of one of your old gals; and this good rifle on my knee for the feather of a goose's wing, my ox's horn for a bottle of ink, and my leathern pouch for a crossbarred handkercher to carry my dinner? Book! What have such as I, who am a warrior of the wilderness . . . to do with books? I never read but in one, and the words that are written there are too simple and too plain to need much schooling . . .' (pp. 137–8). The one book that the illiterate Natty has read is the only one that, since he is illiterate, he can read: the book of nature, of which, for the hunter, all written texts,

including, in this exchange, the bible, are necessarily poor translations, although Natty, who is never consistent in his philosophy, can say elsewhere in *The Last of the Mohicans* that 'the truest thing in nature' is '[t]he holy Bible' (p. 36). What these passages suggest is, first of all, Natty's obsession with language (a central obsession of his, in fact, throughout the Leather-stocking Tales). Next, we might note Natty's valorization (perhaps only logical, since he is illiterate) of speech over writing, of oral tradition, which he identifies with the Indians, over written tradition, which he identifies with the whites. 'I am genuine white,' Natty announces in *The Last of the Mohicans*, but 'I can't approve . . . of [white] customs to write in books what they have done and seen, instead of telling them in their villages, where the lie can be given to the face of a cowardly boaster, and the brave soldier can call on his comrades to witness for the truth of his words' (p. 35). Yet while Natty rejects writing (books), he is, nevertheless, trapped within the figure of the book, as his speaking of nature as a book might suggest. Indeed, elsewhere in *The Last of the Mohicans* we find Natty comparing a 'scalp' to 'the leaf of a book, and each hair [to] a letter', then adding: 'What right have Christian whites to boast of their learning, when a savage can read a language that would prove too much for the wisest of them all!' (p. 232). While Natty's immediate reference here is to Chingachgook's marvellous (even to the naturally well-read Natty) identification of a scalp as specifically that of an Oneida, we must also see this reference to the powers of savage, or illiterate, reading as an indirect statement— Natty does not like to boast—of Natty's own prowess as a reader of the forest, a learning he displays time and time again in the Leatherstocking Tales.

18. Rev. John Heckewelder, *History, Manners, and Customs of the Indian Nations, Who Once Inhabited Pennsylvania and the Neighbouring States* (1819, 1876; rpt. n.p.: The Anno Press, 1971), pp. 376–77, 391, 391–92. Duponceau's reference to himself as 'no sinologist' appears on p. 390. Duponceau separates Chinese from what he terms 'the Oriental languages' (p. 391). In his 1850 introduction to *The Last of the Mohicans*, Cooper appears to group Chinese with the Oriental and says of Indian languages that they have 'the richness and sententious fullness of the Chinese', for they 'express a phrase in a word, and . . . will qualify the meaning of an entire sentence by a syllable. . . .' Thus, Cooper describes Indian languages in the way Duponceau does; but contrary to Duponceau, he includes Chinese in this grouping.

19. Ibid., pp. 403, 405.

20. Ibid., p. 403.

21. Lewis Cass, in the *North American Review*, XXII (1826), 75.

22. Cass, the *N.A.R.*, XXVI (1828), 387. See also Cass's quarrel with Duponceau's translation of *Wulamalessohalian* in the *N.A.R.* (1826), 75–6; and Duponceau's response to this criticism in *Transactions of the American Philosophical Society*, NS III (1830), 79–80.

23. In spite of his ideological thrust, Cass has a few important points to make in his *N.A.R.* essays about the translation of Indian languages.

The two essays are themselves a contradictory combination of ethno-centric assertion, of the kind I have quoted in this essay, and scholarly humility (in relation to the white man's lack of knowledge of Indian languages and cultures, and the difficulty of obtaining such knowledge). The contradictions arise, no doubt, because of the conflict between Cass's avocation of ethnologist and his vocation of government official, who had to deal with the Indian 'problem'. His two essays do, however, focus on the problem of translation as the central problem in under-standing Indian cultures. And he does point out 'the error', even as he commits it, of assuming that Indian languages can be understood solely in terms of Western linguistic models (*N.A.R.* (XXVI 1828), 396). He is also quick to point out in his critique of Cooper that Indians are no more prone to talk in the language of metaphor than any other people, and he suggests that the notion of them speaking this way comes from an assumption that their diplomatic rhetoric is characteristic of their languages in general (*N.A.R.* (XXVI 1828), 374).

24. Lewis Henry Morgan, *League of the Iroquois* (1851; rpt. New York: Corinth Books, 1962), p. 4.

25. Heckewelder, p. 403.

26. Michael Paul Rogin, *Fathers and Children: Andrew Jackson and the Subjugation of the American Indian* (New York: Vintage, 1976), pp. 3, 4.

27. J. G. Wilson, *Bryant and His Friends* (New York, 1886), p. 237.

28. Quoted by Paine (pp. 19–20) from Susan Fenimore Cooper (Cooper's daughter), *Pages and Pictures from the Writings of James Fenimore Cooper, with Notes* (New York, 1861), pp. 130–31.

29. For two recent discussions of these legal matters, see: Stephen Railton, *Fenimore Cooper: A Study of his Life and Imagination* (Princeton: Princeton University Press, 1978), pp. 104ff; and the 'Historical Introduction' to the S.U.N.Y. edition of *The Pioneers*, pp. xxx-xxxi. After opening Chapter 1 of *The Chronicles of Cooperstown* with the observation that '[t]he site of the present village of Cooperstown, is said to have been a favorite place of resort with the adjacent savage tribes, from a remote period', Cooper goes on to give a brief history of the Croghan patent, and later in the text gives an extremely elliptical account of the legal conflict between Croghan's and Judge Cooper's heirs.

30. For an account of how Croghan obtained his land from the Indians, see: Albert T. Volwiler, *George Croghan and the Westward Movement, 1741–1782* (Cleveland: The Arthur H. Clark Co., 1926), pp. 249–51.

31. For a discussion of the differences between white and Indian understandings of the term *ownership*, see: Wilcomb E. Washburn, *The Indian in America* (New York: Harper and Row, 1975), pp. 32–3. In *Red Man's Land/White Man's Law: A Study of the Past and Present Status of the American Indian* (New York: Scribner's, 1971), Washburn comments that '[t]he principal point of dispute between white and Indian historically has been land. The greatest legal gap between the two cultures has been the respective attitudes toward the commodity. Or should one say, rather than "commodity", "sacred and inalienable mother"? The contrast between the two phrases symbolizes, if it does not fully explain,

the basic attitude of the two cultures towards the object which they disputed' (p. 143). Washburn suggests here in noting the problem of contrasting phrases, the problem of translation. I would only call attention to his use of the phrase 'legal gap' and suggest that the gap between the two cultures is a gap created by the problem of translating the term *legal* itself.

32. In the beginning of his discussion of red and white conceptions of land ownership in *The Indian in America* (see note 31), Wilcomb E. Washburn, pointing to the work of Felix S. Cohen and Harold Driver, suggests the possibility of a faithful translation of the term *legal* into Indian languages, before qualifying this possibility to such an extent that it seems severely called into question.

33. Washburn, *Red Man's Land/White Man's Law*, p. 6.

34. In *The Last of the Mohicans* (pp. 127–28) Magua proposes to Cora Munro in what, apparently, we are supposed to understand as English; nevertheless, Cora must translate this proposal for Heyward and her sister, Alice, who, though they hear it, don't seem to be able to understand it, when it is spoken by Magua. In *The Prairie* (pp. 302–3) Ellen Wade stops Natty from translating Mahtoree's proposal to Inez, which Natty, in any event, was going to render 'more obscure[ly] than in the [elliptically metaphorical] original'. Ellen's words in this case are typical of the linguistic boundary separating white women and Indians in Cooper: 'Spare your breath,' she tells the trapper, 'all that a savage says is not to be repeated before a Christian lady.' Here we should note that Cora is not quite a Christian lady, which, in Cooper, we can translate as 'white woman'; for she is of mixed-blood (black and white), and this 'fact' seems to enable her to hear directly the marriage proposal of the savages. In *The Pathfinder, or the Inland Sea* (1840; rpt. New York: New American Library, 1961), a party that includes Natty, Jasper Western, and Mabel Dunham are fleeing the Indians, and overhear their pursuers discussing the possibility of Mabel becoming an Indian's wife. While Jasper and Natty understand this proposal, '[h]appily these words were lost on Mabel . . .' (p. 60). When later on Natty does explain to Mabel that she was in danger of becoming a Mingo's wife, Mabel, typically, replies that 'it would be a lighter evil to be killed than to become the wife of an Indian' (p. 114). Natty and Mabel's father are well pleased with this response.

35. My sense of the history of the Delaware and the Iroquois comes primarily from two sources: Vol. 15 of the *Handbook of North American Indians: Northeast*, ed. Bruce G. Trigger (Washington: Smithsonian Institution, 1978); and C. A. Weslager, *The Delaware Indians: A History* (New Brunswick, N.J.: Rutgers University Press, 1972).

36. James Fenimore Cooper, *The American Democrat* (1838; rpt. New York: Knopf, 1931), pp. 110, 112, 114.

37. Ibid., pp. 112–14.

38. Ibid., pp. 110, 112.

39. For Rousseau's discussion of savagery as the state that blurs or erases the boundary between the literal and the metaphoric, and civilization as

the state that recognizes the boundary see his 'Essay on the Origin of Languages which Treats of Melody and Musical Imitation', *On the Origin of Language: Jean-Jacques Rousseau, Essay on the Origin of Languages; Johann Gottfried Herder, Essay on the Origin of Language*, trans. John H. Moran (New York: Ungar, 1966), pp. 12–13. The French can be found in *Oeuvres Completes de J. J. Rousseau* (Paris, 1824–25), I, 482–83. For Rousseau the savage, ruled by passion, misnames the thing itself by transferring to it a name alien to its reality, thus creating a 'fictitious object' (*l'objet faux*), which the savage takes for the literal. On the other hand, the civilized person, ruled by reason, is able to name the thing itself properly, or literally, to tell the difference, that is, between 'truth' (*la verité*) and 'error' (*erreur*).

40. Railton, p. 85.
41. Ibid., p. 86.
42. James Grossman, *James Fenimore Cooper* (n.p.: William Sloane Associates, 1949), p. 37.

4

Guns Mean Democracy: *The Pioneers* and the Game Laws

by CHARLES SWANN

1

A well regulated militia, being necessary to the security of a free state, the right of the people to keep and bear arms, shall not be infringed.

The right of the people to be secure in their persons, papers, and effects, against unreasonable searches and seizures, shall not be violated, and no warrants shall issue, but upon probable cause, supported by oath or affirmation, and particularly describing the place to be searched, and the persons or things to be seized.[1]

The Pioneers begins with the shooting of a deer, followed by debates about who shot the beast, how it was shot, who owns it, and the question of who has rights to shoot deer. Judge Temple, in his Christmas Eve visit to the 'Bold Dragoon', tells his auditors, in a passage significantly bracketed by discussions of Revolutionary France, that the laws he has been helping to make are game laws, and that he looks forward to 'the day, when a man's rights in his game shall be as much respected as his title to his farm'. Natty Bumppo kills a deer 'out of season' and, as an indirect consequence, is found guilty of having resisted 'the execution of a search-warrant by force of arms' in an accusation which 'particularized, in the vague language of the law . . . the use of the rifle'. Major Effingham, when he finally makes an appearance, in one of his two brief speeches invites the 'gentlemen' to 'dine' and, locked in his nostalgic fantasy of a pre-revolutionary past, tells Oliver to 'Order a repast suitable for his Majesty's officers. You know we have the best of game always at command.'[2]

All this seems to suggest that an understanding of the game laws and the ideologies that inform such laws and the very idea of 'game' are profoundly relevant for an understanding of this complex and brilliant historical novel—yet, as far as I know, there is no real discussion of their significance.[3] Such laws are clearly related to definitions of property, to ideas about the preservation of nature, and to the moral and political questions of man's control over nature—which is to say man's control over man (or one class's control over others). And these issues are patently important to the novel. That some kind of debate about law is central to the novel has rarely been doubted, but the question of who wins that debate, or even of the terms in which it appears in the text, has been a matter of more-or-less fierce disagreement, as has the parallel question of the relationship between historical fact and historical fiction.[4]

I do not attempt to offer anything like a final solution to these problems here, but wish merely to look at some of the acknowledged difficulties through an examination of the relevance of the game laws (and of the political history that lies behind such laws) to the political views embodied in *The Pioneers*. To concentrate on game laws has at least one advantage. As Lund points out in an extremely useful study of American wild-life law, anyone interested in the relationship of law to political ideology finds his task easier than it may be in other areas. The history of game laws *is* a history of class legislation:

> In other areas of the law, subtle insight may be required to ferret out legislative techniques used to beggar the powerless, but early English game law requires no such acuity. Class discriminations were openly embraced from the earliest periods until at least the mid-nineteenth century.[5]

And, as I shall show, even such apologists for 'things as they are' as Blackstone saw and announced this in terms relevant to American political experience, even if this disrupted an otherwise largely coherent political theory of property and its rights.

2

Perry Miller began his section on law in *The Life of the Mind in America* by presenting *The Pioneers* as a novel which 'struck into the very centre of what had by 1823 become a tormenting American dilemma', the conflict between socially necessary law and individual liberty. This is dramatized by Judge Temple's imposition of a game law and by his determination to prosecute Natty for his breach of it, even though Natty has just saved his daughter from a 'painter' and has an impeccable patriotic record. 'Would any society be tolerable', asks the Judge, 'where the ministers of justice are to be opposed by men armed with rifles? Is it for this that I have tamed the wilderness?' (344). The answer comes from Oliver Edwards, the constant mediator between trapper and land-owning gentleman:

> He [Natty] is simple, unlettered, even ignorant; prejudiced, perhaps, though I feel his opinion of the world is too true; but he has a heart, Judge Temple, that would atone for a thousand faults; he knows his friends, and never deserts them, even if it be his dog. (345)

Miller concludes from this exchange that 'the great issue of the nineteenth century was the never-ending issue of Heart versus Head.'[6]

Miller mentions the particular kind of law that Natty has originally broken—a game law both made and enforced by the Judge. But he does not pause to consider the implications, nor to reflect that there is another response to the Judge, one which would not only question how far he can be said to have tamed the wilderness, but which would attach rather more importance and value to 'men . . . with rifles'. This is, perhaps, understandable given his scope and sweep but it is regrettable not only for a reading of the novel but for Miller's subsequent argument. To reduce the conflict about the nature of law to a Romantic clash between Heart and Head (or even lawlessness *versus* law) is radically to distort.

The real conflict is more complex and more interesting, and Miller would not have had to look far to find that the terms of the argument could be, indeed had been, phrased rather differently—in, for example, this gloss on article 2 of the Bill of Rights:

> This may be considered as the true palladium of liberty. The right of self defence is the first law of nature: in most governments it has been the study of rulers to confine this right within the narrowest limits possible. Wherever standing armies are kept up, and the right of the people to bear arms is, under any colour or pretext whatsoever, prohibited, liberty, if not already annihilated, is on the brink of destruction. In England, the people have been disarmed, generally, under the specious pretext of preserving the game: a never failing lure to bring over the landed aristocracy, under that mask, though calculated for very different purpose. True it is, their bill of rights seems at first view to counteract this policy: but the right of bearing arms is confined to protestants, and the words suitable to their condition and degree, have been interpreted to authorize the prohibition of keeping a gun or other engine for the destruction of game, to any farmer, or other person not qualified to kill game. So that not one man in five hundred can keep a gun in his house without being subject to a penalty.[7]

This does not come from any wild-eyed radical Romantic but from St. George Tucker, a prominent Virginian judge and professor of law at the College of William and Mary. In 1803, he issued his highly influential edition of Blackstone's *Commentaries*, an edition which republicanized a text which was already widely known and widely influential. It would take too long to discuss how and why Tucker made the Tory, royalist Blackstone relevant (or, in his words, '*safe*') for a democratic, republican America. It is a remarkably impressive achievement. I shall, however, return to a passage on the game laws. The parallelism between the two passages is striking. Starting from apparently very different points, Tucker moves through the same 'family' of ideas. The associations between them are felt to be so strong that they do not need to be argued (and Tucker was not alone in this). The way in which in both passages Tucker connects democracy, the right to bear arms, and the game laws (as laws of weapons control and *therefore* class oppression) as a 'natural' family of ideas suggests that the clash is more interesting than Miller implies: that it dramatizes potentially explosive ideas about the relationships between power and laws.

I offer Tucker's comment (from a lengthy and important Appendix on the Constitution) as a way of arguing that Cooper's use of the game laws relates importantly to the ideas about the political nature of the law which are so crucial in the novel, and as a way of suggesting that the fact that the rifle is Natty's 'never-failing companion' (153) signifies more than merely that he is a hunter. Natty is doing more than grumble when he says

> I can live without the venison, but I don't love to give up my lawful dues in a free country.—Though, for the matter of that, might often makes right here, as well as in the old country, for what I can see. (21–2)

He is, in however confused a way, making connections between game, rights and laws, and offering an implied criticism of a democratic rhetoric referring to the rule of law which conceals the way in which a would-be American aristocracy is in danger of replicating an aristocratic Europe.[8] I shall return to this point later but it is relevant to note here that Temple's main interest seems to be in the preservation of a great estate rather than in any of the wider political principles of the Revolution. Even if one is sceptical about the Judge's accounts of his actions, his explanation to Oliver of his motives rings (however regrettably) true:

> If the cause of this country was successful, the trust was sacred with me, for none knew of thy father's interest. If the crown still held its sway, it would be easy to restore the property of so loyal a subject as Col. Effingham. (p. 439)

Even though Oliver looks (as well he might) 'incredulous', he has to admit that 'the premises are good.'

3

Before discussing the wider ideological significance of the game laws, I want to mention the actual game laws that had been and were in operation as a way of contextualizing the ideological debate in the novel, of providing a substratum of fact to which that debate can and should be related. Cooper is not referring to any one specific law passed in 1793. Indeed, as far as the preservation of the species is concerned, game laws were no new thing. As early as 1717, Massachusetts had gone so far (and it is really remarkably far) as to ban all shooting of deer for five years. In 1708, the killing of deer in Suffolk, King's and Queen's Counties in New York was prohibited between 1 August and 1 January. This evidence clearly rebukes and refutes any easy rhetoric about the inexhaustible fecundity of American wild-life, at least as far as the North-eastern seaboard states are concerned. While Cooper may not have followed legal history closely enough to have had any specific law of those decades in mind, there were a number of laws passed by the New York state legislature in the last decades of the eighteenth century. The number is accounted for, at least partly, by the piece-meal nature of such legislation. Much was local to a point when one wonders whether parochialism or special interest lawmaking is the more relevant term. And the radical changes in dates as to when animals or birds should not be killed suggests a radical uncertainty about what, how, and why to preserve.

In 1785, an Act was passed for the 'preservation of deer heath-hens and to prevent damages by firing the woods in the county of Suffolk'.[9] This allowed deer to be killed only in September, October and November. Given the way in which Judge Temple links his concern with game to his desire to preserve the woods, it is worth emphasizing that game preservation and preservation of the woods seem to have been felt to belong 'naturally' together in the minds of the historical legislators. (Remembering the fire on the Vision and its causes, 'careless' as well as 'designing' persons were held liable for setting fire to the woods.) The preamble to this Act is typical in that it does not suggest any conservationist concern but rather a crudely economic interest which may again remind us

101

of Judge Temple: 'Whereas many deer in the county of Suffolk are killed in seasons when they are of little value . . .'. More relevant for *The Pioneers* are two Acts passed in 1788 and 1798. Since these Acts are not exactly easy to find, and since their precise formulation bears on Cooper's use of such laws, I give them in full.

AN ACT to prevent the destruction of deer
PASSED the 15th of March, 1788.

Deer, what months killing of prohibited.

Be it enacted by the People of the State of New York, represented in Senate and Assembly, and it is hereby enacted by the authority of the same, That if any person or persons shall kill or destroy any wild buck, doe or fawn, or any other sort of deer whatsoever, at any time in the months of January, February, March, April, May, June or July, every such person, shall, for every buck, doe or fawn, or other deer, so killed or destroyed as aforesaid, contrary to the true intent and meaning of this act, forfeit and pay the sum of three pounds, to be recovered, with costs of suit, in any court having cognizance thereof, by any person or persons who will sue and prosecute for the same; the only moiety of which forfeiture, when recovered to be paid to the overseers of the poor of the town or place where the offence shall be committed, for the use of the poor thereof; and the other moiety to such person or persons as shall sue and prosecute for the same as aforesaid.

And in order the more easily to convict offenders against this act;

Warrant to search for skins, venison etc.

Be it further enacted by the authority aforesaid, That it shall be lawful for any justice of the peace, in any county of this State, and every such justice is hereby required, upon demand made by any person, assigning a reasonable cause of suspicion upon oath, (of the sufficiency of which the said justice is to judge) at any time in any of the months before mentioned, to issue his warrant, under his hand and seal, to any constable of any town or place in the same county, for searching, in the day time, in any house, store, out-house or other place whatsoever, where any green deer skin, fresh venison or deers

102

flesh is suspected to be concealed; and in case any green deer skin, fresh venison, or deers flesh shall upon such search be found, the person in whose custody the same shall be found, or who concealed the same, shall forfeit the sum of three pounds, to be recovered and applied in manner aforesaid.

Hounding of
deer
prohibited

And be it further enacted by the authority aforesaid, That if any person or persons shall at any time, hunt, pursue or destroy any wild buck, doe or fawn or other deer (except in the county of Suffolk) with any blood hound or blood hounds, beagle or beagles, every such person, shall, for every such offence, forfeit and pay the sum of three pounds, to be recovered and applied as aforesaid. *Provided* that nothing in this clause of this act contained, shall be construed to prevent any person or persons from making use of any blood hounds, or beagles, in the hunting, pursuing or destroying of wolves, or other destructive wild animals.

Former laws
repealed.

And be it further enacted by the authority aforesaid, That all former acts and laws of this State concerning deer, shall be, and hereby are repealed.

AN ACT to regulate the fishery in Otsego Lake
PASSED the 31st of March 1798

Preamble

WHEREAS it has become necessary to guard against the destruction of the fish in Otsego Lake at a season of the year when they are of little or no value. Therefore.

Net fishing
in Otsego
Lake

Be it enacted by the People of the State of New York represented in Senate and Assembly. That no person or persons shall fish with a net or seine in the waters of Otsego Lake at any time between the twenty fifth day of May and the first day of October in any year hereafter.

Penalty for
violations.

And be it further enacted, That if any person or persons shall fish with a net or seine in Otsego Lake at any time between the twenty fifth day of May and the first day of October in any year hereafter, and shall be thereof convicted, he or she shall for every

103

> such offence forfeit and pay the sum of ten dollars to
> be recovered by action of debt, with costs of suit
> before any justice of the peace in the said county of
> Otsego or in any court having cognizance thereof,
> one moiety thereof to the use of the person who shall
> prosecute for the same and the other moiety to the
> use of the poor of the town in which the conviction
> shall be had.

What is clear when these acts are set beside the text is that,
in the case of the deer law, Cooper is remarkably close to the
actual historical detail. The fact that the fine for killing the
deer differs is, of course, trivial. The way in which the 'crime'
is to be discovered is so close to that described in the text it is
hard to believe that Cooper had not consulted either this law
or the one in existence in the 1820s.[10] The fact that the dates
the laws are made do not coincide is again a minor matter.
The reason for Cooper choosing 1793–94 must be a matter for
speculation and my guess would be that it has something to do
with the vexed relations with France which surface in the
novel and to which I shall return. But Cooper does depart
significantly from the details of history in his suggestion that
the Acts Temple has so enthusiastically helped to pass have no
precursors, that in their novelty they initiate (if only in
seeming intention) a classless mode of controlling man's
relation to nature. The fact that such laws did exist but that
Cooper chose to ignore this and to write them into his fiction
as a new part of history, suggests that within his narrative
these laws must be read as a crucial political intervention. The
differentiations Cooper makes between his deer and fish laws
reinforce this point; they are a way of dramatizing a concern
that these laws may operate as part of the legislators' plans to
reinforce and extend their class position.

There is a radical difference between the announced intention and the actual function of the fishing law. The way in
which it is presented suggests that neither conservation
(Temple's *announced* intention) nor utility are the actual
reasons for the law's existence. Rather it is a symbol of power;
Temple is making a law to show he can make laws, and
perhaps as a way of preparing for more laws. The very
ineffectuality of this law can then be seen as disarming those

who will be the victims of subsequent class legislation. This is a point of view that seems to me to be reinforced by the epigraph to Chapter XXIII which makes explicit connections between the natural and the social worlds, between game laws apparently passed for conservation purposes, and the (decently veiled) actuality of class rule. Its full weight is felt when Natty appears in court caught in the meshes of the law: 'Help, masters, help; here's a fish hangs in the net, like a poor man's right in the law' (*Pericles*, II.i.116–17). The Judge tells his audience in the 'Bold Dragoon' that 'there is an act prohibiting the drawing of seines, at any other than the proper seasons' (160). What, one may speculate, are the proper seasons? The natural response would be that they would be the times when the fish are not mating and spawning. But Temple tells Elizabeth explicitly and in detail that

> During the winter . . . they are entirely protected from our assaults by the ice, for they refuse the hook; and during the hot months, they are not seen. It is supposed they retreat to the deep and cool waters of the lake at that season; and it is only in the spring and autumn, that, for a few days, they are to be found, around the points where they are within the reach of a seine. (260)

And Cooper has told us that 'the season had now arrived when the bass fisheries were allowed by the provisions of the law, that Judge Temple had procured' (251). 'Procured' is an interesting word; it suggests rather more personal interest in the passing of the law than Judge Temple admits to in the inn.[11] The attempts to defend Judge Temple or his law are feeble in the extreme. McWilliams (perhaps the Judge's stoutest defender) is reduced to forgetting the text, writing that the 'judge's law against the seasonal netting of the bass is apparently not yet in force'. Dekker speaks of the 'new game laws, backed up by concrete police powers and the abstract dignity of the law', and goes on to describe the laws as 'wise and effective', and to say more defensibly that the fishing episode 'best illustrates the chief issues of the novel'.[12] I cannot see that wisdom or effectiveness are helpful terms. If Cooper is not making an attack on Judge Temple's law-making, it looks very like it; he has 'procured' a law which cannot be broken, which forbids seine-fishing when *he knows* seine-fishing to be impossible, and permits it at, presumably, precisely the time when the fish are spawning. He has given a legal sanction to the waste which he claims morally to deplore. The fact that he yields to the excitement of the moment and joins in the slaughter looks at once more trivial and more comprehensible when set against this redundancy, this declaration of his power to make law.

4

As I suggested earlier, it does not take great political sensitivity or theoretical acumen to show that game laws on both sides of the Atlantic were (and are) profoundly ideological, and were (and are) perceived as such both in and of themselves and in the ways they relate to other class-based laws. Game laws can be grouped under four apparently neutral heads: (1) who may kill game; (2) when game may be killed; (3) where game may be killed; (4) how game may be killed. Even from this simple (even simplistic) grouping which I have taken from an encyclopedia of sport, it can be seen that game laws touch some central debates about law and social control. 'Who' involves questions of social qualification, whether these be class or status, and thus raises the problem of law as not equal for all. 'When' is dependent on ideas of conservation, of nature as a resource which needs husbanding. 'Where' is dependent on notions of property, not merely but most importantly in terms of trespass (and here there were radical differences between English and American attitudes and practice to which I shall return). 'How' may seem to refer again to conservation. But there is more to it than the idea that too many animals should not be too easily killed.

On one level this last heading points towards the 'aesthetic' idea of a clean kill and in that demonstration of skill symbolizes a right to be considered a 'countryman'. Judge Temple's use of buckshot and Natty's symbolic criticism when he picks a bird off a branch with a single shot are relevant here, as is the pigeon-shooting episode in a rather different way. There we get a multiplicity of weapons producing mass slaughter opposed again by Natty's virtuous virtuosity. But this slaughter is defensible (however regrettable the extinction of the passenger-pigeon); pigeons are vermin, not game, a categorization which is more than a trivial distinction. They are a serious threat to any agrarian culture as Billy Kirby, of all people, points out:

> What! old Leather-stocking . . . grumbling at the loss of a few pigeons! If you had to sow your wheat twice and three times, as I have done, you wouldn't be so massyfully feeling'd to'ards the divils. (246–47)

On another level, there is a less innocent importance being attached to skill in hunting. It keeps up expertise is the use of weapons and, where these are not available to all, that expertise can be interpreted as being not for national but for class security and supremacy.

There is no need to repeat the English game law debate in any detail if only because it has been so well covered, but the crucial provisions do need to be before us:

> By an act of 1670 a man had to be the lord of a manor, or have a substantial income from landed property, even to kill a hare on his own land. The basic qualification was an income of £100 yearly from a freehold estate, which in 1750 was between five and ten times the property qualification to vote for a knight of a shire.[13]

Nor is there any need to get involved in the various problems about the definition of game (such as the fact that deer were technically not game) since deer were perceived ideologically if not legally as being in that category. The points I want to make are simple and uncontroversial: the game laws privileged the landed gentry over all other country-dwellers, and were so intended. Further complexities come from the fact that it became illegal to sell game, that game came to be regarded as an important thing to be able to give, that game, therefore (in theory if not in practice), transcended the cash nexus and in that transcendence political claims (related to a frequently foggy theory of history) were directly asserted. Opposition to this came from the city, of course. It also came from all those, the vast majority, who lived in the country and were outside the magic circle.[14]

These were predictable opponents. But support for the

attack on class privileges came from a surprising and an influential source, one which gave a theoretical basis to 'the common defence of a poacher' that 'it is very hard that he should be punished for taking what he had as good a right to as any other man.'[15] The most important single figure for the American debate about game laws, Sir William Blackstone, not only asserted that it 'cannot be denied, that by the law of nature every man from the prince to the peasant, has an equal right' of taking as game 'all such creatures as are *ferae naturae* and are therefore the property of nobody' (II, p. 411), but also set his argument in an historical framework which called the political legitimacy of such laws seriously into question. We should remember that Blackstone had been accused (with some justice) by Bentham of being the enemy to all reform, and by Austin of truckling to the sinister interests and mischievous prejudices of power, of flattering the overweening conceit of the English in their own institutions. But on this issue Blackstone parted company with 'our gentlemen of independent estates and fortune, the most useful . . . body of men in the nation' and quarrelled with the gentleman J.P.'s ability to 'exert his talents by maintaining good order; by punishing the dissolute and idle' (I, pp. 7, 8). Given the gentry's obsessive tendency (amply documented by Hay and Munsche) to define these worthy aims as largely consisting of preserving their exclusive rights to game and catching and punishing poachers, it was a serious and fascinating fissure in an ideology. That rupture is the more significant in the authority the text had. It was present, Tucker says, in every American gentleman's library and knowledge of it alone, he regrets, sufficient for successful candidacy for the bar.

5

Blackstone was normally in no danger of being seen as friend to any kind of radicalism:

> There is nothing which so generally strikes the imagination and engages the affections of mankind, as the right of property; or that sole and despotic dominion which one man claims and exercises over the external things of the world, in total exclusion of the right of any other individual in the universe. (II, pp. 1–2)

The reference to the universe is irresistible, but property is not and cannot be universal. Light and air remain, for example, so there are

> some few things, which . . . must still unavoidably remain in common. . . . Such . . . are the generality of those animals which are said to be *ferae naturae*, or of a wild and untameable disposition: which any man may seize upon and keep for his own use or pleasure. (II, pp. 13, 14)

However, because of the tyranny of the Norman Yoke and the subsequent imposition of the forest laws which vested the sole property of all the game in England in the king alone, the law, regrettably, does not acknowledge this:

> . . . though the forest laws are now mitigated, and by degrees grown entirely obsolete, yet from this root has sprung a bastard slip, known by the name of the game law, now arrived to and wantoning in it's [*sic*] highest vigour: both founded upon the same unreasonable notions of permanent property in wild creatures; and both *productive of the same tyranny to the commons*: but with this difference; that the forest laws established only one mighty hunter throughout the land, the game laws have raised a little Nimrod in every manor. (IV, pp. 415–16. My emphasis)

It is a good indication of the importance that Blackstone attached to the game laws that this quotation comes from his final chapter in which he attempted 'an historical review of the most remarkable changes and alterations, that have happened in the laws of England' (IV, p. 407). He doesn't deny that there are reasons for such laws:

> 1. For the encouragement of agriculture and improvement of lands, by giving every man an exclusive dominion over his own soil. 2. For preservation of the several species of these animals, which would soon be extirpated by a general liberty. 3. For prevention of idleness and dissipation in husbandmen, artificers and others of lower rank; which would be the unavoidable consequence of universal licence. 4. For prevention of popular insurrections and resistance to the government, by disarming the bulk of the people: which last is a reason oftener meant, than avowed, by the makers of forest or game laws. (II, pp. 411–12)

While all these reasons have their interest, the fourth is the most relevant for the American debate: the connection between

4 and the thinking behind article 2 of the Bill of Rights needs no analysis (though Blackstone is not the man one expects to find unmasking the ideology behind the law). Whether there are good reasons *now* available for game laws or not, Blackstone is in no doubt about their historical origins and the centrality of history for understanding their social meaning:

> [T]hey owe their immediate original to slavery. . . . [W]ith regard to the rise and original of our present civil prohibitions, it will be found that all forest and game laws were introduced into Europe at the same time, and by the same policy, as gave birth to the feudal system; when those swarms of barbarians issued from their northern hive, and laid the foundation of most of the present kingdoms of Europe, on the ruins of the western empire. For when a conquering general came to settle the oeconomy of a vanquished country, and to part it out among his soldiers or feudatories, who were to render him military service for such donations; it behoved him, in order to secure his new acquisitions, to keep the *rustici* or natives of the country, and all who were not his military tenants, in as low a condition as possible, and *especially to prohibit them the use of arms. Nothing could do this more effectually than a prohibition of hunting and sporting*; and therefore it was the policy of the conqueror to reserve this right to himself, and such on whom he should bestow it. . . . And accordingly we find, in the feudal constitutions, one and the same law prohibiting the *rustici* in general from carrying arms, and also proscribing the use of nets, snares, or other engines for destroying the game. . . . And it is remarkable, that, in those nations where the feudal policy remains the most uncorrupted, the forest or game laws continue in their highest rigor. In France all game is properly the king's; and in some parts of Germany, it is death for a peasant to be found hunting in the woods of the nobility. (II, pp. 412, 413–14)

At this point, when Blackstone is still in full swing, St. George Tucker explodes in one of his crucial critical footnotes which tell America how to read the *Commentaries*:

> An attentive perusal of the preceding pages must be sufficient to convince us, that the game-laws are among the powerful instruments of state-enginery, for the purpose of retaining the mass of the people in a state of the most abject subjection.
> The bill of rights, 1 W. and M., says Mr. Blackstone . . . secures to the subjects of England the right of having arms for

their defence, *suitable to their condition and degree.* In the construction of these game laws it seems to be held, that no person who is not qualified according to law to kill game, hath any right to keep a gun in his house. Now, as no person, (except the gamekeeper of a lord or lady of a manor) is admitted to be qualified to kill game, unless he has 100l. per annum, &c. it follows that no others can keep a gun for their defence; so that the whole nation are completely disarmed, and left at the mercy of the government, under the pretext of preserving the breed of hares and partridges, for the exclusive use of the independent country gentlemen. In America we may reasonably hope that the people will never cease to regard the right of keeping and bearing arms as the surest pledge of their liberty.

Tucker was not alone in looking at the English game laws—and not liking what he saw. In 1808, for example, the Supreme Court of Georgia reflected on the ideology of the Black Act. In part this was a debate about the general relevance of the English common law to America, but the argument was expressed sharply: 'that statute, as is discoverable from the preamble and the context, is founded upon a tender solicitude for the amusement and property of the aristocracy of England'. It was therefore irrelevant in a country 'in which the liberty of killing a deer . . . was as unrestrained as the natural rights of the deer to rove'—and, after all, 'where was the aristocracy whose privileges were to be secured?' The judge concurred with these defence arguments with a force and clarity that would surely gladden the heart of the E. P. Thompson of *Whigs and Hunters*. The intention of the Black Act was quite clear: 'this law is not only penal to a feudal degree, but it is productive of tyranny.'[16]

6

Where *was* that aristocracy? Not so far away, perhaps, if one looks at the ambitions of the great Federalist barons of New York in the 1790s[17]—only as far away, perhaps, as Judge Temple. It is not for nothing that Jones calls him ''duke' repeatedly; Marmaduke has his ambitions to fulfil a semi-feudal rôle. He is both legislator and judge—and patron. He appoints his cousin to be the Sheriff of the county though Jones's only qualities for the position seem to be loyalty to his patron. Dickon's function is clear enough. He aims to extend the powers of 'duke:

> I would have tried law for the saddle, before I would have given it to the fellow. Do you not own the mountains as well as the valleys? Are not the woods your own? what right has this chap, or the Leatherstocking to shoot in your woods, without your permission? Now, I have known a farmer, in Pennsylvania, order a sportsman off his farm. . . . Now, if a man has a right to do this, on a farm of a hundred acres, what power must a landlord have, who owns sixty thousand—ay! for the matter of that, including the late purchases, a hundred thousand?. . . . How is this managed in France, Monsieur Le Quoi? do you let every body run over your land, . . . helter-skelter, as they do here, shooting the game, so that a gentleman has but little or no chance with his gun? . . .
>
> But if I were in 'duke's place, I would stick up advertisements . . . forbidding all persons to shoot, or trespass, in any manner, on my woods. (93)

Jones's ambitions were common enough, but his reasoning is poor, and his cause a lost one. To apply the same principles to the enclosed lands of a farmer and to the unenclosed forest was legally seen as incorrect. As Lund summarizes the issue: 'The American belief in common rights to wildlife was manifested in doctrines that rejected landowner claims of special privilege and allowed free taking even on private lands.' He refers to an 1818 case as typical:

> Having come to the conclusion that it is the right of the inhabitants to hunt on unenclosed lands, I need not attempt to prove that the dissent or disapprobation of the owner cannot deprive him of it; for I am sure it never yet entered the mind of any man, that a right which the law gives, can be defeated at the mere will and caprice of an individual.[18]

The issue was a long-running one; it had been felt to be important enough to enter into debates about the Constitution. For example, the minority at the Constitutional Convention of Pennsylvania argued that the United States Constitution should include these guarantees:

> 7. That the people have a right to bear arms for the defense of themselves and their own state, or the United States, or for the purpose of killing game. . . .

8. The inhabitants of the several states shall have liberty to fowl and hunt in seasonable times, on the lands they hold, and all other lands in the United States not enclosed. . . .[19]

As with Tucker, it is clear that there is a family of ideas which were so strongly felt to belong together as to need no explicit connection, no justification. Natty claims that he has the right to shoot deer. Oliver claims that the law is on his side. Both, it would seem are correct, and it is (to say the least) an open question whether Judge Temple's generosity in giving Natty and Oliver the right to hunt is not merely an empty gesture, the product of his fantasy of feudalism.

That reference to France and its game laws by Richard is more than local colour. Not only was 1794 a time of crisis for relations with France, but also responses to what was happening there radically polarized domestic political opinion.[20] 'France' functions in the novel *both* as a dangerously revolutionary society the terrors (or Terror) of which Monsieur Le Quoi has fled, *and* as an old and valued ally in America's revolution. The Hollisters repeatedly remember the crucial help given by Rochambeau and the French troops at Yorktown (possibly a turning-point for the success of the American cause). France, before the Revolution, had indeed had penal game laws and one of the first decrees of the National Assembly was to abolish exclusive sporting privileges. Horace Walpole was quick to take the political message. 'I never admired game-acts', he wrote to Lady Ossory in 1789,

> but I do not wish to see guns in the hands of all the world, for there are other *ferae naturae* besides hares and partridges—and when all Europe is admiring and citing our constitution, I am for preserving it where it is.

As Munsche points out, some people

> took attacks on the game laws to be the signal for, rather than just a symptom of revolution. . . . 'The Republican party,' [Lord Milton] told Lord Kenyon in 1791, 'has made the game laws the object of their abuse and detestation; in France, the instant they began to overturn the Constitution and level all distinctions, these were the first they pulled down. It therefore seems to me that they should at all times be most respectfully guarded.'[21]

These were not isolated voices and the chorus may suggest that there is a train of association the reader is meant to follow as Judge Temple moves from what he sees as the atrocities of the French Revolution, to game laws as conservation, to a hoped for game law which would radically extend the idea of ownership by converting wildlife into property, and back to the Revolution. It is too often said that Natty's response is principally about the admittedly important question of enforcement:

> 'You may make your laws, Judge,' he cried, 'but who will you find to watch the mountains through the long summer days, or the lakes at night? Game is game, and he who finds may kill; that has been the law in these mountains for forty years, to my sartain knowledge; and I think one old law is worth two new ones. None but a green-one would wish to kill a doe with a fa'n by its side, unless his moccasins was getting old, or his leggins ragged, for the flesh is lean and coarse. But a rifle rings among them rocks along the lake shore, sometimes, as if fifty pieces was fired at once; it would be hard to tell where the man stood who pulled the trigger.'
>
> 'Armed with the dignity of the law, Mr. Bumppo,' returned the Judge, gravely, 'a vigilant magistrate can prevent much of the evil that has hitherto prevailed, and which is already rendering the game scarce. I hope to see the day, when a man's rights in his game shall be as much respected as his title to his farm.'
>
> 'Your titles and your farms are all new together,' cried Natty, 'but laws should be equal, and not more for one than another. I shot a deer, last Wednesday was a fortnight, and it floundered through the snow-banks till it got over a brush fence; I catch'd the lock of my rifle in the twigs, in following, and was kept back, until finally the creater got off. Now I want to know who is to pay me for that deer; and a fine buck it was. If there hadn't been a fence, I should have gotten another shot into it; and I never draw'd upon any thing that hadn't wings, three times running, in my born days.—No, no, Judge, it's the farmers that make the game scearce, and not the hunters.' (160–61)

There is much more than the problem of enforcement here to use to criticize the Judge's plans—including Natty's insistence that the conservation law is redundant, and his version of the argument about the causes of the scarcity of wild-life (seeing change in land-use rather than over-hunting as the principal cause). More important is his repetition of an earlier point that the law has always previously permitted free taking—'who ever heard of a law, that a man should'nt kill deer where he pleased' (25)—and more important still his democratic stress that 'laws should be *equal*'. What the Judge ignores, and what Natty draws attention to, is the question of what happens in 'duke's brave new world to the man whose principal property is his labour. Slotkin makes an important point. The context of Natty's remark

> is crucial. Temple has just been talking of the Jacobin excesses in France, the lawlessness of the mob, and the killing of the king. Bumppo's defiance in one sense associates him with the Jacobins as a revolutionary. From Bumppo's point of view, however, it is Temple who is the law breaker.[22]

Slotkin is right to draw attention to 'the gulf of violence, strife and revolutionary overturn that has been revealed' in this debate over game laws. Nevertheless the sense in which Natty is a revolutionary needs careful analysis; it is hardly how he sees himself. One way is to distinguish between Natty's function and his sense of his own loyalties, to differentiate between his (objective) historical rôle and his (subjective) perception of his rôle. Natty is (if revolutionary at all) a revolutionary on the American, not the French model, a soldier of the revolutionary war and as rifleman an icon of that war. (There was a persistent myth that skill with the rifle had been much of the reason for the States' military success—and George Washington had commanded his soldiers to wear hunting shirts because this garment symbolized the rifleman.)[23]

He is, however, a 'revolutionary' who does not, perhaps cannot, act—except symbolically. (His only real act of rebellion is killing the deer.) While he has fought for a free America, he at the same time feels himself to owe almost feudal service to old Major Effingham. (He is, I think, the only character apart from Captain Hollister to have fought during the Revolution. How, I wonder, did Richard Jones spend those years?) One (though only one) right to carry a gun, to hunt, can be seen as deriving from the fact that Natty is, in effect, the Major's gamekeeper. (Oliver describes him as 'a kind of locum tenens' (441).) But this is not the only right he can be read as standing for; he appeals (with good reason) to custom and to law. At the same time, the vocabulary of natural rights is available (whether or not we attach this to Locke)—as is the rhetoric of the democratic American. It should be no surprise that he cannot act effectively; he is caught between rights deriving from the past, rights embodied in the contemporary radical political language, and rights that, in a sense, are either outside or precede history.

Nevertheless the armed police power of the law is twice brought to bear on him—at first tragically, then farcically. Its first effect is to cause the 'revolutionary'—or, as Jones terms him, 'an example of rebellion against the laws . . . a kind of out-law' (355)—to burn his hut, a defeated minority of 'one to many' (357). The intervention of the posse comitatus (and it is important that it is the posse comitatus not the militia) reduces the 'revolutionary' situation to farce, ending just before tragedy. Here at least Natty is no revolutionary. He has been fighting to protect the representative of the past (which mostly seems to mean concealing the past), Major Effingham, the hidden embodiment of a defeated history, who is given only one chance to speak in the novel. Before that appearance, he is repeatedly referred to, his absence is gestured towards, but who and what is being referred to and what weight is to be put on those mysterious references are matters of speculation for the first time reader. All that is clear is that there is an ambiguous absent authority. His speech is an unconscious anachronism and that reference to having the best of game at his command places him firmly in his history. Effingham is 'living' a time when game was reserved for a class, when it was not a matter for monetary exchange but for gift, and in so doing unconsciously contrasts his feudalism with Temple's modern variant. What better way of symbolizing his loyalty to old England?

The resolution of the inheritance plot does not hide the fact that the central conflict between the man with a gun and the law (Temple's law) is not obviously resolved. To which should moral and political priority be given? The answer, I suggest, lies in decoding, in the light of the historical information I have tried to provide, Major Hartmann's enigmatic words: 'a rifle is petter as ter law' (93). It is a phrase he repeats. The first time is as a critical response to Richard Jones's desire to forbid trespass and hunting on Temple's unenclosed lands. The second time is in response to Judge Temple's concession that Natty has rights and his pious, empty guarantee of legal protection:

> 'Natty . . . has a kind of natural right to gain a livelihood in these mountains; and if the idlers in the village . . . annoy him . . ., they shall find him protected by the strong arm of the law.'
> 'Ter rifle is petter as ter law,' said the Major sententiously.
> (112)

It is a curious phrase that demands interrogation. (Following the *O.E.D.* I take 'sententiously' to mean full of meaning, full of wisdom, aphoristic, since the *O.E.D.* says that the word has only recently been used in a bad sense to mean pompous.) Does it mean merely that the rifle is as good as the law? Or is it to be read as 'the rifle is better than the law'? And in what sense is 'better' to be understood? Stronger? Morally more authoritative? Both?

From my earlier arguments, from such arguments as those of St. George Tucker, it can be seen that the possession of a gun (and by extension the right to hunt) can be regarded as 'a political right as important as the vote . . . a sign as well as a guarantor of political emancipation'.[24] Since laws cannot be made contrary to the constitution, since the right to bear arms is embodied in that crucial guarantee of political liberty, the Bill of Rights, guns mean democracy and in the name of the higher Law of the constitution, the rifle *is* better than the law.

NOTES

1. Articles 2 and 4 of the Bill of Rights (1791), the first amendment to the Constitution. I wish to thank the editor and staff of the New York magazine *The Conservationist*. Without their remarkably generous help and detailed suggestions for reading, I could not have written this piece. I regret I came across Brook Thomas's essay 'The Pioneers, or the Sources of American Legal History: A Critical Tale', *American Quarterly*, 36 (1984), 81–111, too late to refer to it and argue with it in this article. While he is far too respectful towards Judge Temple, his argument is

consistently interesting, as is his discussion of Kent and of the implications of the reform of the New York State Constitution.

2. James Fenimore Cooper, *The Pioneers*, with an historical introduction and explanatory notes by James Franklin Beard (Albany: State University of New York Press, 1980), pp. 160, 365, 437. All subsequent references will be placed parenthetically in the text.

3. E. Arthur Robinson ('Conservation in Cooper's *The Pioneers*', *PMLA*, 82 (1967), 564–78) touches on some of the issues but, as his title suggests, his is a generalist approach and he relies too heavily on secondary sources. Charles Swann ('James Fenimore Cooper: Historical Novelist' in Richard Gray (ed.), *American Fiction: New Readings* (London and New York: Vision and Barnes and Noble, 1983), pp. 15–37) makes an attempt but that attempt is flawed by his ignorance of the actual laws that existed.

4. Among the most important are: Donald Davie, *The Heyday of Sir Walter Scott* (London: Routledge and Kegan Paul, 1961); George Dekker, *James Fenimore Cooper: Novelist* (London: Routledge and Kegan Paul, 1967); John P. McWilliams, *Political Justice in a Republic: James Fenimore Cooper's America* (Berkeley, Los Angeles, London: University of California Press, 1972). Davie makes an interesting point that the opposition in *The Pioneers* 'is not between freedom and law, but between freedom and anarchy' (p. 144), but unfortunately this is never developed. McWilliams usefully documents Cooper's interest in law but does not mention laws or lawyers. When he turns to *The Pioneers* he, unfortunately, relies heavily on Locke. For an acid criticism of his endorsement of the Judge see Wayne Franklin, *The New World of James Fenimore Cooper* (Chicago: University of Chicago Press, 1982). He is also very satisfyingly rude about Richard Jones.

5. Thomas A. Lund, *American Wildlife Law* (Berkeley, Los Angeles and London: University of California Press, 1982), p. 8. I have drawn very heavily from this excellent book.

6. Perry Miller, *The Life of the Mind in America from the Revolution to the Civil War* (London: Gollancz, 1966), p. 100.

7. St. George Tucker (ed.), *Blackstone's Commentaries with Notes of Reference to the Constitution and Laws of the Federal Government of the United States and of the Commonwealth of Virginia in Five Volumes* (Philadelphia: William Young Birch and Abraham Small, 1803). This has been photographically reprinted by Rothman Reprints (New Jersey, 1969). The *Commentaries* first appeared in four volumes between 1765 and 1769. Strong proof of its authority and popularity lies not only in the number of editions (and editors) but in the fact that all these editions follow a common pagination however extensive the editorial commentary. All subsequent references appear parenthetically in the text; the comment above comes from page 300 of Tucker's Appendices to Volume 1 (where Blackstone is allowed only 120 pages). For evidence of the popularity and importance of Blackstone and of Tucker's edition see Julius S. Waterman, 'Thomas Jefferson and Blackstone's *Commentaries*' and the introduction in *Essays in the History of Early American Law*, edited and with an introduction by

Guns Mean Democracy: 'The Pioneers' and the Game Laws

David H. Flaherty (Chapel Hill: University of North Carolina Press, 1969). While it can be proved that Cooper had read Blackstone, unfortunately I cannot prove that he read Tucker's edition.

It is interesting to see how over a long vista of time and space the rhetoric connecting game laws and weapon control remains the same. For example, in 1739 in England, *The Craftsman* declared that 'it would be better for Us, that there was not a *Pheasant*, a *Partridge*, or an *Hare*, in the whole Kingdom, than that they should be preserv'd at . . . the imminent *Hazard* of our *Liberties*.' In 1902, a Californian judge observed: 'He has read history to very little purpose who does not know that game laws . . . enacted and enforced in the interests of a privileged few, have been the fruitful source of the oppression of the masses of the people. . . . It were better to exterminate the game at once than to preserve it for the special benefit only of a favoured few.' So much for the conservationist's tender susceptibilities. P. B. Munsche, *Gentlemen and Poachers: The English Game Laws 1671–1831* (Cambridge: Cambridge University Press, 1981), p. 80, T. A. Lund, op. cit., p. 128.

8. It is only a small point—but American timber is being destroyed to be replaced by European imports of Lombardy poplars—to give 'a show of cultivation', to 'ornament the grounds' (pp. 42, 45).

9. See E. A. Robinson, op. cit., p. 568, for a discussion of laws about timber.

10. I have been unable to consult laws operative in 1823. I quote from James Kent and Jacob Radcliff (compilers), *Laws of the State of New York 1777–1801* (Albany, New York: 1886–1887). They are not easy to find— and do not seem to have been found to be worth consulting. E. Arthur Robinson, for example, says that 'not until 1813 was there a law providing for the issuance of search warrants to constables to look for evidence of illegal killing of deer (p. 571), unwisely basing his opinion on Gurth Whipple, *A History of Half a Century of the Management of the Natural Resources of the Empire State* (1935).

Further evidence of Cooper's interest in precise historical detail is provided by Natty's appearance in the stocks—'the whipping-post, and its companion the stocks, were not yet supplanted by the more merciful expedients of the public prison' (p. 373). 'Those relics of the elder time' were abolished in 1796—see Alfred E. Young, *The Democratic Republicans of New York: The Origins, 1763–1797* (Chapel Hill: University of North Carolina Press, 1967), pp. 526–28. Young is also very useful in setting Judge Cooper's political career in a wider context.

11. It is hard to avoid speculating that Judge Cooper had a hand in the passing of the 1798 law. Cooper is vague about his dates here—but it looks as though the seine-fishing takes place sometime in May.

12. McWilliams, op. cit., p. 108; Dekker, op. cit., p. 46.

13. Douglas Hay, 'Poaching and the Game Laws on Cannock Chase', in Douglas Hay *et al.*, *Albion's Fatal Tree: Crime and Society in Eighteenth-Century England* (Harmondsworth: Penguin, 1977), p. 189. See also P. B. Munsche, op. cit., for an excellent general account.

14. See Hay *passim* and P. B. Munsche, op. cit., Ch. 5, 'Early Opposition to the Game Laws', pp. 106–31.

15. Edward Christian quoted by Hay p. 207. Christian not only wrote a lengthy treatise on the game laws but edited Blackstone's *Commentaries*. He took issue with Blackstone's ideas about game laws—and especially with his idea that ownership was vested in the Sovereign. It was Christian's edition that Tucker used. He makes no reference to his ideas about game—understandably since Christian was all for the game laws. But also Blackstone's views suited the American situation. One simply replaced the sovereign by the state: 'early statutes and all subsequent acts regulating hunting were based on the premise that ownership of all game is vested in the State' (Whipple, p. 106, quoted by E. Arthur Robinson, op. cit., p. 571). And since all state powers derive from the people, here is another reason for finding Judge Temple's attempt to extend the game laws improper.
16. State v. Campbell, 1 T.U.P. Charlt. 166 (Ga. Supreme Court 1808).
17. See Alfred F. Young, op. cit., *passim.*
18. T. A. Lund, op. cit., pp. 24, 121.
19. Merril Jensen (ed.), *The Documentary History of the Ratification of the Constitution Vol. II* (Wisconsin: State Historical Society of Wisconsin, 1976), pp. 623–24. While these proposals were not adopted by the Pennsylvania convention they 'did point the way to other states, which incorporated such proposals in their ratifications', Lee Kennett and James LaVerne Anderson, *The Gun in America: the Origins of a National Dilemma* (Westport, Connecticut, London: Greenwood Press, 1975), p. 72.
20. See Alfred F. Young, op. cit., especially pp. 345–444.
21. P. B. Munsche, op. cit., pp. 125, 126, 127.
22. Richard Slotkin, *Regeneration Through Violence: The Mythology of the American Frontier 1600–1860* (Middletown, Connecticut: Wesleyan University Press, 1973), p. 487.
23. Lee Kennett and James LaVerne Anderson, op. cit., p. 66.
24. Dennis Porter, *The Pursuit of Crime: Art and Ideology in Detective Fiction* (New Haven and London: Yale University Press, 1981), p. 171.

5

Pioneer Properties, or 'What's in a Hut?'

by RICHARD GODDEN

1

Natty Bumppo is an early American literary anorexic; emphatically thin, he advocates merest subsistance. As a hunter he is a minimalist, adopting the aesthetic of the single shot.[1] While others plunder the bass, he spears one laker. The pigeon migrations afford him but one bird, taken on the wing, even as pigeons are cannonaded from the skies. Such events prompt brief sermons on the 'wicked manner' (248) of 'wasty ways' (265), and the benefits of poverty in cornucopia. Restraint is inexplicable to the settlers, their suspicion being shared by the first-time reader for whom much about the Leather-stocking is questionable. For example, when Natty kills a deer or a partridge, the purpose of the death remains enigmatic. The locus of the enigma is the hut to which the game will be carried. The reader never enters the hut, though he is given detailed access to other significant interiors. Doolittle's curiosity and Jones's plots serve only to focus anticipation, as does a temporary tenant—Edwards, a manifest 'somebody' in disguise. The mystery deepens when Natty burns his hut, transferring its contents into the ground. By implication the hut was always an ante-chamber to the grave; Elizabeth offers to rebuild it and is met with the question, 'Can ye raise the dead, child!' (386).

Those permitted to take meat to the place were sworn to secrecy (27) and might submit only the tenderest cuts. Overtones of ritual grace such offerings—particularly as the land in question was called by the Delawares 'Grandfather' (83). Hindsight indicates that gifts were given to a grandfather buried within a Grandfather. Indian coffins modelled on Chinese boxes may seem rather fantastical to those who wish to get on with the story, but as Frank Kermode notes, 'secrets . . . are at odds with sequence'.² Often triggered by key-words (in this case 'mine', 'sources', 'grandfather', 'pioneers'), a secret prompts over-interpretation which molests the plot. Although such words might better be wished away, they can, as they form their own patterns of association, imply alternative modes of causality, other narratives buried in and at odds with the main plot.

Take 'mine': Doolittle and Jones believe that Natty's hut hides gold or silver or, at the very least, implements of excavation. If the hut is a mine it contains a buried source of value. As almost the last resting place of Mohegan and Major Effingham, the mine entombs alternative value sources. Jones digs a 'countermine' (324). Temple, informed as to the probable death of the previous owner of his land, insists, 'talk not of mines' (277). Benjamin hears 'minds' for 'mines' (353), and as a late ramification of the network we learn that the counterfeiters were found 'buried' in the woods (347). The pun eventually infects the title—pioneers are, among other things, miners. Cooper had a taste for Shakespearian epigraphs so perhaps he heard Hamlet as he wrote *The Pioneers*: 'Well said, old mole! canst work i' th' earth so fast?/ O worthy pioneer!' (Act I, Sc. 5). The earth work throws up two 'sources', thereby making problematic the seemingly innocent sub-title, 'The Sources of Susquehanna'.³ If land is capable of double and conflicting definition, the representation of land becomes difficult. As a result the seemingly innocent phrase, 'A DESCRIPTIVE TALE' is not without duplicities. Where the title-page fails to nominate, the novel's troubled preoccupation with entitlement is underlined.

I am aware that in tracing the narrative of a pun, I may seem to be engaged in an exercise more suited to a modernist text than to an early nineteenth-century novel. Locke, rather than Derrida, states the linguistic atmosphere within which Cooper writes; nonetheless, that mode of language which proposes meaning not as a thing, but as an image debated between gentlemen, allows for an argument to occur within a word.[4] 'Mine' is not a released signifier freed from the responsibility of reference; its troubled passage derives from a particular historical debate about, at one level, the right to define the word 'property'. I have described a split referent not a ludic signifier. The double articulation of 'mine', 'source', and 'pioneers' stems from the 'double consciousness'[5] of the Jeffersonian and Jacksonian eras on the subject of land and money.

To nominate two 'sources' for the value of land (gold and title), and to further compress that conflict within a pun on the possessive pronoun, is to activate much of the post-revolutionary debate on the nature of accumulation. Writing in 1823 about 1793, Cooper must have been fully aware of the polarities within a continuing political argument whose goal was the definition of Republican Virtue. For Jefferson the key had been the soil—'Those who labour in the earth are the chosen people of God.'[6] However, the independent husbandman was, for Hamilton, an image of stagnation; only the introduction of a European style political economy could halt the farmer's regression from an agrarian stage of culture to an earlier and more primitive phase associated with the Indian and the hunter. Jefferson's husbandman and Hamilton's manufacturer pass through various incarnations before achieving their Jacksonian form as 'the people' and 'the speculator'. Cooper's hut is a veritable anthology of political iconography— set above a 'mine', and within the sound of farms, it is a charged and semi-prescient image containing blueprints for several of the symbols that were to bedevil political debate for the first four decades of the century. Harrison's log-cabin, Webster's coon-skin cap, Clay's American System and Jackson's monster-bank, can all be made to rise like spectres of the futures-past from Natty's unstable plot of soil.

The figures of Natty and Judge Temple determine the boundaries of the dispute within which puns on 'pioneer' and 'mine' are active. Natty has been aptly (if over-) read as a Lockean hero of the pre-social state. Certainly, upon occasion, he justifies his astringent hunting code in terms of natural law. God informs nature and must be respected via man's use of nature. For Locke God is primarily a 'maker' who holds a right in man as an expression of his 'workmanship'. Just as 'right of creation' puts God in authority over man, so by analogy, man as a 'maker' has a right in his products, and may hold as his own that with which he has mixed his labour— 'The *Labour* of his Body, and the *Work* of his Hands, we may say, are properly his.'[7] However, man's work never erases the divine labour, and therefore no property can be wholly private, in that unless it 'preserves' man its usage violates natural law. Ideally, for Locke, and in part for Natty,

> man should treat the world as a foreign country, using and enjoying what it offers yet leaving everything as it is—with his thoughts on his true home which awaits him at the end of the journey.[8]

Concomitant with Locke's insistence that objects cannot be wholly alienated from God, and must therefore carry within them an ordained social function to preserve man, is the recognition that abrogation of a man's right to use nature is offensive. For Locke the common remains common; one's share of the common may be called property, but that property is not a thing or things. Rather, it is a right to use in accordance with natural laws. For example, in a public transport system the seat belongs to everyone; a ticket buys the right to use, not to own, the seat. As with the seat, so with the deer.

Not so for Temple. Divine patents and common use-rights attached to every tree, beast and stone can only embarrass a mercantile rentier keen to convert trees, beasts and stones to commodity. (It is to be wondered whether Natty was such an unregenerate Lockean when he went to Creation to supply a 'stuffed painter' (292) to the Eastern market.) Temple reads Locke in quite another way, as the secular prophet of the possessive individual—to his eye a natural right to property inspires a natural right to accumulation, and so justifies the natural deprivation of others. Temple's legal scholarship may have been less than extensive, but Blackstone's *Commentaries* were 'an essential part of legal education'[9] in America at the close of the eighteenth century. Blackstone declares it self-evident that

> there is nothing which so generally strikes the imagination, and engages the affections of mankind, as the right of property: or that sole and despotic domination which one man claims and exercises over the external things of the world, in total exclusion to the right of any other individual in the universe.[10]

The utterance is in the spirit of Temple's game laws, which too often are taken ecologically. Temple as conservationist arises exclusively from twentieth-century misreading; his interest in deer, maple and bass, like his interest in coal and canals, expresses a preoccupation with development. The risk taker, whether he instigates a deer law, plans a maple plantation or builds a toll road, is granted exclusive right to the land upon which his new technologies are situated. Morton Horowitz notes:

> As the spirit of economic development began to take hold of American society in the early years of the nineteenth century . . . the idea of property underwent a fundamental transformation—from a static agrarian conception entitling an owner to undisturbed enjoyment, to a dynamic, instrumental, and more abstract view of property.[11]

Temple is prescient. 'Absolute dominion' inspires his concern for wild life. In post-revolutionary America a policy of 'free-taking', though disputed by landowners, recognized everyone's right to take game on unenclosed land. Having shot a deer in Temple's woods, Edwards appeals to his common right in the Judge's hall, 'I must have the saddle myself . . . if a man is allowed the possession of that which his hand hath killed, and the law will protect him in the enjoyment of his own' (91–2). The law stands, but Jones, ever protective of his cousin's estate, immediately suggests the posting of 'advertisements' against 'trespass, in any manner' (93). Temple has no need of posting, since his deer law will go a considerable way to transform the deer on his lands into his exclusive property, and these lands, therefore, into a deer park.[12]

Natty is no respecter of proto-deer parks, for him land and its creatures are common; the killer of the deer owns the deer because he has put his labour into it—but all men must have

125

right of access to the deer. For deer read 'tree', 'fish', 'land', and at once Natty's belief becomes radical, and philosophical discussion graduates into an historical struggle for possession.

Temple fears the 'squatters on the "Fractions" ' (329) and must therefore make an example of Natty, lest 'squatters' become 'depredators'. Poachers are easily transformed into Jacobins, at least by proprietors. Revolution in France is one of the Judge's favoured talking points, his sympathies are Bourbon; during a public discussion of deer law in the 'Bold Dragoon' he alludes pointedly to King killing, 'blood-thirsty Jacobins', and 'infuriated Republicans' (160–62)—the gradation is striking in one who is happy to be known as both 'Duke' and 'King'. Sheriff Jones further escalates the fear of brigands, declaring squatters 'lawless', and calling Natty a 'professed deer-killer' before he has committed his 'crime' against the deer (266). Not surprisingly, beset by forest fires and escaped counterfeiters, 'popular opinion' in Templeton will locate Natty's cave as 'a secret receptacle of guilt' (425). The phrase is resonant; by characterizing Natty not simply as outlaw, but as 'dangerous to the peace of society' (426), the property holders of Templeton can transform their own recent past into the Enemy, and march against their prior selves. In a period of land hunger the squatters are everyone's autobiography—they are the intimate brigands who must be repressed.

The repression of Natty, of his allies and of all that he has been made to stand for, is essential because Templeton is palpably the location of an emergent market economy. E. P. Thompson, writing of English judges in Chancery during the mid-eighteenth century, offers a useful gloss on the spirit of Temple's ambitions for his town:

> The judges sought to reduce use-rights to an equivalent in things or in money, and hence to bring them within the universal currency of capitalist definitions of ownership. Property must be made palpable, loosed for the market from its uses and from its social situation, made capable of being hedged and fenced, of being owned quite independently of any kind of custom or mutuality.[13]

In Elizabeth's words—'The enterprise of Judge Temple is taming the very forests!' (212). Nature will be made to yield,

126

as objects are put into 'value'. The process is by no means complete. The price mechanism is not yet a general system of equivalence—Spanish coin, American notes, counterfeit paper and barter circulate simultaneously. Small land holdings can still change hands 'part cash, and part dicker' (158) at prices set by local arbiters. But the scale of farming is changing. Jared Ransom may believe that sugar will be profitable in 1794 because of 'the many folks . . . coming into the settlement', but his labourer knows that the price of potash will only support a man, 'if they keep on fighting across the water' (229).[14] A growing national market explains Temple's interest in improving agricultural production. His toll roads and his planned canal are part of a determination to lower the cost of commodity circulation and to promote production. Where coal is an abiding preoccupation (222), manufacturers, on a more than domestic scale, cannot be far away.

In detailing Temple's 'bias to look far into futurity, in his speculation on the improvements' (321), Cooper provides a pocket history on the development of mercantile capital as profits taken from land speculation are mobilized on behalf of industrial accumulation. Temple planned Templeton as a city, and already wage labour with its attendant class divisions is apparent. Jotham Riddel sells his farm and turns miner for Jones. He believes that he is on a share of the profits; it is, however, clear from the strategic silence that greets his enquiry that his labour is casual labour for a wage (323). Likewise, Kirby tells Temple that he refines sugar on 'sheares' (229), but Jones knows that he is Ransom's employee.

The writing is on the wall for the 'jobber'. As long as Kirby hires himself out to complete a particular service, so long will he remain his own master. But Temple warns Riddel, 'you must remember that time is money' (159); in that one remark he displaces need and desire from the assessment of value and sets labour in their place as an absolute unit of measurement. Kirby is casual about his work because he works to satisfy himself.

> This fellow, whose occupation, when he did labour, was that of clearing lands, or chopping jobs, was of great stature, and carried, in his very air, the index of his character. . . . For weeks he would lounge around the taverns of the country, in a state of perfect idleness, or doing small jobs for his liquor and his meals,

127

and cavilling with applicants about the prices of his labour;
frequently preferring idleness to an abatement of a tittle of his
independence, or a cent in his wages. (190)

Under Temple's dispensation Kirby's heart and appetite will
matter less than the widening market. Consequently, value
can no longer 'lounge' easy in a man's body, but must derive
from a hidden external system whose criterion is time (labour
time). The gap that opens between experience and economics
deprives a man like Kirby of his indexical relation to himself;
his selfhood ceases to be his body and becomes his labour
power, a power appropriated by another. Likewise his tools
and the objects upon which he works—for Kirby matters of
boast and fantasy—are increasingly taken from him. The axe
and the gun escape the local preserve of tall story, in which
Kirby is still for the moment 'Herculean', 'magical', a
'conqueror' (191)—to pass into the provisional possession of
he who hires.[15]

Kirby stands on the threshold of labour, a threshold that
Riddel has crossed. Such men will grow fewer and seem more
lawless as the rationale of value extends. Temple's internal
improvements will contribute to the centralization of farming,
Riddel will lose his lands, Kirby will 'lounge' less readily, and
occasional day-labour will become permanent wage-labour.
Cooper has a striking capacity to lodge predictive archaeology
in the smallest economic item; for example, the shiftless
Riddel, burned, blackened and in his 'countermine', once
linked to those 'squatters' in the 'Fractions', becomes a
prophecy of the displaced labouring classes, the new 'savages'
so troubling to Adam Smith and Jefferson. Riddel's career,
culminating in a proto-industrial accident about which no one
much cares, typifies Cooper's grasp of the narratives latent in
value and labour.

Riddel is not a riddle to Temple because the judge holds all
the cards: much of the land and most of the laws. To follow
J. P. McWilliams in reading those 'civil laws' as based upon
'moral law' is to declare them innocent of economic interest;
such a declaration misses the political point.[16] Judge Temple
envisions a particular kind of future, and he will have it,
'legally'.

2

Before detailing Temple's legal practice, it is helpful to
consider his purposes; the continuity of one kind of economic
vision is inseparable from the continuity of his blood, albeit on
the distaff. As Nina Baym observes:

> Women [in Cooper's novels] are . . . the chief signs, the
> language of social communication between males; in the
> exchange of women among themselves men create ties and
> bonds, the social structures that are their civilizations . . . and
> thus man has to take them along wherever he goes and at
> whatever cost.[17]

Temple carries Elizabeth back with him from New York to
decorate his accumulations. Cooper is careful to stress the
daughter's economic status; in collecting her the judge also
collects a deer law and title to 40,000 acres (93). The daughter
and the land are synonymous; as the father assures Jones at
their reunion, 'Sell what thou wilt . . . so that thou leavest me
my daughter and my lands' (48). To speak of the father is, for
Cooper, to speak of the land-holder, and to speak of the
daughter is, necessarily, to speak of the future of those
holdings. Natty's double rescue of Elizabeth, first from the
jaws of death and then from fiery immolation, suggests that
Temple's grip on his daughter is, to say the least, careless—
indeed, I shall argue that Natty's resurrection-trick challenges
Temple's paternity by calling into question his property in his
daughter. The manner of Elizabeth's deliverance from flame is
revealing.

Prosceniumed in fire, the daughter is granted a view of the
village and of her father:

> 'My father!—My father!' shrieked Elizabeth. 'Oh! this—
> surely might have been spared me—but I submit.'
> The distance was not so great but the figure of Judge Temple
> could be seen, standing in his own grounds, and, apparently,
> contemplating, in perfect unconsciousness of the danger of his
> child, the mountain in flames. This sight was still more painful
> than the approaching danger; and Elizabeth again faced the
> hill.
> 'My intemperate warmth has done this!' cried Edwards, in
> the accents of despair. (411–12)

Edwards's phrasing is only unfortunate if one expects to hear naturalistic dialogue. Cooper allows innuendo to express a conflict of ownership. The 'intemperate warmth' that ignites Temple's forest (Vision) and threatens his daughter, though stimulated by careless timbering (407), stems from Edwards's passion, in that, as a suitor from Natty's party, he bids for Temple's 'futurity'. His declaration directly counters the daughter's submission to the father. Couched in the vocabulary of flame, which has typified Elizabeth since her first rescue from the panther, his 'warmth' is, however, powerless before the 'heavenly composure' and 'celestial' air with which Elizabeth prepares for immolation:

> Elizabeth moved not. . . . It was plain that her thoughts had been raised from the earth. The recollection of her father, and her regrets at their separation, had been mellowed by a holy sentiment, that lifted her above the level of earthly things, and she was fast losing the weakness of her sex, in the near view of eternity. (412)

Elizabeth achieves self-possession by submitting to possession by the father. She owes her life and her death to him because she owns herself to be only an extension of his power of distribution: 'how dear, how very dear, was my love for him. That it was near, too near, to my love for God' (412). Just as Temple's economy discovers the universal values of price and law in tree, beast and stone, so Temple's paternalism disembodies his daughter, and allows her to find solace in the Father. What Elizabeth murmurs to Edwards is incantation not dialogue; repetitious and internally rhymed it marks her as a supplicant to a closed system, a system of value capable of absorbing each and every particularity. Cooper's writing is here contrived, but its contrivance is in keeping with its discoveries. The daughter's self-sufficiency is achieved at the cost of total artificiality. She becomes merely a sign for The Adoration of the Father. However, at the very moment of her withdrawal into his perfection, Natty interrupts:

> . . . as she thought she was shaking off the last lingering feeling of nature . . . the world, and all its seductions, rushed again to her heart, with the sounds of a human voice, crying in piercing tones—

Pioneer Properties, or 'What's in a Hut?'

'Gall! where be ye, gall! gladden the heart of an old man, if ye
    yet belong to 'arth!' (412–13)

Natty arrives both as an agent of flame and as a deliverer—'red
feature[d]' and with 'his hair burnt to his head' (413), he seduces
Elizabeth away from the realms of abstraction, restoring her
body by 'piercing' her 'composure' (410). The resurrection
carries her from one graveside to another, from her own idealized
'grave' (408), to Natty's far more problematic hole.

Natty's 'mine' epitomizes his attitude to the land: the soil is
an inertia marked by all who use it, consequently the ground is
neither alienable nor transferable. Land, as worked matter,
cannot be owned. No exclusive title can be issued because soil is
particular, containing, sedimented within itself, a singular
history. Cooper's revelation of the secret held in the hole is a
stroke of comic rebuttal on a grand scale; when he finally pulls
several 'sources' from one 'mine' he proves that entitlement to
land, and indeed to private property itself, is a unity imposed on
multiplicity by power.

To steal Elizabeth away from her possessive patriarch to the
brink of such a place, is to threaten most of what Temple, with
his secular-Lockean principles, stands for. Not surprisingly,
once the daughter is returned, Natty's fertile hole must be
stopped in the name of property.

Though 'the public mind' (426) is confused as to what it is
fighting against—squatters, miners, counterfeiters, incen-
diaries—it is plainly at one with the Templeton Light Infantry
in 'enforcing the laws of the country' (426)—laws laying
singular stress on free-hold, albeit in this instance Temple's.
The hill must be recaptured from those who have no right to it
because 'the peace of society' (426) depends upon the protection of private property. However, Temple, armed with the law,
has no need of overt conflict; appearing on Vision he invokes
'justice', and bloodshed is by and large averted:

> 'Silence and peace! why do I see murder and bloodshed
> attempted! is not the law sufficient to protect itself, that armed
> bands must be gathered, as in rebellion and war, to see justice
> performed! (435)

Law has always been Temple's battleground, and with it he
teaches the rules of the market.

131

3

Property is everywhere within Temple's dispensation, and everywhere it is shadowed by law. Law's prevalence should not persuade us of its ethical propriety—in part because Natty's existence persists in posing the question, 'In whose interests were such rights and laws forged?' Natty produces very little that goes to market, and his hole in the ground gives the lie to the institution of private property. According to Temple's 'value' Natty is ill-defined and awkward. Living on the furthest margin of labour, and true to his anorexia, he seems ill-constructed. The reader is invited to ponder whom Natty serves. Questions multiply. What is he to Mohegan? Is he, as rumoured, Oliver's father? If he has scalped has he 'crossed'? Natty is an entity only in so far as he is a composite made up from parts insufficiently named. The contrast with persons in court and market could not be more complete; where they are declaredly equal, he is bounded by unequal and untraceable ties.

The economic subject, like his shadow the legal subject, is isolate because he *freely* alienates his labour and takes possesion of himself as a *will* to *value*. Value, in the form of abstract labour time, grants him his *autonomy* and makes him every man's *equal*. I have italicized certain terms to indicate how extensively the language of the law and the market re-echo one another.[18] As the subject stands in relation to contract so he stands in relation to law. Each institution produces a particular kind of subject and reinforces the subject produced by the other. In both cases a trinity of terms is posited having limited relevance to Natty—'free', 'equal' and 'autonimous'. No theorist, Natty is well aware of the affinity between 'the money of Marmaduke Temple, and the twisty ways of the law (291). The crowds on the road to his trial bear out his supposition; 'the grand juror' is 'a well-clad yeoman, mounted on a sleek switch-tailed steed', his 'elevated' face declares, 'I have paid for my land, and fear no man.' A 'petit juror' walks and does not wear his ownership in his profile (358). To be inferior in property, though not in 'independence', is, when the court meets, to be inferior both in legal 'consideration' and in selfhood.

Pioneer Properties, or 'What's in a Hut?'

The trial offers salutory instruction on the production of a legal subject. In court the circumstances surrounding Natty's 'crime' are abstracted to suit the progress of the charges. An early point of dispute concerns the word 'use'—'you are accused of using your rifle against an officer of justice; are you guilty or not guilty?' (365). Temple intends 'use' to mean 'employ'; for Natty 'use' means the entire act of firing and therefore the intention to kill. As Cooper notes, the language of law is at once 'particularized' and 'vague' (365), its vagueness inheres in its capacity not merely to wield obscuring parentheses, but to transform dialogue into a monologue filled with terms that mean only one thing, and mean that thing to all men. The logic of linguistic equity would be impeccable, were it not that all men are represented in court by lawyers, which lawyers are the only men who can interpret the singular language of law. Double articulations filled with social conflict are anathema. Mr. Lippet is Natty's legal voice, a double who 'instruct[s]' his client in court vocabulary (362), with the result that Natty is found not guilty of an assault on a man he undoubtedly assaulted (Doolittle) and guilty of an assault on a man whom he did not assault (Kirby). Natty protests that, indeed, he 'took [Doolittle] . . . a little roughly by the shoulders' (364); he is silenced. Kirby vociferates that Natty used no violence against him, and is ignored. One could elaborate on the inversions through which Cooper makes his simple point—that law stands reality exactly on its head in search of a story that will protect the agents of property. Doolittle is not a victim, because he did not act as a legal agent. Kirby, for all his protestations, *is* a victim because he was acting as 'a minister of the law' (369). Abstraction is the key to the case; despite talk of 'particularities', the context that would make Natty's defence of his hut meaningful is suppressed, As a result crucial links between property, power and authority remain uninvestigated; for example, the fact that Natty is a 'squatter' on Temple's land, and that Temple's chosen legal agents suspect him of hiding illegally mined ore are deemed not worthy of evidence. Temple knows the facts but omits them to sustain his own 'apparent impartiality' (364). In the absence of the real evidence the jurors condemn and the Judge sentences an abstraction for threatening an abstraction. That neither of the men in question recognizes himself in the decision underlines the power of the law, first to compel amnesia, and then to write another story in the space made by forgetfulness.

As in Temple's court, so in Templeton's market, the subject who contracts is made to forget. The contract is the heartland of a bourgeois economy, in its autonomous space self-possessors meet and are reassured; each mirrors the other in that their agreement declares them equal, if only in their taking of the opportunity to obtain unequal profit. Much must be forgotten before the workings of equity can hold such sway. Temple is persuasive. When he offers $5 for the deer shot on Christmas Eve, he is determined to forget who actually shot the animal. If he has his way 'price' will cancel work, and venison vanish into 'value'. So use-rights become labour time, and the producer submits his claim as maker to the higher claim of the entrepreneur. Temple's patent works in exactly the same way, the measure of its legality being the extent of its historical ignorance. That both patent and deer are still disputed is evidence that value, equity and wage-labour are not yet the very bone and mind of Templeton. Nonetheless, amnesia characterizes the resolution of the novel.

4

The marriage is a crucial act of repression; with it the name of Effingham vanishes into the name Temple. Effectively, the judge manages to engineer a marriage through which he both exchanges and yet fails to exchange Elizabeth. Not only does he regain a daughter but he loses an economic rival and a social threat. In submitting to Elizabeth, Edwards submits, as has she, to her father. Among the flames on the *Vision* he seals their contract with a passionate declaration of amnesia: 'If I have forgotten my name and family, your form supplied the place of memory. If I have forgotten my wrongs, 'twas you that taught me charity' (412). If Edwards can forget his name there is small reason for Temple to remember it; symptomatically, the Judge never uses his son-in-law's proper title, and even Cooper prefers Edwards to the paternal name. By means of marriage the two notional halves of the patent are

reunited and the awkwardly 'composite' character of Oliver
Edwards is sorted out. Gone are the overtones of mixed blood
and uncertain social status. The proliferant paternities die or
go West. Once Edwards is divorced from Effingham, and
more importantly from Natty, the past can be modified to
meet his new integrity as a landlord.

In the final chapter Natty's systematic refusal to fit is
suppressed in an act of substantial rewriting. The troubled
area of his hut is recomposed as a graveyard. Bounded by 'a
circle of mason-work' (449) and 'beautifully laid down in turf'
(450) that location of suspicion is transformed; once monu-
mentalized by 'urn' and 'slab' (450), it becomes its opposite—
the official record of the past, to which future generations will
come for comforts of continuity. They will read inscriptions
that have been rewritten to fit the facts. Natty points out that
Chingachgook's name is doubly mis-spelled (452). Edwards
promises alterations. Cooper's point remains: Temple, via
stone-mason and son-in-law, has mastered both the future and
the past of Templeton.

The marriage plot belongs to Temple more than to the
happy couple. Arguably, he knew who Edwards was almost
from the first, and therefore has a direct interest in promoting
a union that will protect the integrity of his lands. If so, the
sudden largesse of his offers—a roof for life and a secretarial
position for as long as may be—are means to surveillance and
the promotion of affections. I do not have the space to make
my case fully, and instead can provide only a number of
possibly troubling observations. Asked his name by Temple in
Temple's hall, Edwards replies, 'I am called Edwards . . .
Oliver Edwards' (92). The reader has already learned that the
founding Effingham was called Edward (31). Temple, to
whom the face is 'very familiar' (38), will himself refer to
Oliver Effingham's son Edward Oliver Effingham in his will
(443). Are we to suppose that Temple cannot add one Oliver
to two Edwards?

The first announcement of the name casts the Judge into a
silence that Jones fills with a paean to his cousin's ownership.
Meanwhile Cooper salts the text with several jokes about the
political instability of property, the best of them involving
Salic law[19]:

135

'How is this managed in France, Monsieur Le Quoi? do you let everybody run over your land, in that country, helter-skelter, as they do here, shooting the game, so that a gentleman has but little or no chance with his gun?'

'Bah! diable, no, Meester Deek,' replied the Frenchman; 'we give, in France, no liberty, except to de ladi.'

'Yes, yes, to the women, I know,' said Richard, 'that is your Sallick law.' (93)

Monsieur Le Quoi (whose name in translation calls names into question), may be impressed only by Jones's ignorance, but the allusion does more than 'expose Richard's ... pretentiousness'.[20] Under Salic law daughters may not inherit—unless Temple can engineer a marriage plot his daughter may suffer similar disadvantages. However, Cooper's capacity to maintain a subversive sub-plot is not in question; Temple's plotting is the issue of the moment. By binding Edwards to his house he binds him to his daughter. Unless he knows the true identity, why should he remain so unconcerned by Edwards's repeated claims to mixed blood? Marriage between Elizabeth and a palpable gentleman is one thing, support for her interest in a cross-breed is quite another.

As soon as Temple learns, in letters from England, of the death of Oliver Effingham, he writes a will. This, according to Temple, is the document that Edwards eventually reads, and upon the basis of which he exonerates the Judge and marries the daughter. Why should Temple be so immediately 'ill at heart' (275) at the death of a man he has not seen for seventeen years, and who has no legal claim upon him? The benevolent reader, if one still exists, will protest grief and honesty. Cooper denies the second term; a short character sketch of the lawyer consulted in the case submits 'honesty' to 'circumstance':

> ... this man ... was known to the settlers as Squire Van der School, and sometimes by the flattering, though anomalous title of 'the Dutch', or 'honest lawyer'. We would not wish to mislead our readers in their conceptions of any of our characters, and we therefore feel it necessary to add, that the adjective, in the preceding agnomen of Mr. Van Der School, was used in direct reference to its substantive. Our orthodox friends need not be told that all merit in this world is

comparative; and, once for all, we desire to say, that where anything which involves qualities or character is asserted, we must be understood to mean, 'under the circumstances.' (277–78)

Under the circumstances the will is a document drawn up to be produced when, as far as Temple knows, the new Effingham claimant shows his hand, hopefully in matrimony. It is, however, quite possible that this will is not the will read by Edwards. It is written when the liaison with the daughter is going well; subsequently, Natty's imprisonment, Edwards's stormy exit from the household and the prison break weaken Temple's grip on the heir. Even as the mountain burns and the Infantry muster, Cooper informs us that 'Marmaduke was said to be again closeted with Mr. Van der School, and no interruption was offered to the movement of troops' (427). Perhaps, in his closet, Temple is rewriting, preparing a document that will mollify a claimant whom Temple knows to be about to unmask. Only Jones is present both at the writing of the first will and among the persons who gather at Natty's mine. He does not, however, witness the reading of what I would call Temple's second will. Temple dismisses him to fetch a carriage for old Effingham. The task is minor but sufficient to ensure that any discrepancy between the documents cannot be observed.

The will, as the turning point in the marriage plot, must be made to stick. It recomposes the past in terms of equity, and thereby provides a future for Temple's land. The language is 'clear, distinct, manly' (443), with a clarity derived from the vocabulary of quantification ('sum', 'moiety', 'principal', 'fair', 'exact'). The words should worry any reader alert to the legal manipulation of language during the trial scene. Cooper's assurance that the will is the culmination of Temple's 'clear narrative' and as such 'undeniable testimony to the good faith' of the Judge (443), 'under the circumstances', solicits denial by dint of its very confidence.

Yet the question remains, if Temple is wilfully manipulative why cannot Cooper say so? He can accuse the Judge of dishonourable hunting, lying, nepotism and surrogate slave-holding, why then cannot he openly state judicial manipulation of past and future to suit the logic of value. I can answer my own question only by appeal to the ambivalence of Cooper's biography. I would stress that I read Cooper's position within a particular family as a 'class apprenticeship',[21] and not as a psychological case study.

Cooper's parents were socially at odds; his father advanced from 'the disadvantage of a small capital',[22] through legal practice to political power and massive land holdings. He professed himself a speculator:

> Where there is trade there will be money; and where there is money the landlord will succeed; but he should be ever in the midst of the settlers, aiding and promoting every beneficial enterprise.
>
> In this point of view I have often compared the dealer in land to a ship. Money is the element he swims in; without money he is aground; and as a ship that is not afloat is no better than a wreck, so when he ceases to have money his activity and his usefulness are gone.[23]

With this money William Cooper created Otsego Hall:

> a great rectangular stone house with a castellated roof and gothic windows, surrounded by box hedges and wide lawns trimmed precisely by black gardeners, and far surpassing any other home in the old West.[24]

The Hall doubtless gave to moveable capital a secondary status as 'the inorganic body of its Lord'.[25] Cooper's land, or part of it, became Cooperstown, and if the blending of name and land was cosmetic, the judicial and political privileges that arose from a landed estate were not. It is doubtful whether Elizabeth Fenimore was entirely fooled by the guise of the 'Federalist squire'. Her husband's 'modest aristocracy'[26] was too new to persuade 'a patrician who detested the frontier . . . [and] insisted on the primacy of civilized values'.[27] Perhaps her son's marriage into the De Lancey family—'one of the best families in the state'[28]—may have been some recompense, at least until the De Lanceys disowned Fenimore because of his involvement in financial speculation. Caught between gentility and speculation—that is, between the polarities of the emergent bourgeoisie—and writing *The Pioneers* even as his entire landed inheritance was being sold to meet family debt, Cooper recreates a two-faced father. The judge may be read as a speculating entrepreneur or as a benevolent member of the gentry, with one or two advanced ideas. Perhaps he is better read both ways. Temple, like his source, names his town for himself, invests in the transport revolution and lays claim to a ducal title. The decoration—trees imported from Europe and venison to hand—cannot disguise his commitment to an artistocracy of money. And yet his last significant act in the novel is successfully double-voiced; the marriage both asserts the logic of equity and self-possession by means of a will, and simultaneously modifies the dynamic of 'value'. Capital is gentrified. Temple's patent was originally Effingham's; land that in 1793 belongs to the aristocracy of money, in 1775 was nominally retained by a family having 'high court interests' and opposed to 'commerce' (31). The marriage plot restores to Temple's speculative achievements an aristocratic name, while preserving his own name in the land (if only because Effinghamton is something of a mouthful). Nothing has really changed. Effingham may remove his leather-stockings to reveal his silk hose, but beneath both he is a child of 'value', that is to say he is Temple's child. It is Edwards, not Temple, who offers Natty a paper bank-roll against his journey West, thereby submitting Natty's life to the latest fashion in the very measure that the hunter has lived to resist.

Natty's refusal of the money is muted by a marriage that is itself a form of constricted exchange. In marrying Effingham, Elizabeth commits economic incest.[29] The daughter, whom the father may not use but must exchange, *is* exchanged, but only to a man whose own father had been the undeclared source of Temple's 'mercantile house[hold]' (33). The exchange is partial; Temple's plot involves the use of his daughter to concentrate rather than to distribute his own accumulations. Exchange is at once posited and denied, in a solution that marries the polarities of the bourgeoisie. The match is a false mediation, a species of social monster whereby irreconcilable conflicts are disguised. The disguise is thin but allows Cooper respite from antipathy. The fictional marriage enables Cooper to deny Natty and to retain him. Natty is created old, he goes West to die, or at least to re-enact the

139

same struggles with Doolittle who has gone West before him, and then to die. However, Temple's 'future' triumphs only in an impacted form whose social representation is the aristocratic family. 'Value' demands speculation via those forms which Natty has, knowingly and unknowingly, consistently countered. By means of a stratagem of gentility, Cooper mediates class conflict, in that as a manor house the merchant house may briefly shut up shop. It is a solution devoutly to be wished; but just because it is so obviously a wish it offers no solution to the historical conflicts surrounding property—conflicts that articulate and divide the novel from title-page to penultimate chapter.

NOTES

1. J. Fenimore Cooper, *The Pioneers* (Albany, 1980), p. 266. Subsequent pagination refers to this edition.
2. F. Kermode, 'Secrets and Narrative Sequence' (*Critical Enquiry*, Vol. 7, No. 1, Autumn 1980), 87.
3. Even without the pun 'sources' is a problematic term. In the novel's first paragraph Cooper refers to 'numerous sources' (p. 13), while in his 1832 Introduction he insists upon 'but one proper source' (p. 6).
4. H. Aarsleff, *From Locke to Saussure* (London, 1982), pp. 25–31.
5. The phrase derives from Marvin Meyers who describes the 'Jacksonian paradox' in terms of a 'serious tension' between the image of the yeoman and the liberal/laissez faire principle: 'the effort of Jacksonian democracy [was] to recall agrarian republican innocence to a society drawn fatally to the main chance and the long chance, the revolutionizing ways of acquisition, emulative consumption, promotion and speculation—the Jacksonian struggle to reconcile again the simple yeoman values with the free pursuit of economic interest, just as the two were splitting hopelessly apart.' (*The Jacksonian Persuasion* (Stanford, 1968), p. 15.) Arguably, the division was already apparent by the 1790s and early 1800s; Jeffersonian capitalists also spent much time denying the spirit of their occupation, 'it appears that many Republicans wanted what the Federalists were offering, but they wanted it faster, and they did not want to admit that they wanted it at all.' (J. Zvesper, *Political Philosophy and Rhetoric* (Cambridge, 1977), p. 131.) See also D. R. McCoy, *The Elusive Republic: Political Economy in Jeffersonian America* (Chapel Hill, 1980), Ch. 8, 'The Jeffersonians in Power: Extending the Sphere'. Subsequent pagination refers to this edition.
6. T. Jefferson, *Notes on the State of Virginia*, ed. W. Peden (Chapel Hill, 1955), pp. 164–65.

7. J. Locke, *Two Treatises of Government*, ed. P. Laslett (New York, 1965), p. 329.
8. J. Lully, *A Discourse on Property* (Cambridge, 1980), p. 72.
9. P. Miller, *The Life of the Mind in America* (London, 1966), p. 113. See also T. A. Lund, *American Wildlife Law* (London, 1980), particularly Ch. 3.
10. Quoted by D. Hay, *Albion's Fatal Tree* (London, 1975), p. 19.
11. M. J. Horowitz, *The Transformation of American Law: 1780–1860* (Cambridge, 1977), p. 31 and Ch. 2, 'The Transformation of the Conception of Property'. See also R. Cottrell, 'Capitalism and the Formalization of Contract Law', collected in *Law, State and Society*, ed. B. Fryer *et al.* (London, 1981), pp. 54–69; L. M. Friedman, *Contract Law in America* (Madison, 1965), Ch. 1, 'Toward a Working Definition of Contract'; C. Post, 'The American Road to Capitalism' *New Left Review*, 133 (1982), 30–51. For an example of the Temple-as-conservationist approach, see E. A. Robinson, 'Conservation in Cooper's *The Pioneers*', *P.M.L.A.*, 82 (1967), 564–78.
12. See C. Swann, 'James Fenimore Cooper: Historical Novelist', collected in *American Fiction*, ed. R. Gray (London, 1983), p. 22. Charles Swann listened to several versions of the essay as it was being written; his disapproval was always constructive.
13. E. P. Thompson, 'The Grid of Inheritance: A Comment', collected in *Family and Inheritance*, ed. J. Goody *et al.* (London, 1976), p. 34.
14. 1793 was a turning point for the national economy: following the outbreak of the French Revolution, European demand for American raw materials mushroomed; consequently, 'America entered the second half of the 1790s riding the wave of an unexampled and invigorating prosperity tied to the proliferation of its foreign commerce in an era of international conflict.' (D. R. McCoy, *The Elusive Republic*, p. 165.)
15. In actuality the new owner is that 'necessity'—the dynamic of capital— in which 'the form of things is labour, not objects of need representing one another, but time and toil, concealed, forgotten'. M. Foucault, *The Order of Things* (London, 1970), p. 225.
16. J. P. McWilliams, Jr., *Political Justice in a Republic* (Berkeley, 1972), p. 108.
17. N. Baym, 'The Women of Cooper's Leatherstocking Tales', *American Quarterly*, 23 (1971), 698.
18. See E. P. Pashukanis, *Law and Marxism* (London, 1978), particularly Ch. 4, 'Commodity and Subject'.
19. As Temple leads his domestic entourage toward their feast, Benjamin does his version of, 'Can a leopard change its spots?' featuring a N.W. wind and Mohegan. Cooper quickly follows up with the story of Mr. What, a man turned round by fear of two revolutions (French and Haitian)—all in the space of three pages.
20. J. F. Beard, 'Explanatory Notes', *The Pioneers* (New York, 1980), p. 459.
21. J. P. Sartre, *Search for a Method* (New York, 1968), p. 58. Sartre notes that 'the person lives and knows his position more or less clearly through the groups he belongs to' (p. 66); as a founding group the family is that which may 'set up unsurpassable prejudices', (p. 60) and provide,

within parental functions, plots for social conflicts that are realized through the family, but extend far beyond the family.

22. Quoted by S. Railton, *Fenimore Cooper* (Princeton, 1978), p. 42. Subsequent pagination refers to this edition.
23. W. Cooper, *A Guide to the Wilderness* (New York, 1970), p. 8.
24. D. R. Fox, *The Decline of Aristocracy in the Politics of New York: 1801–1840* (New York, 1965), p. 136. Subsequent pagination refers to this edition.
25. K. Marx, 'Economic and Philosophical Manuscripts', collected in, *Early Writings* (Harmondsworth, 1977), p. 318.
26. D. R. Fox, op. cit., p. 136.
27. J. F. Beard, *The Letters and Journals of James Fenimore Cooper* (Cambridge, Mass., 1960–68), Vol. 1, p. 4.
28. S. Railton, op. cit., p. 42.
29. For an oedipal reading of the match, see S. Railton, op. cit., pp. 83–113. In seeking to give economic rôles to figures more often associated with sexual triangulation, I have followed the spirit of G. Deleuze and F. Guattari, *Antioedipus: Capitalism and Schizophrenia* (New York, 1977). They stress that the family is only *one* stimulus, and that everyone has the right to say, 'Oedipus? Never heard of it?' 'The family is by nature eccentric, decentered. . . . There is always an uncle from America; a brother who went bad; an aunt who took off with a military man. . . . The family does not engender its own ruptures. Families are filled with gaps and transected by breaks that are not familial: the commune, the Dreyfus Affair, religion and atheism, the Spanish Civil War . . . all these things form complexes of the unconscious more effective than everlasting Oedipus. And the unconscious is indeed at issue here. If in fact there are structures, they do not exist in the mind, in the shadow of a fantastic phallus. . . . Structures exist in the immediate impossible real' (p. 97).

6

Red Satan: Cooper and the American Indian Epic

by JOHN P. McWILLIAMS

Americans who first conceived of heroic historical romance about the American Indian may have lacked facts about the red man, but they were familiar with conflicting preconceptions of him. Cooper, Bird and Simms had all read historical sources which portrayed Indians as Homeric warriors living on in the American forest. They were also drawn in varying degrees to the Enlightenment belief that the red man had been Nature's noble savage, Man in all his unspoiled virtue. To a generation raised on Homer and Milton, yet exposed to the continuing demand for an American epic in verse or prose, these conflicting images suggested usable literary parallels. To imagine the Indian as hard, solitary, unyielding, ageing and doomed (Hector, Achilles, Turnus, Satan) would prompt romancers and historians to create the Big Serpent, Magua, Mahtoree, Sanutee and Pontiac. To imagine the Indian as graceful, generous, pliable, young and equally doomed (Apollo, Patroclus, Achates, Chactas) would lead the same writers to create Uncas, Hard Heart and Occonestoga. Although these two models of Indian heroism were often were appear as separate characters within one work, the way in which the romancer shaped them became a crucial measure of his attitude, not only toward the American Indian, but toward the nature of heroism in the New World.

Cadwallader Colden's 'Introduction' to his widely read *History of The Five Indian Nations* (1727) is clear testimony to the power of the Homeric lens. Familiar with the red man at treaty signings, but not in the forest, Colden writes of councils of chieftains, feasts, warsongs, rites of hospitality, games and ceremonial burials. Again and again he likens Indians who practice these customs to the peoples of heroic poetry. The red man's willingness to die for his nation exalts him to heroic stature: 'None of the greatest Roman Heroes have discovered a greater Love to their Country or a greater Contempt for Death, than these people called Barbarians have done.' Indian ceremonies of convening prompt Colden to assert that 'all their extraordinary visits are accompanied with giving and receiving Presents of some Value; as we learn likewise from Homer was the practice in Old Times.' The most telling sign of Colden's inability to perceive Indians apart from *The Iliad* is his discussion of the Indian oratory heard in war councils. Although Colden admits he is 'ignorant of their language', he praises the eloquence of Indian speech by asserting 'the same was practised by Homer's Heroes'.[1]

By the 1780s the notion of noble savagery had blurred Colden's rather one-dimensional view. The five-month journey Chateaubriand made through America in 1791 was motivated, he later insisted, by a desire to gather materials for his epic on American Indians, *Les Natchez*: 'J'etois encore très jeune lorsque je conçus l'idée de faire *l'epopée de l'homme de la nature*, ou de peindre les moeurs des sauvages.'[2] The enormously popular prose poems which resulted from this trip, *Atala* (1802) and *Renée* (1803), portray heroic Indians as gentle, disaffected philosophers of the simple way, who almost never seem to have to engage in killing.

The rapidity with which this view of the red man was welcomed in America is apparent as early as Sarah Wentworth Morton's four-canto poem, *Ouabi: or the Virtues of Nature* (1790). Mrs. Morton's title hero at first seems a gentle man of Nature, loving to his wife and protective of his tribe, a figure 'form'd by Nature's hand divine/Whose naked limbs the sculptor's art defied'. As soon as Ouabi appears on the battlefield, however, he hardens into the requisite Homeric stature:

Red Satan: Cooper and the American Indian Epic

Thus before Illion's heav'n-defended towers
Her godlike Hector rais'd his crimson'd arm;
Thus great *Atrides* led the Grecian powers,
And stern Achilles bid the battle storm.[3]

Mrs. Morton, who calls herself 'Philenia, a lady of Boston', evidently remained discomfited by her red Achillean hero. At the poem's end, she arranges for Ouabi to die nobly in battle, relinquishing his gentle wife to an adopted white tribesman, and thereby enabling the softer red virtues to live on into the future.

Despite his calculated bonhomie, Washington Irving was similarly troubled by the issue of Indian heroism. His two essays, 'Traits of Indian Character' and 'Philip of Pokanoket' describe New England's oppressed seventeenth-century Indians as 'a band of untaught native heroes . . . worthy of an age of poetry'; 'No hero of ancient or modern days can surpass the Indian in his lofty contempt of death.'[4] When these essays were assimilated into *The Sketch Book*, their firm accusatory tone, their sense of a lost heroic world, jarred tellingly amid the pretentious modesty of that genial sketchist, Geoffrey Crayon. And yet, Irving was not prepared to embrace the red values he seemed to be condoning. Regretting that the Indian's primitive virtues are still unsung, Irving seems to call for an American Scott to write a *Lay of the Last Minstrel* about our fast-disappearing Indians. Almost immediately, however, Irving compromises the value of courageous resistance by castigating primitivist poets and romancers as sentimental idealists: 'Thus artificially excited, courage has arisen to an extraordinary and factitious degree of heroism' (151).

The more the Indian resembled a Homeric warrior, the more clearly American writers could be sure that their land had known an heroic age. The price of having had an heroic culture, however, was accepting the dignity of the Indian's presumably barbarous values. In 1824 Harvard Professor Edward Everett, who had long been anticipating an heroic American literature, developed 'a comparison of the heroic fathers of Greece with the natives of our woods'.[5] Intent upon proving the Homeric stature of the red man, Everett offered the following evidence:

145

The ascendency acquired by personal prowess independent of
any official rank, the nature of the authority of the chief, the
priestly character, the style of hospitality in which the hero
slays the animal and cooks the food, the delicacy with which the
stranger is feasted before his errand is inquired for, the honor in
which thieving is held, and numerous other points will suggest
themselves to the curious inquirer, in which the heroic life
reappears in our western forests. (398)

The single word 'thieving' here taints our impression of epic
heroism by its inference of savage immorality. Everett's only
hope for extricating himself from this tonal inconsistency is to
claim that 'barbarism, like civilization, has its degrees' (399).

Everett's comparison ends with a sentence which, for a
Professor of Greek who revered *The Iliad*, is a bizarre testimony
to his culture's divided images of savage identity:

> Nations who must be called barbarous, like the Mexicans,[6]
> have carried some human improvements to a point unknown in
> civilized countries; and yet the peasant in civilized countries
> possesses some points of superiority over any hero of the Iliad,
> or Inca of Peru. Though we think, therefore, the heroic life of
> Greece will bear a comparison with the life of our Northern
> American savages, inasmuch as both fall under the class of
> *barbarous*; yet the Agamemnons and Hectors are certainly before
> the Redjackets and Tecumsehs; whether they are before the
> Logans would bear an argument. (399)

Although Logan might even be as great a hero as Hector,
Everett would have us believe that both are somehow inferior
to the civilized peasant who, in other equally unspecified
ways, does not participate in the improvements of barbarous
cultures!

In spite of his shaky logic, Everett is attempting to resolve
the problem of assessing the savage hero by the same device
used in imaginative literature—the gradation of barbarous
qualities among a range of Indian characters. The Indian as
noble savage would prove to be especially useful because he
humanized the harshly stoic grandeur of the fighting chieftain.
Celario outlives Ouabi, Yamoyden's gentleness balances King
Philip's rage, the memory of Uncas seems to outlive the
memory of Magua, Matiwan's humanity relieves Sanutee's
intransigence, and so forth. Although the Roman chief usually

remains the dominant model of the heroic Indian, the doubling of his image with the noble savage heightens elegiac regret while it conveniently assuages the reader's fear.

The activating call for an American heroic literature about the Indian occurred in consecutive articles in the 1815 issue of the *North American Review*. During the journal's ardently nationalistic first year, editor William Tudor solicited from Walter Channing an essay which would have the blunt title 'Reflections on the Literary Delinquency of America'. Joel Barlow's would-be epic poem *The Columbiad* (1807) had evidently convinced Channing that the great American work could not now be written about so recent and so familiar a topic as the American Revolution:

> In the most elevated walk of the muses, the Epick, we cannot hope much distinction [*sic*]. . . . We live in the same age; we are too well acquainted with what has been, and is, among us, to trust to the imagination. It would be an 'old story' to our criticks, for the events transpired yesterday, and some of our oldest heroes are not yet dead.[7]

Convinced that epic literature can only concern the distant past, Channing calls for a complete, celebratory history of American peoples, a work so comprehensive that it vaguely anticipates the heroic histories of Bancroft, Prescott and Parkman.

The renewed hope of Channing's article suited Tudor's purpose exactly. In his Harvard Phi Beta Kappa address of 1815, Tudor had recently reached the same conclusion about the failure of American epic literature, though he had proposed a markedly different solution. Offering his own address as the lead article in the November 1815 issue, Tudor placed Channing's essay after his in a complementary but subordinate position. Like Channing, Tudor begins by attacking the cliché that America must have a verse epic on the founding fathers:

> The American Revolution may some centuries hence become a fit and fruitful subject for an heroick poem; when ages will have consecrated its principles, and all remembrance of party feuds and passions, shall have been obliterated; when the inferiour actors and events will have been levelled by time, and a few memorable actions and immortal names shall remain.[8]

Tudor, however, has no interest either in the gradual winnowing of the true Revolutionary hero, or in trying to prove that Washington could be convincingly decked out in Virgilian clothing. Preferring the remote past, Tudor insists that the wars between the Five Nations and the Algonquins, together with the wars between the French and the English, constitute the heroic subject now pertinent and possible for American writers. It is the Indian, not the Revolutionary gentleman, who 'possessed so many traits in common with some of the nations of antiquity, that they perhaps exhibit the counterpart of what the Greeks were in the heroick ages' (19).

Tudor draws up a kind of literary prospectus specifying the traits common to Greeks and Indians: martial codes of honour, solitary and exalted heroes, feasts and games, eloquence in tribal council, a pantheon of nature deities, and the virtues of 'hospitality, reverence to age, unalterable constancy in friendship' (20). An American writer would be historically accurate if he conceived of Indian eloquence according to the Homeric pattern:

> The speeches given by Homer to the Characters in the Iliad and Odyssey form some of the finest passages in those poems. The speeches of the Indians only want similar embellishment, to excite admiration. (26)

Responding to the romantic affinity for the Natural Sublime, Tudor proclaims that the American Indian epic should contain word paintings of our unspoiled grandeur—particularly 'the numerous waterfalls' and 'the enchanting beauty of Lake George' (15). Episodic adventures similar to the tenth Iliad and the ninth Aeneid should be developed in order to enliven the narrative pace ('These episodes are two of the finest in these immortal Epicks, yet it is only to the genius of Homer and Virgil, that they are indebted for more than may be found in several Indian adventures' (22)). Although Walter Scott is not mentioned by name, his heroic verse romances surely prompted Tudor to assert that 'the actions of these people in war had a strong character of wildness and romance; their preparations for it, and celebrations of triumph, were highly picturesque' (21).

Although Tudor avoids specific consideration of genre, he

seems to be conceiving of an historical romance in verse which would recount the deeds of the French and Indian War around Lake George, and end with a 'prophetick vision' of the Indian's demise (30). Tudor's refusal to restrict the medium to poetry was timely and prescient, because the delivery of his address shortly followed the publication of *Waverley*. Whether Tudor privately had any firm conception of genre or not, his address provides a crucial transition in American literary history. Without the model of heroic literature he somewhat ingenuously offered, the Indian romances of Cooper and Simms would perhaps have developed both later and differently.[9]

'Funeral Fires'

The author of *The Last of the Mohicans* was clearly never deterred by the possibility that an heroic romance about the American Indian should be written in verse by any aged minstrel, red or white. In his tetchy review of Lockhart's *Life of Sir Walter Scott*, Cooper was to contend that Scott's great achievement as a writer had been that 'he raised the novel, as near as might be, to the dignity of the epic'.[10] The epic might remain the highest of forms, but the novel was the only genre through which contemporaries could approximate it. Nor was Cooper disposed to be timid in suggesting that America's one trace of an heroic culture might have passed away with the last warriors of a red tribe. As early as *The Pioneers* (1823), Cooper's approving view of America's expanding settlements had been qualified by condescension toward the gaucheries of middle class progress. In *The Redskins* (1846), Cooper's gentlemanly narrator, Hugh Littlepage, offers a passing slight upon the pretensions of old Albany's new rival, Troy:

> I wonder the Trojan who first thought of playing this travestie on Homer, did not think of calling the place Troyville or Troyborough! That would have been semi-American, at least, whereas the present appellation is so purely classical! It is impossible to walk through the streets of this neat and flourishing town, which already counts its twenty thousand souls, and not have the images of Achilles and Hector, and Priam, and Hecuba, pressing on the imagination a little uncomfortably.

Had the place been called Try, the name might have been a sensible one.[11]

Like Fisher Ames and James Russell Lowell, Cooper was sufficiently appreciative of the inner spirit of *The Iliad* to realize how ill-suited it was to a commercial, middle-class democracy.[12] When the children of the Templeton Academy botch their scansion of Virgil, their ineptitude nicely complements a passage from Cooper's letter to his onetime Yale professor, Benjamin Silliman. After jokingly admitting that he had 'never studied but *one* regular [i.e. Greek] lesson in Homer', Cooper promptly added that he had studied *The Iliad* in 'the latin translation which I read as easily as English'.[13] The probable exaggeration in this statement is not as important as Cooper's desire to have it believed.

If American society truly were as impoverished in ancestral legend and human variety as Cooper claimed in *Notions of the Americans*, then the dying Indian tribes of the eighteenth century could provide the colour and figurative language of poetry. Poetry, in turn, was the *sine qua non* of romantic fiction. In his 1831 Preface to *The Last of the Mohicans*, Cooper asserts 'the business of a writer of fiction is to approach, as nearly as his powers will allow, to poetry.'[14] When Cooper wrote the 1850 preface to the Leatherstocking series, he ended with a paragraph that suggests how the conjunction of these two ideas had led him to attempt (with apologies to Henry Fielding) a tragic-epic-poem in prose:

> It is the privilege of all writers of fiction, more particularly when their works aspire to the elevation of romances, to present the beau-ideal of their characters to the reader. This it is which constitutes poetry, and to suppose the red man is to be represented only in the squalid misery or in the degraded moral state that certainly more or less belongs to his condition, is, we apprehend, taking a very narrow view of an author's privileges. Such criticism would have deprived the world of even Homer.[15]

Throughout the 1850 Preface, the phrase 'elevation of romance' is linked with characterizations of the Indians and of the heroic Leatherstocking, who in many ways resembles them. Homer, the only author named in the preface, provides its closing word.

Red Satan: Cooper and the American Indian Epic

As soon as Hawkeye appears in *The Last of the Mohicans*, Cooper endows him with the knowledge that the days of oral transmission of heroic legend are fading fast:

> I am willing to own that my people have many ways of which, as an honest man, I can't approve. It is one of their customs to write in books what they have done and seen, instead of telling them in their villages, where the lie can be given to the face of a cowardly boaster, and the brave soldier can call on his friends to witness for the truth of his words. In consequence of this bad fashion, a man who is too conscientious to misspend his days among the women, in learning the names of black marks, may never hear of the deeds of his fathers, nor feel a pride in striving to outdo them.[16]

Cooper's own 'black marks' are, of course, the only means by which Hawkeye's complaint against written language can be preserved. Everything that troubles Hawkeye about the removal of white legends from cultural currency becomes many times aggravated when applied to the tribal histories of the Indians, whose oral legends, even if extant in 1757, let alone 1826, have been distorted in translation. Throughout the novel, Hawkeye tells only two oral lays, which concern white soldiers' battle exploits around the Bloody Pond and the blockhouse. From Heckewelder's *Account*, if nowhere else, Cooper had become familiar with the general nature of Indian oral heroic legends, yet he never allows his Indians to tell or invent one.[17] Instead, the void in oral epic legend is filled with the matter of medieval romance. Around the councils and battle scenes which comprise the epic substance of *The Last of the Mohicans*, Cooper fashions escape and pursuit adventures in which the chivalry of rescuing distressed maidens serves as the unifying motif. By thus adapting the captivity narrative for purposes of historical romance,[18] Cooper found a workable, highly popular compromise which avoids patent fakery of Indian legends (Chateaubriand) at the risk of trivializing the stature of his heroes.

The problems of generic adaptation seem to have troubled Cooper less than the dilemma of approving a practicable heroic code. The antebellum American romancer who would find an epic history in the Indian had to ascribe heroic qualities to a race then being dispossessed and killed by the

151

very people who would read his book. To depict the Indian as an inhuman savage lusting to scalp white maidens would be historically indefensible and would ultimately diminish the achievement of conquest—as the hopefully 'epic' poems of Daniel Bryan and James K. Paulding had sadly shown.[19] But to depict the Indian as an aged stoic hero or a noble savage would implicitly deny the justice of the continuing March of Civilization. Throughout the *Leatherstocking Tales*, Cooper would pursue this problem as an issue of daily conduct, as well as of historical displacement. How far could an enlightened author, bent on the *beau idéal* of romance, excuse the 'virtues' of retaliatory justice (scalping, killing in cold blood) and of stoic endurance (sadomasochistic torture scenes) on the relativistic grounds that these were the norms of courage for an heroic people defending their own lands?

The extraordinarily complex and intricate narrative of *The Last of the Mohicans* rests upon a simple symmetrical arrangement of sections:

(1) Exposition (chapters 1–4).
(2) Battle around Glenn's Falls (5–9).
(3) Cora and Alice captured by Magua: Captivity Narrative (10–14).
(4) Fall of Fort William Henry (15–17). End of Volume I.
(5) Cora and Alice recaptured by Magua; Captivity Narrative (18–22).
(6) Rescues of Alice, Uncas and Cora (23–30).
(7) Battles between Delawares and Hurons, Uncas and Magua (31–32).
(8) Dénouement, funeral ceremonies for Uncas (33). End of Volume II.

After the escape and pursuit sequences, the narrative of each volume is resolved in a climactic military action. At the end of the first volume, the fall of Fort William Henry, prefaced with epigraphs from Gray's 'The Bard', reveals white principles of military honour through a panoramic rendering of an historical event. At the end of the second volume, the victory of the Delawares over the Hurons, prefaced with epigraphs from Pope's *Iliad*, demonstrates red war codes as they are practised in a wholly imagined combat. Only by comparing the two battles do the full complexities of deciding upon a code that is both heroic and morally honourable clearly emerge.

In his first paragraph, Cooper emphasizes that his subject is anything but a celebration of the founding of a western empire. The French and the English, 'in quest of an opportunity to exhibit their courage', have learned to make an 'inroad' upon any 'lovely' and 'secret place' in the forest. In the context of international politics, such intrusions serve only to 'uphold the cold and selfish policy of the distant monarchs of Europe' (15). Over the entire narrative Cooper casts a perspective of historical futility by remarking

> the incidents we shall attempt to relate occurred during the third year of the war which England and France last waged for the possession of a country that neither was destined to retain. (17)

Only within this controlling sense of overall historical doom, so like *The Iliad*, are we allowed to appreciate the momentary heroics shown on battlefields or during forest rescues.

Throughout the antebellum era, the presumably humanitarian if not Christian conduct of the white man remained the crucial justification for dispossession of the red man.[20] Nostalgia for the demise of Indian virtues could readily be indulged so long as the white man illustrated his ethical superiority. Unfortunately, none of Cooper's European military commanders conducts himself with the needed combination of integrity and success. General Webb's refusal to send reinforcements is a self-protective cowardice far worse than the flight from battle of the Huron named Reed-That-Bends, who welcomes his own death after he has been ostracized from his tribe. Duncan Heyward may marry Cooper's fair heroine, but he proves so incompetent in the woods that Hawkeye finally tells him that he could best assist by remaining silent in the rear. Although the commanding British officer who is present, Colonel Munro, has the requisite integrity and courage for heroic stature, he proves to be so victimized by chance disadvantages, by the disloyalty of Webb, and by the treacheries of his environs, that he withdraws from the wilderness a beaten, half-senile man.

The hypocrisy of white pretension to ethical superiority is the controlling theme of Cooper's rendering of the fall of Fort

William Henry. After introducing the Marquis de Montcalm as the epitome of refined European gentility, Cooper pictures him offering Munro terms for bloodless surrender which are honourable according to white, but not red, war codes. Because Montcalm then stands apathetically by while his 2,000 Huron mercenaries slaughter every English person they can reach, including women and children, Montcalm's deceit seems the most dishonourable form of barbarism. Intending to qualify the popular memory of Montcalm as a man who 'died like a hero on the plains of Abraham', Cooper asserts that Montcalm was 'deficient in that moral courage without which no man can be truly great' (194). By selecting Chapter 17's epigraph from 'The Bard' ('Weave we the woof. The thread is spun/ The Web is wove. The work is done') Cooper likens the fall of the fort to the atrocities through which Christian King Edward I conquered the people of Wales (179). An analogy less flattering to civilization's march might be difficult to find.

Indian heroic codes prove to be no more commendable than white. However often Hawkeye may excuse Indian scalping and Indian tortures because they are red 'gifts', Cooper always describes them with fascinated disgust. The principle of retaliatory justice may motivate Magua, Chingachgook and Uncas to perform remarkable feats of tracking and endurance, but the principle itself leads only to ever-increasing carnage. Montcalm's cowardice causes the slaughter at Fort William Henry, but the most graphic brutalities, from the dashing of a baby's head against a rock, to the scalping of the wounded, are committed by red men. Inflamed by the sight of blood, Cooper's Hurons far outdo Achilles in their berserk butchery; we are told that 'many of them even kneeled to the earth and drank freely, exultingly, hellishly, of the crimson tide' (190).

The climactic battle of the second volume proves to be the most hollow of triumphs. Because both the Hurons and the Delawares are being used as pawns in an inter-imperial struggle, their fighting against one another, as Magua knows, can only hasten their destruction while it underscores their ignorance. Although the Delawares may have routed the Hurons, the fighting in the woods is confused, desultory, historically insignificant and little like the hand-to-hand confrontations at the end of *The Iliad* and *The Aeneid*. Cora is stabbed, for little apparent purpose, by one of Magua's followers; Magua stabs Uncas in the back because of the frustration of losing his captive; Hawkeye shoots Magua when Magua is immobile and exposed. Like both Achilles and Aeneas, Uncas, Magua and Hawkeye attack their worst enemy to avenge a fallen friend, but all three men attack in a manner that avoids the risk of equal combat. The irony of the Delawares' triumph is emphasized by the epigraph Cooper chooses from Kalchas's prophecy in book one of *The Iliad*:

> But plague shall spread, and funeral fires increase
> Till the great King, without a ransom paid,
> To her own Chrysa send the black-eyed maid. (346)

Lest the reader forget the cost of the Delawares' victory, Cooper thus darkens their triumph by a reminder of the many deaths caused by the demeaning abducting and ransoming of women (Briseis by Agamemnon, Cora by Magua).

The contrast Cooper establishes between his gentle noble savage (Uncas) and his brutal Satanic villain (Magua) proves not to be so total as it first appears. Deprived of their due status as tribal leaders, both Uncas and Magua regain command before the climactic battle. Magua's eloquent accusations of white greed and white deceit merely confirm, in far more inflammatory language, the conclusions reached by Chingachgook, Hawkeye and a tellingly silent Uncas in Chapter 2. Whereas Milton's Satan had sought vengeance against God because of his limit-defying pride, Cooper's Magua ('the Prince of Darkness' (303)) seeks vengeance against the white race because of the tangible injustice done him by Colonel Munro. Uncas and Magua, both of them wronged, and both pursuing vengeance, must be killed together at the tale's conclusion. The red devil who would turn inter-tribal war into genocidal war cannot remain a continuing forest force. But the noble Apollonian hero whose fine feelings 'elevated him far above the intelligence, and advanced him probably centuries before the practices of his nation' (125) cannot be allowed to survive either. Whereas Magua would pose a threat to white conquest through force and cunning, Uncas would challenge white superiority through simple human example.

The determining differences between Magua and Uncas have little to do with their tribal loyalties, their prowess or their courage. Unlike Magua, Uncas has no personal motive for feeling vengeance toward the white man. Uncas's silent acceptance of white authority has its counterpart in his deference to white women. Whereas Uncas even outdoes Duncan Heyward in his chivalrous regard for Alice and Cora, Magua is endowed with the presumably red trait of treating women as serviceable beasts. In spite of the taboo against miscegenation, Uncas proves capable of genuinely loving Cora. Magua's consummate villainy (a villainy which determines the plot) is his decision to abduct Cora three separate times, not primarily to exact vengeance upon Munro, but to satisfy his own conveniently unexplained lust. The protective reverence which the white man and the exceptional 'white' Indian pay to white women thus serves as Cooper's only sure means of upholding the presumed moral superiority of his own 'civilized' and conquering race.

The concluding scene of *The Last of the Mohicans*, surely the finest chapter of fiction any American had yet written, was clearly influenced by the twenty-fourth book of *The Iliad*.[21] The lamentations of Andromache, Hecuba and Helen over the body of Hector, like the Delaware maidens' lamentations over the body of Uncas, precede the climactic short laments of those aged father-kings, Chingachgook and Priam, who know that their nation's demise is one with their son's death. The images of fire with which *The Iliad* closes, a fire that envelops Greek and Trojan, Achilles as well as Hector, conveys the same sense of impending conflagration we find in Tamenund's words: 'It is enough. Go, children of the Lenape, the anger of the Manitou is not done' (372). Just as Cooper was the first American clearly to recognize that prose was the genre for a national heroic literature, so he was the first to recognize that the death of brave men and the end of an heroic age, rather than any panegyric of republican empire, are the true measure of the epic art.

However similar these endings may be in deed and in spirit, the characters of the two mourned heroes differ markedly. Uncas never boasts of his search for personal battle glory, nor does Hector often display Uncas's gentleness and grace.

Neither Chingachgook nor Magua can serve as the Indian for whom white readers could mourn. Wholly committed to red values, these two older chieftains deeply resent the red man's dispossession. Political enemies though they may be, Magua and the Big Serpent are similar in their racial ethos; when they are joined in single combat, Cooper even remarks that 'the swift evolutions of the combatants seemed to incorporate their bodies into one' (123). The warrior to be elegized must rather be the younger red man who most closely approximates, and defers to, the white man's supposed moral sensitivity. Through Uncas's death, the best of Indian qualities can thus be mourned and removed, allowing his less flexible father to remain, a figure of real but lesser challenge to the injustice of dispossession.

Because neither the red man nor the white man practises a code that is both moral and heroic, the closing paragraphs of the novel offer us an alternative that combines yet supersedes them both. The bond between the Big Serpent and Hawkeye, formed over the body of Uncas and beyond the incursions of civilization, is based upon absolute honesty, a mastery of forest skills, and a wordless sense for the divinity of nature. Their heroic life can only be maintained, not by leading either of their peoples, but by separating themselves from any culture whatsoever. The most admirable men of America's heroic age are thus held forth, not as examples for backwoodsmen and Indians to imitate, but as exceptions who represent a promise never fulfilled. The Big Serpent and Hawkeye, like many a semi-divine pair in epic poetry (Gilgamesh and Enkidu, Achilles and Patroclus, Beowulf and Wiglaf, Roland and Oliver) seem to have the ability to perform anything except to escape suffering and mortality. Unlike every one of these pairs of heroes, however, Hawkeye and the Big Serpent represent no community, lead no men, and defend no civilization. Embodying the unrealized potential of two passing cultures, they are nothing more, but nothing less, than the last of their several kinds. In the oldest of extant epics, Gilgamesh forms his abiding bond with Enkidu (a dark skinned 'hunter' from the wilderness) and they undertake adventurous tasks together.[22] Whereas Gilgamesh finally returns to the city of Uruk to guard the walls he has built, Leatherstocking's heroism has been forever defined by his departure from the compromised civilization of Templeton.

By the time Cooper had completed all five tales, the importance of the red man's Greek-like heroism had receded, the bond between the Big Serpent and Hawkeye had become increasingly central, and Leatherstocking had finally become the acknowledged 'hero' of the entire series.[23] At no time, however, did Cooper suggest that Leatherstocking had solved the problem of how to be a Christian hero in the wilderness. In *The Last of the Mohicans*, Cooper twice refers to the Roman worship of household gods in order to convey the acuity of the dilemma. When Magua urges his Hurons to kill Uncas in order to fulfil a tribal custom 'to sacrifice a victim to the *manes* of their countrymen', Cooper admits that Magua is factually correct, but then condemns him for having 'lost every vestige of humanity in a wish for revenge' (268). Shortly thereafter, the psalmodist David Gamut, convinced that unresisting death is better than 'the damnable principle of revenge', tells Hawkeye 'Should I fall, . . . seek no victims to my *manes*, but rather forgive my destroyers' (293). Caught between Christian principle and forest necessity, Hawkeye replies with the fullest account he ever gives of his forest code:

> There is a principle in that . . . different from the law of the woods; and yet it is fair and noble to reflect upon. . . . It is what I would wish to practice myself, as one without a cross of blood, though it is not always easy to deal with an Indian as you would with a fellow Christian. God bless you, friend; I do believe your scent is not greatly wrong, when the matter is duly considered, and keeping eternity before the eyes, though much depends on the natural gifts and the force of temptation. (293)

Hawkeye's statement begins confidently, but soon breaks down into hesitant qualifications and appeals both to 'gifts' and to human weaknesses. Although he may denounce revenge and bloodshed, Hawkeye knows that he must always be ready to fire first in self-protection. The heroism of Cooper's 'magnificent moral hermaphrodite'[24] clearly depends on trying to remain Christian in principle, while surviving by un-Christian, if not Indian, displays of deadly prowess.

The few demurrers from the praise with which reviewers

greeted *The Last of the Mohicans* reflect a failure to concede that fiction might incorporate the romance and the epic. Acute though W. H. Gardiner had been in assessing *The Spy*, he objected to the presumably breathless pace of Cooper's adventure sequences because even a frontier novel should contain 'a little quiet domestic life'.[25] Lewis Cass's accusation that Cooper's Indians were 'of the school of Heckewelder and not of the school of nature[26] was based upon the constricting premise that no author should imagine red men as they might have been during their irrecoverable forest lives. Two years later, Grenville Mellon sharpened the terms of Cass's attack into a critical absurdity:

> The Indian chieftain is the first character upon the canvass or the carpet; in active scene or still one, he is the nucleus of the whole affair; and in almost every case is singularly blessed in some dark-eyed child, whose complexion is made sufficiently white for the lightest hero. This bronze noble of nature, is then made to talk like Ossian for whole pages, and measure out hexameters, as though he had been practising for a poetic prize.[27]

Mellon's probably deliberate conflation of Homer's metric with Macpherson's prose, like his misleading inferences about Cora and Uncas, are of small importance. His blinding error was his refusal to admit either that Indian life might have shared the spirit of the heroic age, or that prose fiction could absorb the spirit of heroic poetry. *The Last of the Mohicans* had already brought both possibilities to convincing realization.

NOTES

1. Cadwallader Colden, *The History of the Five Indian Nations* (New York, 1922), Vol. I, pp. xxii, x, xxii, xxiv, xxviii.
2. Francois René de Chateaubriand, 'Preface' to *Atala, Poésies par Chateaubriand* (Paris, 1881), p. 1. When the full text of *Les Natchez* was finally published in 1826, Chateaubriand assured his reader in the preface that the important conventions of epic poetry had all been convincingly absorbed within his French prose narrative on the American Indian. See *Poésies par Chateaubriand*, pp. 184–85.

3. Sarah Wentworth Morton, *Ouabi: Or, The Virtues of Nature* (Boston, 1790), pp. 14, 19.

4. Washington Irving, 'Philip of Pokanoket', *The Analectic Magazine*, 3 (1814), 509: Irving, 'Traits of Indian Character', *The Analectic Magazine*, 3 (1814), 151–52.

5. Edward Everett, 'Politics of Ancient Greece', *North American Review*, 18 (1824), 398. Everett's best known plea for an heroic American work like *The Iliad* is his 1824 Harvard Phi Beta Kappa address titled 'Oration on the Peculiar Motives to Intellectual Exertion in America'.

6. This seemingly far-fetched comparison would soon become a matter of serious literary concern. During the 1830s and 1840s, the issue of whether North America's heroic tribes had been proto-civilized men of feeling or Achillean warriors would be transferred from the Indian to the Aztec. See R. M. Bird's two historical romances, *Calavar* (1834) and *The Infidel* (1835) and Prescott's *History of the Conquest of Mexico* (1843).

7. Walter Channing, 'Reflections on the Literary Delinquency of America', *North American Review*, 2 (1815), 39.

8. William Tudor, 'An address to the Phi Beta Kappa Society', *North American Review*, 2 (1815), 14.

9. Later calls for epic literature about America's Greek-like Indians include John Dunne's 'Notes Relative to Some of the Native Tribes of North America', *Port Folio*, 30 (1818), 231; William Gilmore Simms, 'Literature and Art Among the American Aborigines' ·in *Views and Reviews in American Literature* (1845) (Cambridge, Mass., 1962), pp. 130–45; Mrs. Caroline M. Kirkland, 'Preface' to Mrs. Mary Eastman's *Dacotah* (New York, 1849), pp. 9–11.

10. James Fenimore Cooper, review of Lockhart's *Life of Sir Walter Scott*, *The Knickerbocker*, 12 (1838), 363–64.

11. Cooper, *The Redskins, The Novels of James Fenimore Cooper* (New York: W. A. Townsend, 1859), p. 96.

12. See Fisher Ames, 'American Literature' (1809) in *The Works of Fisher Ames* (Boston, 1809), pp. 458–72, and James Russell Lowell, 'Longfellow's *Kavanagh*: Nationality in Literature', *North American Review*, 49 (1949), 203, 210.

13. James F. Beard (ed.), *The Letters and Journals of James Fenimore Cooper* (Cambridge, Mass., 1960), II, 99.

14. Cooper, Preface of 1831, *The Last of the Mohicans*, ed. William Charvat (Cambridge, Mass., 1958), p. 9.

15. Cooper, 'Preface to the Leather-Stocking Tales' (1850) in *The Last of the Mohicans*, ed. Charvat, p. 14.

16. Cooper, *The Last of the Mohicans*, ed. Charvat, p. 36.

17. See John Heckewelder, *An Account of the History, Manners and Customs of the Indian Nations, Transactions of the American Philosophical Society* (Philadelphia, 1819).

18. See Richard Slotkin, *Regeneration Through Violence: The Mythology of the American Frontier* (Middletown, Conn., 1973), p. 485 and Michael D. Butler, 'Narrative Structure and Historical Process in *The Last of the Mohicans*', *American Literature*, 68 (1976), 117–39.

Red Satan: Cooper and the American Indian Epic

19. Daniel Bryan, *The Mountain Muse* (Harrisonburg, Va., 1813); James K. Paulding, *The Backwoodsman* (Philadelphia, 1818).
20. See Roy Harvey Pearce, 'A Melancholy Fact', Chapter 2 of *The Savages of America* (Baltimore, 1965), pp. 53–75 and Robert F. Sayre, 'Savagism', Chapter 1 of *Thoreau and the American Indians* (Princeton, 1977), pp. 3–27.
21. See Joel Porte, *The Romance in America* (Middletown, Conn., 1965), p. 40.
22. Alexander Heidel, *The Gilgamesh Epic and Old Testament Parallels* (Chicago, 1970), p. 19.
23. Cooper, 'Preface to the Leather-stocking Tales' (1850), in *The Last of the Mohicans*, ed. Charvat, pp. 11, 12.
24. Honoré de Balzac, review of *The Pathfinder* (1840) in *Fenimore Cooper: The Critical Heritage*, eds. G. Dekker & J. McWilliams (London, 1973), p. 196. On Leatherstocking as a noble savage see Barrie Hayne, 'Ossian, Scott and Cooper's Indians', *Journal of American Studies*, 3 (1969), 75.
25. W. H. Gardiner, review of *The Last of the Mohicans*, *North American Review*, 23 (1826), p. 191.
26. Lewis Cass, 'Indians of North America', *North American Review*, 22 (1826), 67.
27. Grenville Mellon, review of *The Red Rover*, *North American Review*, 27 (1828), p. 140.

7

The Prairie and Cooper's Invention of the West

by GORDON BROTHERSTON

If James Fenimore Cooper may be said to have written history, not the least part of that history must be seen to concern the first settlers of his country, the American Indians. No fewer than eleven of his novels, about a third of all those he wrote, deal with the respective land and other rights of red and white, over a period of two centuries, from Massachusetts to beyond the Mississippi. That these novels may now readily be considered historical is due in part to the recent assessment made of them by, among others, George Dekker, who has meticulously set Cooper into the politics of his time; Charles Swann, who has challenged the mythic reading typified by D. H. Lawrence; and Robert Clark, who theorizes the links between Cooper's fiction, his biography, and the self-image of his new nation, with reference to *The Pioneers*, *The Last of the Mohicans* and *The Deerslayer*.[1] In this perspective, Cooper begins to emerge as nothing less (or more) than the epicist of the United States in its founding days; so that it is now the more possible to question the ideology of the service rendered by him in this rôle. The single most convenient way of doing this is to focus on the third Leatherstocking Tale, the most distinctive if not the best written of all his Indian novels, *The Prairie* (1827).

Faced with Cooper's considerable output on the subject of Indians, we may in the first instance follow the author's own

	Leather-stocking Tales	Littlepage Trilogy	Other
1620			*The Wept of Wish-ton-wish* (1829)
1776	*The Deerslayer, or The First War-path* (1841) *The Last of the Mohicans, A Narrative of 1757* (1826) *The Pathfinder, or The Inland Sea* (1840) *The Pioneers, or The Sources of the Susquehanna* (1823)	*Satanstoe, A Tale of the Colony* (1845) *The Chainbearer* (1845)	*Wyandotté, or The Hutted Knoll* (1843)
1812	*The Prairie* (1827)	*The Redskins, or Indian and Injin* (1846)	*Oak Openings, or The Bee-hunter* (1848)

classification and separate out the Littlepage Trilogy (1845–46), in addition to the fivefold Leatherstocking Tales (1823–41), leaving only three novels unattached. Then, acknowledging the Tales as the main constituent of his Indian writing, we may use them as a yardstick for all the rest. For the Trilogy reveals its hero, the Indian Susquesus, the 'Trackless' of colonial *Satanstoe* and the ally of the land-surveying *Chainbearer*, to be a full albeit much superannuated Onondaga chief among the *Redskins* of the 1840s, and so replays Cooper's obsession with the Iroquois whose lands his father came to possess and who haunt the Tales from their inception in 1823.

Similarly, still among the Six Nations of the Iroquois, the case of the Tuscarora Wyandotté (1843) closely parallels that of the problematic Oneida in the Tales, who came to be no less dispossessed despite their particular loyalty to the United States in 1779. As for the remaining two novels, the *Wept of Wish-ton-wish* (1829) and *Oak Openings* (1848), they chronologically supply a sort of pro- and epilogue to the Tales, insofar as they enclose the life of the eponymous hero Leatherstocking or Natty Bumppo (ca. 1720–1805). The first treats the resistance of Metacom (King Philip) to the Puritans of seventeenth-century Massachusetts, the latter that of his fellow Algonkin Tecumseh, effectively the orchestrator of the War of 1812. In this framework (see table), we may construct a larger narrative that stretches from the foundation of the Bay Company in the 1620s, through the Declaration of the Thirteen States in 1776, to the cries of Manifest Destiny that morally ring already in the ears of Natty as he dies on the prairie, 'miserable and worn out'.

1. What is distinctive about 'The Prairie'

Coming so soon after his literary birth only four years before in *The Pioneers*, and issuing as it does into burial in Indian ground, this death of Natty's is itself one of the distinctive features of *The Prairie*. Another is sheer longitude: on these pages we are transported 500 or so miles west of the Mississippi, to within striking distance of the Rockies, and far further west than Natty or Cooper otherwise ever ventured. The attraction such a western setting could have been expected to hold for Cooper's readers in the 1820s can be variously explained. For example, the prairie and the whole territory of the Louisiana Purchase (1803) had become a hot topic of debate, in so far as its vastness appeared to threaten eastern hegemony. Further, a keen interest was being shown in reports on the territory with its massive buffalo herds and strange horse-borne inhabitants, Biddle's report of the Lewis and Clark expedition (1814) and James's account of Stephen H.

Long's (1823) having been among Cooper's main sources.[2] Also, like many of his society Cooper had been intrigued by the visits of western chiefs to Washington at this period; and his acquaintance with the celebrated Pawnee Pitalesharo in 1821 and 1826 led to the character Hard Heart in the novel. *The Prairie* could then be said to have appeared at a time ripe for the western. Nonetheless, within the scope of Natty's life and Cooper's Indian history, the geographical extreme of the novel does represent a wrench, a flight far from familiar eastern paths. By the same token it assures Cooper's enterprise in the Leatherstocking and associated tales of a continental dimension which distinguishes Cooper from comparable writers of the time, say Washington Irving or W. G. Simms, as they themselves recognized. In this respect it is no less significant that it should have been *The Prairie* that most drew attention, as a model of the westward epic, in other parts of the Americas. (A signal case is that of Domingo Sarmiento's version of the nineteenth-century struggle between 'civilization and barbarism' on the Argentine pampas, which lovingly invokes the novel and which before too long was translated back into the United States.)[3]

Among Cooper's Indian novels, *The Prairie* is distinguished in time as well as space, being as near in the one as it is far in the other. For it is the work where the encounters with Indians effectively lie closest in time to the date of composition, a mere twenty years away. At first sight, this claim might seem more appropriate to *The Redskins*, where the action is more or less contemporary, or to *Oak Openings* where formally the action comes after that of *The Prairie*. Yet in the former novel, though Susquesus goes some way to restoring Iroquois honour it is very much after the event, he being well over 100 years old, isolate, all but a ghost in the war between New York landowners and rioting tenants or 'Injins'. By now the link with the Indian world is as remote as that between the slogans these white Injins adopt, Tammany, and the original Lenape chief Tamenend (who appears, no less superannuated, as an august elegiac presence in *The Last of the Mohicans*). Significantly, the only moment in *The Redskins* when the *Indian* question is rekindled comes when Susquesus is visited by chiefs from the western prairie, a 'welcome contrast' to the local Injins, as Pearce puts it. With *The Oak Openings*, though subsequent to that of *The Prairie*, the action in the year 1812 in fact lies farther from the date of composition (1848); more important, though *The Prairie* provides an epitaph for Leather-stocking himself, it offers a western perspective on the Indian that became wholly current in Cooper's lifetime, even to the extent of encapsulating that of *Oak Openings* as somehow prior and redundant, in the fashion explored below.

With Cooper, the time element demands our attention since, as Robert Clark has shown, so much of his epic was the result of a painful re-casting and re-patterning of Indian history, in a process where greater proximity meant greater anxiety. In the case of *The Prairie* this process can be measured as a matter of scholarly fact, through a comparison between the drafts and the first published version and preface in 1827, and between them and the revised versions and prefaces of 1832 and 1850. Among other points, these rewritings expose Cooper's growing reliance on 'scientific' discourse as an imperial agency, notably in the geology of the 1832 Preface, as well as a nervousness about the eastern hold on the prairie, which he translates from the 'Confederacy' (1827) to the 'American Union' (1832), and about the sheer legality of United States' intentions towards it. For example, while in the draft he had spoken of the Indians as the 'perhaps lawful occupants', for publication he inserted the word 'more', thus admitting the United States' claim in principle; again, in 1832 he omitted the key word 'lawless' from the following reference to 'the red man, jealous and resentful of the lawless inroads of the stranger'. (On all this, see the Chapter 'Visions and revisions' in Överland's study of *The Prairie*.)

A further distinctive quality of *The Prairie*, one intimately allied with those already discussed, is the degree of cross-referencing to the previous instalments of Cooper's Indian history. True, throughout the Leatherstocking Tales we never fail to be reminded of their interconnection, Cooper usually managing to adjust Natty's age to the historical year in question. Rejected by Judith on the Hudson in the 1740s, he is in his twenties; at Fort William Henry in 1757 he is in his mid-thirties, and so on, till he arrives on the prairie, an octo-genarian, in the early 1800s. But in this last novel, despite its actual place in the order of publication, there is a palpable attempt at comprehensive and conclusive statement. Here Natty forever harks back to how it used to be back east, among the Lenape and the Iroquois, when confronting the Pawnee and the Sioux of his new environment, and so it is that he thinks of replacing the lost Chingachgook with Hard Heart for his native companion; and throughout he reflects on the long course of his life, including parts of it Cooper would write up only much later. And here he encounters none other than Duncan Uncas Middleton, who continues the story of both the previous novels: the last name of this character brings back the scenes around Otsego lake, in *The Pioneers*; and the assonant inner one perpetuates the memory of *The Last of the Mohicans*, the young Lenape son of Chingachgook, blessed in his Indian mission by the aged Tamenend, only to perish shortly afterwards. At the same time it was in *The Prairie* that Cooper first developed the character of the bee-hunter who later provided the alternative title of *Oak Openings*. And in so far as Paul, by marrying and settling with Ellen, represents Boden at a later rather than earlier stage of life, Cooper thereby anticipates that enclosure of the *Oak Openings'* action into the broader canvas of *The Prairie*.

Taken together, all these distinctive marks of *The Prairie* afforded it, for all its obvious limitations as narrative, a sense of cumulative memory, an actuality that none of the other Indian novels could claim. It is where Leatherstocking goes 'far towards the setting sun—the foremost in that band of pioneers who are opening the way for the march of the nation across the continent', to quote Cooper's own words at the close of *The Pioneers*; all of which makes of him 'by far the most important symbol of the national experience of adventure across the continent', to quote the loaded rhetoric of Henry Nash Smith's *Virgin Land*.[4] As a result, this novel highlights two functions of Cooper, the epicist of the United States: his co-invention of the western 'frontier'; and his decisive suppression of the Ohio and the old Northwest.

● 2. A paradigm frontier

In its western setting and in its presentation of characters, *The Prairie* sets a pattern for 'frontier' relations between red and white which overrides all other such patterns perceived in his work and United States' history alike, by observers both within and outside that country. As one contemporary reviewer put it, referring to his novels as a whole:

> one thinks of them and is at once transported to the virgin forests of America, to her boundless prairies, covered with grass taller than a man—prairies across which roam herds of buffalo, where the red-skinned children of the Great Spirit hide, locked in relentless conflict one with another, and with the conquering palefaces . . .[5]

Painting a more subtly ideological scene for his day, Roy Harvey Pearce extrapolated this frontier, in his Leatherstocking essay, to the whole question of 'civilization and savagism in America':

> Everywhere in the record of American society in the first half of the nineteenth century there is evidence of a deep compulsion to understand that westward-moving frontier-creating process known, simply enough, as 'civilizing'. . . .
> So . . . the savage Indians entered Cooper's Leatherstocking Tales and furnished the symbolic basis in terms of which the nature of the frontier and frontiersman, of civilization, of progress, and of American destiny westward could be concretely and particularly understood.[6]

Or, putting it another way and bearing in mind the crude material facts of United States' behaviour, out here, on this frontier, conditions of life could with less apparent absurdity be made to resolve the gnawing inconsistencies of a Constitution uniquely framed to defend the basic rights of man but which, in the case of the Indian, did not prevent his massive physical destruction.

In portraying these Indians of the west, Cooper divides them into two groups, Sioux and Pawnee, as he did those of the east, Iroquois and Lenape; and he does so for the same ostensible reason, the convenience of having a readily comprehensible plot: 'In the endless confusion of names, customs, opinions and languages, which exists among the tribes of the West, the author has paid much more attention to sound and convenience, than to literal truth' (1827 Preface to *The Prairie*).

Second, in assigning diametrically opposed moral qualities

to these groups and in continuously cross-referencing them as Sioux = Iroquois = bad, Pawnee = Lenape = good, he again rewrote what he knew to be history. Just as the epithet 'fiendish' attaches to the Iroquois Confederacy which had in fact 'provided a wall of safety for the English colonies during 150 years of national adolescence'[7] and whose constitution served as a model for that of the United States itself, so from the start the Sioux are billed as 'demons', 'devils', 'reptiles', and monstrously treacherous, although they had actually protected United States' soldiers during their first incursions west of the Missouri-Mississippi. Memorable among these occasions was General Leavenworth's atrocious assault on the towns and maize silos of the Arikara, northern neighbours and kin of the Pawnee, in 1823, a shameful event honourably recorded in the various annals (Waniyetu yawapi or Winter Counts) of the Sioux.[8] Cooper also says the Sioux had been oppressing the Pawnee from 'time immemorial' (p. 39) when in fact, according to these same annals, Sicangu (Brulé) presence in the southern Platte area did not much antedate 1803, the year in which *The Prairie* opens, was first typified by the grand calumet or peace celebrations of 1804–5, and became hostile mainly as a result of far severer pressure being exerted on other flanks of the Sioux nation, ultimately by invading whites. On the other side, just as the Lenape ('Delaware'), like the Mohicans, are cast as the white man's best friend while in fact they had stood in the vanguard of military resistance to him as the 'grandfather' of the Ohio-Algonkin nations, so the 'peace-loving' Pawnee are revealed by the Friendship Treaty of 1818, which was designed to prise them out of possible Mexican alliances, to have been guilty of what the United States saw as 'several wanton and unprovoked murders' of its people[9] (Washburn 1973: 2360–361). As for the inverse cross-referencing between Pawnee and Iroquois, it contradicts the common cultural and linguistic heritage alluded to in the longer histories of both nations.

Third, in the west as in the east, Cooper attributes strength and major territorial occupancy at the time of his novels to his bad rather than his good Indians, the better to sanction white intrusion, which is led in the case of *The Prairie* by the latter-day Puritan Ishmael Bush, and of course Natty.

The point now, however, is that this binary opposition of

Indian forces can be elaborated in a yet more conveniently de-historicized space. In *The Prairie*, Natty Bumppo flees west because the east is too 'crowded': as 'a comparative desert . . . aided by no historical recollections' (Preface, 1827), the west can offer a 'wilderness' that is devoid even of trees and their dark memory. Like the imperial Russians moving east to Alaska, in the only comparable seizure of territory in the history of 'Christendom' (changed to 'world' in the 1850 Preface), this migrant Anglo-American finds himself on steppes as vast as those of 'Tartary', a land fit for fierce feathered horsemen and inimical to settlement in more than tents of skin, the 'broad and tenantless plains of the West' that lack permanent human trace (to echo Derrida's term). In the east, with its dense networks of (Indian) towns, its sophisticated and opulent agriculture, and its precise literacy in wampum and Mide scrolls, lawfully writing the Indians off their land had ever proved a formidable task: here on the western prairie it stood a chance of reformulation.[10] The Indians first introduced to the reader are marauding Sioux come to steal Ishmael Bush's beasts, that is animal wealth tamed and owned by 'civilized' whites. According to the Biblical priority enshrined between the herdsman Abel and the agricultural Cain, the local Indian inhabitant is thereby dismissed as doubly the inverse of what he was, the envier of flocks imported from the Old World, not the benefactor in plants genetically perfected in the New which historically distinguish it as the garden of the planet. Clinching the moral, the Sioux are even decried as 'bad-horse-men', that is in both technique ('rude and untrained') and spirit.

So tenuous is the Indian purchase felt to be on their land that it spreads featureless as the sea: 'There was the same waving and regular surface, the same absence of foreign objects and the same boundless extent to the view' (p. 6). As a result, its political geography can be read only at the level of the early neolithic when the great inland sea of North America was draining. In this grand atmosphere, full of the transcendental spirit Wahcondah, the western Manitou, even river names can be freely translated back from the proper to the 'poetic' (Mississippi becomes the 'Father of rivers', Missouri 'The river of troubled waters' and so on). Exactly this abstraction accompanies, to the same ideological end, the western re-siting of

Indian history in Longfellow's epic *Hiawatha* (1856) whose title is Iroquois but whose story is Ojibwa Algonkin; only here, in the finer cadence of verse, the Indians are allowed to have been all good, as well as agricultural and literate, on the strict understanding that they vacate, 'like the mist', even *before* the whites intrude from the east to sully and abuse them.

There can be no doubt that the economy and politics of the Sioux and other western nations were radically affected by their appropriation of the horse, from the southwest and Mexico, two centuries or so before Cooper's tale. Yet this by no means excluded them from the common agricultural and political heritage of Indian America; they partook still of the 'delicious hommany' and continued to honour the four ritual colours of the maize from which it was prepared, for example in the songs they contributed in the 1890s to the major international movement of the Plains known as the 'Ghost Dance'.[11] Moreover, the initial cycles of certain Winter Counts, like the Sicangu count by Wapostangi ('Brown Hat'), indicate how the horse was integrated into a native agricultural and urban system that was much fostered by the import of superior maize to the central Mississippi from Mexico at A.D. 900, nearly 1,000 years previously. Recorded likewise in the Lenape history in Mide writing known as the Walam Olum,[12] and now verifiable archaeologically, this event is alluded to in *The Prairie*, though with the explicit denial of native agency or even presence, when Natty refers to 'the fertile bottoms of the Mississippi, groaning with its stores of grain and fruits' (p. 282). In these circumstances, Cooper's complete silencing of these dimensions of Sioux life (for example, he refers to hominy only as part of the Bushes' diet), and his isolating of them as a race at once powerful, nomadic and evil, cannot fail to be understood as part of the grander denial of Indian land rights that began already with Roger Williams and the Puritan East and which reaches a maximal expression here.

With the mortal disadvantage of being the good Indians, the Pawnee are allowed to be urbane and even urban: their towns provide a sole refuge for the assorted white visitors to the prairie threatened by the Sioux. They are permitted, too, to possess an antiquity and history more venerable than the mere martial exploits depicted on the tent-page of the Sioux leader Mahtoree (p. 336). Yet, just as the good Lenape appeared as it were timelessly scattered, so the Pawnee lack all political credibility in that they have no real idea of the world beyond their own tiny confines. This point is put across with fine perversity by Cooper when he has Natty try to elicit from Hard Heart some sense of common cause between Pawnee and Lenape, only to be disappointed at his ignorance, 'mortal vanity' (p. 329) and blinkered tribal pride. The Pawnee, then, are proposed as circumscribed both physically and mentally when, as we have seen, if nothing else the Winter Counts and the 1818 Treaty initiated by the United States indicate the exact opposite, as do both the earlier Pawnee histories noted by Hyde, and their subsequent participation in the Ghost Dance.[13] Also, the firmly international phenomenon of the calumet has been ascribed in origin to the Pawnee. Thus limited, as the good Indians of the new and true frontier, Cooper's Pawnee are already being prepared for the reservation they were eventually condemned to in 1875, needless to say under great duress.

A further crucial factor in this demotion of Indians, bad and good, as the first settlers of American land, can be found in the fact that as the paradigm frontier the west could also, where necessary, be presented as 'bought'. In *The Prairie* this much provides the substance of the subplot involving Duncan Uncas Middleton who by marrying Ines, daughter of Don Augustin [*sic*] de Certavallos, affirms a prior landright that is not just white but aristocratic and white, one which in the best Cooper tradition would bolster confidence in the idea that the old eastern mechanisms of speculating and capitalizing on land could indeed continue to serve in the west, in the vast stretches of the Louisiana Purchase. That the truly prior occupants might find such a transaction puzzling is got over by the assurance that 'the simple mind' of the Sioux Mahtoree 'had not been able to embrace the reasons why one people should thus assume a superiority over the possessions of another' (pp. 263–64), while in their limitedness the Pawnee are not credited with any opinion at all. Over the Leatherstocking span, this impulse forward to a legitimizing Spain and France in Louisiana and the west is matched symmetrically by the

172

complex castings back to France and England in the east, but far exceeds it in consequence since the power in question is now formally the United States. It reflects a transition to statehood in which the Indians forfeit all civic dignity along with their last notional rights, as Natty's words make plain:

> I have known the time when a few Red-skins, shouting along the borders, could set the provinces in a fever; and men were to be armed; and troops were to be called to aid from a distant land; and prayers were said, and the women frighted, and few slept in quiet, because the Iroquois were on the war-path, or the accursed Mingo had the tomahawk in hand. How is it now? The country sends out her ships to foreign lands, to wage their battles; cannon are plentier than the rifle used to be, and trained soldiers are never wanting, in tens of thousands, when need calls for their services. Such is the difference atween a province and a state, my men. . . . (p. 297)

As a corollary to this political demotion of the Indian 'forever' and retroactively in the west comes the 'scientific' one, for which the mouthpiece is Dr. Battius. Though obviously preposterous, this figure plays his own useful part on the new frontier; and in the last instance his authorities and methods of classification for species, terrain and words, are identical with Cooper's own. Hence, though the reader might first hear it as a joke, there is a relentless undertone to Battius's initial failure to recognize Hard Heart, hidden in the bushes, as of the class mammalia, let alone the genus homo (p. 214). The same is true of the remarkable exchange with Natty on the subject of the possible greatness of the native New World, for which, ignoring even Jefferson's 'prehistoric mounds' and the elementary facts of Indian agriculture, neither can find any 'evidences' at all. Rather, according to Battius the Indian has risen no higher than childhood:

> 'And what see you in all this?' demanded the trapper, who, though a little confused by the terms of his companion, seized the thread of his ideas.
> 'A demonstration of my problem, that nature did not make so vast a region to lie an uninhabited waste so many ages. This is merely the moral view of the subject; as to the more exact and geological—' (p. 281)

By just such means Cooper morally enhances his own geological depiction of an untenanted prairie.

Under this double barrage of new civilized 'medicine', political and scientific, not just the by now savage Indian, but Natty goes under. As an old-style frontiersman he is redundant: the new man and international diplomat Middleton is embarrassed to revisit him among the Pawnee and he cannot match Battius's verbal arsenal any more than Noah Webster's, whose *An American Dictionary of the English Language* appeared within a year of *The Prairie*. In fact Natty's own language disintegrates, as at the end it changes 'to suit the person he addressed, and not infrequently according to the ideas he expressed' (pp. 456–57), and so dismantles finally the persona he had established as *the* mediator between red and white, as the 'Pathfinder', 'Hawk-eye', 'Deerslayer', 'La longue carabine', and so on. Just because he is finished he may decide his last loyalty to be Indian rather than 'a [white] palace on Otsego lake'. Though he spurns the 'clearing of briars' of Pawnee and Iroquian funeral rites (which found an early echo in Rabelais), like Pope's 'poor Indian'[14] he asks for his dog to be buried with him, according to a most ancient and widespread native American practice. And he dies among the Pawnee, intimating the graveyard their reservation would become, before the Indian rebirth of this century.

3. The absent Ohio and old Northwest

Establishing a bridgehead west of the Mississippi in *The Prairie* had the further consequence of enabling Cooper the better to forget what had gone immediately before: the unconscionable rape of the Ohio Valley, the wholesale depredation that was going on, unheard, during the action further east of *The Pioneers*. The neglect of this case remains one of the scandals of United States' historiography even today, on several interrelated counts: the density and organization of the Algonkin nations of the area between Iroquois and Cherokee, notably in Lenape settlement detailed in the Walam Olum between A.D. 1250 and 1410, east from the Mississippi to Wapalaneng (Wabash), south to Makeliming, west to Wapahoning, and north to Lowashkin (Allegheny); the continuity between this settlement and the so-called 'pre-historic' pyramids and earth-works around Chillicothe, Cahokia and other centres; the scale and endurance of Indian (as opposed to French or other) resistance that culminated in the campaigns by Pontiac in 1762–63, who forced the whites back to the Appalachian Proclamation Line, and then by Tecumseh in 1812, who further co-ordinated the Cherokee and Creek to the southeast; the obnoxious rôle of land speculators like Washington in the area, who used the Crown Line as an 'expedient' for both personal profit and Indian destruction[15]; and finally the spectacular savagery of the United States' military incursions led among others by 'Mad Anthony', General Wayne, who heralded the new era of the Indian-killing, maize-burning presidents Harrison, of Tippecanoe fame, and Andrew Jackson. As Makhiakho or Black Snake, who brought 'strong war', Wayne is given a laconic mention in the alphabetic Mattanikum chapter of the Walam Olum, which the Lenape completed before being finally driven from the Wabash as late as 1822, followed by the Shawnee in 1827, the year of *The Prairie*.

Out on the western prairie with Ishmael Bush, Natty Bumppo momentarily recalls how he got there from the east, i.e. via the Ohio Valley and the old Northwest. And in so doing he feels compelled at least to mention what he would rather hide: time spent as the ageing deer-hunter (70-plus) in the service of Mad Anthony, whom, it turns out, Bush also served, coming from what he calls Kentuck and Tennessee. In so far as Wayne was historically the bearer of Natty's very name Leatherstocking, and was still slaughtering Indians at the time of this tale, this amounts to a flash of anagnorisis and crippling regret:

> 'I fou't my last battle, as I hope, under his orders,' returned the trapper, a gleam of sunshine shooting from his dim eyes, as if the event was recollected with pleasure, and then a sudden shade of sorrow succeeding, as though he felt a secret admonition against dwelling on the violent scenes in which he had so often been an actor. 'I was passing from the States on the sea-shore into these far regions, when I cross'd the trail of his army, and I fell in, on his rear, just as a looker-on; but when they got to blows, the crack of my rifle was heard among the rest, though to my shame it may be said, I never knew the right of the quarrel

175

as well as a man of threescore and ten should know the reason of his acts afore he takes mortal life, which is a gift he never can return!' (p. 67)

But that is all. Further dark images from the nether consciousness are inhibited by the present danger of the surrounding Sioux; and structurally the whole intervening history is suppressed as it were below the insistent telegraph between those bad Sioux in the west and the bad Iroquois on the other side of it in the east. Similarly the other direct line between the reservation Pawnee, and the 'scattered Delaware' and Mohicans east of the Appalachians completely cuts out what the unscattered Lenape (Delaware) were actually doing during precisely these years in defence of the Ohio, in alliance with their fellow Algonkin Pontiac (an Ottawa) and Tecumseh (a Shawnee).

For good measure, in the 1832 Preface to *The Prairie* Cooper found a further means of passing over the unpleasant occurrences in 'Ohio, Illinois, Indiana and Michigan', none of which was actually yet a state at the start of his tale; extending his scientism, he contrives historically to acknowledge this region prior to the 'fast settlement' of the United States, once again only at the remote level of that neolithic inland sea, portraying it geologically as the eastern counterpart and prelude to the western prairies. In this he exactly anticipated the strategy of Frederick Jackson Turner who in 'The Ohio Valley in American History' spoke of it as 'the entering wedge to the possession of the Mississippi', a strangely empty zone and 'line of advance between hostile Indians and English on the north, and hostile Indians and Spaniards on the south'.[16]

As if to confirm our diagnosis, when Cooper did return to this lost chapter of his American epic, in *Oak Openings* (1848), he laid bare the most extreme and self-contradictory of impulses. The action takes place during the 1811–12 rising and chronicles the various defeats of the United States, a reason for the 'wilfully contemptuous' review it received[17]; some idea of the array of Indian nations and groups involved and their inner coherence can be gleaned from the persistent references, notably during the grand council at Prairie Round (Chapter 22), to their names and territories, from the Great Lakes to the Gulf of Mexico,

176

among them: the Algonkin Ojibwa, Ottawa, Pottawattamie, Menominee, 'Delaware from towards the rising sun', Shawnee; the Sioux Iowa, Sac and Fox; and the Iroquoian Six Nations and Cherokee. The leader of the rising is several times mentioned by name, Cooper's spelling 'Tecumthe' with the footnote 'a tiger stooping for his prey' (p. 183), while in the measured oratory of the council Indian motives and strategies are directly related to their own time-perspective as this is materially recorded, for example, in a Winter-Count calendar displayed to its members (p. 340). At one point, the notion of their literacy generally is admitted, as it was by Roger Williams, to be equivalent to that of the Bible itself, that great initial validator of the European invasion of America ('Even the Indians have their records, however, though resorting to the use of natural signs and a species of hieroglyphics', p. 264).

All this leads in turn to a certain relativism developing between red and white historiography, particularly through the character Parson Amen, a Methodist whose idiosyncratic version of the Old Testament anticipates the Book of Mormon (1830)[18]; his contention that as errant Israelites the American Indians must be 'lost' leads them to conclude that it is the whites who must be and who should therefore be encouraged to return home.

Details of Amen's argument are often highly evocative, beyond his immediate purpose, and deserve quoting:

Turn to Genesis xlix. and 14th, and there will you find all the authorities recorded. 'Zebulon shall dwell at the haven of the sea.' That refers to some other red brother, nearer to the coast, most clearly. 'Issachar is a strong ass, crouching down between two burdens;' 'and bowed his shoulder to bear, and became a servant unto tribute.' That refers, most manifestly, to the black man of the southern states, and cannot mean Peter. 'Dan shall be a serpent by the way, an adder in the path.' There is the redman for you, drawn with the pencil of truth! 'Gad, a troop shall overcome him.' Here, corporal, come this way and tell our new friend how Mad Anthony with his *troopers* finally routed the redskins. You were there, and know all about it. No language can be plainer: until the 'long-knives and leather-stockings' came into the woods, the redman had his way. Against *them*, he *could* not prevail. (pp. 169–70)

177

In this 'alternative' view, the red Indians are snakes like the
Sioux of western prairie and yet forerunners of their invaders,
Biblically-named Puritans like the Zebulon Pike who succeeded
Lewis and Clark; the covert Leatherstocking identity of white
Natty, Lawrence's 'man with a gun' and 'stoic American
killer', is confessed to; and the third party of the blacks is
introduced as somehow more amenable than the reds to the
Anglo-American economy.

Yet over the full course of *Oak Openings*, the Indians are
made to pay dearly for these privileges, the like of which are
granted nowhere else in Cooper's work. His daring revelations
require all-but constant veiling and terrible retribution, above
all in the final chapter which brings the reader right up from
1812 to the present (1848). Secure now in the avalanche of
immigrants and a far superior machine of military destruction,
alias 'the rapid progress of western civilization' (p. 420),
Cooper writes this chapter in the valedictory tone towards the
Indians, their 'seemingly inevitable fate' now sealed, that
marks the reissue of the Leatherstocking epic, with its revised
prefaces, in 1850. Even so, in this novel he clearly felt the need
to hammer things home. The Indians do not just die off; they
are obliged to convert to orthodox Christianity and to bless
their white dispossessors, being thereby reduced from oratory
and all articulation to a pidgin stammer. Thus the once-proud
hero of 1812, Onoah, now Peter, addresses Cooper and closes
the text:

> 'Tell me you make a book,' he said. 'In dat book tell trut'.
> You see me—poor ole Injin. My fadder was chief—I was great
> chief, but we was children. Knowed nuttin'. Like little child,
> dough great chief. Believe tradition. T'ink dis 'arth flat—t'ink
> Injin could scalp all pale-face—t'ink tomahawk and war-path
> and rifle bess t'ings in whole world. In dat day my heart was
> stone. Afraid of Great Spirit, but didn't love Him. In dat time I
> t'ink General could talk wid bee. Yes; was very foolish den.
> Now all dem cloud blow away, and I see my Fadder dat is in
> heaven. His face shine on me day and night, and I never get
> tired of looking at it. I see Him smile, I see Him lookin' at poor
> ole Injin, as if he want him to come nearer; sometime I see Him
> frown and dat scare me. Den I pray, and his frown go away.
> 'Stranger, love God. B'lieve his Blessed Son, who pray for

dem dat kill Him. Injin don't do dat. Injin not strong enough
to do such a t'ing. It want de Holy Spirit to strengthen de heart
afore man can do so great t'ing. When he got de force of de Holy
Spirit, de heart of stone is changed to de heart of woman, and
we all be ready to bless our enemy and die. I have spoken. Let
dem dat read your book understand.' (pp. 475–76)

The 'General' is the colonizing Ben Boden who gives the
novel its other title, the bee-hunter; a less 'subversive'
amalgam of Paul and Natty himself from *The Prairie*, this
emblematic figure has 'grown with the country' (Cooper's
quotes), has invented a machine harvester that fells, cleans
and *bags* (Cooper's italics) masses of grain, and has taken over
a site named after the double-dealing Government agent in
Indian Affairs Schoolcraft, in the very Prairie Round that the
Indian Council had convened in only thirty-six years
previously, to defend their inheritance east of the Mississippi.

Finally, bringing to light one of the profoundest psychic
shifts of guilt to be found in western literature, one which
underlies Chateaubriand's Indian epic,[19] Cooper actually goes
so far as happily to sacrifice red to white to 'atone' for black:

> The ways of Divine Providence are past the investigations of
> human reason. How often, in turning over the pages of history,
> do we find civilization, the arts, moral improvement, nay,
> Christianity itself, following the bloody train left by the
> conqueror's car, and good pouring in upon a nation by avenues
> that at first were teeming only with the approaches of seeming
> evils! In this way there is now reason to hope that America is
> about to pay the debt she owes to Africa; and in this way will
> the invasion of the forests and prairies and 'openings' of the
> redmen be made to atone for itself by carrying with it the
> blessings of the gospel, and a juster view of the relations which
> man bears to his Creator. (pp. 468–69)

Proving too much even for seasoned Cooper critics, such
embarrassing extremity has been got round as a-typical, and
to be explained in the quasi-theological terms of House:

> Yet the annihilation of Peter's character may well be the result
> less of mysticism than of a movement, on Cooper's part, away
> from Aquinas' theocentric humanism toward a more Lutheran
> emphasis on death and annihilation of the self as vital doctrine.
> (p. 260)

179

It represents Cooper's anxiety to neutralize, once it had been admitted, the whole Indian history of the Ohio and the eastern prairie, which he had otherwise managed to avoid on the continental scale by leaping over it, from New York to the prairie beyond the Mississippi, in what Dekker has called 'the epic of the westward movement'.

4. The invention of the West

In *The Prairie*, Cooper succeeded in both affirming a new paradigm of the 'frontier' and excising from Leatherstocking the rebarbative experience of the Ohio; that is, he helped to invent the West. In so doing, he performed a major ideological service for the ever-fattening United States, told a story it could hear, in so far as its territorial history could now rest on three moments so resonant they could fill the silent spaces between: the first Puritan thanksgiving to and for 'Providence'; the Declaration of the Thirteen States and the 'revolutionary' new birth; and the western frontier that categorically divided civilized man from the savage. During the rest of the nineteenth century and beyond, his lead was broadly followed by historians proper, like F. J. Turner on the frontier as well as the Ohio, and Parkman who openly admired Cooper's capacity to capture 'the very spirit of the wilderness'; by ethnographers, like Schoolcraft the 'mythic' source of Long-fellow's *Hiawatha* as well as author of the dismal *Historical and statistical information respecting the history, condition and prospects of the Indian tribes of the United States* (1851–57), and D. G. Brinton who in *The Lenape and their Legends* succeeded in translating the Walam Olum out of political reality altogether; and not least by fellow 'Indian' writers, to the extent that those who did not no longer fitted in.[20] This point has been eloquently put with reference to W. G. Simms the neglected forerunner of Faulkner who concentrated on the remarkable southern Appalachian society of the Creek and Cherokee, before the westward expulsion of these latter in 1838, according to a criminal and schizophrenic order of Congress, promulgated to 'save them from white corruption'. Specifying the 'obstacles to understanding' Simms, the editor of his *Letters* has testified to the overwhelming power of Cooper's continental story (which

Simms came consciously to distance himself from) in reporting
that critics

> do not grasp the nature and meaning of the frontier in Southern
> life and history. They cannot believe in it, even when they try
> to, because it does not fit the pattern of ideas that they have
> inherited or acquired about the American frontier.[21]

Similarly, she notes how since for Van Wyck Brooks 'Cooper's
frontier is *the* frontier', with Simms he totally fails to understand the enduring commercial and diplomatic relations with
the Creek and Cherokee, and even the actual terrain they
dominated well into the nineteenth century and well east of
the Mississippi; and she detects the same fault in United
States' historians generally who like Cooper have made so
much of this eastern history a 'blank' in 'our historical
consciousness'.

This is a small but agreeably precise and independent
testimony to how Cooper's model of United States' history and
invention of the west has come to persuade even those
academic disciplines whose duty, it would seem, should be to
deconstruct it. In Roy Harvey Pearce's 'Civilization and
Savagism' thesis it has found its grandest expression: following
Cooper's own pointers the western frontier is there extended
back to cover the whole of Indian-white relations in North
America, timelessly and forever, putting the feathered war-
bonnets of the Sioux on every Indian head; and it serves as the
first premise for Pearce's more general study of 'savagery' and
the United States' idea of civilization. And from here, in the
story of what the whites 'know not or conceal' (to quote the
Walam Olum), it is only a step to the discovery made by Jung
upon arriving in New York, one which prompted his notion of
the collective unconscious and hence his break with Freud.[22]
For with his patient Mrs. Miller he unearthed the deepest
trauma in the United States' murder and suppression of the
Indian as 'savage'; so that her dreams took as an available
compensation the psychic antithesis of Cooper's cringing
Peter—a powerful bronzed male from *Hiawatha*, then at its
height as an opera in the city.

In recent decades a whole new initiative in archaeology,
ethnography, map-making and the editing of native texts, has

begun to provide the rudiments of a history of the Indian in North America, to the extent of terminally upsetting the old frontier shibboleth of the savage, with all its tremendous distortions, suppressions and absences. At the same time, surviving Indian nations have begun to recover lost legal ground. Is it too fanciful to relate these facts with the parallel tendency in official United States' rhetoric, e.g. that of Reagan's Olympics, to remove the Indian entirely from the stage and the national story? Consummating the cruelty of those who like Cass and Mellon, so far from recognizing how Cooper had doctored Indian history, sneered at him as an 'Indian-lover' from the start, this update of United States' history removes the whole problematic of the Indian who for that reason can no longer be seriously mentioned even as 'absent'. It offers finally to install, in 'virgin land', that most odious of terms, the 'white American Adam', and provides for that national parthenogenesis whose logical complement has become nuclear flight to the stratosphere and beyond.

Not long before his death in 1808, Fisher Ames predicted that ingesting its newly-acquired western territories would send the United States 'rushing like a comet into infinite space'.[23] By inventing the west of the Leatherstocking Tales, *The Prairie* marks the start of that course which, unlike that of the comet, is apparently without return.

NOTES

1. George Dekker, *James Fenimore Cooper, the Novelist* (London: Routledge and Kegan Paul, 1967); Charles Swann, 'James Fenimore Cooper: Historical Novelist', in Richard Gray (ed.), *American Fiction: New Readings* (London and New York: Vision Press and Barnes and Noble, 1983); Robert Clark, *History, Ideology and Myth in American Fiction, 1823–1852* (London: Macmillan Press, 1984). Quotations from *The Prairie* are from the Everyman edition.
2. On Cooper's sources for *The Prairie* see Gregory Lansing Paine, 'The Indians of the Leatherstocking Tales', *Studies in Philology*, 23 (1926), 16–39; Roy Harvey Pearce, *The Savages of America: A Study of the Indian and the Idea of Civilisation* (Baltimore: Johns Hopkins Press, 1965); Orm Överland, *The Making and Meaning of an American Classic: James Fenimore Cooper's 'The Prairie'* (New York: Humanities Press, 1973).

'The Prairie' and Cooper's Invention of the West

3. Domingo Sarmiento, *Life in the Argentine Republic in the Days of the Tyrants, or Civilisation and Barbarism*, trans. Mary Mann (New York: Hurd and Houghton, 1868).
4. Henry Nash Smith, *Virgin Land: The American West as Symbol and Myth* (Cambridge: Harvard University Press, 1950), p. 61.
5. Quoted in George Dekker and John P. McWilliams, *Fenimore Cooper: The Critical Heritage* (London: Routledge and Kegan Paul, 1973), p. 192.
6. Pearce, *The Savages of America*, pp. 91, 93. Cf. Pearce's earlier version published as 'Civilisation and Savagism: The World of the Leatherstocking Tales', *English Institute Essays 1949*, ed. A. S. Downer (New York: Colombia University Press, 1950), pp. 92–116.
7. See Paul Wallace, 'Cooper's Indians', *New York History*, 35 (1954), 423–46, p. 425.
8. James Howard's recent census of these documents in *The British Museum Winter Count* (London: British Museum Publications, 1979) updates earlier studies by Garrick Mallery, *Picture-Writing of the American Indians* (Washington: Smithsonian Institution, 1893); James Mooney, *The Ghost-Dance Religion and the Sioux Outbreak of 1890* (Washington: Bureau of Ethnology, 1896) and *Calendar History of the Kiowa Indians* (Washington: Bureau of Ethnology, 1898) and others (such as Russell on the Pima and Underhill on the Papago). Together with Sewlyn Dewdney's pioneering census of the Mide scrolls, *The Sacred Scrolls of the Southern Ojibway* (Toronto and Buffalo: University of Toronto Press, 1975), they provide a basis for establishing the common principles of native North American chronology and its relation with that of Mesoamerica. See my ' "Far as the solar walk": the path of the North American shaman', *Indiana*, 9, Gedenkschrift Gerdt Kutscher (1984), 15–29, and 'The Time Remembered in the Winter Counts and the Walam Olum', in *New European Approaches to Indian America*, ed. Jacqueline Fear (Greenwich, Conn.: Greenwood Press, forthcoming in 1985). On the Pawnee in general see George F. Hyde, *The Pawnee Indians* (Norman: Oklahoma University Press, 1974) and on their treaty see Wilcomb E. Washburn, *The American Indian and the United States: A Documentary History* (New York: Random House, 1973), pp. 2360–361. Despite the indifference if not the hostility of the eighteenth- and nineteenth-century mediators quoted by Hyde, Pawnee history clearly has the continental scope and pattern found in that of the Iroquois. For example, the geographical and moral principle of the 'southland' or Mexico is likewise quite explicit in the *Sketches of Ancient History of the Six Nations* written by the Tuscarora David Cusick and published perhaps two years before *The Prairie* in Lewiston, N.Y. In many respects Cusick prefigures Wyandotté, the Tuscarora who, as House rightly points out, was Cooper's most complex Indian character. See Kay Seymour House, *Cooper's Americans* (Colombus: Ohio State University Press, 1965). In their turn these Iroquoian accounts concord well with the native chronology of the Algonkin and the Sioux.
9. Washburn, ibid.
10. See Francis Jennings's caustic look at the *vacuum domicilium* trope in his *The Invasion of America: Indians, Colonialism and the Cant of Conquest* (Chapel

Hill: University of North Carolina Press, 1975), and my article on Roger Williams, 'A Controversial Guide to the Language of America', *1642: Literature and Power in the Seventeenth Century, Sociology of Literature Papers,* ed. F. Barker *et al.* (Colchester: University of Essex, 1981), pp. 84–100. On the scale of the settlement and agriculture of the Seneca and their neighbours see Anthony F. C. Wallace, *The Death and Rebirth of the Seneca* (New York and Toronto: Random House, 1970). Historically, Williams seems to have been the traitor to Metacom and Conanchet whom Cooper, in *The Wept of Wish-ton-wish*, identifies as Indian, a narrative necessity according to House: 'Only Indians can run Conanchet to ground, hunting in relays as they hunted deer.' *Cooper's Americans*, p. 245.

11. Mooney, *The Ghost Dance Religion*, p. 298. Certain of these songs recall the common cultural past of the Mississippi area represented by Cahokia. For the pan-Indian convention of valuing song as an item of tribute, see my *Image of the New World: The American Continent Portrayed in Native Texts* (London and New York: Thames and Hudson, 1979).

12. In the Walam Olum maize is reported to have been brought from 'the maize land to the south' under Taguachi and Huminiend ('Maize-thresher'—whence 'hominy'), ninth and tenth in the series of 40 plus 40 sachems recorded in this word, over a span from ca. A.D. 850 to 1650. (See my 'Time Remembered . . .'.) The Walam Olum was first published in *The American Nations* of Constantine S. Rafinesque (Philadelphia, 1836), 2 vols., and then by Ephraim G. Squire in 'Historical and Mythological Traditions of the Algonquins (1849)' in W. W. Beach, *The Indian Miscellany* (Albany: J. Munsell, 1877), pp. 9–42, both of whom went against the prevailing trend of divorcing the Indians of their day from their own history as this could be read from texts in native script and from the architecture of surviving urban and ceremonial structures. On maize in America see Carl O. Sauer, *Man in Nature: America before the Days of the White Man* (Berkeley: University of California Press, 1975) and *Seventeenth-Century North America* (Berkeley: University of California Press, 1980). On the 900 date, Josephy and Brandon have this to say: 'It is not known definitely how the Mississippian Culture arose; presumably it began locally with ideas and systems derived from the Hopewell Culture, then about A.D. 900 received a strong agricultural base, together with an infusion of new cultural traits, that came from the Huastec area of Mexico via the Caddoan region of eastern Texas. An intensified agriculture, based on new and more productive strains of corn and new implements, supported the growth of the Mississippian Culture, which was marked, also, by . . . more tightly knit social systems organized around new religious beliefs and ceremonies. . . . The new stage appears to have extended westward on to the plains all along the front. . . . In the north, Woodland Siouan-speakers with strong Mississippian influences moved to the middle Missouri Valley.' Alvin Josephy and William Brandon, *The Indian Heritage of America* (London and New York: Bantam Books, 1969, pp. 111, 119.

13. Hyde, *The Pawnee Indians.*

14. From the first part of the *Essay on Man*; cf. my commentary in the 'Solar

walk' article. Rabelais' mocking echo of the Iroquois Condolence ritual can be found in *Pantagruel*, IV, 26, cf. my *Image of the New World*, p. 302.

15. See Washington's letter confiding his schemes to William Crawford published in *Chronicles of American Indian Protest* (Greenwich, Conn.: Council on Interracial Books for Children, 1971). Washington's ignorance of Indian territory at this stage is clear from the Ohio maps filed under his name in the Cambridge University Library. Cahokia features in the ritual time-maps from east of the Mississippi, drawn on skins, that were brought to France in the late seventeenth century and are now in the Musée de l'Homme. As it is recorded in the Walam Olum, Algonkin penetration into the already urban Ohio was at the expense of the Cherokee; this nation claimed for example to have had a hand in constructing Grave Creek, the largest mound in the valley (Haywood quoted by Daniel G. Brinton, *The Lenape and their Legends with the Complete Text and Symbols of the Walam Olum* (Philadelphia: Library of Aboriginal American Literature, 1884), vol. 5, p. 17). Indeed, when this mound was opened by whites in 1840 it was a member of the Cherokee who denounced the sacrilege. See Henry R. Schoolcraft, *Oneota* (New York: Wiley & Putnam, 1845), p. 27.

16. Frederick Jackson Turner, 'The Ohio Valley in American History', in *The Frontier in American History* (1920; rpt. New York: 1962), pp. 166–67.

17. See Dekker and McWilliams, *Cooper: The Critical Heritage*, p. 25.

18. Amen's Naphtali (p. 171) echoes the 'Nephi' of the *Book of Mormon* which was 'translated' from tablets revealed in New York in the same year that Cooper began his Leatherstocking Tales, 1823. A powerful but hazardous outrider of United States' interests, the Mormon church was successively expelled westwards eventually to reach Utah, the meeting point of the continental railroad in 1864. Their colony there, Deseret or Honey Bee, recalls the bee-hunters of Cooper's novels. On the 'lost tribe' the continent over, see Robert Wauchope, *Lost Tribes and Sunken Continents: Myth and Method in the Study of American Indians* (Chicago: University of Chicago Press, 1962).

19. See my article 'Ubirajara, Hiawatha, Cumanda: National Virtue from Indian Literature', *Comparative Literature Studies*, 9 (1972), 243–52.

20. On Parkman, see Dekker and McWilliams, pp. 34–7; on Schoolcraft, see Janet Lewis, *The Invasion* (Denver: University of Denver Press, 1932). Brinton demeaned both the pictographical original of the Walam Olum and the probity of its first editor, Rafinesque, wilfully altering the alphabetic gloss to make *it* appear to be the original in its own right. He also entirely suppressed the Mattanikum supplement that runs from the Swedish settlements of 1650 to about 1800. Cf. Nelcya Delanoë's political hommage to this source in *L'Entaille Rouge: Terres Indiennes et Démocratie Américaine, 1776–1980* (Paris: Maspero, 1982). As for the three historical moments of United States' history supplied by Cooper, they interestingly revise the three pre-western moments suggested to him by W. H. Gardiner at the start of his career. These were 'Founding Fathers', 'Indian Wars', and '1776'. See Dekker and McWilliams, p. 18.

21. *The Letters of William Gilmore Simms*, ed. Mary C. Simms Oliphant *et al.*,

5 vols. (Columbia, SC.: University of South Carolina Press, 1952), vol. 1, p. xxxviii.

22. This much can be deduced from references to 'arcane epics' in his letters to Freud just before the appearance of *Symbole der Wandlungen* (translated as *Psychology of the Unconscious*, 1916) which reads deep into the Hiawatha story.

23. Quoted by Överland, *The Making and Meaning of an American Classic*, p. 49.

Having read a draft of this essay, Roger C. Echohawk has kindly corrected certain details of Pawnee history. He also points out that Martha Royce Blaine, *The Pawnees: A Critical Bibliography* (Bloomington: Indiana University Press, 1980) updates Hyde's *The Pawnee Indians*.

8

Rewriting Revolution: Cooper's War of Independence

by ROBERT CLARK

Since capitalist societies are born in revolution and perpetuate themselves by continuous social transformation, in every phase the ruling class comprises both progressive elements who favour change and who claim their origin in the revolutionary past, and conservative elements who fear their own displacement and represent the past as inherently stable and organically continuous.[1] It is the latter tendency which has usually determined histories of the American Revolution, representing it as a conservative response to British attacks on established colonial liberties and as a unified uprising of innate American libertarianism. George Bancroft, although too rhetorical for later tastes, seems to have discovered the paradigm when he wrote that 'the people of the continent obeyed one general impulse, as the earth in spring listens to the command of nature, and without the appearance of effort burst forth to life.' For him the revolution

> grew out of the soul of the people, and was an inevitable result of a living affection for freedom which actuated harmonious effort as certainly as the beating of the heart sends warmth and colour and beauty through the system. The rustic heroes of the hour obeyed the simplest, the highest, and surest instincts, of which the seminal principle existed in all their countrymen.[2]

187

For Bancroft, the revolution that was to provide an inspiriting example to so many peoples of the world involved no factional division and was motivated by no economic force; it stemmed as naturally from the inmost being of all the rustic heroes as does the plant from the seed.

In non-fictional historiography the first notable challenge to the Bancroft paradigm was Charles Beard's *Economic Interpretation of the Constitution*, a work produced 'during the tumult and discussion that accompanied the advent of the Progressive Party'—in other words, at a moment when the divergence of interests between capital and labour was acutely apparent. Beard's thesis that the Constitution was not the united expression of 'the whole people' but an ideological coup by economically progressive property owners against both loyalists and the common people admitted class antagonism into American historiography. It also prepared the way for the later sophistications of Carl Becker's more persuasive 'dual revolution' account of a war of liberation from Britain accompanied by a democratic political revolution. Whilst history in this century has thus secularized Bancroft's divine will, made money rather than Providence the motor of events, and admitted factional complexity, there remain nonetheless those who repeat the myth of a unified uprising. As R. R. Palmer and others have pointed out, in the 1950s historians such as Clinton Rossiter refurbished the story of Independence as a non-revolutionary and largely non-violent return to original liberties. The purpose of these consensus historians was to dissociate 'the American Revolution from other revolutions by which other peoples have been afflicted'.[3]

To whom revolutions appear as 'afflictions' is not clear in Palmer's account—though it seems a fair assumption that the consensus school wished to prevent anyone imagining that the United States had something in common with those more recent products of revolution, the U.S.S.R. and the People's Republic of China. As early as the Mexican War it was clear that a nation born of a struggle for independence from colonialist exploitation, and proclaiming its right to rebel in the name of a universal right to life, liberty and the pursuit of happiness, would find the history of its own constitution a hindrance to the self-image most expedient to imperial political needs. As Edward Countryman has recently written,

> the measure of the conservative's triumph is that we have forgotten [our] revolutionary qualities, and our forgetting has helped to legitimate the hostility that our government has often shown to revolutions elsewhere.[4]

The irony is that whilst Senator Robert Kennedy believed that the example of the American Revolution should be carried to Latin America and elsewhere, most members of the Kennedy administration did their best to prevent the example being followed anywhere at all.[5]

The kind of 'Cooper' we construct in our university and college syllabi today is crucially informed by these extra-literary factors, great attention being paid to those novels which represent the contradictions of territorial expansion whilst relatively little is paid to those novels which explore the internal class contradictions and economic antagonisms of the United States. In an age in which 'America' dominates the world and justifies its doing so by a binary opposition between good libertarian capitalism and wicked inhuman communism, it is scarcely surprising that critics should find in the novels of the frontier sites for the masked articulation of contemporary anxieties about the relations between the reds and the whites. Making the frontier novels into the canonical texts carries the additional benefit of removing from critical attention those novels which represent domestic aspects of United States history and which puncture the potent, because rarely-voiced, myth of classless non-antagonistic progress. Clearly this aspect of Cooper's writing is most powerfully represented by the Littlepage trilogy and by the novels of the Revolution. It is three of the latter I wish to consider in this essay, pursuing in particular the question of how Cooper represents the American Revolution, and how this knowledge may help us understand the United States today. The conventional way of organizing such a research is to follow chronology and begin with *The Spy*. Here, however, I propose to reverse historical sequence and begin with a less-read novel, *Wyandotté*, justifying my procedure by the precept that the first formulation of a problematic may be more replete in feints and dodges than subsequent versions.

Wyandotté might be classed—although in my view erroneously —as an Indian or frontier novel, as well as a novel of the Revolution. It is set in Cooper's familiar territory, upper New York State, between 1765 and the mid-1790s, and concerns the settlement of a remote valley by Captain Willoughby and an attack on his settlement by rebels at the beginning of the Revolution. The plot in brief begins with Wyandotté guiding Willoughby to an old beaver dam which the Captain drains and turns into a valuable farm estate. The Knoll at the centre of the lake becomes the site for a hut, the interior of which seems as capacious and gracious as a Scottish castle. This is surrounded with a defensive stockade, the gates of which are never properly hung, thus leaving a teasing gap in the phenomenology of seclusion through which the rebel forces may long threaten to invade the family sanctuary.[6] Despite the years which pass, the vague threats of Indian attack and the rumours of revolutionary strife which drift up into the wilderness fastness, there are always trivial impediments to closing this gap. Finally after a band of marauding Mohawks and rebels appears on the valley rim, something is done, but this is so ineffectual that when (many moons later) the rebels finally attack, the gate is easily overthrown and the fort is captured. In the mayhem that ensues many of the major characters are killed, notably Captain Willoughby's wife and his daughter Beulah. However, a party of Continental regulars led by the Captain's son-in-law arrives in time to capture the rebels and save the hero and heroine, Major Robert Willoughby and Captain Willoughby's adopted daughter, Maud. The novel ends with these two inheriting the Willoughby's ancestral estates in England and then in 1795 returning to the Knoll to re-establish the family's American estates and visit their parents' grave.

As in many of Cooper's novels of the 1840s the plot seems dominated by a desire to return to a haven of security (the womb, bosom of nature, a castle or fort), the action consisting in movements out from the circle of seclusion towards the valley crest (a further circle) over which characters disappear in search of history (news of the revolutionary conflict) or at which they are captured and imprisoned by the rebels. Foray, capture, escape and pursuit are the fundamental moves, a basic desire being to remain, like Captain Willoughby, neutral and undisturbed by social conflict, yet at the same time needing that social conflict in order to generate a narrative history.

The writing of the novel proceeds from the same combination of aggression and defence. Cooper announces in his Preface that 'one of the misfortunes of a nation is to hear little besides its own praises', thus parting company with the contemporary tendency to believe everything in the United States the most perfect realization of history, and the subordinate tendency to extol everything that could be associated with Independence as a sign of American regeneration. Cooper's announced reason for saying 'nay' to this paradigm is his conviction that 'there were demagogues in 1776 . . . as certain as . . . there are demagogues now, and will continue to be demagogues as long as means for misleading the common mind shall exist' (iii).[7] The specific addressees of this hostility are, as many critics have noticed, the anti-rent agitators who were leading the tenantry of New York in revolt against a backward system of patroonship in the Hudson Valley. Cooper's novel thus locates itself ideologically as a rupture with Democratic faith, one that aspires to correct 'pseudo-patriotism' by admitting the truth of class antagonism in the revolutionary period in order to warn against similar evils in the present. As a reactionary statement, it stands in an aggressive-defensive relationship to historical change, one that will confuse the complexity of the truth it is so proud to champion.

The superficial polemic of the text is simple. Joel Strides, the seemingly loyal and hardworking overseer of the Willoughby estate, is the demagogue denounced in the Preface; covertly he undermines the faith of Willoughby's loyal retainers and, despite the fact that Willoughby has decided he can no longer remain neutral but must join the American cause, he persuades the majority to desert to the rebels, a piece of low treachery that results in the fort being penetrated and the death of Mrs. Willoughby and Beulah. The novel thus warns the employing classes to beware the dirty reds under their beds.

The confusion in Cooper's representation begins to appear when one inspects the composition of the attacking force: initially described as a party of hostile Indians, they are later discovered by Wyandotté to comprise twenty-two Mohawks, four Oneidas, one Onondaga and forty-seven white men dressed as Mohawks. The historical improbability of this alignment is as evident as the implausibility of their behaviour in the text: as attackers they do nothing for many days except sit on a distant hillside constituting an enigmatic threat (notwithstanding the fact that, as the gates have not yet been hung, the fort is indefensible); they go away and come back again without explanation; they do not attack; they imprison Captain Willoughby's son Robert, a Major in the British Army, when he is sent out to parley, yet let his companion, the Reverend Woods, go off for reinforcements; they make no attempt to discuss terms or signal intentions and finally launch their attack only minutes before Colonel Beekman arrives with his force of continental regulars to take them prisoner.

Story and history are cockeyed. Firstly, why Continental regulars should side with supposed loyalists against irregular patriots is never explained. (It makes sense only if one believes that the class and family loyalty between Beekman and Willoughby is strong enough to stop the tide of popular feeling.) Secondly, as Cooper admits in his Preface to the first edition, 1776 is too early for frontier troubles (the conflict in this area not occurring before 1779). Thirdly, the Mohawks remained staunch allies of the British throughout the War of Independence so would not have supported rebels against a supposedly loyalist British officer. Fourth, the Tuscarora and Oneida were very closely allied tribes so Wyandotté, who is not a Wyandotté but a Tuscarora, is on the wrong side. Fifth, the Oneidas and Tuscaroras did in fact enter the War on the American side in 1777 after violent conflicts with the loyalist Mohawks, so whichever way you look at this gordian knot, something is historically implausible.

As usual in Cooper, the only merit in exposing historical

implausibility is to illuminate the symbolic connections. As far as this gang of rebels is concerned, their unity is obviously given by Cooper's long-standing antagonism to the Iroquois, and to the Mohawks and the Oneida in particular, and by the use of the word 'Mohawks' in the Revolution to designate the 'Sons of Liberty'. In the 1840s the descendants of the 'Sons of Liberty', the anti-rent agitators, dressed in calico and war-paint and went by the name 'Injins' as they terrorized Willoughby's descendants, Cooper's friends, the patroons of the Hudson valley. The attackers therefore stand collectively for the Indians and impoverished whites who claim rights to the land appropriated by the ruling class. Cooper's last history of the Revolution is, as the Preface warns us, a displaced expression of fear at the revolutionary possibilities of the year in which it was written.[8]

This fear also informs the family romance that provides the domestic action of the novel. Whilst the threat of expropriation surrounds the fort, the chief narrative lure is provided by the love-interest between Major Robert Willoughby and Maud, ostensibly Captain Willoughby's daughter but in fact the daughter of an old friend who was killed by Indians shortly after Maud's birth. An associated interest is provided by the potential political disagreements of father and son, Robert being sworn in allegiance to George III, the Captain being an English baronet and a distinguished British officer on the retired list who finds his aristocratic title irrelevant to life in the New World. Beginning the novel determined to remain neutral, the Captain slowly inclines to the patriotic cause and the stage is set for two ruptures in the authority of the patriarch: the son's threat to depart from the father's beliefs and the son's threat to break the incest taboo by marrying his sister.[9]

Of course Maud is not a sister in fact; yet since Robert and Maud make a great song and dance about their not being able to recognize their love because they are brother and sister, the deliberate flirtation around the taboo invites such a reading. Similarly Cooper elides the Oedipal dilemma by having the son remain loyal to the King while the father decides to rebel. The son, who already outranks the father, thus achieves the satisfaction of seeing himself true to the true father—King and

193

State—whilst the biological father reveals his fundamental ignobility. The text thus gives mediated expression to Cooper's own position: the son of a wartime rebel and profiteer, married to the daughter of distinguished loyalists and acting as spokesman for the landed gentry, Cooper has always struggled to disavow his father's origins and manners. In *Wyandotté* the son's desire to displace the father is masked by the gentlemanly agreement to respect each other's honour, proving how well the ruling class behaves in times of stress. The son's desire is nonetheless effectively satisfied by showing that whilst the father is in national terms a patriot, in class terms he is a traitor. The latter is always less easy to forgive.

As usual in Cooper's novels the energy of this central problematic surfaces most clearly in displaced form. Originally entitled 'The Hutted Knoll' the work took on the title *Wyandotté* as this second-order character grew in importance.[10] Wyandotté treats Captain Willoughby as a father but also resents his tyranny for having flogged him at an earlier moment in their history, and for having the incredible ill-grace to constantly remind him of his humiliation. Wyandotté also clearly loves Mrs. Willoughby as a mother because in the past her tender nursing saved him from death by cholera. Wyandotté therefore functions as an Oedipal surrogate for the natural son, someone who can enact the desire to kill the Father (the figure whose very existence perpetually reminds the son of his impotence) and thus allow the son to possess his ostensible sister. Events fall out with that rigged improbability typical of Cooper: Wyandotté saves Maud from butchery by the Mohawks, stabs Captain Willoughby to death, and fails to save Robert's mother and real sister. By commission and omission the surrogate son thus removes all who might prevent or even witness Robert's marriage to Maud. At the historical level his function is to assassinate the patriots (either by stabbing them or colouring them as creatures of duplicity) so that none shall question Cooper's adherence to a reactionary-loyalist politics.

To read *Wyandotté* in this way is to propose that the novel divides around the need to appear patriotic whilst favouring loyalism for reasons of class prejudice. Expressed theoretically, it translates actual political struggles of the 1760s and 1840s into a series of mobile imaginary contradictions from which it produces an imaginary solution.[11] Similar strategies and tensions are apparent in all Cooper's novels of the Revolution, but in *Wyandotté* they are expressed more clearly under the pressure of contemporary events and as a result of the alienation of Cooper's class from the Democratic tendency of the body politic. At one point we even have Cooper nailing unmistakably loyalist colours to the mast:

> It has been said that the English ministry precipitated the American Revolution, with a view to share among their favourites the estates that it was thought it would bring within the gift of the crown—a motive so heinous as almost to defy belief, and which may certainly admit of rational doubts. On the other hand, however, it is certain that individuals who will go down to posterity in company with the many justly illustrious names that the events of 1776 have committed to history, were actuated by the most selfish inducements, and in divers instances enriched themselves with the wrecks of estates that formerly belonged to their kinsmen or friends. (229)

In my reading of *The Pioneers* I suggested that much of Cooper's uneasiness about his own social position derived from his awareness that charges of this kind had actually been laid at his father's door. In the novels of Revolution, however, we find no representation of such base motives in the property-owning classes; rather Cooper's Revolution omits the energetic bourgeoisie whose aspirations gave head to the struggle against colonialist exploitation. In their place he offers us mainly loyalist gentlemen inspired by high principle and lower orders inspired by expropriatory zeal. The characters who mediate between these two levels are actually more selfless and high-principled than the gentry they serve but are perceived as ambiguous and are often accused of treachery. Wyandotté, like Harvey Birch, is persistently suspected of treachery, but excepting his murder of the Captain is loyal to the family throughout. Job Pray in *Lionel Lincoln* is a guileless imbecile whose open avowal of revolutionary sentiments is taken as evidence of his simplicity. These deformed, maligned, apparently duplicitous but highly principled figures stand in the historical place of the real revolutionaries, that complex fusion of urban merchants, artisans, small farmers, men of property and the urban poor that fought for a future free of subjection. Although Cooper frequently echoes the expected celebratory pieties about the Revolution in general, he represents none of this group and indeed seems incapable of sympathizing sufficiently to represent even one truly revolutionary hero. Lionel Lincoln, one assumes, sets off in this direction by following the model of Scott's *Waverley* where the hero, a British officer, enlists with the Highland clans only to discover that feudalism is not as rosy a social formation as it appears to be in *belle lettristic* nostalgia. In order to prepare for a similar change of allegiance Cooper characterizes Lionel as a 'Boston Boy' much respected by the locals and confided in by the revolutionaries in a manner which would strain the conscience of a more credible British officer or result in someone's execution. The respect felt for Lionel derives entirely from memories of Lionel's father, a man whose relationship with the colony seems to have been too brief, fugitive and murky to found such general esteem. No matter how implausible the plot, Lionel is led to his mother's grave behind rebel lines by the aged Ralph, friend of Job Pray and another mysterious go-between. There Lionel promises that if all the dark hints about the family past that have been strewn through the narrative mean what he thinks they mean, then he will turn his back on hereditary rank and fortune and declare for the Revolution. The scene is obviously set for a conversion, probably after the manner of gothic novels where the aristocratic past is revealed as an unholy pit of incestuous scheming, mayhem and vice. Lionel is prevented from having his dénouement by the arrival of a search party but when it all does come out the realization that Job is his illegitimate and elder half-brother, that Ralph is his insane father, and that his wife's grandmother has been prepared to commit any crime to ensure that she or her offspring inherit the patriarchal estates, all this does nothing to persuade Lionel to rebel against the aristocratic system. Rather it has the reverse effect; thanks to a beneficent Providence, the illegitimate, unscrupulous and insane die, leaving Lionel to inherit lands and title, as becomes a man of such inherent aristocracy of spirit. A novel supposed to praise the revolution ends in a gleeful recital of how many honours and riches Lionel and his wife have managed to amass back home in mother England.

It is a justifiable complaint about Cooper's novels that their dramatic plots rarely deepen the significance of their historical plots. Taking *Lionel Lincoln* at face value would seem to bear this out, the gothic pleasure in elaborating family misdeeds seeming to distract Cooper's attention from the political and military scenes he describes so finely in the first part of the tale. Yet beneath the surface, domestic intrigue and political concerns can be said to be curiously in phase; the revolutionary character is imaginable to Cooper only as an unhinging of authority, paternity and responsibility. However high their principles, and however well they compare with the ruder British elements, his patriots are always creatures of obscurity. The Revolution has therefore done enough for Cooper if it replaces such men with a new generation who know better how to exert authority, and how to link means to material ends. We can see this trait leaking out of the text where it extols revolutionary virtues, for it does so by imposing an impossible orderliness; after attending a meeting of the Sons of Liberty Lionel remarks that

> Men on the threshold of rebellion seldom reason so closely, and with such moderation. Why, the very fuel for the combustion, the rabble themselves, discuss their constitutional principles, and keep under the mantle of law, as though they were a club of learned Templars. (80)

The appeal of Cooper's description is that it defuses anarchic violence and praises democracy and restraint. Yet its orderliness is surely as far from actuality as would be its inverse. Cooper is in effect offering an image of revolution that neutralizes its threat by making it into an entirely rational activity, one that is furthermore controlled by a man whose appearance 'denoted him to be of a class altogether superior to the mass of the assembly'. Lionel feels a natural dislike for this man because he appears to be 'abusing his powers, by urging others to acts of insubordination', but he is finally swayed in the man's favour by his open countenance and frank manner. Despite differences of persuasion, they recognize a higher bond, that of social class, and assure each other that they will always meet as gentlemen (78).

The image of rational social unity developed in the description of the meeting of the Sons of Liberty continues throughout *Lionel Lincoln* and sets it apart from the inter-class antagonism of *The Spy* and *Wyandotté*. In *Lionel Lincoln* we find the Bancroft paradigm in the making:

> The male population, between the rolling wastes of Massachusetts Bay and the limpid stream of the Connecticut, rose as one man; and as the cry of blood was sounded far inland, the hills and valleys, the highways and footpaths, were seen covered with bands of armed husbandmen, pressing eagerly towards the scene of the war. (163)

As for the loyalists, 'there were a few, however, among the colonists, who had been bribed . . . to desert the good cause of the land' (168).[12] In the authorial discourse, base motives explain loyalism, not rebellion; but while authorial pronouncements conform to orthodox opinion, the narrative expresses its subversion. As Cooper himself confessed to his daughter, his own sympathies prevented his entering the mind of the revolutionary, biasing him towards stability, hierarchy, loyalty and history as bulwarks against anarchy and dispossession. If his early dread is of a gentleman fomenting insubordination in the rabble, his highest praise for the revolutionary forces comes 'as subordination increased' (425) and they became an army to be feared.[13]

Reading Cooper's novels in reverse chronological order enables us to understand the success of *The Spy* as dependent upon its equivocation, an equivocation which must have been happily in tune with the nation's ambiguous desire for Independence, democracy, individualistic freedom and the right to amass property without fear of expropriation (the Lockean synthesis that had been exploded by a revolutionary war waged in its name). In *The Spy* Cooper had managed to disown radicalism without apparently disowning Independence, and this by representing the antagonism between the possessing classes and the impoverished levelling rebels in a way that provides a singular exception to the Bancroft myth of unified revolt.[14] This contradictory work is achieved by representing the British as divided into good gentlemen of colonial origin (Wharton), bad gentlemen of British aristocratic origin (Wellmere), and semi-legal loyalist guerillas (The Cow-Boys) whose excesses are held in check by disciplined leadership. The Americans, on the other hand, present a starker image, being divided into good Southern gentlemen (Dunwoodie, Lawton), and a horrible bunch of murdering thieves (The Skinners) whose intention in rebellion is to expropriate the rich and take possession of the State. Probably the most exciting and valuable moments of *The Spy* are the descriptions of this class, for by their appearance in a highly successful novel they reveal the dreadful fascination exerted on readers of the 1820s by images of their own extra-legal origins. The negative coloration of the Skinners indicates a desire to repudiate them, and it is one that has not ceased.[15]

The way Cooper supports the Revolution in *The Spy* is by representing the magnanimity of Harvey Birch and Harper; the former by numerous small acts of kindness towards the Whartons and by his refusal to accept payment for his services; the latter by his sagacity in bringing the Wharton affair to a happy conclusion. Neither of these representations has anything to do with revolutionary virtues, rather they are further signs that gentlemanly ethics transcend the trials of fratricidal strife, a meaning that Cooper underlines by quoting as pretext for his story the behaviour of the unnamed agent of the actual war. The original is described as belonging

> to a condition in life which rendered him the least reluctant to appear in so equivocal a character. He was poor, ignorant, so far as the usual instruction was concerned; but cool, shrewd, and fearless by nature. (iv)

In other words, though only one of the lower orders and knowing no Greek, he had native wit and natural aristocracy, refusing to convert high-minded patriotism to mercenary greed by accepting payment for his services.

The fascination of this tale depends upon a double transgression of class boundaries, the gentleman coming dangerously close to breaking the gentlemanly code by employing underhand means, the spy behaving like an ideal gentleman (it is not often so clear that real gentlemen are unconcerned with financial gain). Later, in *Notions of the Americans*, Cooper will make his attitudes abundantly clear when describing the André affair: 'while an officer may communicate with, and employ, a spy, he can scarcely with impunity become one himself.' And,

> among men of high and honourable minds, there can be but one opinion concerning this enterprise. There is something so repugnant to every loyal sentiment in treason, that he who is content to connect himself, ever so remotely, with its business, cannot expect to escape altogether from its odium.[16]

According to these sentences, an officer is allowed to employ a spy but becomes tarred with the same brush in doing so. When the employer of the spy then offers him money his action might be interpreted as attempting to impose a market value on patriotism, thereby to restore the gentleman to a superior station. The spy's refusal of payment removes some of the vulgar taint from the proceedings but leaves the gentleman-employer suspecting that his employee might be ethically superior to himself. It is perhaps an ambiguity of this kind that leads Cooper to malform those revolutionaries who are motivated by higher than base concerns.

Cooper's prefatory repetition of his source-tale invites attention to the changes he has made in producing a novel from it; in actuality there was one spy who was arrested by the revolutionaries, sentenced to death and allowed to escape, thus increasing his *bona fides* with the loyalists whom he was betraying. In Cooper's story the spying is doubled and represented in a low plot and a high: Birch has in the past been arrested and has escaped, then in the course of the novel he is seized by the Cow-Boys but escapes by his own stratagems; it is Wharton who is accused of spying by the revolutionaries, sentenced to death and helped to escape by Birch. The surface irony here is that Wharton seems about to be judged innocent—the court being prepared to accept his explanation that he was merely visiting his family—when Frances's mention of his having met Harvey Birch condemns him by association (321). The meaning of the verdict is that gentlemen should not consort with spies. The deeper irony of the plot is that the person who has actually been spying out the neutral ground is Harper. Although he is the first spy the reader meets, he is the last to have his identity revealed and then he becomes the last person the reader could suspect of conduct unbecoming. Yet is he not in every sense the spy in the piece? And does not Cooper's doubling of his original spy into a gentleman-spy and commoner-spy show that this is Cooper's real concern? Harper is the gentleman condemned by the later words of *Notions of Americans*, the man who does not declare his true colours and is therefore violating the code. He is also the gentleman who works for the revolution, is therefore implicitly involved with the Skinners and with the expropriation of the loyalist gentry, a renegade from his class. Such thoughts cannot of course be voiced because the image of Washington is sacrosanct, but it is of prime significance that Cooper can only imagine the great revolutionary hero in disguise and behaving in a furtive manner.[17] His only saving grace is that by despatching Birch to help Wharton escape he proves that class allegiance takes precedence over patriotism.

Cooper's fundamental concern, then, is to present the gentry with a continuous and undivided history, thereby obliterating the violent divorce in ideology and practice that actually split the upper classes in the Revolution. The lurking implication that Washington betrayed his class is scarcely noticed because the obvious opposition in the text is between the illegal/immoral Skinners and the owners of property; many readers have noticed that the Skinners spend as much if not more energy fighting Lawton and the Continental regulars as they do the British and loyalists. Through foregrounding this opposition Cooper vilifies the nascent proletariat, provides imaginary unity to the gentry, and again absents the radical bourgeoisie whose Revolution this principally was.

One might conclude from this that by the 1820s the Revolution had served its usefulness and the main ideological task was to convince the shock troops they should accept rations limited according to their social usefulness. The same phenomenon can be observed after all bourgeois revolutions. Certainly in the works of Scott and Balzac a parallel limitation on revolutionary ardour is apparent, idealism, passion, social criticism and a tendency to adopt extra-legal methods being represented as needing circumscription. The curiosity of

Cooper's work, however, is that whilst it shares with the work of other historical novelists a desire to represent revolutionary tensions and dangers, and whilst it also represents revolution from a conservative point of view, it finds nothing of value in the radical past. For Balzac, although he sees the Revolution as having displaced true nobility and given pre-eminence to a class of vulgar and foolish parvenus, their wealth and energy are subjects of fascination. The extra-legal outsider, the arch-criminal and representative of proletarian clairvoyance, Vautrin, becomes an irrepressible focus for historical energy. Whilst the survivors of the *ancien régime* retreat to the consolations of the countryside, Balzac remains in the city cataloguing the diverse forms of social life that the Revolution has brought into being. Similarly for Scott, revolutionary ardour is admired for its ability to transform antiquated social systems, provided of course that it knows how to make expedient compromises with political actuality.

Cooper's negative representation of the Revolution, therefore, should not be simply ascribed to the tendencies of his class or genre. Although there is a clear class bias to his work and this did attract some reviewers' attention, the relatively favourable nature of his early reviews and the commercial success of *The Spy* surely indicate a widespread desire to repudiate a radicalism that could only seem to threaten everyone's interests after 1776. A society based on the universal right to life, liberty and the pursuit of happiness, and convinced of the right of its own citizens to possess what they have amassed, did not wish to remember that its Independence was achieved by subordinating its cherished principles to the higher ethical and pragmatic concerns of a violent revolutionary war. If the country were today more mindful of this, perhaps it would take a more sophisticated view of the struggles of many peoples of the world to deliver themselves from far worse tyrannies.

Rewriting Revolution: Cooper's War of Independence

NOTES

1. Cooper himself defined social change as involving 'the struggles of those who would hasten . . . [and] those who would retard, events'. *Gleanings in Europe*, ed. Robert E. Spiller, 2 vols. (1836–37; rpt. New York: Kraus Reprint, 1970), II, p. 184.

2. George Bancroft, *The History of the United States of America from the Discovery of the Continent*, abridged and ed. Robert B. Nye (Chicago: Chicago University Press, 1966), p. 136, p. 161.

3. Charles A. Beard, *An Economic Interpretation of the Constitution of the United States* (1913; rpt. New York: Macmillan, 1961), p.v. Beard's thesis has been critically analysed in Robert E. Brown, *Charles Beard and the Constitution: A Critical Analysis of 'The Economic Interpretation of the Constitution'* (Princeton, N.J.: Princeton University Press, 1956). Clinton Rossiter's consensus theory was advanced in his *Seedtime of the Republic: the Origin of the American Tradition of Political Liberty* (New York: Harcourt Brace, 1953). R. R. Palmer's comments are in *The Age of Democratic Revolution: A Political History of Europe and America, 1760–1800* (Princeton, N.J.: Princeton University Press, 1959), pp. 185–235, p. 188. For understanding of class conflict in the Revolution see Alfred E. Young (ed.), *The American Revolution: Explorations in the History of American Radicalism.* (De Kalb, Ill.: Northern Illinois University Press, 1976); Eric Foner, *Tom Paine and Revolutionary America* (New York: Oxford University Press, 1976); and the works of Edward Countryman and John Shy cited below.

4. Edward Countryman, *The People in Revolution: The American Revolution and Political Society in New York 1760–1790* (Baltimore and London: Johns Hopkins University Press, 1981), p. xv.

5. R. R. Palmer, 'The Revolution', in *The Comparative Approach to American History*, ed. C. Van Woodward (New York: Basic Books, 1969), pp. 47–61.

6. James Beard interprets this as intended by Cooper to reveal the Captain's indecisive character. See his 'Cooper and the Revolutionary Mythos', *Early American Literature*, 11 (1976–77), 84–104. Such a reading recuperates the text for a view of Cooper's writing as intentional, rational, founded in craftsmanship. I imagine Cooper would have approved of this way of making sense of his work, but I think if Beard is right then Captain Willoughby is beyond belief.

7. Page references are to *The Mohawk Edition of the Works of James Fenimore Cooper* (New York and London: G. P. Putnam's Sons, 1896).

8. My reading here runs parallel to that of George Dekker, *James Fenimore Cooper, the Novelist* (London: Routledge and Kegan Paul, 1967), p. 229; and James H. Pickering, 'New York in the Revolution: Cooper's *Wyandotté*', *New York History*, 49 (1968), 121–41. The way the anti-rent controversy appears in *Satanstoe, The Chainbearer* and *The Redskins* can be approached through David M. Ellis's 'The Coopers and the New York State Landholding System', in Mary Cunninghame (ed.), *James Fenimore Cooper: A Reappraisal, Special Issue of New York History*, 35 (1954), 412–22.

203

His *Landlords and Farmers in the Hudson-Mohawk Region, 1790–1850* (1946; rpt. New York: Octagon Books, 1967) is also instructive. Cf. also Alan MacGregor, 'Tammany; The Indian as Rhetorical Surrogate', *American Quarterly*, 35 (1983), 391–407. Cooper's relationship to the Oneida is explored in my *History, Ideology and Myth in American Fiction, 1823–52* (London: Macmillan Press, 1984), pp. 79–95.

9. Eric Sundquist is doubtless correct to interpret the incestuous relationships of Cooper's later works as symbolic of the fear that his social position is illegitimate. See his *Home as Found: Authority and Genealogy in Nineteenth Century American Literature* (Baltimore: Johns Hopkins Press, 1979), p. 19. Cf. Michael Rogin's reading of *The Red Rover*, influenced by Sundquist, in *Subversive Genealogy: The Politics and Art of Herman Melville* (New York: Alfred Knopf, 1983), pp. 3–11.

10. Cooper first called the book 'The Hutted Knoll' then published it as *Wyandotté, or The Hutted Knoll*, the 'or' signifying an alternative between a phenomenology of prominent seclusion (a city on a hill) and the mobility of his seemingly treacherous go-between. See James F. Beard (ed.), *The Letters and Journals of James Fenimore Cooper*, 6 vols. (Cambridge, Mass.: The Belknap Press of Harvard University Press, 1968), IV, pp. 382, 386, 392.

11. The theory on which this reading is based follows that elaborated by Pierre Macherey in *A Theory of Literary Production*, trans. Geoffrey Wall (London: Routledge and Kegan Paul, 1978).

12. The paradigm is picked out by a contemporary reviewer who reports 'he has transfused into his narrative the sturdy spirit of those times, when every citizen was a soldier, and every soldier a patriot.' Unsigned review, *New-York Review and Atheneum*, i (June 1825), 39–50, rpt. in George Dekker and John P. McWilliams (eds.), *Fenimore Cooper: The Critical Heritage* (London: Routledge and Kegan Paul, 1973), p. 77. Strangely Lionel's failure to turn patriot received more comment from British reviewers than from American.

13. Mike Ewart in his 'Cooper and the American Revolution: the Non-Fiction', *Journal of American Studies*, 11 (1977), 61–79, offers an account that complements my reading of the fiction. According to Ewart, Cooper is prepared to justify 'the Revolution as a setting in place of a stable state' but his justification 'denies any *revolutionary* character there might be in this period'. Cooper's own opinion of *Lionel Lincoln* is reported by Susan Fenimore Cooper, *The Cooper Gallery: Pages and Pictures from the Writings of James Fenimore Cooper* (New York: James Miller, 1865), pp. 99–101.

14. James Beard in his 'Cooper and the Revolutionary Mythos' (p. 94) notes that Cooper's representation of the battle for Bunker Hill has proved far more consonant with modern accounts than those of other nineteenth-century historians, many of whom decried Cooper. Cooper's talent for historical research being proved, his misrepresentations become all the more striking.

15. Would that we more knew about actual events. John Shy's essay on 'Armed Loyalism: the Case of the Lower Hudson Valley', in *A People*

Numerous and Armed: Reflections on the Military Struggle for Independence (New York: Oxford University Press, 1976), pp. 181–92, an essay which was written 'in reaction to the "consensus" school of historical writing . . . which treats the Revolution as a more or less unanimous act of the American people (which it most certainly was not)' (181), reveals the *Loyalist* irregulars behaving much as Cooper describes the Skinners. They were ordered to 'seize, kill or apprehend' (189) any rebels and divide any seized property into equal shares. The possibility exists that Cooper is transferring loyalist behaviour to the patriots in a mythical cross-over that parallels those worked on his Indians.

16. Cooper, *Notions of the Americans Picked up by a Travelling Bachelor*, 2 vols. (1828; rpt. New York: Frederick Ungar, 1963), I, p. 218, p. 217. I owe this reference to John P. McWilliams, *Political Justice in a Republic: James Fenimore Cooper's America* (Berkeley: University of California Press, 1972), p. 57, whose reading was helpful in preparing this account.

17. The measure of Cooper's assault on the image is given by the book's reviewers. Here is Mrs. Hall: 'it is offering too great violence to our veneration for this immortal man to exhibit him . . . skulking in a hut to obtain an interview with a pedlar-spy'. Here is W. H. Gardiner: 'It may well be a matter of doubt, whether General Washington himself ever submitted to a personal disguise for the purpose of obtaining this kind of information . . . and, until we see undoubted evidence of the fact, we shall deny it. The whole character of Washington is against it. . . . When such a personage as Washington is made to move in scenes of fiction . . . he should appear . . . only as his countrymen have known and must ever remember him, at the head of armies, or in the dignity of state.' Marcel Clavel, *Fenimore Cooper and his Critics* (Aix: Imprimerie Universitaire de Provence, 1938), p. 78, pp. 84–5.

Notes on Contributors

GORDON BROTHERSTON is Professor in the Department of Literature at the University of Essex and has published extensively on Latin-American, European and Amerindian writing. In recent years his chief concern has been to develop our knowledge of the literature of native America. His *Image of the New World: The American Continent Portrayed in Native Texts* was published in 1979. This work will be extended in *The Book of the Fourth World: An Account of Native American Literatures* to be published in 1986–87.

James Fenimore Cooper: New Critical Essays

ERIC CHEYFITZ teaches in the English Department at Georgetown University and is author of *The Trans-Parent: Sexual Politics in the Language of Emerson* (1981). The essay included in this volume is part of a project entitled *The Frontier of Translation: Language and Colonisation from "The Temptest" to Tarzan.*

ROBERT CLARK is Lecturer in English and American Literature at the University of East Anglia. His publications include *History, Ideology and Myth in American Fiction, 1823–1852* (1984). He is at present working on a study of literary realism in Britain and France.

RICHARD GODDEN is Lecturer in the Department of American Studies at the University of Keele and has published on American writing of the 1920s and '30s. He is currently working on a book exploring narrative responses to late capitalism, part of which appeared in *Henry James: Fiction as History*, ed. Ian F. Bell (1984).

HEINZ ICKSTADT is Professor of American Literature at the John F. Kennedy Institut, Freie Universität Berlin. He has published extensively on American contemporary fiction and on American fiction of the late nineteenth century, is author of *Dichterische Erfahrung und Metaphernstruktur: Eine Untersuchung der Bildersprache Hart Cranes* (1970) and editor of *Ordnung und Entropie: Zum Romanwerk von Thomas Pynchon* (1981).

JOHN MCWILLIAMS is Professor of American Literature at Middlebury College. His publications include *Political Justice in a Republic: Fenimore Cooper's America* (1972) and *Hawthorne, Melville and the American Character* (1984). He is also co-editor with George Dekker of *Fenimore Cooper: The Critical Heritage* (1972).

CHARLES SWANN is Senior Lecturer in the Department of American Studies at the University of Keele. He has published on Scott, alt, Hawthorne, Eliot, Rutherford and Crane. A previous essay, 'James Fenimore Cooper: Historical Novelist', appeared in *American Fiction: New Readings*, ed. Richard Gray (1983). He is at present engaged on a study of English literature, 1830–80.

JAMES WALLACE teaches at Boston College. His dissertation, 'Early Cooper and His Audience', was awarded the Bancroft Prize and will be published in 1985. He is presently at work on a study of the antagonistic relation between literary discourses and discourses of power in American culture.

Index

207

Index

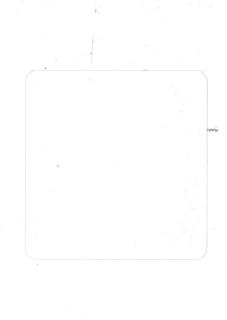